A FOOL, FREE

BEATE GRIMSRUD

Translated by Kari Dickson

HEAD OF ZEUS

Originally published in the Norwegian language as *En Dåre Fri*
by Beate Grimsrud. Copyright 2010, Cappelen Damm AS.

First published in the UK in 2015 by Head of Zeus Ltd.
This paperback edition first published in the UK in 2016 by
Head of Zeus Ltd.

This edition is published by agreement with Rogers, Coleridge &
White Ltd, 20 Powis Mews, London W11 1JN in association with
Cappelen Damm AS, Akersgata 47/49, Oslo, Norway.

This translation has been published with the financial support
of NORLA.

Askews & Holts	

A catalogue record for this book is available
from the British Library.

Paperback ISBN 9781781851944
Ebook ISBN 978178185658

Typeset by Lindsay Nash

Printed in the UK by Clays Ltd, St Ives Plc

Head of Zeus Ltd
Clerkenwell House
45–47 Clerkenwell Green
London EC1R 0HT

WWW.HEADOFZEUS.COM

A *FOOL,* FREE

'Eli's first-person narration of her troubled life, from childhood to middle-age, tugs you into the mind of a schizophrenic... But it's far from depressing, for what shines through is a courageous and imaginative personality, a triumph of optimism over often bitter experience, turning this episodic story of what is – to use the cliché aptly for once – a rollercoaster of a life into a page-turner.'
Daily Mail

'Genuine and humane... This book invades your body and mind. Her voice stays with you and demands attention.'
Expressen

'Everyone knows (or thinks they do) what severe mental illness looks like from the outside. This disturbing novel describes the experience from the inside... an extraordinarily articulate account of something that is seldom put into words.'
The Times

'The most gripping portrayal of the torments of mental illness I have ever read.'
Aftonbladet

'Unique and beautiful. A frightening, yet incredibly liberating read. Grimsrud's language is brilliant. Just as Eli goes to pieces and is mended, it feels as though the words explode and are

BEATE GRIMSRUD is an award-
winning Norwegian author and
playwright. She published *A Fool,
Free* in 2010 to rave reviews,
winning the Norwegian Critics
Prize for Literature. She lives
in Sweden.

A *FOOL,*
FREE

1.

My name is Eli. Which means my God in Hebrew. It can be a girl's name or a boy's name.

I can't stay in the flat. The floor slopes towards the dangerous windows that face out onto the back yard. I live six flights up. The windows pull me towards them. I could throw myself out. I might jump. I'm scared. I talk and can't stop. I am the one telling the story and the one the story is about. The one with voices in her head. The one that they talk in, endlessly. Have to defend myself against what they say. Have to answer their calls. Have to make repetitive movements with my arms in the corner of the kitchen. Again and again, like they tell me I should. What would happen if I didn't do it? I might crack. Fall to pieces. My head might split. The whole flat might crash out of the building like a desk drawer.

I am thirty-nine years old. Have been in and out of psychiatric clinics for the past twenty years. Almost as long as I've made a living writing novels, plays and film manuscripts. Writing is not a profession. It is a way of life. I wrote yesterday. I'm writing today and will write again tomorrow. Wander through words. Feel and get pleasure from sentences and contexts. Find them inside me and give them away. Give away, yet keep them. A gift to grow with. To hold on to when I am ill. To hold on to when I am well. Right now I'm sitting waiting. I've got a new cognitive therapist. The intention is that I'll be able to live at home, after five years in and out of the ward.

I'm sceptical about the cognitive therapist. I've tried so many different treatments. But now I'm going to try something new, and why not? He's my age, tall and thin with a ponytail. He comes home to me instead of me going to him. After all, some of the issues are here at home with me. The dangerous windows. The fear that I will throw myself out. Crash out. Slip out. Be sucked out by air pressure. Without being able to grab the slippery furniture and hold tight. He asks me to write a list of things I find difficult. It's long. He asks me to write a list of what I'm good at. It's just as long, which surprises the therapist. A blip in the illness.

'Where is it most dangerous?' he asks. 'In the bedroom,' I reply. The floor slopes and I'm pulled towards the dark window. 'I have to hold on to the bed.' We go into the bedroom. The window is completely covered by a dark curtain. A big African statue stands behind the curtain as protection. The window is never opened. The curtain is never opened. 'The floor slopes,' I tell him. The therapist takes a small ball out of his pocket. He puts it on the floor. The ball rolls in a circle and then comes to a standstill. It doesn't roll towards the window. We both watch the ball. And I think to myself that our shared understanding that something blatantly wrong is right has now been disproved and is lying there in front of us as the truth. Don't know what to believe, we must have seen the same thing. Then he picks up the ball and puts it back in his pocket. He doesn't say a word.

4

My name is Eli. It can be both a girl's name and a boy's name and means my God in Hebrew. The house is silent. We have stopped screaming. We have stopped running around every which way and making a mess. Mum gave up trying to make us behave ages ago. The flowers in the living room lie strewn all over the floor. We were throwing things around and didn't know when to stop. I am one and a half years old, and my brother, Torvald, is a year and one day older than me. We are strapped into our cots with the harness from the pushchair. We have tried crying several times during the night, but have given up. No one has come to our rescue.

I feel the harness rubbing against my naked body. I twist and turn like a snake but can't break free. My body is wet with sweat and my face is wet with tears. We have managed to take off our pyjamas, underpants and nappies. They are lying on the floor beside the cot. We have thrown out the pillows, blankets and sheets. We have thrown the mattress over the edge of the cot. We are sitting there naked on the bare planks of the cot, secured by the harness, when Dad comes in in the morning. 'Just look how strong they are,' he says.

5

I go to bed early, having taken a handful of sleeping tablets. It's night. Sleep did come, but now it's suddenly vanished again. My leg is shaking. I toss and turn in bed. Lie with my arms outstretched, think that I'm strapped down. Pull with my arms and kick with my legs. The strap is tight over my tummy. I can't open it myself. I think that my hands and feet are restrained too. Someone must have the key to release them. The nurses have it. I shout for help again and again. Can't reach up to turn on the light. It all happens in the dark. I shout again.

I am alone in the flat. In the city. In the country. On the earth. In the world. The Milky Way has crashed in a cloud of gas that has wiped out all humanity. All human life has been destroyed and I am the only one left. Only I am immune to the gas, and all the others who are restrained right now in mental hospitals all over the world. Without a key or any means of freeing themselves. There is still food in the fridge. There are still cars in the car parks. There is still money in the banks. There are still horses in the fields. Still medicine in the hospitals. The pills are still in their boxes. Still schools but no pupils. Still books but no readers. Still flowers in the flower shops. The sun is still in the sky. The rain is still in the clouds. Soon alarm clocks will ring all over the northern hemisphere. And there is no one left to turn them off.

I could make sure things carried on. But I can't get free. The strap is big and wide. I haven't got a chance. I am dependent on people who no longer exist. I am the one who remains when all others disappear. I still have language in my mouth. Sound in my throat. But there are no ears to hear. I shout again. Don't know what else to do. I have words in my mouth, but to no avail. Will I say my last prayer out loud, or silently inside?

Dad is playing with us kids. He creeps around on all fours. Then suddenly he's not playing any more. He snarls at us. Shouting is like hitting with your voice. His hand is quick as a fly swat. We scream. Run and hide. Mum shouts: 'You mustn't play dogs.' 'I'm not a dog,' Dad barks. 'I'm a lion.'

'Focus, focus, focus. Fight, fight, fight.' It's the boxing coach's voice. But it must have been there all the time. Long before I started boxing. I do sit-ups and press-ups. The plank. 'Muscular pain is positive pain. Up on your toes. Boxing is like playing music with your feet!' Punch the bag. The strength isn't in your arms, but in your hips. I have to carry my sparring partner on my back across the room and back. I have a fighting heart. 'Breathe, breathe, breathe.' I think about my new cognitive therapist. We're not supposed to carry anything back. We have to breathe in the present and the future. Not talk too much about the past. Let go of our baggage. Peel it off and leave it behind, bit by bit. Find ways round. Find routines. Find ways forward. Sweat. Grind my teeth at night. What is waiting for me now?

I stand on a chair in the kitchen and recite my poems. The words rhyme. I speak loudly and gesticulate with my arms. Mum and Dad and my siblings are listening. I receive rapturous applause. I bow and jump down from the chair. Run out into the hall and the applause continues. I run back in and bow again. I can see on the audience's faces how proud they are. I ask Mum if you can do that when you grow up, be someone who thinks up poems and has an audience. 'An author,' Mum says. 'That's something you can do on the side.' But I only want to be a writer, and maybe a joiner on the side. 'You are a writer,' Dad says. 'Just you carry on.'

I am six years old. I chat away, can't stop. Repeat, explain, ask, make up, lie and bite my nails. I have long, curly fair hair and big dark eyes. Long eyelashes and roses in my cheeks. I want to cut my hair. Maybe you can decide for yourself when you're seven. I have pale, almost see-through skin. I'm everywhere, high and low, fall and hurt myself all the time. I have a lot of scabs and scars for a princess. A pale brown plaster on one of my knees. Under the plaster, a deep wound. I'm practising riding my bike without holding the handlebars.

It's one of my last days in nursery school. I'm wearing a pretty pink dress that Marit has made. The classroom is shabby. The whole school is just temporary, barracks that were only going to be used for a year while they built a new one. They've been here for ten years now. The sun shines in through the dirty window and our drawings cover tears in the wallpaper. The room is not grand enough for someone like me whose name means God, but here I sit all the same.

I know that there are secret ways out of what they call reality. And soon I will discover there are many. Soon I will have a friend for life. A friend and an enemy. Someone who wants to be good, but who always gets a lump in his throat that then bursts and he can't stop crying. Someone who later in life will remind me that I was once little.

'Who wants to play Espen the Ash Lad?' the teacher asks. My hand is first in the air. We're going to do a play for the parents before the summer holidays. Most of the others don't want to play Espen the Ash Lad. They're too shy to take the main role.

I know that it's mine. I already know all the lines off by heart.

Once upon a time there was a ginormous kingdom. With a king and a queen and a princess who was old enough to get married. The problem was that no one could get her to stop talking. She answered every question with a retort. The king said that the man who could silence her would win both her hand and half the kingdom. There was also a poor family with three brothers. Naturally, Per and Paul wanted to try their luck. The youngest son, Espen, wanted to go too. Per and Paul laughed. You're so dirty, you always sit by the fireplace and play with the ash, you haven't got a chance with a princess.

'Who wants to play the princess?' Nearly all the girls want to play the princess. But not me. The teacher points at me, with my angel hair and princess dress. 'Eli will be the princess,' she says. 'You don't even need to dress up.'

'I want to dress up,' I reply. I want to wear torn clothes and a tartan cap. I want to have a worn-leather knapsack and pick up everything I find on my way through the forest. I want to be the one who renders the princess speechless with my ingenuity and imagination.

I leave my body for a while. I spill out between all the children. See myself from the ceiling. When I leave my body like this, I pull faces and the others copy me and laugh. 'Why do you do all those funny things with your mouth?' I smile over and over again with my mouth without smiling. I can't help it. My dad does the same.

I twist my princess-clad body on the chair. Who decided that I look more like a princess than who I really am? It's everyone at home who dresses me up and displays me to the world. Every family needs someone to put on display. I flop over my desk. Look up and see the teacher pointing at me.

'You're perfect, Eli. You always want the opposite, just like the princess.' And that's true. I don't want to sit up at the front and wait while the Ash Lad shouts: 'I found, I found something!' 'Ugh, throw it away!' his brothers shout. 'It's useless!' 'That's all very well, but you never can tell,' says Espen, and puts it in his knapsack. I found, I found something, I think. One day I will have gathered so much that nothing will hurt any more. One day I will be able to decide everything myself and find a use for everything I've found.

But now it's the teacher who decides. I am the princess and sit straight-backed on a chair by the teacher's desk in one of my prettiest dresses. I have a tiara in my hair and I'm waiting for suitors. The classroom is full of excited parents. They are big bodies on our small chairs. They watch with a smile. I start to pull faces. Blink. Smile again and again. Wait. I need a role where I talk all the time and am part of the plot from start to finish.

Espen the Ash Lad starts at the back of the classroom. He whispers his lines. He fills his knapsack with made-up things that the teacher has put out on the floor. It's all pretend. The boy who is playing the part is usually pretty cool. But not when the room is full of parents. It's only me who takes it seriously. One by one, the boys lie down on their stomachs over the teacher's desk, pull up their shirts and get three gentle taps with the pointer on their backs. The other children are shy and only do what they are told. It's no big deal for them. It's a story.

Per and Paul reach me. They don't know how to court me, so I have the last say. And then it's Espen's turn. We have rehearsed this so many times. He produces one strange thing after another from his knapsack and I ask what it is. He tells me and explains. But unlike all the rehearsals, I keep asking him questions when his knapsack is empty and he has nothing left to take out. The boy who is playing Espen is silent, like I, the princess, am supposed to be. Whereas I just keep talking. There's an audience here today.

I can't stop. A completely new ending to the fairy-tale tumbles out of my mouth. I am not silent. The whole performance is ruined and parents who know the play off by heart don't know when to applaud. The story ended ages ago. We're going to get married and live happily ever after. The teacher has to start clapping to drown me out.

Sometimes we swap places. I move. The princess is just a shell that I can creep out of. I creep in under the tartan cap. Not into the boy who's playing him. But in his place. I am Espen the Ash Lad.

A voice inside me says: 'You are Espen. You're not just Eli. You really are Espen the Ash Lad. And not alone in your body.' Then I stop talking. I am silenced by a voice in my own head. One that decides. That takes over. Gets inside me. Under my skin, in my thoughts. He's in my head. He starts to talk to me and he's here to stay.

He says that I'm him. He is six, like me, an imaginative lad, but very sad. The applause dies down. All the small actors bow and run out through the door into the corridor. Wait for more applause so they can run in again.

I don't run alone. Because now I am two. I see myself from the outside. See the tiara falling off and how we rush back into the classroom. I am Espen and I have the last say. I found, I found something.

Espen pops up again evening after evening when I'm brushing my teeth. As soon as the water is running from the tap, there he is with his gentle voice. We can laugh at each other. There's a grin on my face and no one knows why.

I am beautiful and alive in my far-too-beautiful nightie. Espen is dirty round the mouth and funny. 'Next time, you can play all the roles yourself,' he says. And I spit out the toothpaste. 'I want to be like everyone else,' I say. 'You're not like everyone else. You've got me.'

'I don't know if I want you,' I tell him. 'If I want to be the only one who has you.' My brother Torvald definitely doesn't have a princess in his head like I've got Espen the Ash Lad.

I turn off the water and Dad shouts: 'Are you ready? Shall we read then?'

Can I leave Espen now? In the bathroom. In the water. I can't decide. I have to turn on the water again and then I hear him crying.

'Why are you so sad?'

'It's you who's sad. When the story is finished, the light will be turned out and you'll wet the bed again. You'll wake in the dark and grind your teeth. You'll be frightened and unhappy. Your legs will shake and you'll laugh in your sleep without being happy.'

'Why?' He doesn't answer. I want to be like Torvald. Espen sobs his heart out. I take the hand towel and try to dry the tears. I can't leave him now.

'Come on,' Dad shouts. 'Otherwise there will be no story. Your brother's already in bed.'

When I turn on the water to do the washing up, Espen comes back. He's still only six whereas I'm an adult now. He cries in his little boy voice and says: 'Welcome to reality.'

Should it not be welcome to madness? It's the same thing. Daily life. A line from a poem in my head: *Reality crashing. Without reality born!*

Espen says: 'I see you and will always see you.' I realise that I should be saying that to him. 'You're inside me and will always be inside me.' His tears fall on my warm hands in the water.

He says: 'Why don't you say hello?' 'But I do. I say: "Yes, yes, yes," out loud to myself. That means that I know that you're there. I know that you want my attention and you get it.' 'You have to listen, you have to talk to me,' Espen says. 'Otherwise…' 'Otherwise what?' 'Otherwise you'll break into a thousand pieces. You don't always do what I say,' he adds. 'I do do what you say. Well, mostly.'

But now I'm trying not to be disturbed all the time. Trying to learn to turn the voices on and off. Trying to learn not to do what they say, not to listen all the time. I push the voices out into my forehead. They can stay there and wait while I do other things.

Espen comes and goes over the years. He normally comes with water. Either physically from its feel on my skin or with the sound from a tap, a shower, a river, a waterfall, the sea. I sometimes like him and his tears. I sometimes hate him because he disturbs me. Because he steals my time and closes me off from my life with other people.

We're sitting in the car, Dad, Torvald and me. I've got thirty-five kroner in my pocket. I've been saving for as long as I can remember, that's how old I am. I'm going to buy a leather football. Dad suddenly stops by a shop that isn't the sports shop. He goes in and comes back out. He wants to buy a tin of paint but needs five kroner. 'Eli, can you lend me five kroner?' he says, merrily. 'Say no,' Torvald tells me. 'You'll never get it back.' I looked at Dad's pleading face. But what about the football? He has the five kroner from my hand without me knowing how he got it.

Torvald took a step back a long time ago when it comes to Mum and Dad. He now looks to other adults. But I'm still on their side, because I don't know what else I'd do. We go to the sports shop and Dad talks circles round the assistant and haggles until in the end we take a slightly used leather ball home with us for thirty kroner.

Dad can't and I can't, and yet we can all the same.

The bell rings and Class 1B leap up from their desks and chairs. I take out the football that I've kept in a net attached to my backpack. It's my ball. We're going to play now. We've got the same team as in the last break. The football pitch is enormous. Wide goals. Most people kick the ball when it comes to them. Surprised and without much thought. Some dribble and dribble until they meet too many defence legs and get caught up.

I love playing. I'm on my own with the ball in front of the opponent's goalkeeper. Completely free. It's just a matter of kicking it in. I dribble and feint, but miss the shot altogether. And me who's so confident. A few people laugh. No goal when it's all clear. My team mates have disappointed backs.

A while later I get another chance. And miss again. 'Why don't you play defence?' one of the boys asks. 'I'm playing well,' I say. I want to score a goal, but I don't say that. One of the substitutes pokes me. 'You have to switch. You're no good. We need to win.'

I am good. I think I'm the best. I go over to the ball and pick it up. 'What are you doing?' one of the girls asks. 'Free kick,' someone else shouts. 'Put it back,' a boy tells me. I hold the ball to my chest and say: 'It's my ball.'

'You're ruining everything,' a voice says, and then another and all the children follow me like a long tail as I walk towards the school holding the ball tight against my chest. It can't be helped, I think. I walk faster than all of them and they stop and shout after me: 'Spoilsport!' It can't be helped. I can't stop.

I walk past the school and across the street and into the churchyard. I sit down by a grave. It says Viktor on the gravestone and no one has tended it for a long time. 'Viktor, Viktor,' I say. The tears fall. I'm stupid. When you're playing, it's everyone's ball. I know that. But can't help it.

'Eli's not here,' Espen says. 'She's definitely not here. It's me, Espen. I come in tears, I come in water. You have to score a goal.'

'I can't,' I say. Then I add: 'I know that I can.' 'I, I, I...' stammers Espen. It's Espen who's stammering. Words normally just pour out of me.

'I have to stop crying. I can't go around with tears in my body all day. I'm doing it because you're here. You're floating all around me and taking over. I'm stammering because of you. Because you change direction and place and make a fuss and shout at me when no one can see.'

'Hide,' Espen shouts. 'The janitor's coming. Hide!'

'Good day, little Miss Eli, the prettiest girl in the class and the best football player. Always ready with the ball.' He stretches out his foot and nudges the ball with his toes. 'Why are you sitting here in the churchyard? I thought I just heard the bell.'

'I, I, I...'

The janitor coaxes the ball up onto his foot and gives a few kicks before he misses and the ball falls down dead on the grass. I quickly pick off the scab from a cut on my knee. It starts to bleed. 'Why are you sitting here crying?' the janitor asks, when he's stopped playing with the ball. If only I could say something about Espen. About a voice that shouts without being visible.

'Oh, but you've cut yourself, I understand,' the janitor says. I like him because he gets it wrong. Thinks I'm the best football player when I'm not.

'Yes,' I sob. He gives me his hand. 'Come on then, I'll take you back to school.'

There's a ring at the door. It's my cognitive therapist. He's the one who's asked me to practise turning the voices on and off. He's the one who's asked me to practise not having them around when others are there. We respect them, but they have to wait.

'Say no,' my therapist says. I don't answer. 'Say it out loud,' he says. I say no and nothing happens. I don't crack.

The therapist takes off his jacket and sits down. He has a retro sports bag that reminds me of my bag. He has a file for all the things we talk about. We sit down in the kitchen. I also have a file, and write: Tell them to wait. They can wait, I'm in control. I'm the one who decides.

I tell him about Espen. About how he popped up when I was only six years old. 'You know that Espen the Ash Lad is called Dummerjöns in Swedish,' my therapist says. Even Espen has moved country. I've found, I've found something. But not a new name.

I only notice now that my therapist has cut his hair. His long ponytail has vanished and he has a new image. A fringe, long over the ears and short at the back. I look at him and suddenly he has a name. Jonathan. But how can I trust him?

Dad leans forward. I quickly jump out of the way. I don't know whether he's going to hit me or hug me. I listen to Espen's whispered warnings. He might hit me. A clip on the ear. A shove. A fist. You never know.

Dad does the same thing with his mouth as me. He pulls nervous faces. He stretches out his long arms. Hands reaching through the air. He wants to tickle me. I force a laugh. I run through the house. Dad runs after me. Is today a play day? You never know.

Dad catches me in his dangerous and playful arms. He hugs me close. He is warm and soft and smells of tobacco and grown-ups. But he's not grown up. He wants me to tickle him back.

21

I'm back in the unit again. They've been nagging me for days to have a shower and change my clothes. I don't like getting wet. I like rain, but not the shower. It's not raining and I'm not allowed out. I don't like water on my naked body and then I get cold afterwards and the towel is too small and the room gets chilly as soon as the hot water is turned off.

I lie on my bed and stare up at the ceiling. Listen to music in my headphones. Can't stop. 'You can stop,' Espen says. 'I can't stop,' I say. 'You can,' Espen says. I stand up suddenly, put away my MP3 player and go out to the shower room. There is a kiss mark in red lipstick on the mirror. I turn on the hot water, but don't get undressed. I sit down under the water. Feel my clothes fall heavy against my body. I just sit there and let it continue. I think about nothing.

Then I hear Espen crying. 'You're a grown woman now, you shouldn't be sitting here. You shouldn't be locked up. The doors and windows are locked. How can you just accept that?' 'It doesn't matter,' I comfort Espen. 'I'm just waiting. It'll all be fine again soon.'

I can't explain to Espen why I'm here again. So instead I think about football training sessions in the rain. I open my mouth and drink. The water runs into my mouth and then out again in an unceasing stream. My clothes stick to my body. Espen cries. I wait for him to calm down. Simply disappear one day. That is what he doesn't understand and I keep it secret from him, that one day I won't give him any room. That I want to be just Eli.

But it's not today, because now I can hear him crying and I just have to sit under the warm water and wait. I think about running between cones in the cold and rain. Endless sit-ups. About dribbling with the ball between two lines on the football pitch. That you haven't played football until you've had to sit out. I've sat on the bench. With everyone else's football jackets in a pile on my knees, just praying that someone will play badly or be injured so I can take her place. I would be the cool player with the ball inside the penalty area.

I haven't played football for ten years now. But I'm right there again. In the match. I want to be the one who stays calm in the chaos of all the legs and who dares make the final move and kicks the ball into the net. I turn up the warm water. I was the one who took corners and had hard-hitting free kicks. Don't forget that. I move so that all of me is under the spray. I mustn't get cold. Because I can't leave here. I have to sit here until time turns back and I'm playing football again and have a chance of being selected to the national team.

Winter is my best time of year. I do lap after lap on my skis in the forest behind the house. Someone has built a jump on the steepest slope. I jump the longest of anyone. I dare and I can. I'm out until late in the evening and come home cold and hungry. I'm allowed to do what I like. Come home when I like and eat when I like.

I say that I don't have any homework. Put on my pyjamas and sit in the kitchen eating banana and smoked cod roe sandwiches. I'm in Class 3 and have not learnt to read and write. I, who was so excited about starting school. I was in a rush to learn because I had so many stories to save, now I'm the worst in the class. The teacher says I'm dyslexic. I still love stories and make up my own instead of reading them.

Long after Dad has snapped closed the covers of the books that already exist, long after the light has been put out and my brother Torvald has fallen asleep, I lie in the dark telling stories. Continue the children's books, carry on where the story stops. I'm quite happy for it to be about princesses, but I don't want to look like one any more. I want to be Emil of Lönneberga. With a blue cap and a wooden gun. I've started to dress like him. My long hair blowing under my blue cap.

My brother Torvald can sit in silence for an hour, looking at comics or spinning a globe and memorising the countries of the world. I race around and can't sit still. Torvald doesn't wet his bed at night or make grimaces with his mouth. He doesn't seem to care about the world, outside or in. Or does he, in fact? Know how to live. Counting up all the countries in Africa and

24

feeling happy. I want to be like him.

When we were little, people often said: 'There's the girl, and *there* is the boy.' They would give him a friendly pat on the shoulder and listen to whatever he had to say. They always patted me on the head and said what beautiful hair I had.

Would it have been easier for me if I was a boy? Am I a boy? I'm too nervous. All I know is this. Mum and Dad's bodies are dangerous. Not always. But you never know. Their words of comfort that don't comfort. I can't get what I want when I don't know what it is.

Mum is always tired. She who has to deal with everything. Who can't go to pieces. But is already on her knees. Who has a job simply surviving. Who knows I exist but not what I need. I, who unleash my desperation in piercing cries. Like a bird. Cries that rip through the walls in our small house. It's Torvald who gives me an invisible sign to let them loose. He listens to my cries in silence, but he is the one who has decided that it's time.

Dad is the most dangerous, but also the warmest. When you can lie next to him in bed and listen to him reading, you feel safe. I'm squeezed against the wall and feel his body against mine. Listen to his steady breathing and just want him to carry on reading. When he disappears into the world of the story, nothing dangerous can happen. He doesn't need to be frightened and I don't need to be frightened. No one shouts at us. We're busy.

Torvald falls asleep and I whisper to Dad: 'A bit more.'

'It's your turn now,' Dad says. And I start to tell my story. He listens to me for a while, then slips out. When Torvald opens his eyes, he hears my voice telling the story as if I've been talking all night.

*

25

I hear talk of an American girl who published a book when she was eleven. I want to beat her record. I want to be nine, at the oldest. The book is called *The Stone* and is about Finn-Jon.

I stand beside my eldest sister, Marit, who is sitting at the typewriter. I dictate and she writes down the story. Once we've started, I can't stop. It doesn't matter whether it's time for lunch, supper, children's TV, to get ready for bed, bedtime story or sleep. Just forget it. It keeps coming. I can't stop now.

I'm a real writer. I'm tough, beautiful, I'm full of words and know it. At that same time I wet my bed in my sleep every night and dream horrible dreams. I'm alone in the forest or an enormous house with endless stairs. I keep losing the others. My teacher, my classmates, Mum, Dad, Marit, Hild, Torvald and little Odd. When I turn around they're gone.

I sit beside Dad on the slope up to the church and do a painting. I've been allowed to use proper oil paints, the ones he uses. We each have a palette to mix our colours. But I don't mix mine. Dad says using black is not allowed. It doesn't exist in nature. There are only darker nuances of other colours. So the black has to be mixed with other colours. I only use black. Wonder if white exists in nature. Because then the painting could be finished before I even started.

We paint a church with big chestnut trees and old grave-stones in front of it. I don't get room for the whole church on my canvas. Only the middle of the church. Two big windows. Dad has room for the whole thing, plus the trees and part of a gravestone. I praise his painting. He likes that. And I know that he likes me. I know that he likes me sitting slightly behind him and painting like him. He thinks I'm learning. But I just do what I want and it turns out well all the same. He holds his brush up in front of his face and measures. I hold my hand up in front of one eye. And look. Open my fingers. You don't see half the world with one eye.

It's snowing and winter. I tell stories to the younger children on the street. Their parents ask my mum where they can buy the books I get my stories from. 'They're not published yet,' she says, 'but they will be one day.' I walk to and from school with my classmates. Walking with me is popular. The others listen with curiosity. I've taught myself dramatic composition. When we get close to school in the morning, I finish with a real cliff-hanger. Something exciting so they'll want to hear more. And now it's time finally to go home and for the continuation.

Suddenly I have to sit down. I sit down in a snowdrift and press the heel of my boot against my bladder. I don't stop the story. The others sit round me in a ring. It's the conclusion. It's quite a funny ending. The person in the mask is our teacher. I get up. The others laugh.

But not at the story. They laugh at the yellow puddle in the snow where I've been sitting.

I don't wash. I lie on the bed and wait for a miracle. I'm grown up now. I'm big and I'm small. Can't wake up. Can't sleep. Those who are totally paralysed see nothing.

At the depths of the moment, I tie a small knot. And so life continues. I'm up at night and in bed all day. Short periods back and forth. The world is locked and I'm not there. For better or worse.

I've been out to the kitchen and made myself some coffee and a sandwich. Take it back to bed with me. Start to eat. Haven't eaten cooked food for a long time.

The doorbell rings. It's Jonathan.

'Have you been in bed with the voices all day?' he asks.

'Yes.' I ask the voices to hide me so that no one can find me. So I can't find myself.

'You haven't been following the programme. And what is that food doing there? Look in the file. Your bed is only to be used for sleep.'

Every time the doorbell rings in our small house I think that someone is dead. That it's the minister who has come. If you dare, you can look out of the kitchen window and see who is there. I've seen it on TV. How the dark figure approaches with bowed head, anxious eyes and sad tidings.

I get pains in my stomach. My head feels hot. Tears are waiting in my eyes. Crying. Bird cries. Fractures. No one can die. There can't be a now and a then when everything is different. Where Mum or Dad no longer exists.

I can't bear the world as it is, but it would be even worse if it was different.

I can tear a whole room to shreds. It's impossible to stop the destruction. The cries and tears. It might be a drawing that isn't ready when Mum says it's time to stop. If I can't finish my drawing, I might as well wreck the house. Or the classroom at school. If the bell rings and it's time to go home and I'm in the middle of something, I go to pieces. 'Please stop kicking, hitting, crying and screaming, can't you talk properly and tell us what's wrong,' the adults coax. But that's precisely what I can't do. Not now. Not yet.

But now, now I can tell stories. I am the one who tells the stories and who the stories are about. A writer knows so little, so if she learns something she has to make sure it doesn't get lost.

I write. The only thing we can change is the past, someone once said. Jonathan wouldn't agree with that.

I've just lit the tiled stove in my workspace. I'm going to give a talk about using personal experience in creative writing. We're bad witnesses. Of our own life even. But we're good at creating stories. We make the event sensible. We are filled with what we already know from similar situations.

Memory is also an excellent source when you work with stories, but less so in the courtroom. The more time that has passed since something happened, the more certain we are that we have remembered it correctly. And what were loose threads to begin with, have become a personal story.

I talk on and on. Write down key words. I want to give the students hope. You yourself are a well of stories. Draw from it.

Dad has been working for over a month. Everyone is happy about it. We know that it's payday today. He has his pay in an envelope and has walked up the long hill from the tram stop. He's gone into every shop on the way.

We sit around the kitchen table and see him coming. Mum is uneasy. He stands in the middle of the kitchen and produces a bunch of flowers from behind his back. Mum is furious. 'Where's the money?' she shouts. 'You can't buy flowers when we've got no food on the table. What else have you bought?' Dad laughs, even though he can see that Mum is angry. He wants to put on a show for us children.

'Beef steak.' He puts down a big bloody lump wrapped in paper. We've only ever eaten whale beef at home and get excited about tasting this treat. We've only heard mention of normal beef at the neighbours when they asked if we like beef and we said yes, thinking they meant cheap whale beef.

Dad has bought Pepsi too, something we never normally have, and chocolates for Mum. 'But we've got nothing to celebrate,' she says. She loves chocolate and normally keeps a bar in the top drawer of her bedside table. 'We can find something to celebrate,' Dad says. But there's no celebration.

Mum gets the electricity bill and the telephone bill and demands that he gives her the money. Dad only gives her a bit. 'And you who lent money to that alcoholic last week. You realise that we're never going to get that back, don't you?'

'It doesn't matter if he doesn't pay us back. That's life. What goes around comes around,' he reassures her. Then he dashes out of the kitchen, out of the house and into the garage. He starts up our old wreck of a car with a cough and splutter and drives off. As he usually does when they've argued.

I sit in the kitchen looking at the flowers and the meat and the chocolate lying on the table. I think the same as Mum, what's the point of flowers?

I wake up and I don't want to wake up. Don't want to get up and don't want to lie awake in bed. I've got a cold. It's been a long night. In and out of bed. Then the phone rings. It's a flower shop. I lie there and wonder who they might be from. I go through everyone who might possibly send me flowers, without coming to any conclusion. But somewhere out there, there's someone who thinks I need cheering up. I do need cheering up. I stay under the duvet. A secret admirer?

When the flowers are finally delivered in the early afternoon, it's a gigantic bouquet. At first I don't see the card and the bouquet just stands magnificent in the middle of the kitchen table. I look amongst the flowers again. Then I find the card:

Dear Eli! Congratulations on the publication of your new book. It is a truly wonderful children's book! With best wishes from your friends at the publishers.

I'm lost for words. Has one of my children's books been published today?

How can you forget something like that? Publishing a new book is usually a big thing for me. They write about it in the papers, fresh copies stand on bookshop shelves and in the library. I crawl back to bed and try to feel something. But nothing happens. I go and get the bouquet of flowers and put it in the bedroom. I don't agree with Mum any more, what's the point of flowers? I lie there looking at them. Yes, they're sending out sparks. I catch them and feel: it's worth fighting on.

I sit at the front of the classroom. The teacher is drawing a cow on the blackboard with all its four stomachs and what they are called. I see the outline of the cow, but not the text, what the four stomachs are called. That is what we are supposed to be learning, and I really want to. How can the others see? We have to write it down in our books. I draw a cow, wait for the teacher to point and say the word out loud. But she doesn't.

I've known for a long time. The others see much better than me. But I can't tell anyone. Being dyslexic is enough. I can't say that I can't see the letters at all. And who would I tell? Not the teacher. Not anyone at home. I don't know.

I think to myself that everything will sort itself out when I'm a grown-up. And until then, I'll just have to keep a secret.

It's a sunny day in the middle of summer. We're going to go swimming, the whole family. I've been looking forward to it all day. While I wait, I walk around in the high grass with the scythe in my hand. I'm just going to cut a bit. I'm good with the scythe.

But then there are some hazel shoots. They're far too thick. I take one hand off the scythe so that I can hold the shoots. I swing with all my might and slice the hand that is holding the shoots. I drop the scythe and my hand rushes up to my mouth. I've cut my pinkie. The blood is pouring. My pinkie is almost hanging off. It's nearly cut to the bone.

I run into the woods behind the house. The others can go without me. I hold my other hand tightly round my pinkie. I mustn't be sick or hurt myself. It's Mum who can't take pain. It's Mum who can't take it when things don't turn out the way she expected.

When I'm certain that they've gone, I go back to the house. The blood is still pouring. My finger is thumping. It has nearly fallen off. At home, I try to make a splint to keep it straight. Then use a gauze bandage and lots of plasters. The splint is an ice-lolly stick from the drawer. It's longer than my pinkie and juts out. I break off the top. It has to look like a small cut. The blood seeps through and I have to bandage it again. It heals over time, but will now forever be a slightly crooked pinkie.

The bell rings. I open the door in my pyjamas. It's midday. I spent most of the night writing.

It's Jonathan. I rush into the bedroom and put on some clothes. We sit down at the kitchen table. I'm not as curious about Jonathan as I have been about my previous therapists. He tells me about himself over time and is not particularly secretive.

We write down everything we do. Draw up lists and anxiety management strategies. There are always two sides, problems and solutions. Advantages and disadvantages. I have a form to fill out every evening about how I think the night is going to be, on a scale from one to ten. The next morning, I have to fill in how it was, on a scale from one to ten.

I see Dad sitting in the car in the garage having a sneaky cigarette. Because he's stopped smoking.

He has a rope round his neck. I wrench open the door. He puts his finger to his lips and says shhh. Then he stubs out the cigarette. 'Don't tell anyone.' 'What are you going to do?' I ask and point at the rope. He doesn't answer. He's not very good at talking. Except for when he's telling funny stories.

There's something dark in his eyes. He starts the car. 'Where are you going?' 'Nowhere.' 'Can I come too?' Normally he lets me. But not when they've been arguing.

'I'm not going anywhere,' he says in a hard voice, and pushes me out of the car, then locks the door. He lights another cigarette. I stand with my face to the window and stare in. 'Dad, Dad,' I shout.

When he's finished the cigarette he suddenly starts the car and I have to jump out of the way. He reverses out of the garage at full speed. Spins round and races off out through the gate. I run after the car down the street, waving my arms and shouting: 'Stop!'

He probably won't manage to hang himself. There's so much he can't do. He can't keep down a job. He can't help in the house like Mum wants him to. He wants things to be neat and tidy, but in his own way. When we're going to go anywhere, he gets all us kids into the car hours before we leave. But there's lots of things he can do. He's a good carpenter, he makes paintings and sings. He calls in strangers from the street to come and look at his paintings. He reads books. He reads out loud for us children.

He and I can stop grimacing. Stop flaring up for nothing. Stop going to pieces.

I sit on the snowdrift by the gate and wait for him to come back. I feel the cold and damp seep in through my trousers, through my tights, knickers and right into my bum. I wet myself. I'm wet from the outside in and now from the inside out. I move from the yellow patch in the snow and find myself somewhere new to sit. It looks like a dog has been here. Mum calls out that food is on the table. I don't go in. I wait until it gets dark and then I see the car creeping slowly up the road. And I hurry in. Dad mustn't see that I was waiting. That I was scared he might die.

Events wait to become stories. The sculpture sleeps in the stone. I'm writing about my childhood again. At first I thought that memory was a photograph that became a painting as I wrote. And that the painting then replaces the memory. But the more I write, the more I realise that the memory was never a photograph to begin with. There is no original. Does creating involve both writing and erasing at the same time? I don't think so. I think that the past is a swirling torrent, but you can still wade out into it. I normally say that I have experienced everything I write about, because when I write it down with the full range of emotions, I have experienced it. But it's wrong to think it was like that from the start. Memories don't stay where you left them. You've dragged them around with you into every nook and cranny of life. Like pulling a sledge, a lot has fallen off and more has been added.

It's Christmas Eve and I'm all dressed up and waiting. I do somersaults in Mum and Dad's big bed. I do somersaults from the bed down onto the floor, several times. And then, crash. I land on one of Dad's paintings. It's standing on the floor with a few others that he's done, leaning up against the wall. The glass breaks and the painting gets torn. What will Dad say? What will he do with his mouth? And his arms? Will I get hit?

I can run round and round in the deep snow out in the garden. Without seeing the sunlight and rabbit tracks. Just run. Run until I'm dizzy and can put up with anything. Dad might come after me.

I'm too big to be tied to the bed, like when I was little. I'm too big. How will I be punished? How can I somersault backwards again so that it never happened? 'Cut yourself,' Espen says. 'Blood, courage.'

I pick up a piece of glass and start cutting my arm. Now I've ruined Christmas Eve, I think, close my eyes and cut a deep wound in each arm. The blood runs down onto my white dress and down onto the white wooden floor.

It's Granddad who finds me. He looks at my arms. 'That needs stitches,' he says, and gets Mum and Dad. They look at the cuts and say nothing about the painting. Silently they pick up the pieces of glass. They start to discuss whether I really need stitches as it's Christmas Eve and we're about to eat Christmas dinner. But in the end we go, just in case.

There's nearly no cars on the road. It's five o'clock and we wind down the car windows to listen to the church bells ring in

Christmas. At A&E there are Christmas decorations, but nearly no people. The people waiting there are silent and all dressed up. Apart from one man who comes in on unsteady feet with blood on his face. He stinks and he's left to sit in a corner and talk to himself.

The doctor is kind and asks why I have done this to myself. To which I don't have an answer. She says that she will get me an appointment with a child psychiatrist. Someone to talk to. I get nine stitches in one arm and seven in the other. I get some stickers of Santa Claus to share with my siblings, who have been quiet and good in this horrible place.

Then we go home again. Eat Christmas dinner and sing Christmas carols around the tree at midnight. And then, finally, I get to open my presents in my pyjamas. I've got a piece of white material from some relatives where I can embroider the letter E with flowers all around it. I can't embroider and don't want to learn. My eyes are too bad. I want the same things Torvald gets.

The good presents must not be overshadowed by the futile anger I feel about the ones that are wrong. It seems so pointless to get something you don't want when there is so much you do want. I get a box that Dad has made and decorated with a traditional Norwegian rose painting. I like it. I'm going to hide all the things I don't like in it and bury it in the garden until summer. I've got a special place for things I don't want to be found.

After Christmas, Mum and I meet a child psychiatrist. She has toys and a sandpit in her office. Mum tells her all about my screaming and crying and bird noises that really pierce your ears once I get started. And that I can wreck a whole room if you just turn your back. That I wet myself at night and get hysterical about things that Mum doesn't understand.

I say nothing. Me, who is normally bursting with words. The

child psychiatrist asks Mum to go out, but that doesn't help. I've got nothing to say to this woman I don't know. Nothing about this. Nothing about the difficult things. I'm used to making things up and telling stories, but that's not what this woman wants to hear. I can't mention Espen. He's a secret.

The psychiatrist asks if I want to come back and play in the sandpit. I don't want to. She writes out a prescription for some pills that I'm to take every evening. I don't know what the pills are for and Mum doesn't either when I ask her. Next time when Marit goes to the chemist to pick them up, she asks and is told they're for nerves.

'I'm nervous.'

'Yes, I can see that,' Jonathan tells me.

'I'm nervous about the jab tomorrow. Haven't been able to sleep all night. Everything inside me says that I don't want a depot injection of anti-psychotic drugs. I keep trying to tell my doctor, but he says that it's a preventative measure. My little boys inside say don't, full stop.'

'I know that they make a fuss and don't want to. But it's not them we should listen to,' Jonathan says.

'My doctor told me that I've got a chronic illness. Wasn't much fun to hear that.'

'He's both right and wrong, really,' Jonathan says. 'Childhood is also chronic. It depends on how you deal with it, there is always a healing power. If we only did what our mothers did all our lives, the world would come to a standstill.'

'I don't want to have neuroleptics in my body, now that I'm well. I think it would be good to only take them when I'm psychotic. But being given the injections instead of pills, just because the doctor thinks I'm skipping the pills, makes me feel powerless. I want to do that. I want to be well now.'

'We're working on it,' Jonathan assures me. 'We'll show the doctor that what we're doing is better than medicine. We're working towards you being drug-free. You've had your dosage halved since last year.'

'But I don't want to take anything at all.'

I close my eyes and throw the chronic label over my shoulder, behind me, where it belongs.

Mum and I are going to go skiing. Mum has promised me some hot chocolate at a teaching college by the edge of the forest. Mum has new skis and new ski pants. Yellow like Big Bird, with a ribbed yellow woolly hat. She looks very smart. We use the wrong wax, but don't re-wax our skis. Just set out on skis that are slippy. We have to cross a big road before the forest starts. When I'm on my own, I normally ski to a café further into the forest. But Mum can't face going that far. I always turn back at the café. Don't go into the warmth and buy something. I just stamp my card so I can show them at school that I've been there. The teacher then writes the number of kilometres down on a squared sheet that hangs on the wall. My column is the longest. The teacher has had to tape on an extra piece of paper to write up all my distances.

There is a high snowdrift by the side of the road left behind in the wake of the snowplough. The road has been gritted so you have to ski down the drift at an angle and stop abruptly at the bottom to take your skis off. Mum stands on top of the snowdrift. She gingerly puts one ski down. Instead of doing the plough, she leans on her sticks. The whole of her upper body is leaning forwards. The skis slip away from under her. I can see what's about to happen.

Mum falls hard on her back. She slides down to the road and then just lies there. I follow her. Stand there. 'Did you hurt yourself?' I ask. I saw how hard she fell. She says nothing. I give her my stick and she hauls herself up with great difficulty. I see her wince and put her hand to her back. 'Shall we go home?' I ask.

'Absolutely not,' Mum says. 'I've promised you a hot chocolate.'

We ski across the fields towards the forest. Mum is in pain but doesn't give up. We make slow progress. I don't race ahead. I move my skis in slow motion, turn around and see Mum is straight as a poker and determined. I want to go home.

We get to the college. We have to go up three floors and there's no lift. Mum can scarcely walk. She stops on every step and I can see how much it hurts, but she says nothing. We find a drinks machine in the corridor and buy a hot chocolate each. Mum drinks hers quickly. Mine is too hot. I burn my mouth. I don't chat away like I normally do. I say nothing and Mum says nothing. I'm sure that Mum wants me to enjoy my warm chocolate, but I don't. I force it down in small gulps. Mum wants everything to be as planned. But it's not.

When we go back down the stairs again, Mum is in terrible pain. Pain is not allowed for us children. And not for adults either. She goes down a step then stops. Down a step then stops. Slowly we make our home across the fields as dark falls.

Mum doesn't sleep all night. She is tired and stiff at breakfast. She says that she's going to go to the hospital, that it's nothing to worry about but she just wants to get it checked. She comes home after having had to wait for a long time. Three ribs are broken. Espen shouts: 'Ouch! Ouch!' No one hears him. I say: 'No!' It doesn't exist. Pain doesn't exist.

'Maybe you should call your mother,' Espen says. But I don't want to right now. 'Maybe you could make her laugh a little,' he says. I bang my fist against my head.

'Maybe I could make myself laugh,' I say.

'Good,' says Jonathan.

The doorbell rings. It's not the minister, it's the boys from the street. They want to play football or go skiing with Mum's little wild princess. But one evening the doorbell rings and it's dark and there are no children outside. I can feel in my whole body. Someone has died.

No one opens the door and the bell rings again. The sound tears through my body. I lean forward to look out of the kitchen window and see a dark shadow. It's the minister. I open the window and try to say hello. I can't get a word out. I'm visible in the brightly lit kitchen.

'Is your dad at home?' asks a voice in the dark. I close the window. It's Mum who decides. I don't want to let him in with his horrible message. I run and hide in the cupboard above the garage. I crawl under some soft yellow glass fibre matting. Whoever isn't at home has died. Who isn't at home?

Then I hear a voice that isn't Espen. 'You're not alone. You're not Eli any more. You are me, Emil,' the boy's voice says. 'You don't need to be so frightened of death any more.'

'What should I do then?' I whisper with a pounding heart. I feel death all through my body. It's very close. 'You'll cope with death,' the boy's voice tells me. 'I'll help you. As long as you play football nothing scary can happen. I'm ten, just like you. I'm the best football player in the world, just like you. You can hide in the game.'

My chest burns when he speaks. 'Don't believe that the grown-ups see you because you've got long angel hair. They only see the hair. You're not who they think you are. You're also

48

Emil. Every time the doorbell or telephone rings, or whenever I want, I'll be there. Every time someone is about to die, I'll be there.'

Then there is silence. I rub my head and hair on the glass fibre. Then I hear the voice again. 'Eli, Eli,' he calls. I say: 'Yes, yes, yes.' 'Don't tell anyone about me. I'm your secret.'

I leave the cupboard and sneak back into the living room. Marit is sitting at the table with the sewing machine in front of her. 'I'm making a dress for you,' she says. 'Emerald blue.' 'Who was it at the door?' I ask, still frightened. 'It was the tramp. Come over here and try it on.'

I stand on the floor in front of her. Hold up my arms and let my big sister undress me and dress me again like a doll. 'It was only the tramp?' I ask, my heart still racing. Our tramp, as Mum and Dad like to call him. He always asks for Dad. Because he gets five kronor from him, whereas Mum only gives him two.

I wriggle in the blue dress. My body starts to itch. 'Take it off!' I shout, and Marit and I both try to get it off at the same time. I've got a red rash all over my arms, neck and face. 'What is it?' Marit asks. 'Don't know.' 'Where have you been?' 'The cupboard.' 'You didn't touch the glass fibre matting, did you?' 'Yes.' 'That's what it is then. You'd better have a shower.'

I don't want to. I stand there in my knickers. The itching is unbearable. But I don't want to have a shower. Don't like having a bath or a shower when I'm not on my own any more and can be with Espen. His tears start to fall as soon as the water starts running.

And now I've got Emil as well. Someone who plays and has promised to help me cope with death. I will need lots of time to be with them. Marit says something at the same time as both Espen and Emil. It's hard to hear their voices and chat when I'm supposed to be normal and answer other people's questions.

49

It's too much. But I'm going to have to learn how to do it.

I run into the bathroom and pick up a brush. Rub it all over my body.

I want to have my picture in the local paper. I persuade the boy next door, Bjarne, to come with me and sell raffle tickets for a good cause. We've just heard about a volcano in Iceland on the news. We decide that we're going to support the children affected by the catastrophe. I steal a vase from my second sister, Hild's collection. It's going to be the prize.

We have a notebook, a pen and a plastic bag for the money. Everyone who opens their door recognises us and wants to help. 'What thoughtful children,' they say. When we get home again, we find a hat and put as many folded pieces of paper with a number on it as there are names in the notebook. Bjarne mixes them all up in the hat. I close my eyes and pull out a piece of paper. It's number thirty-three.

Old Mrs Vangen has won. We barely know her as she hasn't got any children. We've never been in her house, just in her garden to steal apples. All the children on the street are a little bit scared of Mrs Vangen. She's obviously a miser. She only bought one raffle ticket today.

We ring the doorbell and have to wait on the doorstep for a long time. Eventually Mrs Vangen comes and opens the door a crack, then peers out cautiously. She has a security chain that needs to be opened. No one else has that.

'Oh, is it you?' she says, sharply, though perhaps it was meant to be kind. 'Come in.' We stand in the hallway. It's dark. 'You, you, you've won,' I stammer. 'Oh,' she says, surprised, takes the vase and carries it out into the kitchen. 'Now let me see if I've got something for you.'

We want to go. Why do some people live on their own? No one who has children does. And we only know people like that.

'I thought I had some chocolate, but no.' 'It doesn't matter,' I say. 'The children in Iceland are all that matter,' I say. Mrs Vangen strokes my blonde curls. 'What beautiful hair,' she says. I twist away. It's cold in the room. 'We really have to go now,' I say.

'Here, why don't you take an apple each.' We each take an apple and hurry out. When we're back out on the street we start to giggle. The apples are wrinkly, having been stored all winter. We throw them as far away as we can. 'Let's go back to my house and count the money,' Bjarne says.

We sit in his room and empty the plastic bag of money out onto the bed. We count. It comes to three hundred and forty-seven kronor. 'I'll ask Mum to call the paper tomorrow,' I say. There's a pile of magazines on the desk. 'Do you read them?' I ask. 'They're for grown-ups.' 'We get given them,' Bjarne explains. 'My granddad does the crossword. I read about a downhill skier called Erika. She was in the Olympics and is from Austria. She changed sex and christened herself Erik. But then she couldn't take part in any more competitions, either as a man or a woman.'

Bjarne finds the magazine and I stare at the pictures of the downhill skier before and after the operation. She looks pretty similar in both pictures, with short dark hair and a fringe. Bjarne starts to talk about something else. But I can't take my eyes from the pictures. Before and after. Erika and Erik. Man, woman.

I'm going to do that, I think. Maybe that will save me from growing up. I have to be allowed to be a boy before I grow up, at least. The princess is going to turn into a prince. But I can't say anything to Bjarne. They might write about it in a normal magazine, but I realise that it's more complicated than that. That it's a long secret journey. But I store the possibility somewhere deep inside and think about it nearly every day for the rest of my life.

The next day we take the money down to the local paper. We are photographed. And we're interviewed as well, but it's only me who speaks. I say that we've started a club that's going to collect more money for those who need help. I want to give examples but can only come up with the poor children in Iceland.

Our photograph is in the paper the next day. I'm so proud. But my brother Torvald teases me and says that there aren't any poor children in Iceland. That it's one of the richest countries in the world. That I should have said Biafra.

I'm going to give a reading in Bohuslän. I take a train and then a bus and then another bus. There are fewer and fewer people on the bus, and by the time I get off there is no one left. I don't like travelling to places I don't know on my own, and it's always a huge relief when I arrive at the right place. My bad eyesight means that I can't see signs and timetables and what's written on the front of a bus. I don't dare to ask for help due to pride or shyness.

I've ended up on a small square edged by some shops and public sector offices. It's the middle of the day. Not a person to be seen. I spot the library and go in. It's empty in there too. I see a poster of myself advertising the reading this evening. I meet the librarian, she makes me feel welcome. She drives me to the hotel and says that she'll come back and pick me up at six.

I sit down on a sofa to wait. Then a woman comes. She introduces herself as the hotel manager. 'Do you serve lunch?' I ask. 'I'll sort something out for you. I've got a whitefish. Would you like that?' I nod. 'Go and have a sauna in the meantime, while I get things ready.'

I'm in the sauna for a long time. When I go back up to the dining room, a table has been set with a white tablecloth and a plate with a big fish on it. And lots to go with it. Potatoes and vegetables. The hotel manager comes and keeps me company. 'You're the only guest in the hotel,' she says. The only guest. I remind myself that we live in a sparsely populated country. I remember the time I was in Greenland on a research trip. I took a boat along the west coast and every time we stopped in a small town, they made an announcement about something unique that we had to go and see. 'You will find the only fountain in Greenland here.' I got chatting to a Swede. He was going to cover for a Dane and would be the only psychiatrist in Greenland over the summer. I met him some weeks later in Nuuk. The problem was that he didn't understand the Greenlanders' broken Danish and they didn't understand his Swedish.

The hotel manager chats away. 'The owner called me and said you have to come home and take over the hotel. I was living in Gothenburg at the time. And I haven't regretted it for a moment.'

Why do we move and why do we move home? Everyone thinks about moving away and everyone thinks about moving home again. From the country to the city, from the city to the country. From country to country.

'I'll have dinner ready for you at five. I just need to pop out and do some shopping first. Is there anything you don't eat?' 'I eat everything,' I reply. It's good that I'm here. I make a difference.

I go up to my room, stuffed, and lie down on my bed to rest. Then I practise reading the texts and look at the key words that I've written about what I'm going to say. I know the texts more or less off by heart so I don't need to worry about bad lighting. I'm going to talk for one and a half hours. I'm looking forward to the evening. Only hope people will come. I gave a reading in Gothenburg yesterday and there were over a hundred people there.

Dinner is the same as lunch, only even more food. I can choose between several dishes. It would be impossible for me to eat it all. The hotel manager keeps me company again and tells me what it was like to come back to her hometown after twenty years in the city. I'm given a key. 'The door can be quite difficult.' We go out and practise. 'Here's my mobile number. I only live a stone's throw away.'

The librarian picks me up. Around twenty people come. Some to listen to me, others to meet people. There's a good atmosphere and they laugh a lot and ask questions. They get even livelier in the break when coffee and cake are served.

When I get back to the hotel I can't open the door. I try again and again. Suddenly the hotel manager appears out of the dark. 'I knew that you'd have problems,' she said. It's ten o'clock. We say goodnight. 'Breakfast at eight,' she says and then goes home. I go into the big building and think that I'm going to sleep in here all on my own.

I wake all sweaty from a dream and get up to drink some water. Think that I'm all alone in this big building. It would have been different if the building had been smaller. There are meant to be lots of people here. I am lots of people.

Espen starts talking. He's been woken by the water from the tap. He cries and says that he's frightened. That someone will lock us in an even smaller room in an even bigger building. I try to console him. Do I have to be the adult? Do I have to be the one who's not scared?

I go out into the dark corridor just to test myself. I feel my way. I walk along to the end and back. Then I get into bed again. Emil can't help reminding me about a hotel corridor in a sky-scraper in New York. I pressed the button to call the lift. It took some time. Then the doors opened and I saw a policeman and a nurse and a black rubbish bag the size of a person on the floor. I froze and watched the lift doors slide shut again.

I can't sleep. I've got small holes in my eyelids. Close them and I can still see. The dark. And an even smaller room in a small house. I've been locked in the toilet. I'm five years old.

The door has a key that can lock the door from the inside and the outside, but the light switch is only on the outside. I've been throwing things around and screaming from deep down in my belly. High pitched like a bird. I'm carried, screeching, into the toilet. Everything will end up in small pieces. My frustration and anger know no end. I cannot be comforted. The key is turned and the light switched off.

I am to calm down in there in the dark. There's nothing to break in there in the dark. I hurl myself against the walls and door. I know that it won't help. What helps? I flush anything that's lying loose down the toilet. I fumble around in the dark. Soap and toilet paper. I can keep flushing until the toilet breaks. I can turn on the tap and let Espen weep in the running water.

I am blind. I am confined. I am wound up like a propeller. Then all the energy drains out of me, there's nothing left to break. Empty of screams and tears. But I will have to stay there for a while, I know that from experience. Mum lets out a sigh. I think. And Dad is sitting somewhere in a meadow painting the landscape. Marit, Hild and Torvald will have to pee behind a bush in the garden. They wait. Are worried and wonder how long I'll be locked up. Odd is still in nappies and if Mum is lucky, he sleeps between crying.

I turn off the water. Dry my swollen blotchy face with the hand towel and sit down on the floor. There's a cupboard I can't reach. Tried to climb up on the sink. There are plasters, bandages, creams and pills in it. I wrap myself up in the hand towel. And start to tell stories. I tell myself stories. One day I'll tell them to the whole world.

There's a knock on the door at half past seven. A personal wake-up call from the hotel manager. I get dressed without having a shower and go down to the dining room. In amongst all the empty tables is one with a white tablecloth, set for one. The food has been laid out on the sideboard. It looks like it's the middle of the high season. There are several boiled eggs. There's scrambled eggs and bacon. Sausages and yoghurt and porridge and pineapple and other fruits and a basket of warm bread. Where shall I begin?

I'm standing in the kitchen at my gran's. My gran is massively fat. They say it's because she's got diabetes. I'm eight and it's the first time I'm visiting her and Grandpa on my own.

Marit once knitted Gran a stripy waistcoat for Christmas. It was so big that there was room for Torvald, Hild and me inside it. It was too big for Gran as well, which must have upset her. I've certainly never seen her wearing it.

Grandpa built the little yellow wooden hut. He's a carpenter. There's a workbench in the cellar with all kinds of interesting tools. I can potter about down there if I want. And Grandpa has a drawer of building blocks that you can build anything with. I'm going to stay the night. I don't know them really and they don't know me. I'll wet myself. But they don't know that yet. I haven't said anything and Mum hasn't told them.

I'm standing in the old-fashioned kitchen. I want to get a glass of water. The tap is directly under the water heater. Gran is right behind me. I hold out my glass and turn on the water. It's boiling hot. It hits my hand and I drop the glass. A reflex. I hear it smash. Gran hears it smash. My hand is burning under the boiling water.

Then there's an explosion. Gran's hand slaps me hard in the face. The shards of glass have just stopped tinkling. Ow, crash, slap. Ow, crash, slap. I run as fast as I can. Out of the kitchen, out of the house, out of the gate. Down the street and into the park. I hide myself in some bushes. Sit there shaking. Ow, crash, slap.

I sit there until it gets dark. Then Grandpa comes to find me. He holds out his great carpenter's hand and I take it and get up.

I'm glad that Grandpa found me. I wasn't looking forward to spending the night in a bush.

I can't apologise to Gran about the glass. Because I didn't mean to do it. Gran has such a hard voice. Even though she's lived half her life in Norway, she still speaks bad Norwegian. I'm far from home and know what's going to happen. I'm going to sleep on the sofa bed in the living room and I'm going to wet myself in a strange bed. I stuff my pyjama bottoms full of towels. Don't drink anything all evening and try to stay awake. But in the early hours, I need to pee.

I've had my ears pierced. I stand in Mum and Dad's room and look at myself in the mirror. Two small pearls nearly hidden by my hair. I tuck my hair behind my ears. I'm a bit proud of my blonde, thick, curly hair, but I also hate it. It has become a part of me that isn't really me. From the outside it's me, but not from the inside. Grown-ups always comment on it and pat it as if I were a dog.

I don't know how it ended up on my head and nor does Mum. Her hair is thin and brown, just like my sisters'. Mum loves plaiting it. My hair is like a special little person for Mum. But it's going to go soon. To make the truth visible.

My doll-like face. The big brown eyes. Then I see what's wrong. I don't want a hole in each ear. I want two holes in the same ear and nothing in the other. How can I explain that to Mum? I start with the hair. 'Mum.' 'Yes, what is it?' 'Sit down,' I say, and Mum sits down on the kitchen sofa. 'I want to cut my hair short. A bit longer on one side than the other, with a long sloping fringe and short at the back, and two earrings in the same ear.' Mum stuffs her hands into her apron pocket. 'I won't let you,' she says. 'I'll do it anyway.' 'Do you have to?' I nod, and feel sorry for Mum.

'Ask Marit,' she says. Marit is happy to help me with any-thing, but this time she doesn't want to. I sit on a stool with a towel round my neck. It's Mum who has to cut my hair. First she makes a plait that she then cuts right off. She's going to keep it. Then she starts to style it. Slightly longer on one side, and Mum does it as well as she can. At least we're saving money by not going to the hairdresser.

When she's done, I look at myself curiously in the mirror. Mum is standing behind me with the scissors in her hand. She says in a thick voice: 'You look like a little troll.' Her words warm me. I headbang. Play the air guitar. Run my hand through my hair so it stands out in all directions.

'You're Emil,' a voice inside me says. I shoot myself with my hand in the mirror. I shoot Eli and the princess and all that has been. I purse my lips, narrow my eyes. Slowly, slowly I let my hand fall and put the revolver back in its holster. I make a little clicking sound with my mouth. As if the baddy has been rendered harmless.

As an adult, I dream a recurring dream about changing sex. I meet all sorts of doctors and psychologists. They ask me questions and I'm measured and weighed. Open wide and say aaaa. I tense my small biceps and have to pick up a doll and cuddle it. I have to look at myself in a mirror and try on different caps and hats. I have to be a goalkeeper and do a goal kick. I have to open packages and they observe my reactions. But most of all, there are corridors, rooms for bureaucracy and different forms for different alternatives that have to be filled out. I find all the paperwork challenging and have to ask several times. Fill them out in different languages I don't really speak, but pretend to. Crumple the paper into a ball and throw it away. Do it again. When I finally get to the form where I'm asked which sex I want to become, I can't answer. Can't decide which one. And so just put down a question mark. More masculine, more feminine?

I am ten and Marit is seventeen. We're skiing from cabin to cabin in the mountains. Just me and my big sister alone in the mountain kingdom. We're carrying enormous rucksacks. I keep banging my head on mine and start to cry. It's so heavy and uncomfortable. I can't move my neck normally. It's an adult's rucksack and my back is too short. Marit doesn't complain.

After our first night, we eat breakfast and make a big packed lunch. Then we do what all the other guests do. Study the map and choose our route for the day. We decide to go to the Grimsdal cabin.

The sun is up and it's going to be a glitteringly glorious day. We head off along the ridge. We can see the peak we need to go over, which we know is deceptive because it looks very close. Which it isn't. After a short rest, we start to climb, several kilometres of herringbone in order to reach the top.

Finally we're up. The summer cairn is as good hidden in snow. Only the top stones are showing. 'It's downhill all the way from here,' I say blithely. I'm going to hold a downhill position the whole time. I've been looking forward to this all the way up all the slopes. Marit doesn't dare. 'See you down at the Grimsdal cabin then,' I say, and turn on the spot. It's almost a straight ten kilometres downhill. Marit slowly puts on the heavy rucksack. Amongst other things she's got a reindeer hide, knitting and a book in it. I'd forgotten that the stupid rucksack got in the way of my head. But all that matters is the downhill now. No way am I going to stop. I turn round and see that Marit is nothing more than a red dot on the mountainside.

There's a rushing in my ears. Kilometre after kilometre. The snow is hard and I'm going really fast. My legs are shaking. A pleasant pain warms me. The sun has gone behind a cloud. The snow is blue-white and everywhere. When I get down into the valley the tracks fork. I go to the right and follow the valley floor. Here and there, dwarf birches poke up through all the whiteness. I should see the cabin soon. But I don't see it. There are no cabins to be seen.

I have forked off from the tracks several times and my trail has become thinner and thinner. I don't meet anyone. Ski slowly into the dark. There's no tracks under my skis any more. I'll be there soon. Be there soon, I think. I can only see the tips of my skis in front of me sliding on the hard snow.

I'm exhausted and the rucksack is rubbing against my back. I say: 'Yes, yes, yes,' to myself. The wind howls. The hour it should have taken to ski down the mountainside has long since passed. I want to fall down and just lie there. I want to call out across the snow. There is an eternity of grey-blue air around me. An eternity of snow and air.

'If you lie down, you'll die!' It's Emil talking. 'Is that what you want?' That's Espen's voice, thin and teary. I sneer. 'Yes, yes, yes.' That means that I hear them. 'Is that what you want?' says Espen. Don't know. Maybe I could just sit down for a while. 'If you sit down, you'll freeze to death,' says Emil. I start to ski in a big circle. If I go straight ahead and that's wrong, I'll never meet anyone. The mountain plateaus here are endless.

Emil says: 'Sing something, or you'll die.' I sing 'Fair is Creation', like in church. Espen sings along. He's got the kind of beautiful boy's voice that I would love to have. I'm not alone. I ski in a circle for hours. Together with Espen and Emil. Every step is one too many. My disquiet evaporates for short moments. Deep tracks in the snow. It's not as hard here as up on the mountain. I just need to turn round to make sure that I'm still alive.

Marit must have got there a long time ago. Marit knows nothing about Espen. No one does, except me. The world is so full of people, but there's no one I can tell. You live in the same air. But are completely alone in your own body. Like a balloon. The air outside and the air inside the thin shell that can burst. You just have to avoid the pin that is a constant threat. Which means that one day it will all just go pop.

'Lie down then. Lie down on your rucksack and die. They'll miss you. But they'll get over it. They'll remember you as you never were. They'll believe that you struggled all night. But you didn't. You just lay down. They'll find you frozen with your thumb in your mouth.'

I can't face going round and round all night. It would be easier to die. But I can manage a little more. Maybe I can manage to do it all night. Maybe I do want to live. If Espen says I can't then I can. Emil says I can. He's a bit stronger. He's like me. But the rucksack is too big. It's rubbing again. My legs are completely numb. My back and neck ache. I'm hungry.

Is it better to exist than not to exist? I try to stop thinking for a while. I'm not thinking now. But I'm thinking all the same. Wonder what Marit is doing. Sitting in a warm cabin, having soup and waiting for me. I should have got there first. Wonder what Mum is doing. I want to eat sweets.

Suddenly I notice that they're not here any longer. Espen and Emil have gone. It's empty. Only me, who can feel them sinking away deep inside me. Only Eli is in me. Espen and Emil don't want to die with me.

There's a hole in reality. That's where I am now. On the edge. See myself from outside. The big rucksack in the dark. It must be night soon. Reality is not here. It's in the warm cabin where

66

Marit is having soup and wondering where I've got to. I pull off my hat. How could Marit be so stupid as to let me out of her sight? Just because I'm a better downhill skier. How could I think that I would know the difference between left and right down in the valley?

It starts to snow. White snowflakes falling out of the dark. Dancing around in the air. I stick out my tongue and taste them. Then I hear a voice through the dark, shouting in the distance far away. 'Eli! Eli!'

'Here,' I shout back. It's not Espen. It's outside. 'Eli!'

'Yes!' I head towards the voice. 'I'm here!'

Then a dark shadow appears on the snow. A small skier. We're in each other's arms. It's not me with the rucksack who's the heaviest. It's Marit, her arms hanging round my neck. She lets loose her tears, great rivers. 'I'm here,' I whisper. My voice barely carries. It dissolves in the air. 'I got lost,' I say. 'But I'm here now.' We fall over in the snow and Marit is still crying. It warms me right through. Does she really love me that much? I feel sparks in my stomach. This magical warmth is worth all the pain. Marit really loves me.

We stand up. I follow my sniffing sister all the way back to the cabin. It feels like I've won something. It feels fantastic. Marit says nothing, but halfway she takes the rucksack. When we get to the cabin I can hardly stand up in the warmth of the room.

We crawl up onto the sleeping platform. There are grown up skiers there too, snoring. When we're lying next to each other, Marit says quietly: 'Let's not tell anyone about this.' I close my eyes and fall asleep.

I sit on the edge of my bed in the psychiatric ward. My favourite nurse on night shift is sitting beside me. He's an auxiliary and will soon finish his law degree. The hospital will lose a real pearl.

'My head is splitting in two,' I say. One that sees badly and one that doesn't see badly. Don't tell anyone. 'It's splitting open. The blood is pouring out.' He puts his hand on my head. 'It's just as whole,' he says. 'No splits, no blood.' 'It's splitting,' I say. He takes my hand. Puts it on my head. 'Feel,' he says.

Marit is emigrating to Australia. She has a boyfriend from down under. When the day comes for her to leave, the whole family goes to the airport with her to say goodbye. Marit is going to fly to London and from there, take an emigration boat all the way to Australia where her boyfriend is waiting. They need labour there.

The year is 1974. It is the last migrant ship to sail between London and Sydney. After that, unemployment catches up with Australia as well. The passage is free. But you have to stay there for at least two years, or repay the ticket.

We stand by the check-in desk. Marit looks younger than her eighteen years and has put on far too much make-up. It's not in to wear make-up. This is the heyday of feminism. Marit is wearing an unfashionable home-made fitted suit. Maybe she's already in Australia. On the other side of the world and a grown-up woman. The rest of us are all dressed in the same light-green long-sleeved t-shirts and dungarees.

Mum goes to the ladies' to cry. She has had to sign the emigration papers as the legal age is twenty. She's away for a long time. Marit checks in her enormous suitcase. She's packed an entire lifetime. Dad asks a woman to go into the ladies' toilets to get Mum. She's not allowed to finish crying. Mum refuses to come out. Dad takes a photo of us children with Marit in the middle. He sends another woman in to get Mum. When she finally comes out, it's a hasty farewell. Then Marit disappears through security control.

In the car on the way home, Dad tells us about a friend of a friend who flew to Sydney. Disembarked. Picked up his luggage. Went out onto the road outside the airport, was run over by a bus and died. I don't want to hear, but Emil does.

Granddad moves in with us. He doesn't want to live in an old people's home. His second wife has now died and he has never made a sandwich himself. He thinks Mum should look after him. He's going to sleep on the sofa in the living room.

He wants to be called MP, main person, and likes to show us that he's got an entry in the encyclopedia. He was one of the best chess players in Europe between the wars. He designed IQ tests and sold them to newspapers and was a professor in mathematics. He was a working class boy who got scholarships all the way through school because he was so gifted. He's nearly ninety. Wanders around at night confusing nursery rhymes and mathematical formulas. Round and round from the living room to the hall to the kitchen. When he passes through the kitchen he turns on a hotplate, and when he comes back through again looks at the glowing hot plate and swears. He's scared of burning to death.

I'm woken by his singing. When he sees me he says: 'Three point fourteen, two times two, big devils and five small demons ahoy.' He looks completely different and his speech is unclear. Then I notice for the first time that he hasn't got any teeth at night.

Dad is wrestling with my little brother, Odd. The chairs go flying and they roll around on the kitchen floor. Suddenly Odd starts to cry. Dad is too strong. Dad is the strongest of us kids. Dad can't fill in a form at the post office, we have to do it. Most often Torvald. It's best to have him with you. Dad doesn't know our postcode or telephone number. Sometimes even Odd is lifted up onto the counter and little Odd rattles off the numbers that Dad doesn't know.

What is it with Dad? When he goes to pick Odd up from the nursery, he can sometimes come home with the wrong child. When he's driving the car he can't decide where to go. He just follows the car in front, turns when it turns. Sometimes he gets in behind parked cars and waits for them to move. No one in my football team wants to drive in Dad's car to away games. Because there's a risk you won't get there.

Dad has lost his job as the janitor at school. Mum won't say why. Suddenly he was back home one day. And the pupils liked him so much. It's the grown-ups who think that Dad doesn't do what he should. He gets a job as a swimming instructor. He stands on his hands on the diving board, bends slowly backwards and flips into the water. The children are there to learn, not to watch him show off. He loses his job as a swimming instructor. He's at home when we come back from school. He cooks fish without cleaning it and we won't eat it. 'You have to eat,' he shouts. We pick at it, clean it and eat a tiny bit and Granddad gets a bone caught in his throat and after that always gets his food in a container from the home help. Ready chewed.

Mum starts to study. She doesn't want to be at home with Dad and Granddad. Dad paints a picture, flowers in bright colours, trees in a winter landscape. The little money he manages to scrape together, he uses for glass and frames for new paintings and yet more new paintings.

The doorbell rings. 'It's the minister,' says Emil. It's not the minister, it's not the tramp, it's not the boys from the street. It's Jonathan.

We sit down at the kitchen table. I haven't eaten breakfast. Don't want to. Don't want to do anything. My body is heavy from all the medication. I don't think he can help me. I can't either. I'm an adult now and I should be able to look after myself. 'I'm just sitting out on life,' I say. He's already started with the paper and pens. 'Write that down, just the other way round.' I start to scribble. 'No,' he says. 'A bigger piece of paper and a thicker pen, so you see it every day.' I write: Don't sit out on life. We put it up by the fridge.

'Yes, yes, yes,' I say. 'What are they saying?' he asks. 'They're saying that I should go into the corner of the kitchen and move my arms up and down. 'Say "no, I can't",' Jonathan says. I get up. 'Sit down,' he says. I sit down.

'Yes, yeeees.' 'Say no.' I say: 'No. I won't do it right now. I can't.' 'Why can't you?' Jonathan asks. 'I'm talking to someone else.' 'Who are you talking to?' 'Jonathan.' 'Good.' 'You have to wait.'

I sit there. I have managed not to obey my voices. I sit at the table and my leg shakes. My therapist is pleased.

Winter is here again, with snow, sun and skiing. I win the Nordic combined competition at school. Cross-country and jumping. I jump in a clown costume that Marit made for a carnival. One trouser leg is red, the other blue. The wide jacket has big red polka dots on a blue background. The collar is like a big flower. I also wear a clown's nose. A red ball. It doesn't matter whether I'm making a fool of myself or if the others think it's cool. I don't care. I could be a trendsetter, I could be an outsider.

I stand up on the highest platform. 'Go a bit further down,' Espen whispers in my ear. But I think quite the opposite. If it was possible to get even higher, I would. I manage to work up a good speed and give it all I've got. Make a perfect Telemark landing. Carry on down the outrun with my arms in the air. Thirty-two metres.

I stand on the top rostrum and am presented with a medal and a laurel wreath with long ribbons.

I'm in sixth grade and have extra classes in Norwegian. On one of the last days of term at the end of primary, my teacher starts to cry. She had forgotten to skip me when we were reading out loud one by one round the class. I stammered on every word and got stuck in the first sentence. Could only see black and couldn't differentiate any letters. Then I started to guess what was written there. She hastily asked the person next to me to take over. All of a sudden she starts to cry and no one can understand why. 'I've been teaching you for six years now. You are the first class I've ever taught. And the idea of sending anyone on to secondary school who can't read is terrible.'

My support teacher has no tears when she tries to drum into me the difference between short and long vowels. 'Double consonants, bounce the ball so you can hear it.' She has one lying on the desk. And a rubber band for words with long vowels and single consonants. I stretch the rubber band and bounce the ball. But still I get it all wrong. I practise one word one day and the next day it's as though I never knew it. I mix up B and P and G and K and jump over letters in the words or write too many.

'Well, that's us done now,' she says one day. 'No doubt you'll get another support teacher in secondary. Have you thought about what you want to be?' 'An author,' I reply without hesitation. 'An author,' she says, surprised. 'I think you can forget that.' 'And a playwright,' I continue. 'And maybe I'll act in some of them myself in the big theatres. And films, I'm going to write for the cinema and TV. And draw the covers for my own books.' I find it hard to stop, there's so much I want to do.

'I think you can forget the idea of ever being an author. Not only do you have to be good at writing, you have to be able to read as well. You can't do either. Think of something more realistic, it will make things a lot easier.' 'It is realistic, because that's what I want to do.' 'I see,' the support teacher interrupts. 'Well, good luck in secondary school.'

I look up and study the support teacher. Suddenly I feel very sorry for her. Sorry for someone who doesn't know that you can be whatever you want to be. Perhaps I've been sitting here with someone who didn't want to be a support teacher. I know what I want.

There is a new youth worker at the Christian Junior Club. He's called Arild. He's much older than the other workers, thirty-something maybe, with a full moustache, untrendy clothes and sweaty hands. Seems to be lonely and very religious. He's new in town and appears to only know God.

I am thirteen and my friend Lena is fifteen. We go to visit him in his small rented flat. We go to tell him about everything that's bad. To confess and have our say. It was Arild's idea and we're hungry for someone who will listen.

Lena's dad is in prison. He helped the North Korean embassy with a big alcohol smuggling job. I've been there and helped to carry boxes down into a secret room in their cellar. She wants to know if you can be called a child of divorce when you're nearly grown up. She's asked me. But I don't think my answers were good enough.

I confess that I drink alcohol, even in the mornings, and about the hash and pills. For my thirteenth birthday I wanted two things. One was hash. The other was a yellow and black tracksuit. I went and bought that myself and my parents paid for it. It was harder to get the hash. I didn't know anyone who smokes hash. Who could I ask to give it to me? I just knew that I wanted to try. It was something to do with God. A longing for something else. I gave the task to an older boy, and he was successful.

Arild listens. I wonder if I'm talking too much, but carry on. 'Everyone at home is like a solid wall. You can't talk to them. They never ask anything.' They hold up daily life like a roof. Because the rain mustn't get in. Fall to pieces.

'And Granddad's moved in permanently now. He can't cope on his own and we can't cope with him. We're not used to having a main person in the house. He's constantly asking what the time is. Just about every five minutes. I'm the only one who contradicts him when he says it's his son Bo on the TV. The others tell me to shush and just say yes. "Nod and agree."' It makes me uneasy that it's not true. Nervous about lying.

Arild gives us tea. We're not used to drinking tea. Not used to sitting and talking about everything. 'I'm scared that I won't be a proper grown-up,' I say. Arild looks very earnest. He quotes some Bible passage and prays for us. Put his hand first on Lena's knee then on mine. He says our names out loud and calls on the Lord to see us. When he's finished he says amen and closes his eyes.

We sit in silence and almost get a fit of the giggles even though we don't want to. It's serious in a way we're not used to. It's the first time that we've told an adult any of this. I look at Lena. I can see that she's still a child too, with her round cheeks, bleached hair and heavily made-up eyes.

Then Arild says that the only way is to accept God. And suddenly I want to do just that, even though I've always been so against Him before. I just don't know how. In this almost empty flat. With this stupid man I don't know. I really don't understand the first thing about how to find God. Even though I've been going to the Junior Club for years now and have been to countless prayer meetings. I've sat and thought about other things, thought that soon the prayers and sermons would be over and the activities would begin.

I take a sip of tea. It does down the wrong way. I cough and start to cry. My head splits. It's Espen inside me who's crying. Arild starts to talk in tongues. All foreign words. They pour out of his mouth. He folds his hands, hard, and I do the same. Bow

78

my head. Espen says: 'No, no, no.' In a language I understand. I open my fingers so that God can see that my hands are properly in prayer.

I don't need to tell anyone at home where I'm going. I'm just not there. Peter and I go into the woods. We smoke hash. It's a home made bong. An empty toilet roll with a hole in it and we put hash in a tinfoil holder.

At first we don't feel anything. Draw the smoke down as far as we can. Cough. Then I lie down on the ground and start to float. Out of my body, away and up into a new world where the details take on a new dimension. The soughing in the treetops. You could easily think you were lying up there in the sky looking down at the ground.

Peter starts to laugh. There's nothing to laugh about. I lie in my bubble and hear nothing. I look at my fingers. I fold my hands. I believe that God has seen me. My body spreads. My arms come loose and move on their own. A dog appears and sniffs around, I jump up. My nerves on the outside of my body.

I have to smoke more. Peter has to pee. He doesn't just open his flies. He lets his pants and trousers fall to his ankles. He stands there naked from the waist down and pisses. Then he comes towards me with his with trousers down and his hand on his cock. I've lit the bong and ask what he wants. 'I want to smoke with this,' he says and waves his willy around. 'Do you like it?' I don't answer. I don't want to see his willy. 'Do you wish you had one?' 'No way.' He pulls up his trousers. We smoke, cough. We lie down on some pine needles and fall asleep. It's chilly, but we don't get cold.

When I get home I can't find the key and have to ring the doorbell. It's Dad who opens in his pyjamas. I'm wearing my new tracksuit. 'Have you been out running?' Dad asks. I nod and totter into my room.

I stand at the fountain in the square by school. I've just walked down the hill from school and across the square for the last time. I'm never going back to my school again.

This autumn I'll start at the secondary school that's on the other side of the town. Something new is waiting for me. I don't want to get old. Don't want to grow, don't want to cry. What is it that's waiting? I don't think I'm finished with childhood yet. I want to be looked after. It's too late now.

It's better to be the biggest amongst the small, than the smallest amongst the big. I watch the water spouting out in great arcs. Listen to the noise. Then I hear someone crying. Espen is here. Children know things they can't express.

I'm afraid that Jonathan is losing hope. We're sitting by the kitchen table. I want to get out our file but he says it's not necessary. That we're not going to write lists today.

I've had a relapse and been in hospital again. It wasn't supposed to happen, not now when things were going so well. 'What am I doing here, when you just stay with the voices?' he asks, disheartened. I want him to be here. I have to be with the voices. But I still want him to be here. He normally says that he's always here. That he's at the end of a telephone. That I'm not alone.

Now I'm alone. It feels like he's lost hope. He puts some old snus back in the tin and pops in a new pouch. 'Would you like some coffee?' I ask. He hasn't taken off his hat. The yellow one with the Arsenal emblem on it. He sinks down into the low kitchen sofa.

He is the first therapist I've had who's shown his emotions so clearly. He's been let down. 'What shall we do today then?' he asks. 'I don't know. Yes, yes, yes.' 'What do they want?' he asks.

I don't answer. I get up and stand in the corner and make repetitive movements with my arms. He lets me do it. We've written lists of what I should do, hour by hour. Which even includes spending time with the voices. No list is going to help me today. They're not enough. They can't save me. Don't lose faith, Jonathan. Don't lose faith. We just have to keep fighting.

Peter and I are standing in the toilets just by the Christian Junior Club. There's only one youth club and it's run by the church. We're necking spirits. Then we go in again and the sermon has just begun. Ascension Day is coming up. Filip and Terje, two of the youth workers, are nineteen. They volunteer here and are very kind, good-looking and devoted Christians. And naive. They see it as their mission to save us. I wonder if they've noticed that they're not managing. They have run the club for years. We were children to begin with, now we're teenagers.

It's a mixture of prayer, songs and activities. After the sermon, we watch a film by a revival movement in the USA and after the film Peter and I go back out to the toilet and take a few more swigs of vodka. But instead of going back in, Peter wants us to lie down on the sofa in the cloakroom. We lie very close together on the narrow sofa. Gospel singing can be heard from the club room.

Peter opens his flies and strokes my cheek. 'What do you want?' I ask. 'To see if you're a girl or a boy,' he says. 'You're so beautiful. You're so cool. You dress like a boy. I think you're a girl. But how can I know for sure? Maybe you're some strange mixture. Let me have a look.'

'You can't,' I say. I'm drunk and have no will. 'Let me see, just once,' Peter says.

A strange mixture. Is that what people think about me? Somewhere deep down I know that it's right, but I still feel insulted. Don't know myself what I want them to think either. Peter pulls down my trousers with force. The button pops off.

But he's not particularly interested in looking that closely. He quickly pulls down his own trousers. He pushes his penis into my vagina. 'Don't,' I say. It hurts. He pushes even harder. 'It won't work,' I say. 'I'm too tight.'

Peter thrusts and I scream. The gospel singing stops and the door bursts open. Terje the Christian worker, Terje the innocent, just stands there and stares.

I think that I'm tied down. I'm lying with my arms out to the side. A waking nightmare that I've conjured up many times. I'm lying in bed. I try, but I can't move. I try to talk, but can only stutter. I want to say that there's been a misunderstanding. That I'm well and healthy. That I'm not going to harm myself or anyone else. I throw myself from side to side. I stammer: 'Help, help.'

It's the staff in a psychiatric clinic who have tied me down. People I trusted and confided in. Someone pulls out a knife. They circle the bed in silence. Then someone slices the knife through the air and the blade catches the light. It slashes over my face. Close, but doesn't touch. I scream. Then they make a cut on my forehead and the blood pours down over my eyes. They tear off the blanket and cut up along my inner thigh towards my genitals. I piss myself. I shout: 'No, no, no.'

85

I write and write, full of mistakes, but I know what it says. I know my texts off by heart. It's easier to write your own book than to read one. I am the one telling the story. I force my sister Hild to write the texts on the typewriter, while I dictate. Marit is not here and I miss her. She was the one who used to type for me. Now we get postcards where she describes her wild life with her new boyfriend. I write letters back. Try to say something grown up, and she notices and replies: You're getting so big now, my little princess.

It's quiet at home without Marit. She used to shout and make a noise and say what she thought. Hild says nothing. Isn't seeing anyone, just sits in her room and smokes. The trouble with Hild is that she's dyslexic too. Of all us children, Marit is the only one who isn't.

But Hild types as well as she can. Mum corrects it and Hild has to redo it. Mum laughs out loud at the spelling mistakes. She's not laughing at us. She just thinks that spelling mistakes are really funny. She's the sort of person who likes to get books of spelling mistakes from the papers for Christmas. My book, *The Stone of Finn-Jon*, is ready. We send it off to the TV. I never hear a peep in reply and have sent them the original. But I continue to write.

I start to write about old people. Every morning, Mrs Vangen slowly pulls a cart up the road. She has done the paper round. Her back is stooped. I compare her bent back with the old apple trees in her garden. In my story I call Mrs Vangen Mrs Evensen. This gives me the freedom to write down all the thoughts I have about her life and my own. I write an entire short story about Mrs Evensen. I send it in to the radio. I even write a poem called 'Letter Box'. Which is also about an old woman. She goes to the letter box every day to see what's in the post. She looks into the letter box, full of hope. She lives in hope. 'But the spark of life in her eye quickly fades, when day after day, month after month, she gets nothing.' The poem finishes like this: 'The letter box is green, small and not particularly nice. It stands on a frame and could have brought joy to an old woman's life.'

Both manuscripts are accepted by the radio. But not by the youth programme that I sent them to. They end up in a programme for the elderly and are going to be read by a real actor. I'm to go to the studio and be interviewed.

I've been looking forward to it all week. The day arrives when I go on my own into town and up to the radio station to give my first ever interview. Imagine being on the radio. Now everyone will know who I am.

I have to wait in reception. Then a woman comes to get me. We walk down endless corridors.

I get a microphone and headphones. 'The people interviewing you are sitting elsewhere,' the woman explains, 'so you'll hear their voices in the headphones and then you can answer, once we've got the microphone sorted out. Would you like a glass of water?' 'No thank you. I'm going to speak to someone somewhere else? Won't I see them?' 'No, the programme is made in Bergen. Could you just say what you're called?' I say my name over and over again. Then they say that they're happy with the microphone check. The green light goes on and a voice starts talking in my headphones.

'The short story we have just heard was written by Eli Larsen, who has just turned thirteen. And we are lucky enough to have her here with us today. Welcome, Eli.' 'Thank you,' I say, quietly.

87

'So, here we have a young person who writes about old people.' 'Mmhmm,' I reply. 'To think that there are young people in this country who really care about old people.' 'Mmhmm.' 'Where do you get your ideas from?' 'The kitchen window,' I reply. 'It really is heart-warming and gives hope that such a young person actually thinks about the elderly in society.' 'Yes,' I say, still quiet. I haven't really got started yet. 'More young people should do the same, don't you think?' 'Mmhmm.' 'You describe these people with such insight, you must know a lot of old people.' 'Yes,' I lie. 'Well, we'd like to thank you for your lovely pieces and for coming to talk to us today. We hope that you continue writing.' 'Yes,' I squeak.

The light shines red and I take off the headphones. They lead me back through the endless corridors. I sit on the tram home, devastated. I had thought that I would finally be able to say what I think and feel. All I managed to say was yes. I could only agree.

At home, the whole family has listened to the radio. 'You were so good,' Mum says. I don't answer. 'Chin up,' Dad says, 'you've been on the radio. That's more than I've ever been.' 'It wasn't me,' I say. Then my brother, Torvald, who has been leaning over the table with his head in his hands, wakes up. 'If you're going to be a writer or a politician or anyone else who gives interviews in the future, can I give you a tip?' he asks. 'Don't answer the questions. Just say what you want to say.'

I'm on tour in Germany with my latest book. Travel from town to town with an interpreter and sleep in a different hotel every night. I manage to say what I want to say. I talk and read from the book and the interpreter interprets. I mix seriousness and humour. It's a kick to stand on stage. To enthral. To concentrate. To believe that the texts are good and that what I'm saying is touching. I enjoy it. Almost as intoxicating as writing.

In one place, a man comes forward to where I'm sitting signing books after the reading. He says that he's staying at a hotel nearby. He's a travelling salesman for jewellery. He normally sits on his own in a pub or his hotel room in the evenings, but then he saw a poster about a reading by a Norwegian woman he'd never heard of. 'Could you wait here for seven minutes until I get back?' he asks. He comes back with a silver ring with a green stone in it. 'You have given me something special this evening,' he says and gives me the ring.

In Kiel, there is a man who wants to come up on stage and ask me a question. 'You said that you played football.' 'That's right,' I say, feeling cocky. 'Can you juggle?' 'Yes, I can.' 'Then I challenge you to a game of keepie uppie.' He doesn't produce a ball. He takes out a keyring and says that I should put it on my foot. Kick it up in the air, lean forwards and catch it on my back. I try. The keyring flies out into the audience. I try again. Get it up in the air, catch it on my back but then it crashes to the floor. Then it's the man's turn. He flicks the keyring into the air, leans forwards and catches it and the keys stay lying on his back. The audience applauds and he does it again.

I'm fourteen. I'm a child and I'm grown up. I start doing a paper round in the morning to get money for alcohol and cigarettes. I get up at half past four every morning.

Sometimes Dad comes with me. He's out of work again and proud that I'm working. We take the car then. Otherwise I cycle. Collect the papers down at the tram stop when it's still dark. I deliver the papers to the blocks down by the playing fields. When you get to the top of one stairwell in one building, you can go across the roof and down the stairs in the next.

I always meet an old man drinking up there on the roof. They say he was in the war and never got over the shock. But that was forever ago. He says hello and asks for a cigarette and a paper. Which I give him. He calls me 'sonny'. 'Hey, sonny,' he says, and I like it.

One Friday when I'm delivering the weekend supplement as well as the normal paper, something special happens. When I get home, I open the paper and the weekend supplement falls out. I found, I found something. The whole front page is one big painting. I recognise it. I painted it.

My picture has won a competition and is going to be a stamp. It's a four-leafed clover with four children's faces, one on each leaf. One yellow, one red, one black and one white. They're laughing. They're supposed to represent children from each corner of the world. I personally wasn't particularly happy with the picture, thin stripes of watercolour had run from the faces. I thought it had been ruined. But the jury obviously though it was charming or artistic. My prize is that the painting will be on a stamp for letters abroad. I'm very proud of that.

At the Junior Club, we go round to all the pensioners living on their own in the neighbourhood and give them Christmas decorations. It's a candlestick with moss and gnomies. Then we share all the sweets we get and have a nice evening. I choose to go to the old lady who lives farthest away. I've talked to her in the mornings when I deliver newspapers to the blocks of flats. Her front door is usually wide open when I get there around six and she's already been up for hours and baked and made enough food to feed an army. 'This will make them happy,' she chuckles to herself. Freshly baked bread, buns, soup simmering on the stove. She must have looked after a big family.

If I get there a bit later, sometimes she's completely broken. It's as if things become clearer for her, the longer she's awake. As if the loneliness she lives with suddenly becomes real. Then she goes and lies down. Angry with everyone who isn't there. I know that she'll do it all again first thing tomorrow morning. Up at the crack of dawn, twittering and baking for those who aren't there.

I decide to go and give her the Christmas decoration. I go on my own all the way down to her block of flats, the others go in twos to the houses near the church. She doesn't come to the door at first. I think that maybe she's asleep. Or dead. I consider leaving the candlestick outside the door. But just then the door opens cautiously. 'What do you want?' I hold out the candlestick. 'I wanted to give you this.' She opens the door fully. 'It's me, Eli the newspaper girl.' 'Boy,' she says. 'Boy, we can say boy. How are you?' She doesn't answer. We go into the living room. It smells old, not of food. There is nothing in the flat to remind you of Christmas. She seems different, more severe. Is this the evening version of her? She doesn't look at the candlestick. I leave it standing in the middle of the table. Realise that she's never going to use it, and that's probably just as well as she might burn the flat down.

We sit there and I chat away for quite a while. She doesn't seem to be particularly happy that I'm there. Suddenly she says: 'My husband was fun, he was. He used to hide behind the door. And when I found him we laughed and laughed.'

'What did you get?' the others ask me later. 'Nothing.' 'And you stayed there all that time. She must be mean.'

She wasn't mean. She didn't know who I was and who she was and that it was nearly Christmas, and didn't even notice the Christmas decoration I'd brought. I have no idea what kind of person she thought I was, coming there and disturbing her peace. As long as she was whistling and singing again in the morning. I think I came at the darkest time of day.

'Eli, listen, we have to talk about how you get on with yourself,' Jonathan says. I've told him about yesterday evening. How I went to bed in the afternoon. How I live in one world when someone is here or when I'm out with people and how I live in another world when I'm by myself. The flat becomes a little bubble in space. And I float around without a mooring.

'You have to start liking spending time with yourself. With the writer, the sports girl, the philosopher, the playful child in you. The angry person, the sad person. I think it's something you can practise.'

'Yes, yes, yes.'

'What are they saying?'

'They want to be part of it.'

'Say no, they can't. We're talking now.'

'I'll give you half an hour later,' I say.

'Being on your own and feeling lonely are two different things.'

'I want to die,' I say.

'You can carry on living and still be with the dead people inside.' Maybe I can. He knows who I'm thinking about.

'Look in the file. We've already gone through things you should do when you're on your own. If you start to behave in a certain way, you should try to change tack.'

It's not because I'm lazy that I can't follow the plan. I put my hands to my ears. 'What is it?' 'Nothing.'

So much of me is in my head. I force the voices back. Jonathan has someone to be with in the evenings. So how can he understand? He laughs and pats me on the shoulder. Looks at his watch. 'Come on then!' I know that I will come on then.

We're going to make a film in the Junior Club. Super 8. None of us have made a film before. First we have to write the script. But when we go out into the forest where we're going to film, someone has another bright idea: let's film someone hanging themselves. Eilert gets the role. First we film him standing on the ground with a rope round his neck. His head is tilted to one side and his eyes are closed. We only film his upper body and the rope hanging from a gently swaying branch. Then Eilert hangs over the branch with his upper body and his legs dangling in the air. We only film his legs.

We send the film to be developed and we're going to make the cuts for the film the next time we meet. We disagree about which clip should come first, the upper or lower body. In the end, it's the lower body.

Arild is alarmed. The original manuscript was about someone who was saved. Terje and Filip are more enthusiastic and feel that we have at least understood something about what it means to make a film. I have understood something about what it means to make a film.

Soon after this the Junior Club fizzles out. We've got new interests. In the end, the same people are Christian as when we started, more or less. Despite the fact that the youth workers have worked on our salvation every week. I concentrate on football and partying instead. My friend Lena, whose father is in prison, has had a baby at the age of seventeen. And the baby's father is Arild. They get married. Move into her grandmother's old house and have another child. Then get divorced.

Two friends and I decide to get drunk. We've got beer, vodka and some pills that I've stolen from Granddad. We sit out in the park. It's still light. We've started early, it's no later than five.

We sit on the swings and pass the bottles between us. The vodka tastes disgusting. I have to rinse it down with some beer. I cough and almost throw up. We take a break and compete to see who can swing highest. Then we sit in the sandpit and I take out the pills. The boys don't want any. It's Valium that Granddad takes for his nerves.

I take all thirteen pills and swallow them down with beer. At first I don't feel anything. Sit there making a tunnel in the sand. Then things start to spin. It becomes hard to control my mouth. It's as if I'm sucking my cheeks into my mouth. Feels like my face is twisted. I try to light a cigarette, but can't inhale the smoke.

One of the boys has a moped. They want to go and all three of us get on. I'm at the back. I fall off straight away and start to run after them. I fall, get up and run a bit further. They disappear up the road. I have to pee. I squat down on the nearest piece of grass. Pull down my trousers. 'What are you doing?' says a voice. The janitor from primary school is standing in front of me. 'Pull up your trousers,' he says. I fall over when I try to stand up and lie there on the janitor's lawn with my trousers down. 'Oh, is it you?' he says. I pull up my trousers and look drowsily at him. Hunker down and then fall over. He gets hold of me, shakes me. 'Not you, Eli, no. You're not going to be one of them. A drunk, a druggie. You're the best football player in the school. I've seen you take a corner. Bend the ball in from the right with your sensitive left foot. Even the boys' team is jealous of that foot. Do you understand? Come here.'

He drags me across the lawn and into the house. I sit on one of the kitchen chairs stammering. I tell him about the pills and the alcohol. I'm given a large glass of water that I drink in one go. Then I have to throw up. I run out into the hall. Where is the toilet? I stay in there for a long time and then wash my face. Look at myself in the mirror. Is my face all twisted?

I come out and we sit down on the sofa. I start to shiver and he gives me a blanket. The janitor isn't as angry any more. But he says again that I mustn't become one of them. I have to promise him that. He never wants to see me in this state again. I have so many positive sides. I'm going to be a great football player who the whole city will be proud of.

I sleep on the sofa for an hour. Then he gives me some hot chocolate and a sandwich before walking me home. He stops at the gate and gives me a timid hug. He understands that he can't ring on the doorbell and talk to my parents. I have learnt my lesson. Or have I?

I have started to write in all earnestness. I've dropped the pensioner theme and write punk texts. Texts to be spoken. It's the sound of the words. How they jostle each other and create new meanings. How they sing and rhyme. The rhythm. I sit in my room and read the texts out loud. I take pleasure from it, saying the same sentence over and over again.

I start to sew my own clothes. I'm tired of the princess dresses that Marit and Mum made. I will never wear a dress like that again. I have designed an outfit with a yellow and brown monk jacket and yellow and brown trousers with one leg in each colour; I'm going to wear it to a birthday party. Hild and Mum help me as much as they can. It's in jumbo cord with knitted details.

I go to the party in my home-made creation. From the top of the hill I see the house and garden below and all the girls in almost identical summer dresses. Only for a moment do I think that I've made a mistake and should turn around. I was there last year and blended in perfectly. I take a step and then one more. I am absolutely certain. I am right and I am good. I am Eli, I am Emil.

I go to jumble sales and buy strange hats. I go to school in my creations and Hild and Mum sit at the kitchen window and watch me go, scared that I'll be bullied. 'I would never dare to stand out like that,' Hild says. And she never stands out. She's barely noticed. That's her strategy.

I'm not bullied. Not that I notice anyway. I start a hat trend and get several of the girls in the class to go to jumble sales and find old things instead of buying expensive brand names. I feel like I'm starting to grow into myself, create myself, be myself along with the boys' voices, and they are happy.

Slowly the thought that I am no longer a child grows in me. It's frightening. I look at my body in the mirror. I am slim and curveless, with small breasts, one slightly larger than the other. Breasts can wait, I think. I'm not ready. I don't even know if I want to be a woman. I need more time. I hide myself in the boys' voices.

'Be yourself,' Espen sniffs, who doesn't want to play football, but is happy to play with the doll's house. Then Emil also wants to play with the doll's house and that confuses me. 'You are me,' he says. I write Emil on all my school books in big, far too childish letters.

Jonathan rings the doorbell. I haven't slept for two nights. We sit down by the kitchen table, and I tell him how things are.

'Okay, go into the bedroom then,' he says. I get up and go into the bedroom. What is he going to show me now, I wonder. Another ball? He follows me in. 'Lie down under the duvet,' he says. I lie down under the duvet. What is he trying to tell me? 'I'm going to turn off the light,' he says. 'Then I'll lock the door and drop the keys in through the letter box.'

'No, don't go.' I sit up in bed. He leaves. I lie down again. Listen to the silence in the building. I had been looking forward to a break in the silence. I lie there wide awake. What am I doing here with my clothes on? And it's not even just any old clothes. I'm wearing pink stripy trousers with zips everywhere. A tight pink top with a thick polo neck. Pink, which was once my most hated colour, has now become my favourite colour. It has changed from being an expression of helplessness to being an expression of strength.

I don't want to be alone. That's the hardest bit. Because that's when the boys come, the violent fantasies. Sleep won't come. I know that. I wanted to sit in the kitchen talking to Jonathan.

I'm in Class Eight and have written a piece with the self-chosen title of 'Free Will'. It's so good that the teacher reads it out loud. She wants to use it in other classes and thinks I should send it to a paper. But the text runs red with corrections. She writes institutitution up on the blackboard. Asks me to come up and rub out letters so that it says 'institution'. I don't manage. I read the syllables in my head, but can't see from the word where it should end. The teacher sighs. I sigh, but it's not as deep. I will never learn to spell. I understand that. But it doesn't matter. I can write, and there are so many other people who can spell so I will always get help.

When I am fifteen, I want to get a moped licence. I have to have an eye test. I have to look at rows of letters on a board. Can only see the first row.

'How have you managed?' the optician asks. 'I manage fine, I just need to get my licence,' I reply. The optician goes to get his father who is also an optician. They put various lenses in the strange frames and with great effort I manage to read the second row.

'But your eyesight is damaged. We can't correct it with lenses. It seems that you've got a congenital defect in your optic nerve. It hasn't developed normally. We can't correct that. It's like trying to get a glass of water to jump. The basic pre-requisites just aren't there. You can only see with one eye at a time and no depth perception.' 'Can anything be done about it?' 'Not now. It should have been done before you were ten. I'm sure they'll give you a mobility allowance instead of a licence.'

I shake my head and run out. I have to manage. And I, who thought it would all resolve itself once I was older. I have to be even older. I have to run even further. I don't want to have glasses. I don't want to have damaged eyesight. I just have to decide.

I only get confirmed because Torvald is getting confirmed. I pretend to myself that it's because I don't want to sit at his party watching him get presents. But in reality it's because I'm curious. I have too many feelings and need to invest them somewhere. I think of religion and alcohol as more or less the same thing. It makes your body tingle. It makes your head spin and makes you warm under the skin. A bit like scoring a goal.

I want to test everything there is. Euphoria, kick, salvation. Torvald is getting confirmed because you should and it's what other people do. Torvald's goal is to be normal. Granddad says he can only cope with one confirmation party, so we're doing it at the same time.

I want the minister and his wife to see me. We have meetings at their house. I want to be seen by everyone. Seen by someone. Before I go in, I drink a quarter bottle of vodka. I want to smell of it. Want to be thrown out and discovered and people to feel sorry for me, to be reprimanded. I want to be judged and not get what I so long for. Security. I slur my words and say I can't read the Bible.

'You can't read?' the minister's wife says. 'But you're in eighth grade.' She doesn't say that I smell of alcohol. I ask if God can see us and she says yes. But God doesn't say anything about what he sees and I can't borrow his eyes even to read the Bible. Torvald promises not to say anything at home. But the minister has noticed. As we're leaving he takes me to one side. He does not have a warm voice. He doesn't want to know the reason why I've done it. He says: 'If you've been drinking next time, I won't let you into my house. Do you understand?' I am only trying to be visible. Not even the minister sees with eyes that want to save me.

Next time I go, I am sober and ask questions they can't answer, and the minister is forced to say that we don't have time for so many questions, because then we won't get through the study material. We talk about morals. 'Christ does not judge himself, he is the judge,' the minister's wife says, and I don't understand. I want to know if Hell exists, but that's not part of what we're supposed to learn. The strange thing is that I'm not too worried about Hell. It's the present that matters, because everything will be easier for me later, when I'm grown up. At the same time I don't want to be grown up yet, because I don't think I'm ready with being little. But I am convinced that things will sort themselves out. That I will be like Torvald. That I will be normal.

What about Heaven? It seems unreal. I think about Gran who gave her whole life to faith. Who lamented the fact that Dad and those around her were not believers. She sang and prayed for us. But when I went to see her when she was nearing the end and should have benefited from her faith, I could see that she had started to doubt. She said that she suddenly had a strong feeling that nothing existed. She was filled with a great fear of death. She no longer found comfort in the comforting songs she had always sung. After a life of deep faith, she became an atheist two days before she was able to let go and die.

There are examples of the opposite. I think about the thief who was sentenced to death on the cross. He embraced God at the moment of death. Imagine if it's true that there's salvation and eternal life. That it was possible to go around your whole life doubting, to live like an idiot and even deny God. And then, when it really counts, whimper a yes. How much a tiny second, one single small decision can mean. I believe in will. But is it free?

*

On the day we're going to be confirmed, Mum suddenly notices my shoes. They're small brown men's shoes. They're Emil's shoes. 'You can't wear those. The only thing you can see under the confirmation gown. And now that we've bought lovely new clothes as well.' Mum stops in the middle of all her preparations for the party. She looks at me in a way she doesn't normally look at me. 'What's going to happen to you, Eli?' she says, with a little sigh. Then she turns around and takes the cups out of the cupboard. She counts the cups out loud.

I wear the neighbour's shoes and we get confirmed and the meal is successful with Granddad MP sitting at one end of the table and Torvald and I at the other. MP holds a long and incomprehensible speech about the good old days. He's ninety-five now, and sees no future. Mum holds a speech for both of us and we each get an unchipped plate from the plate rack in the living room, the only two that survived our wild behaviour when we were younger. Torvald and I who are so unalike are bound together. Mum is so proud of what we have become and wishes us all the best on our journey onwards in life.

Jonathan and I are standing in my bedroom. We look at the dark curtains that have been hanging in front of the window and not been opened for a year now. The window has not been opened and the room aired in all that time either.

'Do you think it's time?' I ask.

'What do you think?'

'Yesterday I thought that if I opened the window I would throw myself out.'

'But if we do it together?'

'Just test it?' I say. 'No, I don't want to. I don't know. No, I don't dare.'

'Well, you can start by cleaning in here and changing the curtains. They're very dark,' Jonathan says. 'I can help you.'

'Okay, I'll start by buying new curtains, then we'll see.'

'At least you've started to think that the window isn't dangerous,' Jonathan encourages me. 'Maybe one day you'll be able to open the curtains. There's no rush, after all.'

I'm not at home on the afternoon when the minister does ring the bell. I come back from football training and don't notice anything in particular before I'm standing out of breath in the hall. I've run all the way home. Am thinking about having a bath. Covered in mud from head to toe. It's October and wet. Then suddenly I notice a pair of unknown shoes in the hall next to where I've kicked off mine. We never have visitors. There's something in the air. I see an unfamiliar coat on the coat hooks. I listen to the house. Not a sound. It's never silent in this house. There's no one at home. Just a guest.

A thought charges through me, I don't want to go up. I want to go back to the football pitch. I don't hear the sobbing until I go upstairs to the living room. Mum and Dad, Granddad, Hild, Odd and Torvald are sitting there, and in their midst, the minister. It's my little brother Odd who shouts out as soon as he sees me: 'Marit is dead.' I stop and stare at the others who all look down. He says it again: 'Marit is dead.'

His voice is shrill. How can he know that? Little Odd. He can barely remember Marit, because she's in Australia. Odd's words cascade from my skull, through my head and straight through my body. The others are crying. I want to kick Odd. Why did he have to say that? It would be better if I'd never been told. I look at Torvald. He's sitting beside Hild, who has her arm round him. He's chewing his sleeve. I do what I normally do. I look for signs in Torvald so that I can react, but don't see any.

But I knew. I already knew when I was down in the hall. No, I didn't know. On the stairs? No, I didn't know. I've known many times that something terrible might happen. Emil has warned me. I've been afraid that Mum and Dad would die, but not Marit. Marit will always be with me, there to explain things that are difficult.

'Hi Eli,' the minister says. I haven't seen him since my confirmation. He's wearing a dark suit and dog collar. He's trying to tell me something with his body, sitting there on the sofa in the middle of my family. He doesn't belong here. He reaches out his arm and wants to take my hand. He's got nothing to do with us. He can go to hell. With his wife and forgiveness and the church and all. He doesn't know Marit.

The minister sits there like a dark and dangerous island, like a misunderstanding between us that has made us cry. I want to run back down to the cellar. I want to hide. I don't want to be with this sorrow. I scored a goal with a header today, why can't I tell them that? There are coffee cups on the table. Who made the coffee, I think, and squeeze myself onto the sofa in my muddy clothes between my little brother and Granddad. He's sitting there shaking. Odd is rocking back and forth.

I usually say that I have three siblings and a sister in Australia. Is that because I feel that Marit has already been taken away, in the way she has now? Thoughts can't change things on the other side of the world. No one looks at me. They don't look at anything.

'What do you mean, dead?' I ask in the silence. It's the minister who answers. Mum sits with her head in her hands. 'It was a diving accident,' he says. 'On one of the islands. We were told by the consulate. It will take a week for the body to get here.' The body? Don't I have a sister in Australia any more? Marit is the body. Marit, who hasn't been home for three years. Who has sent us letters and postcards about everything she has done and experienced. She has only told us about the fun things. Not a word about anything else. She hasn't had the money to come home again and we haven't had the money to send her so she could if she wanted to. We haven't had the money to go and visit her there.

Granddad stands up. He goes out into the hall to the toilet on unsteady feet. We sit and wait for him to flush. To come back so we can be together again. Only once in those three years have we spoken to Marit on the phone. We stood in a row and talked to her one by one. She spoke Norwegian with an English accent and everyone said hello but didn't manage to say much more. I want to ring her up and say that she doesn't have an English accent. I want to ask her not to go to the pub and to save enough money for a ticket home.

Granddad flushes the toilet now. MP comes back. Bent back and thin, so his clothes hang off him. It could have been him who died. I wonder if that's what he's thinking. He bumps me when he sits down. It feels like punches to my body. I expect to start crying. The screaming and bird noises from when I was little. Nothing comes. Why don't I get up and smash something? The lamp over the coffee table. I hit it. Only Odd sees. He moves his head as he follows the moving lampshade.

What comes instead of tears is a big solid lump of fear. My leg starts to shake. It's not true. Nothing is going to happen. I'll go to bits if Marit is just a body that will be returned in a week. I say: 'No, no, no.' I talk to the voices. After all, Emil has promised to save me from death. 'Is Marit dead?' I say. 'Yes,' Hild replies, irritated, as if I'm slow to understand. I know now, I think. I know now. No, I don't know. I only know it with my head, so I don't believe it.

I hear some strange sobs coming from Dad. Is that how he cries? Mum doesn't lift her head from her hands. Has she noticed that I've come back? She should maybe hug someone, but doesn't. Doesn't hold anyone's hand. Doesn't touch anyone. Everyone is crying alone. Something makes me realise that it's just us now. Everyone except the minister, who might get up at any moment and go out into the warm rain and disappear.

Suddenly Mum reaches out a hand and grabs a coffee cup. She takes a gulp, swallows it the wrong way and starts to cough. Dad has to pat her on the back. Dad, who doesn't take anything seriously, is totally serious.

Marit got straight off the plane and went out onto the street and was run over and died. 'It's Dad's fault,' Emil says. She never really made it to Australia. You can be away for years and then really disappear. She hasn't been there in the meantime. The minister asks if we should sing a psalm. 'Sing?' Dad says. Mum nods through her tears.

It's my first funeral. I'm wearing the same clothes that I wore to my confirmation, only I've got football boots on my feet. Everything has a meaning. I had to wear football boots in order to survive. To be who I am.

Lots of Marit's old friends are in the church and it said in the paper that they should wear colourful clothes. When we walk up the street to the church, I think that Marit could just as easily be in any of the houses that we pass. Or still in Australia. Gone so long and then gone forever.

I talk to Emil a lot. He says that I'll cope. But I don't. He says that it's him and me and Espen now. It feels lonely. I sit beside Hild in church. We each have a red rose in our hand. Mum passes down tissues and throat sweets. All my tissues are wet. My lap is full. My eyes just keep running and running. I can feel it in my throat as well, that my crying will come out as hiccups. Hild moves closer. I think that Hild is my big sister now. But Hild is not the same. She's not as safe as Marit. If Marit had been here now she would have made decisions and sorted everything out. She would have told Mum and Dad what to do.

Mum has got up. She thanks everyone for coming in a loud, clear voice. The whole of Marit's old class is here. She wants to say to the young people: 'Look after each other.' Then her voice breaks and she sits down.

'I'll look after you,' Emil whispers. I squeeze Hild's hand and wonder who will look after her. The funeral finishes with those of us who were closest to Marit going up to the coffin and putting our flowers on the already flower-bedecked coffin. While one of Marit's favourite songs by the Rolling Stones is being played on the organ.

My new life begins. I've moved away from home. I don't have much in my tiny room. Travelled to the school on my own by train. A cassette player, a football and a few clothes. I'm sixteen years old. No one knows how I am here on the edge of this small town. No one knows who I am.

The pupils sit side by side on chairs in a big hall. It's eight o'clock in the morning. The register is called. Row by row. If any chairs are empty we have to say, along with the number of the person who's missing. Everyone has a number. I'm number forty-three. Forty-four is my corridor neighbour. I saw her on my first day at school. She didn't say what she was called or hello, didn't nod or hold out her hand. She shone like the sun. Looked me straight in the eye and started our friendship by saying: 'I have been given a thermos by God.'

It's the first prayer meeting of the day. We're pupils at a Christian boarding school. It's the last year of the seventies. An extremely charismatic teacher starts the term by saying: 'Cast aside your prejudices and stand naked before God.' He has seductive brown eyes under a dark fringe. I'd like to have those eyes close to me so I could see them properly. So that they saw me. I am open, but am trying to close myself again. I'm about to let go, but then decide that if there's anything I should keep hold of here, it's my prejudices. The prayer starts. The words God and Jesus pierce me. I know that there are others here who don't hear. Who just let it pass. Who have heard this since they were a baby. I haven't. Only at the Junior Club, but it's more penetrating here. More dangerous. I can't keep the words out. I'm

114

used to taking words seriously. They gnaw and scrape. I have to feel it. I have to understand. Why else have I come here? I need something. No, I mustn't let go.

I sneak out. Instead of going to my room, I go up into the loft above the hall. There I lie down on the floor, in the dark and dust, and I listen to each word from down below. I cover my ears, but the message of God's mercy finds resonance in me. The words 'The Lord sees you always' vibrate under my skin. Am I a sinner? What does that mean? I want to be small and not know anything. We can only know one thing about God. He is what we are not. If God exists, he has already punished me. If God exists, he has taken Marit from me.

I hear singing from the hall below. They are together. I am alone.

Then another voice starts to speak inside me. 'You are not Eli. It's me, Erik, that's who you are. I'm sixteen, like you, and a rebel. An irresistible strong rebel. I can fool anyone and physically I can do anything. I'm the one you're scared of and that you miss. I'm going to frighten you and give you strength. Fill the void, otherwise God might get in there. Sneak down from the loft. Go to the woodwork room and find the thinner.'

I sit on the floor in the woodwork room and sniff thinner on a rag. I'm pulled into a dark tunnel, like a ghost train at the fair. Scary, masked people jump out in front of me. 'We're going to get you. We're going to eat you. Believe in us.' I'm sweating and the hairs stand up on my body. I start to shake. The nerves under my skin start to move. Someone shouts for me in a horrible scream. It sounds hollow.

At the other end of the tunnel is hell. I know that it exists. I belong to hell. I'm on my way. 'You don't want to go there,' shouts Young Espen. 'Yes,' replies Big Eli in Erik's voice. 'Are you sure?' 'Absolutely sure.' I want to have a look. I want to be tormented.

115

I ask Jonathan if Erik came to save me from becoming a Christian.

'If it was to save you, he certainly did that. I think he came because he was needed. But he's no longer needed. The most important thing now is that he no longer decides. He can be there, but it's you, Eli, who makes the decisions. You have to take the reins back from your voices. They can be there, but they can't dominate. They are part of the problems and conflicts you had back then. We'll work towards allowing them more limited space in your life.'

'Yes, yes, yes.'

'What are they saying?'

'It's Erik, he wants to fight.'

'You have no reason to fight.'

'Yes, I have to show that I'm strongest.'

'There is strength in not doing it.'

I'll break something when Jonathan has gone. I'll bang my head on the wall. Or should I just not do it?

As the weeks pass, I pray to God to not become religious. 'Dear God, please don't let me become a Christian.' I lie with my eyes closed and my hands folded under the duvet. Am I wasting energy going around not believing in something that doesn't exist? It's Erik who gives me orders. His deep, almost grown up voice cuts through. He rules over Espen and Emil as well. He keeps them at bay. These are new times. I'll soon be grown up. I'm in the process of deciding who I am and who I want to obey. It's we who decide, Erik and I.

I sit through the morning register and prayer. You can close your eyes, but not your ears. There are no eyelids for the body. The teachers take turns in talking. I don't believe them. But something else in me says that you can never be sure. I am filled with unease. With longing and defiance. Because I haven't decided. Maybe you can take a peek? Stand on the threshold? I want to have some of what they claim to have. I want to know what it means to believe in something greater. Not to have all the answers yourself.

'You have decided,' Erik says. 'You're on the outside. Full of voices, but not God.'

Soon I start to tell the other pupils that I'm called Erik. They call me that straight away, and start an Erik fanclub. The teachers continue to call me Eli. I cut off my hair, which has grown long again, and dye it red and green. I stick a needle that has been frozen on ice straight through one ear and put in a silver ring next to the other one. Now I've got two earrings in one ear and

117

none in the other. I wear an old tuxedo waistcoat with badges that say *Punk Rules OK*, and on the back of my leather jacket it says *Nuclear War is Bad for Business*. I'm elected as spokesman for the pupils' council.

I have a blue book with a skull on the cover where I write down all my thoughts. I think a lot about writing, how I write, and that by formulating and expressing myself in a certain way I am the person I want to be. I think the others relate to things that have already been written. I talk to myself, can barely read, an unopened treasure. Dress myself up consciously, with clothes on the outside and words on the inside.

I understand that I have to be who I am. Otherwise something terrible might happen. I realise that I could fall apart. But who's going to fill the hole? 'I found, I found something.' I want to be taken home in big hands. I want to do something with this year, but I don't know what. I might fall. I might… I fall asleep to the Clash on the cassette player. I might fall deep and pull myself up and go even higher.

'I don't want to give up my world.'

'You don't have to give up your world, you just need to take more control,' Jonathan explains. 'You might have needed the voices then, but you don't need them any more.'

'It's not me who decides. They want me to change sex. I can't get rid of the thought. It's the others, society that has decided which sex I should be. It doesn't come from me.'

'The question is whether it would make you any more secure. I don't think it's the answer,' Jonathan says.

'That's what everyone says.'

'You have to let Eli come forward first. The more you do that, the more confident you'll feel about who you are and what you need.'

'Everything's too fast. I've started to question the voices and say no and to say what I'm doing instead. Who I'm talking to and why I can't speak to them.'

'Good.'

'But they just harangue me when you've gone instead. At night when I'm alone.'

Jonathan gets up. 'It will be a long journey.'

I ask Dad if he will drive me back to the folk high school. I've been at home for the autumn break. Absolutely not, is his answer. Then he wakes me in the middle of the night because he's changed his mind.

I pack a whole lot of things. A poster of Marx and my slalom boots and skis. We stop at a petrol station in the middle of the night. Dad doesn't manage to pay using the machine. He gets stressed and nervous. I stay in the car and do nothing to help. I see Dad pulling faces and trying to feed in the notes. Finally, he gets into the car, swears and suddenly starts the car, then drives off with the pump still in the tank. He brakes abruptly and jumps out. He's filled the car with diesel. I'd noticed but didn't say anything. I thought that it would probably be okay. I know nothing about cars and petrol. I should have thought. I should have taken responsibility. After all, I'm with Dad.

We only manage to drive a kilometre from the station. The car starts to cough and then comes to a complete standstill. Dad tries, but it won't start again. 'Is it okay to use diesel?' I squeak. 'Diesel?' he says. 'No, doesn't work.' I have to get out. He's angry. He's not going to any folk high school. He's going home. He's going to sit down and paint in the dawn light until the rescue services come. We'd spotted a telephone kiosk further back, so he's going to go there and call them.

It's still dark. I drag my luggage with me along the country road. I try to hitch a lift, but there are practically no cars at this time of night. I eventually come to a train station. The first train is not for a few hours. I collapse on a bench and fall asleep.

The other pupils try to save me and pray for me. But I am Erik and I hold on to my prejudices. I try to get them to join a green organisation called Framtiden. I don't do very well, but do well all the same. I like staying at the school and am surprised to find I don't miss home.

I nearly get together with a boy called Thorkild. He's the one who started the Erik fanclub. He's made membership cards with a picture of me on them, which he gives to anyone who wants to join. He's the quiet type and seems to admire me, to hold me in awe. He asks if he can be my boyfriend and I say maybe, then he doesn't ask again. We're in the same class and he sits beside me at mealtimes. We hang out with the same group in the evenings, the non-Christian group. I can't really be his girlfriend properly, not as Erik. Thorkild doesn't understand that I'm carrying too many secrets. I keep him on tenterhooks.

When I'm at home in the holidays, I steal my granddad's tranquillisers. I keep them safe. I collect them. Need to take at least ten to have the desired effect. Preferably with hash, alcohol or glue.

I sing in the compulsory choir. One day I take ten tablets and smoke a little hash before practice. I stand in the middle of the choir and am fired with enthusiasm. I sing louder than normal and continue to sing when the others stop. I move my body to the music as if I was in Harlem and not in a free church school in the middle of Norway. I relish praising the Lord with my voice. It's going to happen, I think. I can feel that I'm close to something sublime.

121

The singing teacher wants to talk to me after practice. I just laugh and can't stop. My body is wonderfully woozy. I wave my arms in long arcs. He says that he's heard a rumour that I take drugs. I deny it. He says that they are going to search my room and goes to get some more teachers. I'm absolutely certain that they won't find anything.

When they find the pills, I say that they're fluoride tablets. They wrap them in toilet paper and don't dare to try them. Soon they find my hiding place in the corridor: a small lump of hash is nestling in the smoke alarm. Someone must have told them. I'll be expelled from the school, me, who doesn't want to be anywhere else.

They phone home. Granddad answers. The principal tells him that I've been caught high on drugs and alcohol and have therefore been suspended. Granddad obviously didn't understand what they say because no one ever confronts me with it. Once I've packed my bags, I am driven to the station where I arrived seven months earlier. I cry for the whole train journey. When I get home, I open the back door which leads straight into the utility room where Mum is doing the washing. 'I'm home,' I say. 'So I see,' she replies.

The school let me go back after a month. I have to sign a paper that says that I won't drink alcohol or take drugs. Not even in secret.

I don't believe in God, but am scared he might exist. When the school year is over, it's been one of the best years I've had. I don't want it to end. The handsome teacher holds an end-of-year service outside on a beautiful May day. We won't meet again. In a few hours, we'll leave and go our separate ways to all four corners of the country. He says: 'Thank you for this year together. We'll meet again in heaven.'

After folk high school, I soon move away from home again. I move in with Hild who is living in Granddad's empty flat in the centre of town. I get the big bedroom. Hild sleeps in the old maid's room behind the kitchen. The room is dark and you can barely fit the bed in. She lies there for days on end. I've got friends and football, think it's exciting living in the city and can't understand why she just stays in bed.

I start sixth form college. I'm elected as the class representative and then as the spokesperson for the student council for the whole school. I focus on Operation Day's Work, go round all the classes and talk about collecting money, which is going to Eritrea this year. I'm happy, talk a lot in the classes, ask questions and make suggestions as to how to improve the teaching.

One day the principal comes to the classroom and wants to talk to me. 'I don't think you really fit in here. You're too disruptive. Perhaps you should go to a Steiner school. You need extra resources that we don't have. I'm afraid you can't continue here.' I, who thought I was getting on particularly well here.

I decide to study for my end of school exams independently. The problem is that I can't read. I contact an adult education college, but the principal says that I'm too young and immature. All my life I've been told that I'm immature. It was in my school report at the end of Class One. Immature, lacks concentration and unmotivated. Mum got angry and complained to the teacher. 'Eli might be immature and lack concentration, but she is certainly not unmotivated.' In fact, I was perhaps a little too motivated.

I go to various classes at the adult education college, sit right at the front of the room. Say to the teacher that the principal has said that I can join halfway through term, but that I have to sit my exams independently.

Dad wants to help me. I go home nearly every day. He gets fired from work at the same time that I'm kicked out of college. We've got all the time in the world to improve ourselves. He is convinced that I can be what I want to be, which is a writer. We lie on his and Mum's big bed and he reads the history books to me. We read about the French Revolution. Dad puts the book down and tells me about what was going on in Europe at the time. I ask questions, listen, and enjoy learning. I've got a good memory and find it easy to see the big picture and put two and two together, you have to be good at that if you find reading hard. The French Revolution comes up in the exam and the words just flow out of me. I get top marks.

I wake up bright-eyed. Unusually well rested. Light, as though sleep had never come. Even though I have a sheet with all my routines for the whole day written down, it's really only in the morning that things go automatically. If at all. Sometimes I slope back to bed as soon as I've finished my morning routine. Or I just lie there and don't get up at all.

I run out into the kitchen and put on the coffee. Go back into the bedroom and get dressed. Don't shower. I shower after I've done my training. Go back into the kitchen and pour the coffee into a thermos. Go back to the bathroom and wash my face. Rub in some face cream and put on some rouge. Have a coffee and smoke a cigarette. Make up two slices of bread. Eat.

Can I write today? I think I'll go to my workspace early. Light a candle. It's November. I turn on the radio, it just whines. 'Take a step to the side,' Emil says. I think about what Jonathan has told me. 'I'm eating,' I tell him. 'I'll do it later.' 'Get up,' Emil says. I stand up, take a step to the side, then sit down again. 'Do it again.' I do it again. 'Do it again.' I do it again. 'Do it again.'

'That's enough.' Jonathan has said that we have to share the space. Then I pick up my bag, tie my shoes and walk to my office. It's dark outside. The shops haven't opened yet. There is no one else around when I get there. I turn on the computer and go out to the kitchen to make some more coffee. I look at the kitchen clock. It's one o'clock. One o'clock in the morning.

I'm not early and I'm not late. I'm wrong, I'm out of time. No one will be here for hours.

125

I can't stay here alone all night. I have to go back home and sleep.

I walk back through the city. Feel confused. Agitated. I could do with talking to someone but don't dare to phone any of my friends in the middle of the night. They might think that I'm ill again.

Espen keeps his eyes trained on the ground as he walks. He always finds things. 'I found, I found something.' He sees things that no one else sees. He picks things up, takes them with him and I make collages or small glued things. But I don't always let him stop. As I would never get anywhere then.

He's found something again now. I can't face it. It's a great find. It's a stop sign. 'Ach, no, throw it away,' I say, 'it's just rubbish.' 'It might well be, but I'll keep it with me,' he replies, and I pick up the sign and carry it home. 'You could use it as a tray, or a sideboard on the balcony,' Espen says, happily. I throw the sign into a corner in the hall. Take off my clothes and go back to bed.

'You know that you must never trust the people at the hospital,' Erik says. 'They make you ill.' I try to close my eyes but it's my ears that are the problem. Can't sleep. 'They make you ill,' Erik says again. 'They're tricking you. The people you know there who you like so much. They're tricking you.' Then Espen starts to cry. I dry his tears on the duvet cover. 'Get up and make something with the sign,' he says. Then Emil says that Espen is a crybaby.

I have to talk to someone else. 'Don't phone,' Erik says. But I do phone the ward. It's the young German nurse who answers. He sounds happy. Always happy. It's different every time, depending on who answers. Sometimes they are strict: 'Go to bed. We can't help you.' 'I just want to talk a little.' 'Not now. Goodnight.' Click.

But tonight the mood is open and easy. I say: 'The voices are

126

telling me that I shouldn't trust you.' 'It's the voices you shouldn't trust,' he replies. 'We only want what's best for you.' And when he says that, I know he's right, that he's telling the truth. They only want what's best for me.

I don't know how I should use my good marks. University perhaps. In which case I could imagine studying things like politics, followed by training in the foreign office and a career in the diplomatic service, in embassies around the world. I am of course still going to be an author, but you're only ever that on the side.

I get a job as a cleaner at a fire station. Do a newspaper round before I start at eight. I write. I have to get away. Can't live with Hild when all she does is stay in bed. The whole flat is dark, full of Granddad's furniture, and steeped in the past and passivity. I've got ants in my pants.

I've been headhunted for one of the country's best women's football teams. I go from being the best of the worst, to the worst of the best. I, who's used to taking all the corners and free kicks, have to sit out. We're going to Taiwan in the autumn for a football tournament. Just when I'm about to start training for a place in the A team, I dive from the seven metre board and hurt my back. No football trip. I go to Copenhagen instead and stay in a squat. It doesn't turn out the way I thought it would.

I'd seen part of a film on TV about young people living together and they made soup and ate happily round a big table. I want to be part of that sense of belonging. Where I end up, confused children and teenagers lie on mattresses on the floor and sleep off their high. They've run away from home. There's plenty of drugs and no one can be bothered to make soup. I try to talk to them without much joy. I tidy discreetly. We're wading in rubbish.

Older people who don't actually live in the squat come by and preach politics. 'You have to go underground. Get rid of your ID numbers so the authorities can't trace you.' One day the house is raided by the police. They ride down the street on police horses, with shields and batons and helmets with visors. We've made an underground tunnel from our house under the road and up into a house on the others side. Some people manage to escape through the tunnel. Not me. I'm standing by the window ready to jump when the police storm the flat. My whole body is shaking. I, who has always thought that the police are something good that's there to protect us, am terrified. I've never felt so frightened and helpless. How can I get away? I'm on the wrong side. I haven't recognised the gravity of what I've done. I've got a lump of hash in my pocket.

I'm whacked across the back with a baton and fall to the floor. Two policemen are immediately on top of me. I'm as small as a sparrow in their enormous hands. I try to hit the visors. My punches sound like tapping. They quickly catch my arms and twist them up behind my back. Put on handcuffs. Am I a terrorist, a thief, a criminal? I don't understand. I'm just frightened. I'm carried down the stairs with the imaginatively painted walls. Into a police van which is already full of other young people. 'Deny everything, keep schtum, don't say your name.' The words of the older anarchist leaders echo in my head.

I tell them everything. I shake and cry when I'm being questioned. I'm locked up on my own in a cell. Feel like a tiny child and put my thumb in my mouth. My name is Espen. I want someone to come and get me, but don't know who. Someone I don't know. At home they think I'm on holiday in Denmark and staying with some friends.

I lie on my own in the cell all day and the voices are not good company. Erik is threatening and says things that frighten me.

I'm never going to be able to see a policeman again and feel safe. 'Bang your head against the wall.' I bang my head against the wall. No one comes.

On the second day, a prison officer comes in with some magazines. One is a literary magazine which makes me curious. I read modern Danish poems that I don't really understand, but like. They give me the energy to think. I only know the old Norwegian poets who rhyme. And in amongst all the poems I see an advert. It's for a writing course at a Nordic folk high school in Sweden. I've never heard about writing courses before. I find a piece of paper and write down the address. I write 'important, contact them' on it and stuff it in my pocket.

I'm released on the third day. I've barely managed to eat, just been lying there in a fog of fear. Imagined that they would nail me to the wall, crucify me. Imagined that I wouldn't get out of that cell for years. Imagined that some huge policemen would stamp all over my fingers. Erik sneers and Espen cries. Emil tries to think of as many riddles as possible. I solve them all straight away and once again time is silent and threatening.

On the boat back to Oslo, I am so relieved. I will never go near another squat, amphetamines or lumps of hash. I sit up on deck. The wind blows through my hair. I can't get home soon enough. Once I'm back at Hild's, everything is as before. She lies in bed all day and I do my paper round and clean the fire station. My back is better but not good enough for me to start football training again. One day I find the note in my trouser pocket: 'important'. I don't remember why or what it is. But it says that it's important, so it must be. I write a letter and get an answer.

2.

2.

My name is Eli. I found, I found a new country. I am twenty-one years old. Have moved to Sweden to do a writing course at a Nordic folk high school. I had to send in a piece of writing to get in. I was late, they had probably filled all the places. I think that the most likely reason that I got in is that I'm from Norway. I am the only non-Swede in the class. I've been at the school for just over a month. It's been a bit of a roller-coaster. I've never met other people who write before. Who talk about poetry, literature and film. As well as the new and terrifying joy of hearing someone talk about your writing, I'm surprised by how little Norwegian the other students understand. I dress like a punk and they ask me if there are rock bands in Norway. I have Nationalteatern, the Swedish TV series *Learning for Life*, ABBA, Ebba Grön, Cornelis Vreeswijk, Bellman, Bergman and Astrid Lindgren in common with all of them. But they have nothing Norwegian in common with me. I point out that Karius and Baktus, the tooth trolls, come from Norway. One guy says that his dad used to tell him that all the old bangers in Bohuslän in summer in the sixties and seventies were Norwegian. A lot has happened since then in a country that was one of the poorest in Europe only a century ago.

But now I am in the country of true legend. My parents have always revered Sweden. Mum because of the 'Swedish soup' that was given to schoolchildren in Oslo during the war. It came on the train from Karlstad every morning. In Sweden, children get food in school. Everything is slightly better there. And now I'm here.

*

Three days ago I drank a half bottle of vodka and smoked hash. Haven't slept since. I haven't come down yet. I went to Norway to see everyone. I met a Samí at a party who saw straight through me. I was more frightened of him than the police. The next day I hitchhiked back to Sweden with some Finnish construction workers who were drinking vodka in the car. When it got dark, we discovered that the lights on the car didn't work. I didn't have a krone to my name and couldn't just get out.

Today I've been at school and spent hours throwing darts at a dartboard. I walk around my room at night. I've seen top ice hockey players moving around on the wall. A match between Canada and Sweden. Red and Yellow. It's over now, but the players continue to move around outside in the dark between the trees by the student accommodation.

A school friend grabs hold of me and asks how I am. 'I haven't slept,' I say. 'Have you tried going to bed?' he asks. I think so. I'm shaking. 'I think it's best if we go to hospital,' he says. I don't want to. I get scared. He promises that it will be quick, that I'll just get something to help me sleep. He orders a taxi to the psychiatric clinic.

I can't explain what I've done or how I am. A whirlwind of questions storms out of the doctor's mouth. There's a paper tablecloth between him and me, which I tear into tiny, tiny pieces. I concentrate on the white pieces. I want to make them as small as possible. Everything else is unclear. The school friend who brought me here, the doctor, the nurses. They have thrown their bodies into the air. Like the ice hockey players around the houses. They are ghosts, transparent and at odd angles. They talk to me from far away.

Is there really someone sitting opposite me? Which of the bodies are real? The doctor asks about alcohol and drugs. I grin. I'm nearly falling from the chair, I'm so tired. 'Tell, tell me.'

This is new territory for me, talking to someone I don't know. Only single-syllable words come out and they are meant for no one but me. I say: 'Yes, yes, yes.' I'm talking to my little boys. Slowly my head splits into two pieces. I jump between the two.

The doctor asks if something has happened. I don't know. 'Tell me.' My thoughts stack up. I can't get the words out. Don't know what's significant. The person who is Eli isn't really here. I've ended up outside myself. Just want to sleep. Disappear. Gather myself.

When I was at home in Norway this time I saw what I had left behind. The Sami's serious eyes and words tumble around in my head. Does someone know something about me that I don't know? About lines and curves on my hands, about a whole load of wounds and breaks. He had dark, dangerous eyes and claimed to have knowledge that I didn't understand. He threw

135

out words like fate, judgement, prophecy, blame, demons and pain. In the Samí's eyes, I felt like I was wearing my inside on the outside. I had no story about myself to retaliate with. I was like a new-born, in the present with a big hole on either side.

Is there a fate waiting for me that will leave new marks on my hands? A new country, new people. I can be anyone here. I have started writing in earnest.

I tear the paper tablecloth between us into tiny, tiny pieces. The words are to be found in the pieces. I pull them apart. I'm shaking and restless, stand up then sit down. Bang my head on the table, repeatedly. Then I think of something. 'I'm good at skiing. All categories,' I tell them. I want to save myself. 'Your friend here says that you haven't slept for three nights, is that right?' I nod, gather up a handful of what was once the table-cloth between us and cram the pieces into my mouth.

I have to stay at the hospital. I just want to get some sleeping pills and go back to the folk high school. Have got hung up on the words 'something to help you sleep'. But they'll only give me sleeping pills if I stay. I'm ushered into the day room. Think it's empty, but the TV is on, in the middle of a Norén play. The words boom out of the actor's mouth. I haven't a clue what he's saying, but I'm drawn in and copy him. I move my mouth and say the words slowly. 'How are you?' 'Like normal, only worse.' I copy their voices and there are no words in my head other than those that belong to the actors. They shout and I shout. I don't know why. One day I'm going to write a play myself.

I start to hit the TV. I start to kick. The room is filled with nurses and I'm hauled out.

There are more patients in the dormitory. Sleeping lumps under duvets. Then they wake up and walk around and talk manically or cry. There are nurses in the room all the time. See through. I am the only one alive. I am half deaf. Don't know if anyone is talking to me. I'm in a secret, unreal space, like a dream. 'How are you?' 'Like normal, just worse.' I grin. No one knows me and I recognise no one. Are the others real? Is everything a stage set, a play where I'm supposed to feel uncertain?

They take a blood test and a urine test. I deny that I've smoked hash and say nothing about the fact that I've also taken LSD. They whisper and say that they know. What do they know about me? I'm surprised that everyone is speaking Swedish and that I've moved here. They don't understand my Norwegian. I wave my poems around, but don't find any readers. I've got sores in my armpits. Think it's due to all the drinking. I pick off the scabs and the sores persist. Every day a nurse cleans them with alcohol. I'm not even allowed to touch the bottle. They pour it onto some cotton wool, then lock away the bottle immediately. I feel like a ghost, I exist but I'm not visible.

At breakfast, food is served to everyone individually on a metal tray with separate sections, like when you fly with Aeroflot. I get buttermilk for breakfast. I'm used to having bread. Notice that some other patients get eggs. I take the buttermilk for a week before I ask why I don't even get a small slice of bread for breakfast, or perhaps an egg. Even the dining room smells like the inside of an Aeroflot plane. Maybe I'm on my way somewhere.

'You filled out a breakfast menu when you were admitted,' is the answer. I feel upset and unsure. Didn't even know my own eating habits when I was admitted. How could I have ticked something I don't like? I haven't been with myself at all. I don't know who I am and I can't trust myself. But I get bread and an egg the next day.

I'm sectioned and put in a locked ward. The others' inner life disturbs me. The patients and staff scarcely move and I don't know who's who. I also move very slowly. My thoughts get jammed and seem to stick together only then to be reshuffled. Sentences are broken into pieces. Cut in two. All sounds are amplified and bombard me as if they were messengers of doom. One beautiful day we'll all come loose from everything.

I don't talk much. And not many people talk to me. I sit beside a young guy who tells me that he's there for an amphetamine detox. Am I on some kind of detox? No one has told me. He spends days drawing Chinese characters with elegant hand movements. One day he's suddenly gone.

I don't know who to sit beside with my metal tray in the dining room. Then an old man with a beard and kind blue eyes comes and sits down beside me. His good-natured appearance reminds me a little of my father. But is he as unpredictable as him?

'We've met before,' he says. 'Don't think so,' I reply. 'I don't know anyone in Sweden.'

'I lived a normal life with my wife and children before I got the third eye.'

I look at him, see two eyes, but incredibly also perceive the third eye. Perhaps it's grown over, I think. 'Ended in divorce,' he says. 'I've got the third eye and the shaman's touch. The psychiatrists don't understand it. It's an unusual diagnosis which they change all the time.'

I get up in the middle of his story. I want to listen, but can't. 'Keep on fighting,' he says. I keep on fighting.

He sits down next to me again the next morning.

'Have you heard about the Mayan Calendar?' I think I know, but don't know. 'It runs until 2012. After that there's something new. Then things will get sorted.' He laughs a little. 'Things will get sorted is something I've decided, you see.'

The nurse comes round with the medicine and interrupts us. I take what she gives me and swallow. When she's gone, the man spits out his pills. 'They'll have to think of something other than pills. I just keep them under my tongue and then spit them out as soon as the nurse has gone again. What do you take?' 'Haldol and Trilafon and Cisordinol.' 'Do you know what Trilafon is often called? *Trill ifrån*, or roll away. Watch out. Keep your Norwegian accent. It will make you well again.'

I think about the Norwegian Samí who read my palms and terrified me. This man doesn't frighten me. He can have as many eyes as he likes. He still doesn't threaten me. He doesn't claim to know anything about me that I don't know. I'm sure he's just like my dad, kind and funny, ill and well.

He sits opposite me at breakfast the next day and the next again. His eyes are heavy and his body is heavy. 'I dreamt I was out in space last night. New stars were being lit,' he says in a thick voice. Then the tears fall. They slip silently down his old face. 'The scientists don't understand. They know too little about spirituality.'

I reach out my hand and take his. He squeezes my hand with the hand he's just dried his tears with. I get some of his wet tears in my hand. But can't cry myself. Don't understand what's so sad.

I'm shaking. Jonathan asks me to lie down on the sofa. He sits down beside me on a chair. I close my eyes. 'Concentrate on your toes,' he says. 'Just be there. Then your feet. Then your ankles, knees. Buttocks, thighs, abdomen. Fingers, palms.'

He goes through my entire body and I feel small parts of myself one by one. 'You can do this yourself before you go to sleep. Focus. Relax.'

I get up slowly and I'm not shaking any more.

I don't see the autumn that is blazing outside. But then there is suddenly the opportunity of an outing. I can go swimming with the others. I've been inside for over a month and not been allowed out. Except for some short walks in the grounds with staff.

No one knows that I'm here. Not even me. I weigh nothing on the inside. I listen and practise speaking Swedish. New words creep in. I get stuck on *fåtölj*, *hoj* and *doja*. I'm sleeping better and better. Even though I wake up every morning and wonder where I am, everything is a little clearer now.

We drive into Uppsala in one of the hospital cars. I think that we're going to the library. It says *BAD* in big letters on the wall of the building, which transforms into ABC in my mind. I'm going to be forced to borrow a book. An easy reader, like in primary school. We hire swimsuits, but mine is far too big. I dive in and my breasts jump out. I quickly get out of the water, say to one of the nurses that I want to swap swimsuit and run down to the changing rooms. There, I get dressed and then leave the building that I still think is the library.

I walk for several blocks. I wander for hours, doing the same circuit. When it gets dark, I go into a restaurant. I have no money, order a glass of water and say that I'm waiting for a friend. I sit next to a family that are celebrating someone's engagement. They're laughing and having fun. After a while they ask if I want to move a bit closer. And I want to. They ask if I would like anything to eat. 'I'm called Eli,' I say. And yes, I am hungry. They have ordered a selection of small dishes that everyone can just help themselves to. They come from Poland. 'Would you like a beer?' 'Yes, please.' One more? Yes, please.

I drink and chat with the Polish family. I sit beside the mother. She's fat and wearing a flowery dress and pearl necklace. She speaks broken Swedish, but smiles good-naturedly. 'Marek, Marek,' she says and blows a kiss. 'Isn't he handsome?' Marek is her son. He radiates bliss from where he sits next to his pretty fiancée and orders more beers for the whole table. When the restaurant closes, they say goodbye to me outside. Everyone gives me a hug. I'm not used to being hugged.

I have no idea what to do or where to go. I know no one in Uppsala, have no home to go to. The folk high school is miles away. I walk in a circle, as I did earlier in the day, or rather, a large square. I look at the people who belong here. How will I get out? I change route. Only one part of the town exists for me at any one time. I have to take possession of it. Maybe the whole of Uppsala collapsed and was raised again as a labyrinth while I was eating and drinking.

I can't sit down on this cold November night. I have to save myself. But how? God, where are you? What should I pray for? The wind blows. The streets are empty now. And in the midst of a whirl of leaves and rubbish, I see what I think is an animal do a somersault. I'm frightened, don't know which direction to run. It's a white plastic bag. I kick it. Pick up a branch and wave the bag around in the air. It frightened me and now I'm going to hurt it. It doesn't work.

I want to go home, somewhere. Everything is so eerily silent. As if I was walking amongst paintings. It's the witching hour. I'm completely exhausted. I haven't seen anyone for ages. I turn into a side street. There's a lone taxi standing there and the light on the roof is on.

143

I go up to the car and ask the driver if he can take me to the mental hospital for free. I'm a patient there, but don't know where I am and have no money. He's an immigrant like me, and at first I don't understand when he says I should jump in. He just looks at me. I'm shaking. 'Could you just point out which direction I should go?' I try. Then he opens the door. I hesitate, he's opened the door to the passenger seat. Should I sit in the back? 'Come on,' he says. 'I'm just sitting here resting. Not a good night. Not for you either, eh?' 'Yeah, not bad.'

My right leg is shaking. It won't stop. And I whisper: 'Yes, yes, yes.' It's Erik who's talking. He's saying: 'Get out of the car. It might get lost.' I stay where I am. It's good to be sitting in the warmth. The driver looks at me. 'I ran over a fox cub,' he says. 'Flat as a pancake, it was. Its guts had kind of spilled out and lay in a bloody pile on the road. It was so small. And now you.'

He starts the car. 'The mental hospital,' he says. 'Do they look after you there?' 'Yes,' I reply. Look after me. I don't know what that means. I'm just there. 'In Gambia, where I come from, we look after any mad people in the family ourselves. What does your mum say?' 'She doesn't know that I'm there.' The dark, kind man looks at me. He takes one hand off the wheel and puts it on my shoulder. 'Then you should tell her,' he says. 'You should tell your mother.' I stiffen. He removes his hand, but it was good while it was there.

When we arrive at the mental hospital, I don't know where we should stop, in front of which building. I've only been inside. I get out and say thank you. The taxi drives off. I watch the lights disappear.

All the doors are locked. I start at the first building and ring on the bell. The voice that answers doesn't recognise me and won't let me in. It's cold. It'll soon be dawn. Finally a door opens and a nurse comes down to get me. At first he says that he shouldn't really let me in, as he can smell on my breath that I've been drinking. Then he says that I've been sectioned and that I left the swimming pool without permission.

We take the lift up to a unit I recognise. 'You ran away,' he says. I nod. 'Why?' 'I don't know. I wanted to get out.' 'You'll get no more leave for a while now.'

I go into the smoking room. There are two nurses there, playing chess. I want them to talk to me. I try to say something, they don't give me much attention. But they sit staring at a chess board with great concentration. I am just air. I look out through the window, see the day dawning. I smoke a cigarette and stand beside the nurses. There's a strange silence. As if someone invisible has come into the room. Something is going to happen.

Then I kick the chess board and send all the pieces flying. The air can do that. To see if anyone is alive. I grab a chair and try to smash the glass door out onto the corridor. It's unbreakable. I hit it and hit it, but it doesn't even crack. I throw myself at the door with the chair in my arms. The alarm goes off. Suddenly a whole lot of nurses appear and tackle me to the floor. I hit and kick. I'm not going to end up like the little fox cub, beside myself in a pool of blood.

There are too many of them. My trousers are pulled down. I'm given several injections while I'm lying on the floor. I'm lifted up and restrained on a bed. Thick leather straps round my arms and legs and stomach.

145

I don't wake up for forty-eight hours. When I try to open my eyes, everything feels glued. My throat is dry and my jaw is stiff. I can't talk properly, my tongue keeps getting in the way. I'm terrified. This has happened to me, this has happened to me, echoes round and round my head. My whole body is stiff. I've been broken and changed. They've injected me into a permanently different state. A strange unknown body. I will never be like normal again.

A girl is lying whimpering in the bed beside me. Her father is there the whole time. I think she's tried to commit suicide. The telephone out in the corridor starts to ring. I think it's Mum. Something jumps inside me. What if she can see through the receiver? She mustn't know about anything. I'm invisible and alone. It has to be that way. I've been changed forever.

It was Erik who wanted to break the glass door. He told me to do it. But I can't get out of bed. I try, but I'm unsteady. Lie down again. A broken glass door would replace the pain. What is inside would flow out into the shards of glass. That's what he thought. But now it's me who aches all over. Who has been broken. It's almost like the first time I saw a child who was drunk. A twelve-year-old girl. I couldn't imagine that she would ever be sober and normal again.

The doctor apologises and says that in the chaos that ensued, someone managed to give me too high a dose, but that I'll be given something for the side effects. I get more injections. I don't understand why I can't use my muscles like I usually do.

Why does no one tell me that I will be normal again? That

I'll regain the ability to speak and move again. I lie petrified in my bed and wonder how I am going to explain to the others at home that I've changed. That I fought like a baby fox against a car and ended up outside myself.

In my dream I'm doing an enormous jigsaw puzzle. I'm at home with Mum. She says that maths is the queen of all science. 'Some people think there's no use for maths. But I think that in the same way that we solve maths problems at school, we can later solve all problems in life. Remember, there's always a solution. With a bit of effort and patience, you'll find it. It's the same with everything, even a jigsaw puzzle,' she says.

We each put down one piece at a time. Pictures grow in the picture. From all my most secret nightmares. Things that I don't want to tell Mum about. We don't say anything. I see what it's going to depict, it grows into a picture of a bound-up girl. I try to put down another piece. One that will protect and conceal. But it too fits, fits perfectly into the awful whole.

'My advice for sorting the pieces is to divide them up into corner pieces, side pieces and normal pieces,' Mum explains. 'They're the ones there are most of. Then there are all the irregular pieces. And there might be some even stranger pieces, thicker and thinner. I think of them as odd.'

I look around the living room, at all the things that we children have made. My drawing from the newspaper of the four faces from different parts of the world that became a stamp and the front page.

'It's you who's odd,' says Erik. 'It's you who sits there and is different. The body is the I's outside.' I say nothing. Mum says nothing. I put down the last piece and the picture is complete. 'Now we can destroy it,' I say.

'Hearing voices is not sick, in itself. It's about how you deal with them. People have heard voices since time immemorial. Philosophers, wise people, and artists,' Jonathan says.

'And mad people,' I say.

Jonathan laughs. 'I've got a much freer attitude to voices than you. I don't think it's sick,' he says.

'It's your job,' I say.

I stay in hospital for a few weeks more. Am given Antabuse for my alcoholism and anti-psychotic medication. I ask for talking therapy, but don't get it. I really feel that I need to talk to someone. I both want to and don't want to. There's something I don't understand. Something that's there, pressing me, confusing me.

Back at the folk high school, a girl gives me all her attention. She's there all the time. She's from Stockholm, popular, smart and the most attractive person at the school. What does she want with me? She asks what I did in hospital, what it was like and how I am now. Her name is Lolo and she tells me that she's started to dream about me.

Her boyfriend gets angry and splits up with her when he finds the poems she has written about me. They're about Eli under the hat, Eli in the leather jacket and punk paraphernalia, a terrifying armband with 20 cm nails. A dangerous beauty. Someone who seems to be mysteriously kind. Eli from Norway. Who stands out in the converted stable and reads out long poems that rhyme, that sound like music that no one can understand, but that lull you like a lullaby. Eli who plays floorball better than the boys. Who plays in a white tuxedo shirt instead of a tracksuit. Eli who radiates a primal energy mixed with super sensitivity. Who can smash the world to bits and go to bits herself. Eli who fascinates you and makes you warm and curious. Someone you can't leave once you've become her friend.

I'm astonished, elated and feel seen. I've always thought of Lolo as out of my league. A snob. I'm curious now. Who is she?

*

Lolo and I go on a trip to the mountains. We go skiing and she looks sweet in her yellow beret, with her bright blue eyes and thick blonde hair. She's beautiful in much the same way as me, only it suits her better. I wear an armour of accessories and attitude, which doesn't allow what could be described as beautiful to shine through. I've shaved one side of my head and permed my hair so that it stands straight out on the other. She laughs and listens when I tell her how you should dress in the mountains. Wool against your skin. Several layers and then something windproof. Lolo wants to wear nylon tights under everything. 'Are you crazy?' I exclaim. 'You'll freeze to death.' For my part, I've taken off all my punk gear and dress as though I was going to spend the night in the snow. Lolo listens to all my advice, but does what she wants in the end. She goes skiing like a Stockholmer, in other words, someone who's only been skiing a few times in the winter break. We go cross-country. She's out of shape, but shows stamina going uphill. On the downhill she falls frequently but always gets up. She struggles up the mountain on slippery skis, but doesn't complain. She's tougher than I first thought. We laugh a lot. We eat freezing sandwiches in the wind. Go back to school and are together all the time.

One evening we're getting ready for a party. We have a little to drink. I've stopped taking Antabuse and it's important for me to show Lolo that I can drink in moderation. She seems so confident. So controlled. So normal. So considerate. A city girl. We get done up and sit in her room in the accommodation block. Her unabashed closeness makes me so nervous that I brush my teeth with hand cream instead of toothpaste. I spit it out and drink some water. Lolo is worried but then laughs. She wants to put a necklace round my neck. I pull back, suddenly terrified that she's going to strangle me. No one is allowed to touch my neck. My sudden movement makes her back off.

'Sorry, I didn't know,' she says. How could she know? I didn't know myself. How can I give her a hug, or anyone else for that matter, if I'm so frightened of being strangled?

> *'Under bunnen, nede i undergrunnen, går mennesker
> omkring uten smil om munnen. Underfundig i grunnen.'*

> Underground, under the town, people walk around wearing
> a frown. Underhand, really.

I'm standing in the old hall reading my poems. They are long, rhythmic harangues. I intone them in sing-song Norwegian. The audience listens. I've caught them. These are political texts, angry texts full of wonder, youthful texts. We do writing exercises and have talks from visiting authors. I write a piece about Marit's death, which I don't dare to show. At first I'm shy about talking about other people's writing and my own, but that soon passes. I had no idea you could read so much into a poem. That there's another short story behind the short story. That sometimes it's good to fail. I read, make associations, make my own formulations. More than anything, it's exciting to hear the thoughts that your texts trigger in others. How a reader helps to shape the content.

I write and write and dare to get closer to my own language. I start to experiment, listen to the previous sentence, immerse myself in the language. But it comes as a surprise that the other students not only write, but also read. I feel inferior when they talk about important authors who I haven't even heard of. Or about literary trends. I've barely read a book and can't suggest any Norwegian authors when they ask. My defence is that I'm anti-literature.

153

We have a lot of time during the day for writing and then there are the long weekends when the others go home. I stay behind and don't know what to do with myself. I want to create all the time. One late evening, when I've been drinking and am stumbling around between the old oak trees, I stumble upon my writing teacher. I've got a studded belt and spiky armband so everyone can see that no one can touch me. But my teacher has understood. 'We didn't ask you to come here,' he says. 'You behave as though you're at some kind of special needs school, under duress.' Then suddenly, in the dark of the old building and trees, so drunk that I can barely stand on my own two feet, I realise that I have in fact chosen to come here myself. That I've got something to learn.

I think, as I always do, that things will get better now. But behind my back, the teachers start to consider whether I should be expelled. A media teacher recognises my impatience and talent and suggests to the principal that I should instead get individual tuition from him. I learn to take photographs and develop them, to film with Super 8 and to cut films. I've barely held a camera or seen a film before. Have no examples, but I'm keen and full of ideas. Can scarcely sleep at night.

The teacher is patient, he praises me and helps me navigate my ideas. I have never come across such an enthusiastic teacher before. He applauds all my mad suggestions. He helps me to believe that I've got something of value to tell. Encourages me to do it in my own way.

We take a picture of me with Emil's cap on, with white make-up, and enlarge them to life size so we can make a film. *Him and the Other Boy*, where I play both boys. One who talks all the time and one who is mute, in other words, the photo. They're hitchhiking and tell the same story, each from their own perspective, to the drivers who can't be seen. Him wears Emil's cap, the other boy doesn't. I alternate between acting with the cap and without, against the photo of me. The one sitting in the front seat is the one who does the talking while the one in the back is silent.

The end result is a forty-minute film and the whole school crowds into the gym hall to watch it. The person who was almost expelled has won. The media teacher is proud, and I understand that I have gone from being the worst to being the best.

I sit by the kitchen table and wait for Jonathan. Flick through one of my scrapbooks. Used to do things like that. Read art periodicals and foreign fashion magazines. Cut and paste. Make collages. I've got several thick books, full of ideas. Night would fall and I'd continue.

It's a long time since I last did it. I've made several films for TV and cinema, and each film has a book of story boards and visual ideas. The film work has dropped off a bit right now. I look through a book with ideas for film sequences where the image size is distorted. The film was never made. I carry on to a poster I've called 'Matter Out Of Place'. Where objects are placed in the wrong position and therefore display an outsideness. A queer theme. That hasn't amounted to anything either. Making collages is one of the things on the list of anxiety management methods that Jonathan and I have written in our folder. I've got as far as buying a new book and writing the year on the front in big numbers. I look forward to starting to fill the book one night.

Torvald is coming to collect me from the folk high school. The year is over and I'm going back to Norway. I can't leave. I can't finish, just when I was getting used to it. I've never had it so good. I've met lots of people. I've met Lolo. I can't say goodbye to anyone. I've been seen and encouraged.

I drink half a bottle of vodka. I pull all my stuff out of the drawers and cupboard and throw everything on the floor. I can't pack. I find a whole lot of empty bottles. 'Yes, yes, yes. What is it?' 'Smash them,' Erik says. I smash one bottle after the other on the floor. Now I can't pack. I drift between the buildings and watch the others carry their things out to their parents' cars. See that they want something new. That they dare to let go. How easy it has been for them to be here. No depth. I want to stay. They can't leave. I haven't put any shoes on, am walking around in my socks. What's going to happen to me now? Just when I've started writing in earnest. When I've dared to find a story that's mine. When I've learned to talk about my own writing. When I'm just learning to talk about other things too.

Torvald is alarmed by the mess in my room. He gets a rubbish bag and starts to tidy up. There are bits of glass in all my things, so he has to pick them out with his hands. I sit on the bed crying. 'Stop it,' he says. I stop. He pulls down the Karl Marx poster that I'd put up upside down. What does the old man mean to me? Nothing. Just something I took with me from the last folk high school. I rip it to shreds. The white hair and beard, no one will be able to put it together again. A shiny picture of Jesus also hangs upside down. He's got a halo around his head and his hands on his burning heart. It's on such thick cardboard that I can't tear it at all. I take it outside and burn it. Not going to collect men any more.

'I've been in the nuthouse,' I say to Torvald. He doesn't answer. 'Help me,' he says. 'I've been in the nuthouse this autumn.' 'Did it cost anything?' he asks. 'Well, they didn't say that it did,' I reply. 'Do you know why I was there?' 'No,' he says. 'Neither do I,' I say. 'They locked me up. I took pills.' I want to say, what if it happens again? But Torvald wants to talk about something else. 'It took me eight hours to drive here,' he says. 'Can we eat before we go?' 'You don't need to pack, because I'm not leaving,' I say. 'Let's just pack everything and go anyway,' Torvald says. Typical. Like a dad, but then Dad wouldn't have said that. Like a big brother. I've always done what Torvald said, and will do it again. But not this time.

'I don't want to leave,' I say. 'I understand, but that doesn't stop us leaving, does it?' he says. 'I'm not leaving.' 'What are you going to do then?' 'Stay here.' 'But everyone's leaving. You can come back to see them another time.'

I hit my head with the heel of my hand. 'Yes, yes, yes.' I'm scared. Scared of going home. I'm a stranger here, but not any more. I'm not a stranger at home, but will be when I go back. I get up and walk out, still without shoes. I walk out to reception and ask to talk to the principal.

'I can't leave,' I say. 'If you're wondering why, I can't tell you.' 'But hasn't your brother come to collect you?' 'Yes, he's here.' 'And you can't leave?' 'No.' 'But do you want to stay here when everyone else has gone?' 'For a while, then I'll get used to the fact that they're not here any more.' 'You've not been drinking, have you? You've got no shoes on your feet.' 'No.' 'Because you know, artistic souls like yourself can't take alcohol.' I know.

'What's an artistic soul?' 'Someone who takes life very

seriously indeed.' Then I know that I'm not going to leave. 'If you think it would be better for you to stay a while, then you can work on the grounds for a few weeks,' the principal says. 'There are summer courses here, so the canteen will be open.'

I go back to my room. Torvald has nearly finished packing. 'Eli,' he says. 'Please don't ever say that again.' 'What?' 'What you say about the nuthouse. You must never tell anyone.'

I hold my tongue and I hold my tongue. I tell Jonathan just how much I've held my tongue. 'Your family must surely know,' he says. 'I'm pretty sure that they don't,' I reply. 'Are you sure? All these years.' 'Quite sure.' 'Why have you kept it a secret?' 'Because they don't want to know.'

I could have done with Marit now. Maybe I would have been able to tell her. Tell her that I'm ill. That I'm not ill. Maybe she would have said that it was okay.

When I've finished the few weeks' work in the garden at the folk
high school, Lolo and I go to West Berlin. We stay in a huge
squat together with other young people from all over Western
Europe. It's an international work camp. I, who promised myself
I would never go near another squat again, have changed. And
also I'm with Lolo. Somehow it seems that that's allowed. The
people are older than when I was in Copenhagen and there are
no druggie children who've run away from home.

We get board and lodging free in return for helping to reno-
vate the building. We paint the stairwells in bright colours. We
build a barbecue in the garden. We shop in the nearby market
and take turns making food. We visit the Berlin Wall which is
covered in graffiti and take a train to East Berlin to buy cheap
film. Look at the small cars and grey houses, and the people, we
want to talk to them, but can't speak German.

Lolo and I are inseparable. We hold hands. One of the
German helpers wants to know if we're together. We don't know
what to answer. 'It's what they do in Scandinavia,' a girl from
England says. 'They hold hands.' We sleep in a big room. With
an enormous bathroom done out like a living room with armchairs and big plants. Or do we have a bath and toilet in our
living room? I read a piece for Lolo there in the Berlin night.
She's very taken. 'You've got something there,' she says.

When I drink alcohol I start to shake. I lie on the bed and
shake all over. I stutter and only manage to stammer out single
syllables over and over again. My thoughts get stuck.

'You really are damaged,' Lolo says. 'What happened to you?

I don't know if I dare be with you. Either, or,' she says. 'Either I leave you or I never leave you.'

Welcome at the right time. I'm nervous and bursting with hope.

I've moved into a box room in a flat with Lolo and her cousin in Stockholm. I don't think it's alcohol or drugs that are the problem. They're more a case of self-medication.

The problem is that I need to talk to someone. The problem is that I'm about to break. That when I get a problem in one reality, I move to another. That the boys' voices inside make me stop mid-step and say: 'Yes, yes, yes' and listen to their constant demands. That my thoughts stop on the verge of an empty abyss. That sleep won't come. That my stomach aches.

I go to a doctor and have to swallow a long tube. They examine my stomach. I've got a stomach ulcer. The doctor asks why. The boys say I mustn't tell anyone about them. Or I'll be punished in the most terrible way. Can I find help to get help to get rid of them? I don't know if I can carry on living.

I have to save myself. I'm a scream. I'm twenty-two years old and I get in touch with the mental health services. Lolo encourages me to call. She doesn't want to watch me shaking and stammering and falling to pieces on her own. Lolo talks to them on the phone. She says that she can't bear to see me like this. 'Throw her out,' says the voice. 'You can't look after an alcoholic.' 'She's not an alcoholic,' Lolo says. 'I've promised myself not to abandon her. She won't survive on the streets.'

I get an appointment far too far into the future. We wait. I have far too much faith that someone will be able to help me. That there's an adult somewhere, a warm person who knows something I don't know. How to make it better. What is wrong. But there's a misunderstanding. I'm convinced that

163

I've come at the right time. I'm nervous and bursting with hope.

From my medical journal: *Pat did not turn up for appointment yesterday. Have received copies of her medical journal from Uppsala. Appears to be a case of extensive alcohol and hash misuse by a vulnerable person. Will wait for pat to say whether she is interested in continued contact.*

Note, afternoon: *Pat comes in at around 3 p.m. in intoxicated state. Says that the time suits her better. I tell her that it is not what we agreed, which she eventually accepts. Comes back to reception again just before closing in the same state. Is offered another appointment, but says she is not interested. I am of the opinion that we will not be able to help this pat.*

Note: *Have consulted the senior doctor about pat. Pat rang and asked for a new appointment. We will prob not be able to offer her much, but will give her a new appointment on Tuesday.*

New appointment: *When I ask her whether she has been admitted before, she looks at me blankly, but when I push her a little, she says she was in hospital because she had a sore stomach and was very unhappy. When I ask about drugs and alcohol, she looks very surprised and says that she does not use them. When I ask what she does for a living, she replies: nothing, don't know where the time goes. Says the reason she has come is that she wants to start psychotherapy.*

Pat makes an odd impression. Is well padded with scarves and sweaters and a couple of shirts. Does not sit still for more than a few secs at a time. Pulls apart a pen. Sits drawing in a notebook. Looks down at the floor. In general, gives the impression of motor restlessness. Is also very reticent in giving information about herself. When I press her, she tries to remember when and where various things happened, but is rather confused. On the other hand, she says several times that she wants psychotherapy. When I tell her that I think she is not ready for it at the moment, she becomes agitated, says that she knows what is best for her. Thinks that she has wasted fifty kronor if she does not get a referral for therapy. I try to explain to her that it is important for her to have more structure in her daily life. To find a job and somewhere to live. It transpires that she does not live at the address given in her medical journal, but she does not want to say where she is staying at the moment.

Assessment: *Clearly disturbed young woman, with extensive history of substance abuse from early puberty. Claims that she does not use drugs now, but hard to tell. Was clearly under the influence when I met her here. We cannot give her any more help.*

I'm so upset when I leave. I don't feel we've talked about what's important. About the pain. The voices kept interrupting me and I was so terribly nervous. Wanted to show my best side. Wanted to convince the doctor that I needed help to survive. I'm not under the influence, just frightened. And now I've fallen to bits.

When I come out of the room and realise that the doctor will do nothing more than humiliate me, reprimand me and tell lies about me being high, I try to kick in the lift door. Several people rush over and take a firm hold of me. They escort me down in the lift and show me to the door. I stagger out onto the street. Where should I go now? I decide to go down to Lake Mälaren and drown myself. Freeze to death. I can jump off the bridge into the icy water. That's what I'm going to do. First fall through the air, then hit the thin ice and break through. First cold, cold, then warm, warm and then death.

I'm never going to be a proper adult anyway. I've always known that. I want to be a child and grow up again. No crying, no growing. I can't carry on from here. I'm raging with the doctor. I want revenge. I am disappointed with life. I won't stand on the railings and hesitate. I walk with determination. Now, you bastards. I feel almost triumphant. I don't need to hope any more.

Then I hear someone calling me. 'Eli, Eli!' I don't stop. No one is going to stop me from dying. No one at all. It's Lolo, she runs up beside me. 'I suddenly felt so worried about you,' she says. 'I'm going to die,' I say. 'I'm going to drown myself. There's no help to be had.' Then the tears come. 'I'm here,' Lolo says.

'I'll never leave you.' 'You will,' I sniff. 'I can't,' Lolo says, 'and you're not going to die.' She gives me a long, hard hug. 'You are the most precious thing I have.' I want to say 'you too', but she's holding me so tight that I can't get the words out.

No one has such wonderful cheeks to hug as Lolo. She is cool and soft. She's wearing her yellow beret. She fixes the collar of my jacket that's all twisted and inside out, and says: 'You're going to write.' I've written all my life, I think. 'You've got much more to give. You've got much more to get. I promise. We'll go home and make lasagne and then you can show me some of your new work.' She takes a step back. I don't move. Lasagne or dying in the water? We usually eat pasta with fried cabbage or carrots and garlic.

What finally persuades me to let Lolo put her arm round my shoulders and lead me away, is that I desperately want to read my latest piece to her. Once again I'm like the fox cub. I've been run over, but Lolo has stuffed my innards back in. A mince lasagne might even be nice.

We create a tiny writing space for me in the minimal room that Lolo and I share. I start to do a paper round again. I write full time. Feel my way into the language. Have found a form for my wonderment and a language in which to wonder. You can learn something from yourself. I don't write in the way that I thought I would write. I write in the way that I think when I write. I am inspired by the sentence before. Images and rhythms just flow. I say the sentences out loud. Over and over again. It's like sucking on sweeties. I find my own pattern. Feel like I'm sewing the text together with a thick red thread. It's a young person's journey into the world, dreams and life. A young person who has just opened their eyes. Someone who doesn't know how things normally are. She moves through story after story and tries to the best of her abilities to understand what is around her. The question is not who am I. The question is who are the others.

One of my pieces is published in a magazine. Then Bonniers, the publishing house, ring and ask if I have any more, and I do. 'But they're in Norwegian.' 'Could you translate them into Swedish yourself, do you think?' I answer as I always do when I don't know. I say yes. My friends from the writing course tell me that publishers don't usually contact you. Normally you submit something, have it returned, then submit again and have it returned.

Tim and Sonja from the writing course help me to translate. They learn Norwegian and I learn Swedish. I start to speak Swedish as well. Feel like I did when I was little and stood in front of the mirror speaking English. Perhaps I should stay in this country. Then I would blend in and not always be a foreigner, someone who's here on a visit. I'll be able to go shopping without the shop assistant saying *akkurat* and *guleböj*.

One day when I'm out walking in the woods, the title pops into my head. I say it out loud. It just came to me. The writing goes on all the time without me knowing. Buzzing through my body until it suddenly gives me a sentence. The book is going to be called *There Are Limits to What I Don't Understand*. Could be the title for my entire life.

I contact the Swedish Association for Sexuality Education, RFSU, about my confused sexual identity. They tell me to come in for a chat. Then they tell me I have too many underlying problems for them to help. I'll have to try elsewhere.

After trying for several years to get state-subsidised therapy, I start going to see a psychologist privately, who somewhat hesitantly takes me on. It costs five hundred and ten kronor a time, which is roughly what I have left once I've paid all my bills. I'm full of hope. Can she save me? Can she show me something about myself that will make things easier for me?

She wears sweaters with pictures of cats on them, the tails (surely they're not real) hanging down from the stomach. I think they're expensive designer clothes. They frighten me, but I'm not sure why. She looks frumpy, with round cheeks and small eyes. Old-fashioned haircut and old-fashioned ladies' shoes with a heel. I decide that she's from Romanian aristocracy and that she speaks French at home. If she ever goes home. I always think of her sitting in her fine armchair, day and night. She is nowhere else to be found when I'm not here. When I have money myself, I'll start to buy my clothes in designer shops. Find my own style using brands from London and Japan, and Swedish designers. I'll get my own tailor. But that's not now. For now, it's more a case of charity shops and skips.

I find it hard to talk. I like her, but we come from different worlds. I think that every sentence I utter tells her there's something wrong with me. And I don't think there is. I'm proud of being Eli. I'm not like the psychologist, that's for certain.

Sometimes I have a beer in a pub nearby beforehand. Or a whisky. I'm not used to talking about my parents. Don't want to show them in a bad light. Say that everything is fine, that everything has always been fine and that I don't understand where the anxiety comes from. I say I only see the difficulties. Why do I do that? I don't say anything about the voices. One day she says: 'Tell me, do you think of your father as sacred?' That sticks. The only true answer is yes. No one is allowed to say anything bad about him or Mum.

I tell her nonchalantly that I found a suitcase in the skip outside her door. That there were lots of people at the bus stop who watched me rummaging around in the skip. The case is red and old-fashioned, just the kind I like. She can't understand how I dared to look through the rubbish when so many people were watching. I don't understand that that could be a problem. She thinks that I have funny, big shoes that are not at all feminine. I'm ahead of fashion, but can't expect her to understand that. I think she's got sad, fat feet that are squeezed into high-heeled red patent shoes. I think that she's trying to make me more feminine. I'm not just a woman and I wish that she could accept and appreciate that. Maybe she's trying to be a feminine role model. But she's too peculiar for that. Or I am. She's reliable and has authority, just not enough for both of us.

But I relish the fact that she cares. Feel strongly that she wants to help me. But can she? Over time I learn to talk more. I think I learn things in secret. She shows me that I have holes inside. Difficulties that have to be fixed. She says that I'm like a worn blanket and we're trying to patch up the holes. The question is whether there's enough material between the holes to do this. If there's any material left to pull the thread through. Sometimes both she and I doubt it. She suggests that I should consider admitting myself to hospital for a while. I don't understand

172

at all. That's not the point. I'm nearly better again.

I want to talk about my writing instead. How well it's going. I tell her how I work and edit and rewrite. 'You rewrite?' she asks. 'Of course. I work every day. I sand and polish and listen and rewrite.' She doesn't seem to understand what being a writer means. I realise how poorly we communicate when I give her a card for Christmas. It's a picture I found in the paper and I feel that it says a lot about who I am, in a humorous way. A young man, it's Erik, it's me. He's smiling in the mirror. Perfectly combed hair and white teeth. He's standing there putting a tie round the stiff collar of his nice white shirt. The text reads: 'Anyone could see that I was on the verge of a nervous breakdown. But I wasn't anyone.'

The psychologist doesn't laugh. Simply takes the card and says thank you. She just doesn't understand me, I think to myself. Or does she, in fact? The next time I try to tease out a laugh, I tell her about the time I had to get home quickly after my appointment. As I have to pay for the therapy myself, I can't afford to take the bus or underground, so I walk through the city. When I got home I discovered that I had one of the hooks from her designer coat stand sticking up from the collar of my jacket. How could I have walked all that way without discovering that it was in my jacket? I couldn't take it back and I couldn't keep it at home, so I gave it to my friend Lisen. 'You'll have to look after this. It's a symbol,' I said. And every time I've been there since, I've seen that the hook is missing. So finally I've decided to confess. I'm so full of laughter that I can scarcely get the words out. She listens as usual without the hint of a smile and does not ask to have it back. I'm disappointed. I have a piece of her hidden away with a friend. Her big warm body, her untrendy haircut and her cautious smile.

*

One day when I get there too early, I can't sit still and wait. I pace back and forth in the waiting room. There are magazines there. They irritate me. After all, I can hardly read. Three colourful vases stand in a row on one of the shelves. Suddenly I've grabbed one of them and thrown it to the floor. I sit in the middle of all the pieces of glass and pick one up. I start to cut my face. The blood runs down my throat and onto my clothes, my hands are bloody. The skin on my face is so thin.

The psychologist comes out to call me in. She gets her colleague and together they manage to force open my hand and take out the piece of glass. They get paper towels and wipe the blood from my face, neck and hands. They cover as much as possible with plasters.

Then I go into the psychologist's room and have nothing to say. The next time I go to see her, I deeply regret what I've done. I offer my sincerest apologies and ask if I can continue my treatment. I can.

My first radio play is going to be broadcast on the radio. I've already been commissioned to write another. I started writing it at the folk high school with support from the media teacher. He's the one who sent it in to the radio.

I'm woken up by the director the day after it's been broadcast. 'Have you read the papers?' I don't read the papers. 'They've written about you and your play. The captions are "crystal clear enigmas" and "magical signals".'

I didn't know you could get in the papers for writing. Thought it was only when you were involved in politics and sport. This encourages me even more to finish the book. I get a lot of help with the spelling and Swedish. The former students from the writing course have started a forum where we read each other's manuscripts and give constructive criticism. Then I sit down and do a rewrite.

I talk to the typewriter. Say the words out loud and taste them: she is beautiful, much like me, but on her it's more visible. Time is like thought, thick, you could almost rest your arm on it, like on a shelf. We're not old enough yet to not believe that someone sees us. In the depth of the moment, I tie a small knot.

I get a job as an assistant for a blind boy. What is it in me that compels me to say yes? Total denial. A total blackout. I could do with an assistant myself.

He's studying at a further education college. We sit towards the front of the classroom. It's an English lesson. I can't spell a single word in English. It's mostly conversation. Difficult words are written up on the blackboard. The whole point is that I write them down in the blind boy's book, but the only thing is, I can't see what's written on the board. I pretend to write something. He pops his vocabulary book in his bag, happy in the belief that we'll see each other again in two days.

When I get home, I tell Lolo. She understands the situation and takes over the job.

I get a new job, as a carer, and start as an hourly paid temp. Sometimes at night, sometimes during the day. I like helping, cleaning, tidying, dusting and hovering. Washing grumpy old men in intimate places is worse. Changing shitbags on people's stomachs is not much fun either. One day, an old lady grabs hold of my breasts and squeezes them. 'Look after these two when you're on holiday in Norway,' she says. Lots of old ladies only seem to have one thing on their mind: swearwords and genitalia. They call those of us who work for them cunts and whores. Have they carried these words around with them all their lives and never been able to say them? So now they've let go, the words flood out in great streams.

Others have stories to tell, are funny, grateful and happy.

Many of them have lost it slightly in a rather charming, but sad way. I sit with a woman at the kitchen table and every time she looks out of the window, she says in surprise: 'But that's my view.'

One day I find a woman dead in her bed. I try for quite some time to wake her before I realise that she's dead. Then the room turns cold. It's death. I run back and alert the boss. Later, a hearse pulls up slowly outside the house. That's that. The end for her. And after that, I'm scared every time I ring the bell and no one answers.

One weekend when I'm working night shifts at a home, Sussi suggests that we do one night each instead of doing two together. I go to work and do the medicine round. Everything is fine. We use the small bedroom in the staff flat as the smoking room. I hear someone knocking on the window. There's a man outside who I know is a drug addict and the grandchild of someone who lives here. She's his mother's mother, the only one in the family he can stay with. I open the window. He asks for Lilian. 'She's not at work,' I say. Then he brandishes two forks at me in a threatening manner. I quickly shut the window and leave the room. As I close the door, I hear the glass in the window breaking and the man stumbling into the room. I rush back and lock the door. Stand on the outside and hear him moving around. He tries the door handle, I see it going up and down.

'Close your eyes,' Espen says. 'Go and lie down,' Emil says. 'Sleep, sleep, don't be here,' Espen says. 'Fight back,' Erik says. 'No,' says Espen. 'Think about something else,' Emil says. I take some cushions and go and lie down on the floor in the day room, which is also the office. I think so intensely about disappearing, I fall asleep immediately, with a little help from the boys.

I'm still asleep when the day staff come at a quarter past seven. There is glass and chaos everywhere in the smoking room. Anything that wasn't attached has been stolen, lamps, cushions, ash trays and books. 'What did the police say?' The police. 'I didn't speak to the police.' 'Why didn't you call the police? After all, you were responsible for over thirty pensioners, safes and medicine.' 'I just didn't think,' I whimper. And I really didn't. All I thought about was pretending it hadn't happened. 'Where is Sussi?' We both get the sack. Since then, I haven't had a normal job.

The telephone screams through the night. The rings mean danger. It's my sister Hild. 'Mum didn't dare call you because you're so sensitive,' she says. 'But something's happened. Dad's had a brain haemorrhage and is in a coma.' The thought that races through my head is: I can do this. No matter what, I can do this. Dad, I won't go to pieces.

I wake Lolo and cry. 'I think he's going to die,' I sob. When I get to Oslo, I'm met by Kristin, my best friend in Norway. I'm wearing the blue boiler suit that I got from Dad. 'It's too big,' I say to Kristin. I stuff my hands in the pockets and wave the legs around to demonstrate, then I start to cry. We go straight to the hospital. The rest of the family were there, but have just gone home again, so I'm alone with Dad. He's lying there with all these tubes and equipment. Kristin waits outside. I talk to one of the doctors. He says that they haven't managed to stem the haemorrhaging yet, so there's only a slim change that he'll survive. Kristin and I go to Hild's, and I cry the whole way, and after we get there, Hild hugs me. 'Why are you crying?' 'For Dad,' I sob. 'Stop crying,' Hild says. 'The rest of us aren't crying. It is what it is. There's nothing you can do.'

But you can cry. Someone has to cry in this family and it's always been me. So I carry on.

I go to the eye hospital. There's not much to be done with my poor vision. I can only get about 15 per cent normal vision wearing glasses. But they do give me aids. I'm one of the first people I know to get a computer, with an enormous screen that I would never have been able to afford. I get opera glasses and magnifying glasses and encouragement. And most important of all – an audio book player. The whole of world literature is now open to me and I will forever rank the audio book above the wheel, in terms of human invention.

'What do you want to do?' 'I'm a writer.' Here, the work psychologist could have said that that's what everyone wants to be, but what are you going to do? But he doesn't. He's read one of my pieces and says: 'Good idea. You can use a room here and we'll teach you how to use the computer and you can stay here until you know what you're doing.'

And I get started straight away. A few months later, a new short story is published in the country's biggest national paper. 'We backed the right horse,' the psychologist says, proudly. 'Your aids certainly won't be left in the loft to gather dust.'

I ask Jonathan how you can know what sex you are if you're sitting tied to a chair, with a blindfold over your eyes and have lost your memory.

'Is that one of your fantasies?'

'Yes.'

'You should just know,' he says. 'You know.'

'I don't.'

'How do you feel then?'

'I feel like a child. A sexless child. I denied puberty.'

'Why?'

'I wasn't ready.'

'You didn't have the security and tools you needed to take the next step.'

'I heard on the radio today about a man they found in the south of Sweden. He'd lost his memory and spoke poor English. He didn't even know what his mother tongue was. And I thought, mother sex. How do you know that?'

'We'll have to talk more about your sexuality,' Jonathan says.

But we never do, there are always other fires that need to be put out.

181

I get an internship at the Kungliga Dramatiska Teatern, arranged by the eye hospital. The idea was that I would be a set design assistant, but the play is shelved. I'm moved to lighting and plugs and sockets. Learn more about electricity than the theatre, as I had originally hoped. Occasionally I operate the follow spot for performances. My job is to follow the main character, but often I can't see him. So I point the spot straight up at the ceiling.

But mostly I tramp the corridors between the different stages. I don't know what to do with myself. Hide myself away in various corners. Get there late and try to make the day pass. As an intern you're not really a worker. No one counts on you. When I'm in Oslo over Christmas I get sick, Tim calls Dramaten to say I can't come to work. The message is received with panic. Can't come! Is she an actress? A stage manager? An important person? They look me up, but can't even find me in their papers. No one misses me. I can be ill for as long as I like.

Half a year passes and I potter about. Then my book is published. I get fantastic reviews, lots of attention and they write about me in the papers. I'm immediately transferred to the literary department and given responsibility for a drama competition in connection with the theatre's two hundredth anniversary. A month later I have my first reading, on Dramaten's smallest stage, it's Imprisoned Writers' Day. A man comes up to me afterwards and invites me to a dinner reception. Can I take Lolo with me, who was in the audience? Of course. We are guided along service corridors and through public rooms. There are women in white aprons everywhere. Crystal chandeliers on the ceiling and silver candlesticks, paintings and antiques. 'And you can sit here,' my host tells me, and shows me to a place in the middle next to an elderly gentleman. The food is served on silver platters. As soon as you've taken a sip of wine, someone is there to refill your glass.

I notice that as soon as my table partner opens his mouth, everyone falls silent. He talks about Ingmar Bergman's stomach. Which isn't that interesting really, but silence reigns. Then he says politely to me: 'I've seen you at Dramaten. You work there.' You could hear a pin drop. Then I say loudly: 'Do you work at Dramaten too?' It is even more silent, if that's possible. He says yes and laughs a little. I get up and go to the toilet and soon I have a gaggle of women around me. 'How could you say that? Erland Josephson is Sweden's best actor. Right now he's playing the main role on the main stage and is in Tarkovsky's film *The Sacrifice*.' Oh shit.

Making your debut is a bit like finishing a long education, I get lots of job offers. I'm asked to write articles in the country's leading papers, to write plays and film manuscripts. I get a writer's stipend and live off my writing. My internship at Dramaten has finished. I walk past a sports stadium every day and suddenly one day I go in and say that I want to play football again. I, who thought it was a passing phase, and that culture was now my focus, am back in the women's team. It feels right.

I'm worried about Dad. Worried about getting the articles written on time. Newspapers have deadlines. I'm not used to that. I get invitations to take part in debates and readings. I say yes. I say yes to nearly everything. Criss-cross the country. Until one day the radio call me and ask what I think about the interest rates. Then I realise that I have to choose which offers to accept. That I have to slow down.

It's the 30th of April, Walpurgis Night. I go to meet my friend Sonja, her husband and their little boy. We're going to meet by the bonfire. There's a lot of people there. I can't find my friends, and start to circle the fire. I'm convinced that I'll spot them. At any moment, that everything will be fine. People are sitting on blankets on the grass, eating and drinking. This is the evening when teenagers often get drunk for the first time. I walk round and round the bonfire for hours and can't understand why I can't find my friends. If they had been here, we would have bumped into each other. I've made myself as visible as possible. But I can't give up. Can't understand. It was agreed.

The place starts to empty as families leave. The bonfire burns down. Only a few groups of young people left. I walk round the dying fire. It's dark and the air is heavy. I've got stuck. I only live a few hundred metres away. I walk further up into the park. Have got it into my head that I have to walk. That something horrible will happen if I don't carry on. 'Yes, yes, yes,' I say. 'Yes, yes, yes.' It's Emil and Erik who want to talk to me. I acknowledge that they're there, but don't want to engage in a conversation. 'You can't go home,' Erik says, and I've already heard that. 'You have to look until you find them. You have to stay in the park all night.'

'I want to go home to bed.'

'You're lost.'

It's true. I'm lost. I don't know where I live. I try to guide my feet out of the park, but don't manage. Where is my bed? At the top of the building somewhere. Suddenly all the paths look so unfamiliar. As though I had never been here before. I normally run in this park. The air solidifies in front of me, I'm forced to walk in zigzags. It's not me that's deciding my direction. The April evening is chilly and I start to freeze. Night takes over the park. No street lights. No fire. Only witches. Only Emil and Erik. Words, words, birds, birds. The dark hangs in the air like a threat.

I eventually lie down on a bench with my hands under my cheek and pull up my hood. Hear the teenage gangs making a racket in the distance. My sensitivity to sound increases, their voices get closer like rockets. Fired off from far away and exploding in my head. I'm freezing, I fall asleep and start to dream. My friends turn up in my dream. They disappear when I reach out my hands to touch them. I wake up several times during the night, frozen to the bone and frightened.

My dad survives. He has lost nearly all power of speech. He can't paint any more, as he dreamed of doing full time when he became a pensioner. He can't figure out money and numbers. Forgets all the time. Can't remember what he's just done or what happened yesterday. But he knows who we are, that we belong to him. He's much calmer and more good-natured.

After a year of therapy, he slowly regains one ability after the other. But he still can't paint. The walls in the house are full of his paintings. He lies on the sofa and looks at them for hours. Talks about them. The composition of colours. Points and shows that there's an invisible circle in the square paintings. He starts doing woodwork instead. He still fumbles for words and can't count. He starts to cry at the slightest thing. Is that the illness or grief?

Mum, who has said she looks forward to spending her old age with someone she has so many shared experiences with, now has a husband who can only remember things from the time before they met. But he still has his sense of humour. He has more brain haemorrhages, some bigger, some smaller. When he is no longer able to make things with wood, he starts to make rag rugs and work in the garden. Vegetables and flowers. When he can't read any more, he looks at books with photographs of art and listens to the radio. When he can no longer speak, he starts to sing.

'Where are we, and why? I'm not quite with you,' Jonathan says.

'The voices have been going on about it raining all weekend. Over and over again they say the word rain, rain, rain.' Outside the snow is lying white and fluffy. The trees have soft white muscles. Why do they insist that it's raining? 'Do you think they mean crying?'

'In psychodynamic therapy it could be interpreted that way,' Jonathan says. 'But I don't know.'

'The crying could be my dad calling.'

'What does he want?'

'We're sitting together, I can't look in the mirror any more and be him. See him in my thoughts and go in.'

'You need to get up from that table in that little Norwegian house and walk away. Sit here with me in the kitchen and be an adult instead. Torvald had already left your childhood kitchen back then. Now it's your turn to leave.'

'When Torvald is faced with problems, he lets them go, walks around and carries on, whereas I stand there banging my head.'

'Stood there banging your head. You now have an alternative.'

It's a wonderful day. It's the season's first football match on grass. The one you long for after winter training. It's wonderful until about twenty minutes into the first half. I've been playing from the start, have been on top form, get a fantastic chance. The ball rolls towards the other team's goal, there's only one obstacle between me and the goalie, a huge centre back. In my head I'm already past her. Feint to the left, around. I even feint the goal keeper… but before that the centre back has no doubt been told to think *clearance* in a tight corner. She must have got to the ball first, a leap forwards and then THWACK! Everything goes black. I get the ball with her foot behind it in my face. The black is splintered by white and then the sky.

I ask: 'Can I carry on playing? Do I need to leave the pitch?' 'You're off the pitch,' the trainer says and looks down at me. I put my hands to my eyes. I've played in glasses for fifteen years and it's always been fine. I'm bleeding from cuts all over my face. The glass and frames have cut the skin in several places.

I sit in a car with two men I don't know and press the towel to my face. It sucks up the dark red blood. The men are the boyfriends of a couple of girls on the team. When we get to the hospital, one of them says: 'We'll get back just in time for the second half.' I realise then that they're not coming in, that I've been substituted for the whole match and won't be making a comeback in the second half. I'm dispensable. I'm abandoned at the entrance to A&E. A voice in reception asks me for ID. I lower the towel. She sees my bloody face. I say: 'Ball in the eye.'

From then on I get full service. I'm the only one who is

allowed to lie down. I start to enjoy myself. Everything's great here in A&E. I close my eyes. Fall and fall, as if I was coming from a party. I've got a little inflatable swimming ring round my arm that someone keeps blowing up. Everything is great and beautiful. I can relax. I imagine that I'm lying in an architectural gem. I smile. The only thing is that I'm ravenous. Then I see a trolley being wheeled in. The person pushing it is an old-fashioned nurse, maybe a kind Nurse Ratched from *One Flew Over the Cuckoo's Nest*. A little white cap with a red cross on it. The trolley is full of soft white sandwiches full of air and cheese. I imagine reaching out and threading ten sandwiches on a straw and then popping them in my mouth and sucking on them like you do with wild strawberries.

I'm plastered and sewn up in several places on my face. Then I'm rolled along corridors under the hospital. I lie in the bed on wheels and continue to wax lyrical about how beautiful everything is. I end up in the intensive care ward, with tubes in my arms and a drip. I'm now wearing a white nightie. My football boots and strip are on a chair next to the bed. I'm obviously spending the night here. It's one of Sweden's largest hospitals, and yet everything feels small and pretend. Pretend serious. But comfortable, absolutely. They ask if I can remember the actual impact and if I lost consciousness. I can't answer. Just say that I'm interested in architecture and that it's so beautiful here. It's actually a very run-down hospital.

They ask me my name and I don't know. I don't know where I've got this positive feeling from. And all this beauty, where do I see it? In reality, I am confused and frightened, but it's a lovely feeling that Sweden doesn't want Ball in the Eye to die. That Sweden wants me to be comfortable, wants to help me, to look after me. Here I lie, barely able to recognise myself... and am looked after. Not because of who I am, but just because...

because I exist, or am... broken. Outside the window, because I'm quite high up in the hospital now, I can see all the houses I've stayed in. Even my lovely little workspace. I look onto my desk and see to my delight that a lot has already been written of the feature film manuscript that I'm working on. And I've been struggling with it. At a complete standstill. An endless starting block.

Everything seems to be going my way at the moment. I see my flat. My childhood home. The garden with the gnarled apple trees. The folk high schools. The low accommodation blocks. I see the water. It moves in waves and I close my eyes. Which pulls at the stitches. My heart pounds. Where am I? I don't dare ask the question. I just say thank you and smile. Why am I thanking everyone? I'm scared. Everything's fine, I tell myself over and over again. This is just a dream. Soon you'll wake up. I ask the woman in the bed beside me what's wrong with her. 'Bitten by a cat,' she replies. The ward for minor injuries, Ball in the Eye thinks. The woman adds that she might have to have an amputation.

I open my mouth, always hungry. 'No food for you,' says the nurse. 'You've got a drip.' I feel hungry to the marrow. I look out of the window and don't see the low building where I lived. I see instead that I'm high, high up. I haven't spoken to anyone I know. I haven't remembered any telephone numbers so the staff can call. I'm not Eli. I'm not the boys. I don't know who I am. Other than Ball in the Eye. I'm not happy any more. I'm frightened.

They say it was a mild concussion and that I'm not in any danger. Why am I so confused then? They don't understand. 'Think about it, then you'll know,' they say.

I think: I'm in a bed in a room with unfamiliar bodies and voices. Exposed. In a room with machines and strange smells.

I'm lying free in the air. My body is resting on nothing. It's flying without a pilot. I have cuts on my face, which is starting to swell. People crying and shouting for help. No one knows that I'm here. It's a long weekend. Lolo is in the country and thinks I'm playing football. The football trainer, where's he? Why hasn't he come to see how I am? Could I have died?

It's time for me to go home. I put on my football strip, have new plasters put on the small cuts and a big white bandage over my forehead and right eye. My face is swollen in several places, the blue blending into yellow. I think I look worse now than when I came in. It's the body's way of healing, creating disharmony in order to fall into harmony again. I feel unsteady on my feet after several days in bed. It's not dangerous, I tell myself. But the thought of an inner landslide doesn't let go. The air has changed. It lies in front of me in great lumps that I have to shy away from. And she who shies away is layer upon layer of me. Ball in the Eye, the boys and so deep inside she's almost invisible, Eli. The fact that the health services can't see the difference between concussion and psychosis is appalling.

I walk down the slope and out onto the street. Think about food, about gnawing on a hard bone. Think that I could eat a whole pig now. Crunch it between my teeth. 'Hello,' a voice calls. I don't want to meet anyone, I want to go home and eat a whole pig. 'Hello,' the voice says again. I don't want to show myself, I don't want anything to stop me. I look down, and a hand is stretched out towards me. I take it and slowly raise my eyes. From the heavy boots, the dirty workman's trousers and jacket, and finally to the face. It's like looking straight into the mirror, he looks wild. He has exactly the same bandage as I do round his head and over one eye. Bruises and a black eye. I shake his hand and say: 'Ball in the eye.' 'Fell with my hands in my pocket,' he replies. We stand looking at each other, until he says: 'Want to come for a coffee?' I shake my head. Black coffee, the very thought makes me retch. I can't say that I'm more interested in a whole pig. I turn and walk away. He shouts after me: 'Maybe not worth it, people might think that we're married.'

Two weeks later, I go to Oslo to meet the producer of the film that I'm supposed to be writing. I tell her the truth, that I haven't managed to write much. 'But goodness, what's happened?' she interrupts. 'Nothing in particular, really.' 'I mean with your face?' 'Oh that.' 'Did someone beat you up?'

I tell her the whole story. I sit up. Can tell that the producer is listening. She's with me, nodding, smiling. I only tell what is glorious and funny. Say nothing about the fear, that I still haven't got over the feeling of being abandoned. That the psychosis is still here, humming inside. That the fear is still there. That I'm floating in a room of strangers and can't see anyone I know. Can't tell whether I'm awake or dreaming. Can't tell whether I'm dying or in the midst of life.

But I tell the story with great animation, horrible experiences can become great art. You just need to work on it. I tell her about the guy on the street. That it was like looking into a mirror when I saw his face. That we were like twins. And when I say that he shouted after me, 'Maybe not worth it, people might think that we're married,' I find myself adding, without giving it a thought: 'And that is the opening of the film.' 'Great,' the producer says. 'All you need to do now is go home and write the rest of it.'

I'm also in the middle of working on a documentary film about my life as a football player. I've written the script, and am going to direct and play myself in the film. We've auditioned and filmed lots of little girls to find the right one who can play me as a child. Most of them were too complete. They had been in countless adverts and were confident in the wrong way. Then I found a little girl with fair hair and big dark eyes and a mischievous smile and something that I perceived as a crack in her lovely face. She walks around in the film with a ball under her arm, as though it were a doll. Difficult to direct, but absolutely right. It's a huge challenge for me, as I'm not used to directing.

Everything goes well to begin with. But before the summer break, the producer gets nervous and wants to replace the cinematographer, who I like a lot. She wants a more experienced head of photography. We leave it for the moment and I hope that she'll forget what the problem is.

I get staphylococcus in one of the cuts on my forehead which won't heal. It turns into a visible scar above my right eye. Erik is happy. 'Now your doll-like face looks like it's lived a bit,' he says.

Lolo and I go to Italy with a big group of people. Lolo and I share a double room and a double bed. One of the group is called Alexander. He plays the guitar and sings Russian songs. He grew up in Sweden but has a Russian mother and a Greek father. I would love to have that cultural heritage. I can see that Lolo is attracted to him. The three of us sit at the same table for breakfast and I get the feeling I'm invisible. I move table. Sit down and talk to another guy from the group, a composer from Norway.

One evening I come back to the hotel and am just about to put the key in the lock when I hear moaning from inside the room. Someone's fucking in there. And I know who it is.

I clutch my key and slide down to the floor. I don't know where to go, suddenly feel completely adrift. It's the end. The end of everything I know. I think of leaving immediately, leaving everything and everyone behind and never going back to Sweden or Norway or Italy. I don't know where to go. Out into the world. Out in the empty nothing. Away. Alone. Out into the air. Run away. Australia. Not Australia. I will never come back to anything I know.

The feeling of a completely empty present and a totally unknown future is so powerful that I start to shake. I'm going to pack my bags and go. Not tell anyone who I am ever again. Not let anyone save me from taking my own life like Lolo did ever again. I listen to the sounds behind the door. I will only ever be an observer in the world. Invisible.

Then there is silence. I don't knock on the door. I stay sitting where I am and fall asleep, leaning against the wall.

I wake in the morning, my whole body is stiff. Is it time to leave now? I go to the restaurant to get a cup of coffee. There I meet the composer from Norway. He has plans for some new projects we can do together. I can't plan, can't think about anything in the future. After all, I'm going to leave. He says we can go to a hot spring and swim. I say no, but then go all the same. My stiff body could do with some warm water. There's no sign of Lolo and Alexander.

It's not until early evening that I can talk to Lolo. I cry and say that I'm going to go out into the world, anywhere, and I'm never coming back. She, of all people, manages to persuade me to stay.

It's the weekend and Jonathan's not working. I send him a text all the same. 'Help,' I write. Get a swift reply. 'Fight for your life,' it says. 'I'm with you.'

At the end of the summer, we start filming again. The producer forces through a change of cinematographer. The new cinematographer and producer are a team, they know each other from before. I'm inexperienced and full of ideas, but no one supports me. When I act in front of the camera, the cinematographer says I'm too stiff. Which makes me even stiffer. But I don't give up. This is going to be a good film.

I show them my drawings, thoughts and texts. We film the winter training sessions and things get a bit better. I'm awake at night and write *Ball in the Eye* and another screenplay, which is set in the mountains in the fifties. I'm caught on a wheel and work day and night. I end up in conflict with the producer about payment for the film script, and meet her together with a lawyer. Two strong women. Or are they mad? They shout at each other, and it's about me.

I feel warm and my whole body is shaking. The walls are radiating. I'm falling. Breaking up. When I come out from the negotiations, everything has somehow changed. People are like shadows. They walk in front of me on the pavement, not to be trusted. They want something from me.

I sit on the metro and see that they're all staring. Even the ones looking down are staring. They whisper to each other when they think I can't hear. Everything they say and everything they do is to confuse me. They communicate in sign language and think I don't see.

*

One day at the psychologist's I get really frightened. Something is released inside me and everything is dangerous. I have to hide. Think that the psychologist is going to hit me. I run out into the tiny waiting room and hide behind an armchair. She comes out. 'Don't hit me,' I scream. 'Don't hit me.'

She doesn't hit me. In a gentle voice, she says: 'No one's going to hit you any more.' I walk home on unsteady legs. She phones and says that we need to take a break in the therapy. She says that I'm not well enough. She wants me to get more help than she can give. It's the last time we speak.

I've baked the traditional saffron buns and celebrated St Lucia's Day with my colleagues at the workspace, to mark the winter solstice. Drunk a lot of *glögg*. I go home in a taxi. Wake up on the kitchen floor with my clothes on.

Today I'm going to the dentist, and then travelling to Oslo to receive a prize and then hold a thank you speech at the dinner. My head is splitting: I can feel the two separate halves pulling each to one side, the blood spurting. My hair is warm and wet. I have to find a hat. I left my special hat at the party. I have to have that one, the snowboard hat. As protection.

I phone Tim, who has a car. Can't move naturally until the hat is in place. He doesn't answer. I creep out into the hall and tie a scarf round my head, put on my jacket and leave the flat. The air has changed. Banks of thicker and lighter air drift around each other. I crash into them and have to zigzag my way forward in order to avoid them.

When I'm lying in the dangerous chair, which today doesn't seem to be so dangerous, the dentist asks in a friendly voice if I'm not going to take my scarf off my head. 'No,' I reply, and open my mouth. I've got other things to think about. Have to prepare my speech for this evening. I'm giving an after-dinner speech at my publisher's big Christmas party. I call Tim again. 'I have to go to Arlanda airport via my work to pick up a hat.'

Tim is long and lean. He is one of the smartest people I know. I met him at the creative writing course at the folk high school. He gives me a hug. I feel like I'm floating through his body. That it's not a real hug, but rather an examination. A test I have to pass. I rattle around in the flat. I have to pack. I'm not packing, not changing my clothes. What will be will be.

The workspace looks as it did when we left it. Bottles, glasses, saffron buns and cigarette butts everywhere. I find my hat, take off the scarf and pull on the hat. 'Eli, how are you feeling?' Tim asks. I think he's changed. I don't know if he's real. If he's here. I tell him that my head has split in two and the blood keeps pumping out. He says that maybe we shouldn't go to Arlanda. That perhaps I should cancel the whole trip. I fly into a rage. What's been agreed has been agreed.

Then Lisen comes in, who has the room next to me. We sit on the sofa. I massage a raisin between my fingers. Lisen talks to Tim. At first I don't understand what they're saying. They fall silent every now and then and listen to my chatter. I've started on my speech, and compare a man with a pair of slalom skis. 'Shall we go?' I say, and get up. 'Or should I write down some key words first?' 'Forget your speech,' Lisen says. 'Did you sleep at all last night? Are you hungover?' 'I slept on the floor.' Tim takes my hand and looks into my eyes. I look down. 'Have you been smoking hash?' he asks. I shake my head. 'What is it then?' 'I don't know.'

'What day is it today?' I shout from the back seat. I've pulled my hat right down over my eyes. They're talking together in the front, whispering. Suddenly they pull off the motorway and turn around. When the car stops we're back at Södermalm. 'We think it's best if you stay with Lolo tonight.' 'What do you mean, I have to catch the plane.' 'No go,' Tim says. 'I don't know, but I think you're ill.' I reluctantly follow them up. Lolo is surprised to see us. 'Are you not in Oslo?' They talk in the kitchen while I lie down on the big bed in the living room. I've taken off everything except my hat and underpants, and Lolo has lent me a vest.

'Should we not contact the hospital?' Tim asks. 'Absolutely not,' Lisen says. 'They only make things worse.' 'But what are we going to do?' Lolo says. 'I think we just need to be there.' 'But I've got work tomorrow,' Lolo says. 'Then I'll come over,' says Tim. 'We can make a rota so that there's always someone here. She just needs to sleep and rest,' Lisen says. 'Then it will pass.'

Lolo comes into living room with some fortifying tea for me. I sit up in bed. I've become someone else. My right ear is itching. A new voice has taken root there. Two voices. Two women who are not me. Three voices. Right at the bottom of my ear there's a tiny man shouting. I don't say a word about it.

The day after, Tim comes back, and Sonja and Harald. I've got lots of friends. They take turns. Someone watches over me the whole time.

What I know is that I missed the party at the publishers and didn't hold my after-dinner speech. What I don't know is that my friends are starting to disagree about how to look after me. That Lisen is consistently the one who is most opposed to medication. She's a vegan and doesn't trust conventional medicine. My other friends are uncertain. They want the old Eli back. The smart, funny one.

How can someone change in this way? It's frightening, both for them and me. Is there a kind of security in them being with me all the time, or doesn't it matter? Can they face it? Should I have medication and professional help? Would it not be better to have me admitted to hospital? Sonja thinks so. Lolo is not sure. She so desperately wants their love to be enough to make me well.

Harald gives me a massage. Sonja sits on the edge of the bed and holds my hand. 'Why have you withdrawn? I want you to share my world with me. Why have you locked yourself away in a world where we can't get in? Wake up, Eli, wake up, be here with us. Please. I need you. Don't let go, I won't let go,' she says, and squeezes my hand.

One evening when Lisen is not there, we go to the hospital all the same, five of us in a people carrier. I still feel like my head is splitting in two. The first question the staff ask is who is ill. We all laugh. After a short conversation with the doctor, I'm admitted. And won't be released for nine months.

But my friends don't let go. They make up another rota and I get at least one visitor every day. But I'm not very good at having visitors. Can't concentrate for even four minutes at a time. They pretend to leave, wait outside the hospital for twenty minutes and then come back for another four minutes.

What is there to talk about? There's nothing here. Except beds. The cold walls, the corridor, the others' bodies, ramblings and screams and tears and movements. I don't care what it looks like here. Wouldn't want it to be pretty. Just quiet. Think that the few paintings out there in the corridor are disturbing. I have enough colours, shapes and voices inside.

Lolo says that she regrets that they didn't take me to hospital sooner. She was quite simply not sure. My friends meet to talk to each other, support each other. Something breaks in some of them too when they realise that something is broken in me. The hospital doesn't consider them to be family, so they have no contact with the medical staff. They come to visit, but the staff won't talk to them and hide behind professional confidentiality.

I have a longer conversation with a chatty doctor. I draw an ear and explain where the voices are sitting. Two women at the top and a man at the bottom. It's not the boys this time, Espen, Emil and Erik. I don't mention them. And unlike them, these voices are not me. They come from outside, not from within. They don't have names or know me. They shout at me, call me different things. They think that I'm some kind of superhuman. Maybe even God.

The doctor listens. Then suddenly he says: 'You've got an open toilet seat to the dream world, it's open all the time. For most people, it's closed during the day, and only opens at night.' An open toilet seat? I think I understand.

It's Christmas Eve. There are mainly locums working on the ward. I've been asking all day if I can go to midnight mass at the local church. The answer is no. Then I ask the night shift and the answer is: we'll think about it. We're served slim pickings for Christmas dinner, not even low-alcohol beer. There are hardly any patients here. Most of them have been allowed out to spend Christmas with their families.

I put on my coat and sit by the door. At half past ten, a student lets me out into the snow storm. I walk between the buildings to the church. Groups of people hurry on their way, all in black, brown and navy. All in the same direction. It's quiet. The snow swirls around on the pavement. Then a Santa Claus comes towards me. He's wearing a mask and a beard and red hat and waving stiffly with one hand. I wave back. Turn round and watch him stagger on. The church bells start to ring. It's possible to hear a faint ringing of bells from other churches too. I press on against the wind. The silent dark patchwork of dressed-up families heading towards the church doors. Everyone has someone except me.

I accept the psalm book. The church is already full. I find a seat in the middle. An old man kindly moves his coat and I slip into place. I normally never go to church. I had an overdose of religious meetings at the folk high school in Norway. But something stuck. A longing. I fold my hands. It's magical and beautiful inside the church. There are decorations everywhere. A huge crystal chandelier hangs from the ceiling with real candles. 'I hope that you've prepared for Christmas within as well,' the minister says.

She reads the Christmas story from St Luke. My right leg is shaking. Can't sit still. Can't stay here. Luckily it's time to sing a carol and everyone stands up. I join in the chorus. We sit down again and the sermon begins. It's beautiful and festive, but far too long to sit still. The minister thanks the Lord for sending us his beloved Son. She gives thanks for the fact that we are gathered here tonight to celebrate the birth of Jesus, Son of God, conceived by the power of the Holy Spirit, born of the Virgin Mary. She gives thanks to the Lord that he sees each and every one of us. At this point I stand up and then sit down again. Haven't heard those words since I was at folk high school. He can't possibly see me now, when I'm in church hidden amongst all these families.

I want the living to see me. The minister to come down to me. Push her way through the people on the pews, lift me up in her cape and carry me back to the hospital. I long to be back in the unit, the staff who turn their backs, the ugly, tired yellow walls. In the smoking room with a lighter on a chain and a TV that's fixed to the floor, the torn beige faux leather sofa and armchairs.

The bells start to ring again. Everyone stands up, pretends not to rush, but still presses forwards a little too forcefully out of the church. I wait until it's almost empty. The minister is standing by the door and shakes everyone by the hand. She says 'God bless you.' I go to her. Lots of people want to stop for a word. Some come back after they've already gone out, having mustered their courage to come in again. To be near the minister. This is the minister's parish. She has a small smile on her lips. But no sign of doubt. She wants to greet everyone and then go home to her own family. I'm at the front of the queue now. What shall I say? I'm the one who doubts. I don't need to say anything, just hold out my hand and nod. But I need something more.

The minister is gentle and masculine in her wide gown. I

stammer. 'Yes, well, I, we, we just wanted an intercession.' 'I don't have time right now. Could you perhaps come back another day?' I shake my head. I'm never coming back. The minister has more hands to shake, but she can't say no. She points to the nearest pew. God has ordered her. God has seen me this night. I rest my head against my knees and both my legs are shaking. I'm forced to be alive. If God is so idiotic as to give people free will and they then abuse it, isn't it all then a fabulous failure? God is shaking me.

Eventually the minister comes over and prods me. I promptly sit up. 'What's your name?' she asks. 'Eli.' She places her hand on my head, asks what it is that I want her to pray for. I had thought of saying peace. But instead say: 'I want you to pray for the new year. That I will feel at home in myself. That I will start writing. That I will find someone to live with. That I will have a family. That I will feel free. That I am the only one who rules me. That I will never hear Erik, Emil and Espen talking in my head again. That I won't need to lie down and spend hours with them. That the new voices will disappear. That the air won't settle in front of me like an impenetrable sheet of ice. That I won't go to pieces. That my family in Norway won't find out about anything and that they think that I'm on holiday in Portugal right now. Pray to God that I won't need to fight against him any more. Pray to him that I won't turn all religious. That he should close his eyes when he sees me and fix everything with his invisible hands. That my head will be emptied of all my brooding. That I won't get lost. I want to go home, but not be lonely.'

I look up. Her hand is still on my head. The hand that has shaken so many other hands today. It's all mine now. I look straight at her. She has round, lovely cheeks. She's pale and has no make-up. I know what I want. I want the minister to hug me tight in her divine cape.

'That's quite a lot,' the minister says. 'You just need to pray that I'll be released from hospital,' I say. Then she takes her hand from my head and sits down beside me on the pew. She puts her hand on my shoulder. 'Have you come from the hospital now?' I shake and nod. 'Then I think that you should go back.' She puts her hand on my head again and says *Our Father*. Then she says something very quietly that I hope contains a lot. It occurs to me that I'd like to ask her about Marit. If she could pray for her. The minister takes my hands in hers and asks the Lord to look kindly on Elin. Elin is someone completely different from Eli. If God doesn't have his eyes shut then he'll be looking somewhere else right now. He'll be looking for Elin.

'Now, you get back as quick as you can,' the minister says, and stands up. 'Promise me you will?' I don't answer.

It's almost empty outside the church. I don't want to walk back through all the flats and buildings. I want to walk where things don't get in the way. I choose the widest street. It's rush hour. Everyone wants to get home now. It's still snowing and windy. Suddenly everyone is gone. I'm the only one left on the pavement and a few cars illuminate the snowflakes in their headlights. The new snow has whirled through the town like a cleaner. A voice can be heard in amongst the sounds of the cars. I can't make out what she's saying. She's mumbling a kind of chant. Is it the minister? I did want her to pray especially for me. But she just said a general prayer. I'm nothing special. I don't know who I am.

The mumbling is in my right ear and is quite comforting to begin with. Then another woman's voice starts to mumble at the same time. It's the women who appeared a few weeks ago and sit at the top of my right ear. They talk from the outside and the inside. Not like the boys. Suddenly all midnight masses are over, all family festivities. Even the cars have vanished. The road is empty. Now the voices are behind my back and very clear. 'Jesus, I love you,' says one. 'I love you, Jesus,' says the other. I walk a bit faster. 'Jesus, I love you.' 'No, I love you, Jesus.' They both shout at the same time. I can't protect myself. I can't turn round. 'Jesus, I love you.'

I've got the wind on my back and drag my feet to whip up the snow in front of me. My entire being is a sail for their love. I'm forging ahead. Leaving clear tracks in the snow. It's beautiful. It's my favourite weather, but I can't enjoy it. 'Turn around.' 'Look at us.' 'Save us.'

I can't. I cross over to the other side of the street. Their shouts are cold like snowballs on my neck. I am completely covered in snow. Stick out my tongue to taste it. Do you think their arms are reaching out? That they could touch me at any moment? I shouldn't have gone to church. I'm nearly at the hospital. There they are again, chorusing: 'Jesus, we love you.' 'Stop!' I shout. 'There's been a misunderstanding. Stop!' Then I start to laugh. I want them to hear, but don't dare turn around and laugh in their faces. I laugh to myself and think ha, ha, Jesus certainly doesn't love all of you. Jesus doesn't love you back... ha, ha...

When I get to the hospital gates, I turn round. The women aren't there. I am open, cold and empty. Just snow in front of me. Just the city and me. That's just how it is, and how it cannot be.

Every night, a Finnish angel appears in my room. She comes tiptoeing in. How can she know that I'm awake? She seems to embrace the whole room with her calm voice. I can barely see her in the dark. I tell her I'm a writer. Say some sentences. Steal some of Erik Lindegren's lines and say: 'Reality crashing. Without reality born!' Then say some of my own Norwegian sentences: 'Do you know the world the way it looks at you? That is reality.' The angel listens with curiosity. She says that she likes what I write, because that is what I need to hear.

She comes with warm milk and honey. I'm full to the brim with sleeping pills, and still can't sleep. The Finnish lady disappears just as angelically as she came. Now I can sleep. She comes back in the dark the next night, in white hospital overalls. With milk and honey and a voice that embraces. Milk and honey and whispers. I give her new words and sentences, she listens. I hold my hands round the warm cup and drink. She waits in the dark. Doesn't the angel know there are sleeping pills in one of the largest hospitals in the north?

Kristin comes to visit me from Oslo when she hears that I'm ill. Lolo phoned to tell her. She's a student and broke, but borrowed the money for a plane ticket from her sister-in-law. She stays in my flat and comes to see me in hospital every day. I'm allowed out for a few hours on New Year's Eve. I want us to be together at midnight, but we can't. I have to be back by eight o'clock. We go back to my flat for New Year's dinner. I've almost stopped eating. Kristin knows that. I say that I'm full before I've even tasted the food. It's too noisy to eat in the unit. Kristin knows that. She's someone who always knows everything in advance. Who sorts things out and meets your needs before you've even said what they are. There's a quiet power in this. I let her decide, let go of my adulthood a bit when I'm with her. She's like a home. A house, a familiar bed. The part of me that's broken rests in her closeness. She talks to Lolo and my friends. Says that I should have as little stimulus as possible. That I shouldn't write. Sonja doesn't agree. She writes herself and knows that you just have to.

I don't want dinner or to sit by the kitchen table. 'You're not going to sit by the kitchen table, you're going to sit on the sofa in the living room,' Kristin says. I turn on the telly and Kristin switches it off. She comes in with a plate with the tiniest amount of food decorated with parsley. It's not more than a mouthful. I look at it with curiosity. It looks tempting. 'Are you not going to taste it?' Kristin asks. I shake my head. 'You could at least taste it.' I taste it and the whole thing disappears. She goes into the kitchen and comes out with something else. A minimal little titbit. I shake my head. She tells me what it is and my mouth starts to water. I take a bit and the whole thing is gone. She comes in with one more, and another. Marinated prawns and avocado, and raw beef and parmesan and basil, prosciutto and rocket, crab and aioli, gravlax on rye bread. I must have eaten about fifteen miniature courses in the belief that I've eaten nothing. I'm smart, but Kristin is smarter.

'Happy New Year.' We raise our glasses of water and I ask if we're not going to have champagne. 'Not this year,' Kristin says. 'There will be other New Years.' We have to go back to the hospital. It's dark and fireworks are already exploding, some people can't wait. We go into Tantolunden, to the highest point in the park. 'This is where you need to stand at midnight,' I tell Kristin. 'This is where we would have stood and watched the fireworks together.'

'I'll come with you back to the hospital, then I'll go home to bed,' Kristin says. 'I've come here to see you, not to see the fireworks.'

I found, I found something. A line of poetry has popped into my head and I say it over and over again, all the time. I write it down on a piece of paper and hang it up on the wall. I am completely obsessed with this line by Erik Lindegren: Reality crashing. Without reality born! Another patient, a depressed secondary school teacher, reads and records poems for me and I listen to Erik Lindegren and Karin Boye. It goes straight to the heart of my stomach. What is difficult and what is good resonate together.

Long, wasted days. I wear an ink-blue, far too big tracksuit with Landstinget written on it. The trousers are so long that I don't need socks and shoes. I stand out on the small fenced in balcony. It's strange to stand behind the wire and look down at life on the street. Like a bird in a cage. Then a woman comes out and says: 'Hello, my friend.' We're not friends. 'Can I get a cigarette?' 'You've already had two, so that's a no.' 'Can I get one later?' 'You can buy your own.' 'Yes, I can. But I prefer to be given them.'

I get a hug from one of the guys. He keeps saying: 'I believe in miracles.' He's been saying that for several days. Every now and then he shouts: 'I've only got good intentions.' He hugs everyone all the time.

I've got to know a nurse who's on an hourly contract. She's looking for a job as a therapist with drug addicts and working here in the meantime. She's got cropped blonde hair and a vest that shows off her muscular arms and tattoos. It's easy to talk to her. She seeks me out. And that's what the staff have to do with me, because I don't try to talk to them.

A woman is lying on the floor waving her arms and legs in the air. She's done it before and no one seems to bother. She's taken off her top so that everyone can see that she has only one breast. 'Help me get her up,' the hourly paid nurse says to the other staff. 'No, let her lie there,' they say. 'She can lie there until she's done.' The nurse gets so angry that she shouts: 'What kind of a place is this? Is that how you treat people?' She dashes into the storeroom and gets a patient's gown. Two other nurses eventually lift the woman up onto a chair. I've heard that there's some bad feeling amongst the staff. It wasn't there before. It affects all of me. They are them and we are us.

I'm sitting waiting for a new doctor who might become my doctor. He's known to be very good. I'm twenty-six years old and my name is Eli. I'm a woman. But the boys are still inside me. I have to talk to them. The exits from reality are more and more frequent. And I don't come back into myself afterwards. I end up somewhere diffuse and halfway. Partly the one, partly the other. Espen is crying. Emil wants to play, hide in the game and forget. Erik wants to smash up everything around him. I pull my hat down over my forehead and play football with Emil. My body feels for all the world like I'm ten years old and a boy. I hold the ball in a special way. Lie down on the hospital bed and become Erik. In my mind I destroy everything around me. Am restrained, released and do it all over again. I've dyed my princess golden hair red, have clear dark eyes, long eyelashes and a fringe that stands straight up. I'm dressed in leather. Black leather trousers and a black leather jacket. I've got a leather armband around my wrist with extra long nails.

We go into the doctor's office, it's big. Bookshelves and books everywhere. He greets me and indicates that I should sit down on the chair in front of the overflowing desk. I don't know what to say. The words stack up. There are so many of them. Completely naked and disconnected from each other. Have I said my name? I think about sand, grass and snow. Places where you can play. I think about the boys, Espen, Emil and Erik. Did I greet him properly? I wouldn't mind wrestling with the doctor. Not talking.

'You are Erik. Sixteen years old. You are invincible. You are strong. You are a skier, a footballer, a boxer, a wrestler, you run great distances on the beach and warm up. You have to show your good side now.' I really want this doctor to be my doctor. My best side. What is that? No words can change my facade. It's actions that count. I have to show what I can do. That I'm balanced.

I lean forwards over the desk. Put my hands down amongst all the papers, lower my head and forehead. Lift my body slowly up over the desk into a headstand. I don't lose my balance. I stand straight up and down and look around the doctor's room. The doctor says nothing, so I stand steady for a while longer. Then I lower myself down again. Slowly, without shaking. We did it. Now the doctor knows who we are and the way things are.

I've started bowing. I've started to wear a white dinner shirt and have taken off my armband of nails. The belt as well. You can't wear that many nails when you spend so much time in bed. I've started stretching. Combing my hair and nodding politely to everyone I meet, no matter whether they're staff or a patient. Feel someone pushing out from inside. I'm randomly looking through a book of old photographs and see a picture of Prince Eugen. It's me. He is me.

'You are Prince Eugen.' A voice cuts through my thoughts. 'You are twenty-six years old and one of the most stylish people in the world. A royal rebel. Someone who wanted to paint rather than cut ribbons and represent his country. Who wanted to go to Paris to meet like-minded people.'

I have found myself. 'You have to show them who you are,' Prince Eugen says. I take a copy of the picture and hang it on my door to the hospital corridor. I have my own room. I am royal. Unique. I am not only a writer, I am also an artist.

I zip up and down between ages like a lift. Jonathan wants to talk to the adult Eli. But the boys are there. 'I'm the lift that they come up in. It's their ideas about me that I can't shift.'

'It's good if they don't feel safe,' Jonathan says.

I don't understand. Their insecurity makes me insecure.

'Imagine that they've moved out and only come to visit. How would that be?'

'I do sometimes think about that as I'm going up to the sixth floor. What if they got out on different floors? Espen lives in the cellar near the water pipes so he can cry himself dry. Emil lives on the first floor, and you can barely squeeze into the hall because of all the balls, skates, skis, toboggans and football boots. Erik lives on the second floor. You can always hear him out on the stairs there and catch the sweet smell of hash. Prince Eugen lives on the fourth floor. He has nice pots with plants in them outside his door and an embroidered sign that says: No junk mail! And I live on my own on the sixth floor.'

'Good. You keep thinking, more and more often, that you go up and down in the lift without them getting in.'

'But they've got a key!' I say. 'They can come in the evening, the middle of the night, whenever they like.'

'Just tell yourself that you've changed the lock. That they don't have a key any more. You invite them in, not the other way round. So that maybe one day, you won't want to carry them around any more, even if you can.'

That's Jonathan's idea of me. That I can shift them. Throw their keys down the drain. Full control. Just invite them in when

I need them and want to. They came because I needed them to survive. So is it essential to get rid of them? Jonathan answers that I should just keep telling myself: 'It'll take time.'

One evening I lose my single room. I come back from a rather stressful release, when I didn't even manage to sit in a cinema and ran out halfway through the film. I've been drinking whisky. My things are all stacked up in boxes in the corridor. The picture of Prince Eugen has been taken down from the door. A woman in a wheelchair has been admitted and needs my room. She jumped from the old Katarina Lift at Slussen and survived.

I'm thrown out of what was mine. It's like a landslide. My place is gone. I grab the thing closest to me, a chair, and smash it against the wall until it breaks. I throw myself against the door. My head splits. I muster all my strength, Espen, Emil, Erik, Prince Eugen, get everyone to help. I have to break my skull. Have to annihilate myself. Have to change. Espen is crying. We split, my head splits in two. I feel the blood gushing out. The alarm goes off.

There are six nurses around me. I lash out and kick with all my might, hurl myself against the door again. There's a little plastic Christmas tree nearby. I lift it up and throw it to the floor. I stamp on all the baubles. Another patient arrives who wants to join in the fray. I'm wrestled to the floor, carried to a bed and restrained with straps around my stomach, hands and feet. I throw myself from side to side, but can't get loose. I'm too big to be restrained. It's not Mum and Dad who do it any more. It's the nurses, who I like. My trousers are pulled down and I'm given four injections. Immediate and slow release anti-psychotics, tranquillisers and something for the side effects. I shout when I talk. Is someone trying to calm me down? I don't hear it.

A nurse sits down on a chair by the bed. When you're restrained on a bed, someone always has to sit watch. He picks up a magazine. 'Think yourself fit and healthy,' he reads. 'I am fit and healthy,' I say. 'Curvaceous mothers have smarter children,' he reads and laughs. 'Eli, there you go, your mother must have been curvaceous.' I can't make a joke about it. I have to pee. More nurses come into the room. They pull down my trousers again, so that my lower body is naked and uncovered. I'm the wrong sex. I'm Prince Eugen. It was Erik who wrecked everything and Prince Eugen who's punished. Maybe he was also the wrong sex. They put a bedpan under my bum. It's like ice. I can't pee. They don't put the covers back. I lie there on the cold bedpan with my trousers down. Everyone in the room can see my sex. Maybe the whole thing is being filmed and will be shown to the police. Or to my teenage friends who asked: 'Let's have a look at your bits. Are you a boy or a girl?'

When they finally put on my trousers again and pull up the covers, I wet myself and have to stay there all night. I try to throw myself from side to side even though I'm restrained on the bed. Can't sleep, despite the injections. Can't give in. Can't calm down. Know that I just have to persevere.

'Walk,' Mum says, 'walk!' I'm six years old and the family is walking from hut to hut in the mountains. We're going to be there for seven days. I'm carrying a rucksack with my sleeping bag and clothes. It's far too big. The mountains are steep. The air is cool. I've got blisters and a tummy bug. But I mustn't let it stop me. Not when we're out walking.

We walk for ten hours every day. No one is allowed to give up. There's no way out. Just stones and mountains, moss and dwarf birch, and the odd burbling stream. I have to be coaxed the whole way. Behind every next peak there are raisins. I know that it doesn't help to complain, but I still cry. I'm bribed and harried on. I'm sick along the path. 'Look at the others, they're walking like troopers,' Mum says. Odd is the only one not walking, he's in a carrier on Dad's back. But Marit is walking, Hild and Torvald are walking. When I see the hut that is today's destination, I break into a run. Then Torvald starts to run too. First to the hut, which is still only a dot in the valley.

'How can you run when you're sick?' Mum asks. I can do anything.

From my medical journal: *Pat says that the only thing she wants to do is fight, with anyone. After a while, pat then instead starts to say that the only thing she wants is for someone to hit her, to be kicked in the head…*

The undersigned has been called to Ward 93 because Eli has become very aggressive, restless, and is hitting herself and the staff. The staff were forced to restrain her because she wanted to hit herself on the head, as she herself said: to break her skull. Asks to be killed.

The day after I sit in the smoking room. My whole body is stiff after the injections. My speech is delayed. It feels like I've got rubber bands in my jaw every time I try to open my mouth. A man comes in who is just as stiff. He's terribly thin and the hospital tracksuit hangs off his body. Haven't seen him for a few weeks so I guessed he'd been discharged.

'Hi,' I say. 'What brings you back here?' He sits down with great effort. He's got a boyish, gangly body that's grown old. 'I pissed on a tree and had to pay a six hundred kronor fine. There are plenty of people who've pissed on that tree in Katarina Bangatan.' He rolls a cigarette. He looks up. He's changed his mind. 'Nope, I was thrown out. Was hammering all night, but not many people heard it.' A woman bangs open the door to the smoking room. 'I don't smoke,' she says. 'Just want to come in for a chat. But I'd actually rather go out. Run around the streets shouting: take me from behind, take me from behind.'

An older man that the police found wandering around the town is sitting out in the corridor. He's been a concert pianist and has just played beautifully on the piano. He's a black American. He's wearing a baseball cap, which only the Americans never get too old to wear. Someone asks: 'Are you glad that you came here now?' He looks away. Doesn't want to answer, but then says: 'At my age, you are glad to be anywhere.'

I've got my bike in my room and cycle up and down the corridor. There's something I want to say. But can only say it by hitting.

Or losing the power of speech and just lying there shaking. My manner changes and becomes wild. Madness and a wealth of ideas. Am I writing or not writing? Am I alive or sleepwalking? Something is thumping inside. I'm locked into several bodies, layer upon layer of Eli and the boys. Don't know how they're trying to help me. Is it just a matter of time? Just to wait. The months pass.

We bake buns in the unit kitchen. One of the nurses suddenly turns round. I jump out of the way. Hunker down. My hands up in front of my face. 'Don't hit me, don't hit me,' I shout.

'Hide,' Espen shouts. 'Run away, burn,' Emil whispers. 'Kick,' Erik screams. 'Tell them who you are,' says Prince Eugen.

The nurse bends down over me and wonders what's wrong. He doesn't dare hold out his hand. I kick him away. Don't come near me. I cover my head with my hands. I don't remember, but can't forget.

The first thing I say to Jonathan when he comes in the door is: 'I can't sleep.' I slept badly for several months and say so every time we meet. I sit up eating crisps and sweets and smoking. The floor in the flat is full of sweet wrappers. I throw everything around. If there are no sweets, I can sometimes wake up to a floor covered in sugar. Wander around. Talk loudly with the boys and wave my arms up and down, up and down. Sit in the corner of the kitchen. The safest place in the flat, drag my pillow and duvet over there and lie straight on the hard lino floor. Try to sleep but then jump up. Think that I can't.

'You're not allowed to start our conversations by saying how badly you've slept any more. Say something positive instead,' Jonathan says. 'Say something good about the hours you did sleep. Say I'm a champion at sleeping. I can sleep.' We write a contract about what I'm not allowed to do at night: smoke, listen to frenetic pop music on the headphones. Eat chocolate. Write, unless it's absolutely necessary. Make compulsive movements. Indulge in violent fantasies. Take any pills, like ten Heminevrin, in the middle of the night, only the normal dose of sleeping pills before going to bed. Don't go to bed hungry. Don't drink coffee.

Instead I should do this: concentrate on anxiety reducing methods, such as audio books and the radio. Beautiful, peaceful music. Do some exercise in the evening. Phone the hospital. Phone Lolo after six in the morning. Listen to relaxation tapes. Think about what I'm writing. Develop positive fantasy worlds and use them to replace anxiety. Do everything that reminds me that it's night and do nothing that might indicate that it's day. Believe that sleep will come.

'Because it will. It's like the postman. He comes no matter what. But you don't need to stand there waiting for him.'

I see that there's a trolley full of glasses outside the dining room. I pick one up and weigh it in my hand. 'Smash it,' Erik shouts. 'Smash it.' He throws it onto the floor so hard that shards fly. He smashes five glasses at a furious pace. It's great. Something is released. 'Cut yourself,' he shouts, agitated. I sit down on the floor in the middle of all the glass. Pick up a piece and press it as hard as I can into my forehead then cut down. The piece of glass is thick, but not very sharp. Put as much force into it as I can. Feel the blood oozing out. 'More,' Erik says. I manage to make four deep cuts. Not so that they'll be visible later. Just for that moment, to feel that I'm alive. To shift the attention.

The nurses rush towards me. I'm overpowered. I'm holding the piece of glass tight in my hand. They push back one finger at time, I hold them closed as tight as I can. The glass has cut deep into my hand, the blood bubbles out. 'Take another piece,' Erik shouts. I manage to free myself from the nurses and grab a new piece, squeeze it in my hand, fist tight. They open it and force me onto my stomach on the floor, with hands that press hard against my back. There are splinters of glass everywhere. I try to press my cheek against the glass. I want shards of glass all over my body, but am pushed clear. I like the firmness of the nurses' grip, but would rather have glass. Feel something.

There are maybe five nurses there now and things happen fast. When I'm lifted up, I'm very light. I try to make myself heavier by fighting. 'Take a piece of glass with you,' Erik says. But I can't. I can't get to them and I'm not Eli any more. It's Erik who is carried down the corridor to his room. Is laid down on his stomach while the nurses hold his arms and legs. He tries to struggle. The sister comes, pulls down his trousers, and Erik gets five injections in the bum. Then the restraining bed is rolled into my room. Because Erik has vanished, and it's me, Eli, who is lifted onto the bed. Alone. Erik, where are you? You who are so strong. I've got no strength. Lying on my back, restrained by belts around my wrists, ankles and belly. It's impossible to scratch yourself or turn round or sit up. Then Erik comes back. 'Next time take a glass with you to your room,' he says. 'Put it on the floor with a pillow over it then smash it, so that no one can hear. Then you can cut yourself in peace.' Or smuggle in a razor blade in your shoes, I think. I got that tip from one of the patients in the smoking room the other day.

When I wake up, I'm no longer restrained and the doctor comes in to look at the cuts on my face. It's too late to sew them. They put plasters on. 'Run,' Espen says. 'Escape,' Emil says. 'Hit them,' Erik says. 'Make yourself attractive, cut your hair, get white gold hoops for your ears,' Prince Eugen says.

I will never lie restrained on a bed again. I will not listen to Erik and the little boys. I will listen to Prince Eugen. I will make myself elegant. Be both a prince and a princess.

From my medical journal: *Eli is agitated and bad-tempered after being restrained and has been at odds with the night staff for several nights. Wants them to come and sit on the edge of her bed when she's feeling anxious. The night staff don't think they can do this any longer and are worried that she might get used to having their support nightly. Eli wants them at least to come in and say goodnight. It's agreed that the undersigned will try to negotiate with the night staff and arrive at an appropriate compromise where both parties give and take and the current deadlock is broken.*

As Eli is experiencing such huge mood swings, I am of the opinion that we should try lithium.

I tell Jonathan that I've been watching the children's programme *Bolibompa*. That they were teaching them the emergency number. Mouth, nose, eyes. One, one, two. So I rang it.

'Why did you ring it?'

'Because there's radiation coming from the walls.'

'When you use mobile phones and electrical equipment, there's always a minuscule amount of radiation in the walls.'

'But there's loads. It's the police, they're scanning me. They want to catch me, restrain me, prevent me from moving freely.'

'The police are not interested in you. They never have been, not as long as I've known you. You should ring us instead.'

'The police have been after me for a decade, and I can't get away.'

'Listen to us now,' Jonathan says. 'We think about you. Remember, we're only a phone call away. Forget the police, and think about me instead. Learn my number off by heart.'

Instead of a prayer meeting in the mornings, we have a morning meeting for all the patients and staff. The theme is open, it might be about a flower or a bird, and time is always left to celebrate anyone who has a name day. I sit there more or less in my own world. Nothing of value is said, it's simply become one way to start the day.

In the evening, one or more of my friends come to visit. They read out loud for me or talk soothingly. I don't sleep well at night. Wake up with a start at nothing and am wide awake. Scramble out of bed, go out into the corridor where the staff are sitting wrapped in blankets in the armchairs. 'Go back to bed.' 'Can't. There's radiation coming from the walls. There's someone watching.' 'No one's watching. There's no radiation.' My body spasms. I walk back and forth. 'I want to talk to the priest.' 'You'll get an injection to help you sleep.'

I run down the corridor, bumping into the chairs that stand up against the wall, knocking them over onto the floor. 'You'll wake the others,' one of the night staff shouts, and runs after me. I have to talk to the priest. I'm falling to pieces. The sister comes after me with an injection. 'I don't want an injection,' I scream. 'Shhh.' More of them come and carry me back to my room.

Once we're in the room, they let me go and I throw myself at the screen between the beds, head first. There is a thump and the old lady in the bed bedside me with her grey hair elegantly piled on her head and her own nightie, jumps. She sits up with terrified eyes. She was an opera singer. Her name is Esmeralda. How could her parents have known that she would

229

be an Esmeralda? She's started to lose her memory and is sad-
dened by her circumstances and the fact that she needs to be
in this awful room. She wants the lights to be turned off when
she wants them off. She starts talking about it in the morning.
'We have to make the best of the situation,' she says. That means
that she decides. She's been in the room longer and that gives
her the upper hand.

More nurses run in. I wave my arms around. I have to escape,
to save myself. Before the police come, before anyone discovers
where I am. God, where are you? I'm wrestled to the floor. One
arm is forced back. I throw myself forwards and up. The grip
on my arm is hard. I fall on my back, arm first. Ow, it hurts like
hell, but I continue to struggle. The pain makes me even wilder.
I bang my head on the floor. The restraining bed is rolled into
the room. I'm lifted up and restrained. I throw myself from side
to side. My arm hurts, but my rage blankets everything and
numbs it. A nurse sits down beside the bed with a newspaper.
He says nothing.

Perhaps it's better to be restrained than to go to pieces. Perhaps
the belts keep everything in place. I wanted to destroy everything
until there was nothing left. I can't sleep. After an hour, the nurses
swap places. I say that my arm hurts. 'We'll have a look when the
doctor comes back, but that's not for another three hours.'

Finally imprisoned. Finally restrained. A pain in another
pain in another pain. Body after body, like a Russian doll. The
ultimate punishment, locked doors and windows, locked hands
and feet. Only the innermost doll can't be opened. If anyone
tries to gnaw at it, they'll only get sore teeth. Everything that is
me has to be stuffed into that little doll in order to survive. This
is what I have feared.

When the doctor comes to release me, my arm is blue and
swollen. He can see immediately that it's broken. A nurse and I

spend all morning at A&E. I'm restless and walk back and forth in the waiting room. My arm hurts. I move it up and down in the air. Erik says: 'Serves you right. It's the police's fault.'

My friends are furious that I've been restrained again and about my broken arm. Sonja contacts the staff. They are a little more cooperative now, frightened that we might report the incident. Sonja says that if I go wild again they should call her straight away. Night or day. 'I can get here in five minutes,' she says. 'And I think I can calm Eli down so you don't need to restrain her.' Lolo comes with flowers, which I love. I throw the vase to the floor. Want to break it, but it's made of plastic. Which frustrates me at first, but then I later think it's good, and I can enjoy the flowers.

The staff slowly start to work with my friends. They realise that they want to help me get out of hospital as soon as possible.

Sonja, Lolo, Harald and Tim have a meeting with a doctor, but are none the wiser for it. I'm still not allowed to go out on my own, but get permission to run with Lisen twice a week along the lake, in order to get rid of some excess energy. I run fast, despite the heavy medication. I haven't had a period for five months. Is that because of the stress or the medicine? One of the other patients has started to produce milk, even though she hasn't had a baby.

Sonja visits me frequently. She leaves her husband and child and sits with me for hours. Sonja can just sit in silence in the room and be present. She demands nothing of me. Sometimes we talk about writing. I show her my book where I've scribbled page upon page. It's chaotic. It's what the voices say. I've written what I think. The same thing over and over again. Sonja thinks it's good and that I should continue.

She tells me about an insect. I think it's a male. One of its wings is broken and it can't fly. It bites off one leg and takes off. 'Will I find a way to get out of here?' I ask. 'Why do you ask?' she says. 'We know each other. So I don't need to say any more.' Typical her, I think. Was it the wing or the leg that he bit off? 'Tell me again.' Sonja tells me again.

Then she sits on the edge of the bed and reads Gombrowicz's diary to me until I fall asleep. Read, Sonja, read. I feel better now.

I'm allowed to leave the unit for a few hours every day, as long as I say where I'm going and when I'm coming back. It's Prince Eugen who goes out. He's going shopping. Completely wild. Prince Eugen feels exhilarated when he shops. He doesn't try clothes on, he slips into them. Expensive suits are like putting on better self-esteem. He looks good in everything. Admires his elegant, supple body in the mirror. He, who feels so different inside, is understood by a whole host of designers. His body is perfectly proportioned. He suits colours, feminine cuts, silk shirts and finely checked ties. He buys flowers, household goods. Is delighted to find a pillar box-red dish signed by Sigvard Bernadotte, or even better a coffee thermos. There's something seductive about coffee thermoses. He has a kitchen full. He also buys bits and pieces on sale and in second-hand shops, like duvet covers, tablecloths, computer equipment, CDs, uniform details, electric drills, and lots of painting things, of course. He collects coffee sets from the fifties and already has enough to open a café. He feels contented, with his entire being. Pays, and leaves with his bags and boxes. The more, the happier. Secretly happy. Like a thief stealing from himself. A stolen joy. To think that I can afford all this. That I am a prince.

Jonathan comes into the flat and discovers that it's entirely changed. I've got a stipend and want to do something new. He stands in the middle of the room. The walls have recently been papered. By an artist who has decorated the walls with thin strips of eight different wallpapers around the whole room. In blue, turquoise and a bit of red. The wallpapers are from different periods, but mainly from the fifties. It's not possible to hang any pictures, as the walls themselves are a work of art. I've stored Dad's paintings away. Feel a bit guilty about that. Might put them up again when I get a bigger flat.

I tell Jonathan that I'm going to live in this room with the new wallpaper for a while longer. Then one day, when I've written something that sells really well, when I've met someone, when I've been left an inheritance, then I will move to something bigger. Then I will have open, light surfaces. A cream medicine cupboard from the forties with all my red fifties cups and saucers visible behind glass doors. A chandelier. And I will almost only sleep in the bed. I won't greet Jonathan by saying how badly I've slept. I'll tell him the truth, that I've slept well. That I'm considering whether to stop taking sleeping pills altogether. I'm fine now and things will only get better. Things will go my way.

Jonathan listens to my plans, and hears and sees that the new wallpaper has created strips of light inside me.

I'm tight-lipped on the train home. I've been in Ludvika and thought that I was going to get a place in a clinic there. I tried to make a good impression. Really made an effort during the interview to be the model patient, someone who quite simply would fit into their programme. This was my chance to get away from the hospital. I had never imagined that they would not want me. I was the only one who could say no. It was too rural. Too cosy-cosy. The train journey was endless. Did they really not want me? I could perhaps move there all the same.

I get off the train and walk straight across the road. A car brakes and toots. Well, I don't want them either. People are sitting at tables outside the cafés. What a fucking awful spring. I go into the nearest place. Order a beer and a double whisky. I don't go out into the sun and sit with the others. I stand inside by the dark bar and down the whisky. I drink the beer in great gulps. Laugh. Is one not allowed to laugh? What did it say in my journal? 'Unmotivated laughter.'

I walk back up to the hospital, ring the bell and the door opens. The kind hospital priest is standing a couple of metres away. He has prayed for me. He has spoken to me. He has listened. He has lit a candle in a church abroad for me. I run towards him and punch him as hard as I can in the chest. He falls backwards onto the floor and lies there. The staff rush out and grab hold of me. I'm lifted and carried back to my room. I want to see if the priest has stood up or if he's been hurt. I didn't mean to. Of all people, not him. I've floored the kindest

236

person of all. I'm restrained. Sleep all afternoon and think that it's morning when I'm released in the evening.

I'm not allowed to go to the workshop in the next corridor. I'm seen as being too unstable. But one day they let me. There are looms, a pottery and mixed materials. I choose the latter. I'm going to make a bust of myself from medicine cups. Four times a day, medicine is handed out in small plastic cups. White in the morning, yellow at two o'clock, blue in the evening and red at night. I mould some chicken wire around my head and shoulders. I manage to wriggle out and keep the beginnings of a bust of me. The idea is to attach the small coloured cups to the chicken wire. Red for the hair, yellow for the face, blue for the eyes and white for the body. I make two small holes at the bottom of each cup and then attach them to the chicken wire with steel thread. It requires patience. It will take weeks, but that doesn't matter. The other patients start to save their medicine cups and give them to me. It's a waste of resources, really, putting pills in a plastic cup then throwing the cup away.

The plastic cups that start to cover the chicken wire stand out at right angles and make the bust far bigger than me. Gabriel has been sitting beside me for weeks. First turning a vase and then decorating it with a beautiful pattern. Gabriel jumped from the Skanstull Bridge and survived the freezing cold water. He's been in here for several months and says that he will wander the hospital corridors until he dies. He doesn't get dressed during the day, but walks around in his white hospital nightshirt. He says that he's the youngest heterosexual in Sweden with HIV. He had just started in his final year at school, hadn't had any relationships before, but then chatted up a woman from Botswana on the town late one night. He only discovered he had HIV when he went to give blood. Gabriel is convinced that he's going to die soon. There's no cure for his illness yet. He reads Shakespeare's poems in English at night and tells me that he's read my latest articles in the paper.

The vase becomes more and more beautiful. He sits there and engraves the pattern with a thin engraver's needle. One day he suddenly smashes it to pieces. I'm devastated and want to comfort him. The staff intervene and say that I should put my energy into my own creation. That patients mustn't get emotionally involved with each other, which we do all the time. 'Sometimes you have to destroy the thing you treasure most,' they say. But it was almost finished. I can't understand why he had to destroy it. I am too materialistic. I want to comfort him, but am not allowed to talk to Gabriel. I carry on with my own thing. Every afternoon I walk down the corridor to my room with my medicine cup bust, which grows and grows and gets lots of attention.

From my medical journal: *Starts by saying that she wants to stop taking her medication, that she thinks it makes her ill. As an example says that she was supposed to go to a screenplay writing course last week, but didn't manage as she felt restless and unfocused. Pat has had major conflicts in connection with the completion of her film. Pat bitter that the producer sold herself as an artistic producer. Pat is of the opinion that the producer has never shown any interest in the content, and has only been concerned about saving money. Pat describes feelings of anxiety after a meeting between the hospital and the film team last week. 'The world came from outside and inside me.' Pat describes other feelings of anxiety as 'sounding like two plastic bags being rubbed against each other.' When the pat describes the frustrations she has experienced in connection with the film project, her symptoms are more comprehensible.*

I get boxing gloves from Tim, which the staff are none too happy about. I punch everything and everyone. But they will prove to be a very useful present. We're filming the last scenes of the football film in my room at the unit. I go to the cutting room for a few hours every day and write and record the voice-over. I, who previously thought that I'd drawn the short straw, now feel that I have greater control over finishing up the film. It opens: 'I dreamt that I had been playing football for more than twenty years. I woke up. I had been playing football for over twenty years.' The film is a fifty-eight minute declaration of love to football. It ends when I give up football. And that was the intention. I did that in reality too. Finally. I think I have played myself out. I'm a grown woman now. Someone who works with culture, not sport.

But then I get the boxing gloves. The need to move. I walk past a window where some people are sparring. You can't be a proper woman until you've tried boxing, I think, and before I know it, I'm in there and before you can say Bob's your uncle, I've started boxing. Boxing is defence and attack at the same time. To punch and not be punched. Mind and body. No time to waste. Always on your toes. The boxing trainer screams: 'This is no Disneyland. Come on! You can't fool me, you can only fool yourselves. I'm just shouting.' The training sessions are demanding in a good way. Obey, suffer and play. The ache in my muscles is positive pain.

I help to start the first boxing club for girls in the Nordic region. See it as my mission to document my life, so shortly after I decide that I should film the whole thing. From the point where we get a run-down cellar space and put together a boxing ring, sew punching bags from coarse tarpaulin and fill them with rags. Our stomachs and breasts shrink. Soon you can see the hard muscles in our bodies. Punch, don't get punched. Intellectually, boxing feels ridiculous, but emotionally it feels absolutely right.

I make two films about boxing and one wins a prize for best documentary.

When I leave the hospital after nine months, I leave the medicine cup bust behind in the staff room. It's called Healthcare Victim. I say that it's a self-portrait of the painter Prince Eugen. It stays there for six months until I'm asked to come and collect it. I don't know what to do with it, don't want to have it in my flat. The whole point of it was the patience needed to attach each cup to the chicken wire. I understand Gabriel now. I want to smash it.

But a fellow patient suggests that I should submit it to the spring exhibition at Liljevalchs Gallery. Healthcare Victim is accepted and is exhibited for all to see. When the exhibition closes, I take the bust to my workspace in a building that's due to be demolished. When I move out, I leave Healthcare Victim and the large desk behind and they end up in the jaws of a bulldozer.

3.

I found, I found something. Five good years. Harald moves in with me so I can be discharged from hospital and live at home. I learn to make food from scratch. Harald learned from his mother and so it's goodbye to fried cabbage and garlic. We eat food from all corners of the world, Harald experiments. He lights candles and the conversation round the table stops when the candles have burned down.

Harald moves out and Tim moves in. He, who is trained as an engineer, now works as a translator and can sit at home or in an office and work whenever he likes. Which is generally late in the evening and at night. He told me once that he was studying for a PhD and shared an office with only men. During a coffee break one day he suddenly thought: I can't sit having coffee with these sort of men for the rest of my life. Tim's theory is that if the patriarchy disappeared, the world order would change entirely. So he signed up for the writing course and that is where we met. At home, he walks around in a loincloth rather than trousers. He thinks, and always takes a long time before he answers a question. He has thoughts about everything. Solutions to everything from the state of the world to technical appliances in the home. His mind is free, and moves in all directions. I enjoy talking to him about mathematical problems and life. He should be an inventor. He should be a poet. He should be everything. But he's not the type to progress from thought to action.

My birthday is coming up. Tim talks about the various dishes he's going to make. He's a fantastic cook. He has plans for a big dinner. 'Not too big,' I say carefully. 'Sirloin steak, and what about champagne and strawberries for breakfast?' I try to rein in my expectations, because I know Tim. But maybe this time, I think as always. He asks what I would like. I hardly dare to answer, because there's so much. 'I've got the money,' he says, and throws open his arms.

On my birthday, I'm woken by Tim moving around in the kitchen. I close my eyes and pull the duvet up over my face. He'll come in soon. Best to pretend that I'm sleeping. I wait, but don't hear any more sounds from the kitchen. He's gone out to buy fresh bread, I think, and look at the clock. It's nine. He's gone a long time. I try to go back to sleep, but can't. I listen for his footsteps. It can't take over an hour to buy bread. I can't bring myself to get up. Lie there with the feeling that I'm waiting for someone who's not going to come. He will come. He doesn't come.

I get out of bed at midday. How stupid can you be? There's no note in the kitchen. He's had a cup of coffee and breakfast. I head off to our shared workspace. 'Hi,' he says, happily, when I come in. I burst into tears. 'What's wrong?' 'I lay in bed for three hours waiting for a stupid cup of coffee,' I sob. 'Oh, I thought you wanted to sleep so I didn't wake you.' How the hell could he think that I wanted to sleep?

In the evening, Harald comes to the flat and makes an improvised buffet. Lolo comes with a present. If everyone was the same you'd only need one friend. In the future, I will be invited to countless dinners by Tim, who has changed from a pretty normal guy to a poet and inventor, and then back to a pretty normal guy.

'You've got a monkey on your back,' Jonathan says. He's come to my workplace. 'Your violent fantasies. Your past is a monkey on your back. Have you ever heard that expression?'

'No.' I'm shaking.

'You're not being threatened now. You're free.'

'Eli's not here,' I say. 'It's Erik. I am Erik.'

'Yes, yes. But when I'm here, Eli has to be here. Can you get her out please?'

I guffaw.

'What are you laughing at?'

'They say you don't know them.'

'Of course I know your voices and I respected them from the start. Their names are even in the programme. But only at certain times. You've not been following the programme. You should always contact someone at the weekend. You should start the day the same way. Turn on the light and the radio. Write.'

He gets up. I normally sit on the bed when someone is here. It's got a duvet and blankets. But Jonathan says no. I have to sit at my desk while we talk. Jonathan stands and looks at the bed. 'What can we do? So you don't go and lie down as soon as I've gone.' He takes two big pieces of wood and places them in a cross on the bed. 'It'll get a little dirty, but now you know that you're not allowed to go to bed.'

I laugh.

'What are they saying?'

'That I'm falling apart.'

'You're not falling apart. You've never fallen apart.'

'Yes, I have. Lots of times. When I lose myself, it feels like I'm falling apart. That's what I'm afraid of.'

'But you're stronger now. Stronger than the voices. You said it so well yourself last time, that you've been reading your journals and seen a pattern. The voices talk about the same things that they did twenty years ago. They've not kept up. You've grown and developed, they haven't. Who decides? You decide. Say it out loud.'

'I decide.'

Lolo and I buy a summer house in Roslagen. She's too nervous to do the bidding so she leaves that to me. 'We won't get it anyway,' she says, and escapes to the cinema. I bid and bid, ten thousand at a time. Threaten the other bidders by saying that I'm bidding with my emotions and won't give up. Which means that I don't have a ceiling. They back down. The house is ours.

I can't get hold of Lolo to tell her that she's now the owner of a nineteenth-century *torp*, with an outside loo and twelve-thousand square metres of land. I would actually rather have a cabin on a cliff by the sea. But we don't have the money for that. The thought of a cabin in the forest has made me anxious, and now I own one.

Lolo and Harald use a chainsaw and tree after tree is felled. Eventually it's possible to see fields and meadows and the sun can get in. Harald and Tim build a little guest house on the site so there's room for everyone. They all think that I've bought it as a place to write. That I sit there at my desk for days on end, looking out over the fields. But it soon transpires that there's loads of work to be done on what will become the garden, and I have to hide away up in my room to write in short bursts. Before more wood has to be chopped, more water has to be fetched, bonfires burned, branches broken, weeds weeded, meadows mown and delicious dinners prepared.

I start a project called 'Instead of a Novel'. I spend the whole summer putting together a shed and the next renovating second-hand garden furniture. Lolo has an eye for colours and paints the whole house in linseed paint. She's quick and not very careful. I am slow and meticulous. We complement each other.

To think about text, to write text, to talk about text. It's the best thing I know. I enjoy it with my entire being. Sonja and I give our manuscripts to each other. We take turns in taking each other out for a meal. We were on the writing course together and have continued to share our writing with each other since then. Every line, every book from the beginning. We talk about structure and content. Associations, possible ways forward. I normally draw small patterns on the paper alongside her poems, to illustrate how I read them. I myself show her things at a very early stage. The fact is that I have barely written anything before I want to show it. Believe that with only the vaguest idea of the very first sentence the novel is finished and want to send it to the publishers. Sonja holds me back. She pulls me further and further into the writing. She shows me that I'm only at the start of a long journey.

I'm a sprinter taking part in a marathon. I want to stop after only a short distance and be applauded. I want to have thoughts and feelings, others' aha moments. I want to give them something they never would have thought of if they hadn't read my text. When I wrote about my childhood and the publisher wanted to publish it, Sonja just said: 'You can do better.' She thumped the pile of paper down onto the table. Ordered a cognac that I was paying for. I was angry for a week, but then started working on it again. It took six months and became a far better book.

It's a matter of giving a little more and a little more. Like boxing, but it's not boxing. It's no Disneyland. It's not a charter

251

tour. It's a lonely long-distance run, and you have to pull in the odd spectator to wave a flag and give you some water during the slog. It's about remembering all the trainers I've had over the years and their encouragement never to give up, you can always be better. And after better, will, will, will. Muscle pain is positive pain.

I go to see Kristin in Oslo. 'You're so thin,' she says. I eat like a horse the whole weekend. I'm tired and I eat. Go to the loo and eat again. 'There's something wrong with your metabolism,' Kristin says. She looks at my thyroid gland. 'Promise that you'll go to the doctor as soon as you get home?' I promise, but don't do it.

My body isn't working. I, who didn't weigh much to begin with, lose twelve kilos in six months. Don't have the energy to box. Eat constantly. Make stews in the morning that stand simmering all day. Think about an old Norwegian folktale where they chew on a boulder. Think I can hear the crunching sound between my teeth when I eat.

I need some encouragement. I go to Mensa's homepage, the organisation for people with the highest IQ in the country. I start doing their tests. I love trying to work out which shape fits into the series. I love the maths and the logic. Sit with my stew in front of the computer. Go and lie down for a while and ponder the problem. When I send in the test, I'm sent an invitation to join Mensa. I knew it. I'm proud as a peacock, I'm one of the smartest people in the country. Until I see that the test should have been done in an hour and I used the whole day. Smart, but slow.

I go to see Kristin again, and am told that I'm not so smart. Not smart enough to go to the doctor. She's a qualified doctor now and gives me a blood test the next day. I've had hyperthyreosis for nearly a year. Back in Stockholm, the doctor says that my values are like those of ninety-year-old. 'How on earth did you manage to get up the steps to Söder Hospital?'

After taking medication for a year, I'm well again. Start boxing again. Carry stones for a wall at the cottage and get a slipped disc. But I'm healthy. I'm not psychotic.

It's a beautiful spring day. I'm going out to the cottage and taking my bike with me on the bus. I fly along the cycle path, but in the wrong direction in the wrong lane. Suddenly there's a bang and I'm lying beside my bike. Beside another bike and a large man in a police uniform. I stand up without a scratch. Pick up my bike, which is intact. The policeman's bike is more like an accordion. I almost start to laugh. The front wheel is completely twisted. The light smashed. The policeman has a hole on one of his uniformed legs and blood is seeping out. He screams at me: 'That was your fault. Look where you're going, you idiot!'

'Yes,' I say. 'It was my fault. I'm sorry.' He immediately pulls a pen and pad out of his bag. 'Write that down here,' he shouts in an authoritarian voice. 'That it was your fault.' Does he have to shout? He starts to draw where he was and how I swung onto the cycle path in the wrong lane. I agree with everything.

I've come straight from my therapist's small room, which I feel might be a disadvantage. The world outside is somehow new. Even traffic regulations. With my reduced vision I'm probably not supposed to cycle at all. I couldn't get a driving licence. I have very little in my favour. I've crashed into the worst person you can crash into. A policeman. He asks for my name and telephone number. I write it down, but don't check it. Don't see what's written there.

Then I take my intact bike with me on the bus out to the cottage. On the motorway, I see a man crouching down, his back to the busy motorway, picking coltsfoot. I write on the piece of paper I got from the policeman. I write over his name. Think I might need the coltsfoot-picking man who's going to such effort more than the name of a policeman I would rather forget. The policeman rings the next day and wants more details. He rings all summer. The birds sing, and I can hardly hear the phone. I run in from all the greenery. It's the policeman. He is obviously not able to fix his bike. Nor is anyone else. He tells me about all the bad luck he has all the time. About the leaks and the fact he can't sleep. About his job as a mounted policeman. About the horse that kicked him. About the friend who has abandoned him. And now the broken bike. I promise to pay if he sends the bill. I feel that I have no power against a policeman. He would rather talk than sort it out.

In the late summer, he's still calling. New misfortunes all the time. Eventually he manages to press a charge for careless behaviour in traffic. In August, I'm sent a fine and the bill for the bike. He calls me one more time to tell me that he's had vermin in his cupboards and has had to pull out his entire kitchen.

Suddenly the window in the bedroom is open. Even though the dark curtains are still drawn, I immediately notice that something is different. There's fresh spring air in the room. I open the curtains. Close my eyes and close the window. Then I notice that the other half of the window is still open. I freeze. Should I do it? Should I die? There's a pull in the pit of my stomach. The air is right outside my walls and window.

In fact, there's always a danger. Part of me wants to stay in the world and the other wants to jump out and lose everything. The whole flat could tip out like a drawer. Or I could fall out. Not choose to do it, just do it. Because the air is calling. The fall. I pull my head in, reach out with shaking hands and close the window. It's not been open for over a year.

I hold on to the bed. What happens if I open it again? How did the window manage to open itself? I had thought of giving it a grand opening when either Jonathan or Lolo were here. As a sign that everything was better. As a small triumph. But now it's not a triumph at all.

One day it will be opened again. I'm determined. The dark curtains will be taken down, the windows will be washed and be ordinary windows that give light and air. Not a dangerous black hole. But I'm not there yet. It's evening and I just hope the feeling of falling out won't keep me awake.

Then I realise what has happened. One of my mental health workers was here. We were cleaning today. Morgan was in the bedroom, he's the one who draws while we're talking and leaves behind little men all over my papers. He's the one who helps me fix bits and bobs in the house. He's the one who always has a good answer to all my difficult thoughts. He's a handyman, even in his mind. Does he not know how dangerous the windows are? Or is he testing me? I ask him when he comes again. He tells me he'd thought of closing it again, but forgot. 'Sorry.'

One day a kitten appears. A so called street-mix from the streets of Bergen on the west coast of Norway. She comes in the middle of the night with Hild. She's stowed away in the car. She's curled up in the food basket, exhausted after the long journey, with the remains of the chicken. I look down at the tiny, weary grey creature and think, what is a pet? I have never had one. What is this creature that's going to be mine? But it's me who becomes hers.

I think that she's tiny and sweet, but not much more. To be honest, I think that she's quite… empty. But how could I know? Quietly she pads around and creeps into me. When I have my back turned, she stretches inside me. Up and across, she just grows.

In many countries and for many people, a cat is just something to keep the mice away. She becomes family for me. I become a curling cat mum. We start to hang out. Play and cuddle. Kiril comes racing to the door to meet me when I come home. This meeting makes me burst with joy. I stroke her back. She runs into the living room. Lies on her back and stretches into infinity. Rolls over and does it again. I tickle her tummy. Kiril is training to be world champion in the full stretch. She's a master at recovering. Kiril knows that muscles grow when they relax. After stretching, she lies on the window sill above the radiator, or under the duvet in the bedroom and rests. I sit for a long time looking at her as she sleeps. Or lie down beside her and am simply with someone.

I tell things to Kiril, talk all the time, and she does to me too. This means that I talk less to the voices. I lie in bed in the

259

mornings with a piece of bread and cheese and a cup of coffee on my bedside table and Kiril on my stomach. To think there's a person stuffed into every body and a cat in every cat. I need more people to love and now I have one.

Mum and Dad come to visit me in the country. I've booked a room for them at a guest house nearby. Dad doesn't want to stay in a guest house, he wants to stay with me. I know him. He wants to sleep in my bedroom, be amongst all my things. Not with strangers.

He's not feeling very well after the journey and lies on the sofa in the kitchen. They've taken the train from Oslo to Stockholm and then the bus out here. The bus journey takes two hours and Dad thought he had to entertain everyone. That he had to speak Swedish. He's exhausted. Our garden appears to make him think of his own. He says: 'The grass at home, do you think it will have grown?' 'At least half a metre,' I joke. Which I should never have done. He gets up from the sofa. 'I have to go home and cut the grass,' he says. 'Lie down. You cut the grass yesterday.' 'I have to. I have to go home now. The grass is growing.' He gets up again. 'But we've just arrived,' Mum says. 'And now we're going to go back to the guest house and sleep.' Dad twists his mouth. 'The grass,' he says. 'The grass is growing.' He begins to fumble with his trousers, undoes his flies and takes out his willy as he totters towards the door. He gets out onto the step just in time, before he starts to pee.

At night, he wakes up and cries. He goes out into the corridor and wakes up the manager of the guest house. 'Please, let me go home,' he says. 'I think perhaps you need to see a doctor,' the manager says. 'I'll get an appointment for you tomorrow. And of course you don't have to stay here if you don't want to.'

Dad is given tranquillisers by the local doctor, but is not

examined beyond that. Mum so wants everything to be as she planned, that they'll have the nice holiday that she's been looking forward to. Stay in a guest house, get food served. Meet me and Lolo and all Lolo's family in the summer houses round about. She wants to see the sea, if at all possible. Dad lies in my bed and is left alone in the house while we go down to Lolo's relatives for a coffee and to look at the sea. Mum takes her swimsuit with her. She wants to have a quick dip at least, if nothing else. When we get back, Dad is crying and wants to go home. He's shaking. I'm torn between Mum's desire for a good holiday and Dad's desperation and breakdown in unknown surroundings. I had also looked forward to showing them my life. But there's no space.

'Your dad actually looks like he's dying,' one of Lolo's cousins says, and she's right. He could die at any moment. Even on holiday. Mum has now at least seen the sea, had coffee and tasted Lolo's relatives' fantastic sandwiches and cakes. She has now dipped her swimming costume if not her body in the brackish Baltic water. 'We have to call an ambulance,' Lolo says. 'Either your dad has accelerating anxiety or he's had another brain haemorrhage.' Mum thinks that an ambulance sounds too scary. 'We'll take the bus back to Stockholm,' she says, 'and then we can change our train tickets home.' And that is what happens.

It's horrible to see Dad so shaken and Mum so disappointed. I both want them to stay and to go home at the same time. Once we've explained to Dad that he's going to go to Stockholm, then spend the night in my flat before going back to Oslo the following day, he immediately improves. He gets up and shakes less. His speech is more articulate.

The bus journey is long, but Dad doesn't do the entertaining this time. He sits there dozing. I really regret saying what I did about the grass, that it was half a metre high. But he normally jokes like that himself. At home in my small flat, he gets into my bed. Mum and I sit in the kitchen. 'I so wanted to go to a restaurant before I went home,' she says. 'There's one in Tantol-unden, just over the street. Dad can stay in bed. Maybe we can take some food back for him.'

We have to wake him and say that we're going, so he won't feel abandoned when he wakes up. 'We're going out to eat in a restaurant. But it's just over the street,' I say, and go back into the kitchen. 'It'll be fine,' I say to Mum. Then Dad comes out of the bedroom in his lovely beige summer suit. He looks so elegant. Though his white hair is unkempt and doesn't really go with the suit. 'Where are you off to?' Mum asks. 'To eat in the restaurant, of course.' And so all three of us go.

The next day, I go with them to the station. Dad seems to be happy but tense. In the evening I speak to Mum on the phone. She tells me that Dad got better and better the closer to Norway they got. It's the last time Dad goes on holiday.

'Move your arse and your mind will follow,' Jonathan says. He wants me to take action. Participate. Follow the programme. Get out of bed. When I was a child, I always found things to do. Not only as a child, but up until only a few years ago. I, who didn't understand how anyone could be bored, can now spend hours sitting there doing nothing. Lying in bed with the same commercial radio station thumping into my ears.

'You have to build a life that involves more than just writing,' Jonathan says. I'm fine on weekdays, when I go to my workspace, write and meet colleagues. Then I go to boxing. But at the weekends there are hours of: what do I do now? A long silence. An empty space. If I don't go out to the country. 'You could write a bit at home at the weekends too. Write about different things than you do during the week.'

'I can't write at home.'

'But surely the words come from inside you and not the workspace?'

Doesn't seem like that.

'It says in your file that you should call someone. Do you?'

'Sometimes.'

I look up at the cartoon on the fridge. Two men sitting looking out over a depressing landscape of factory chimneys. One says: 'We're all going to die one day.' The other replies: 'And on all the other days, we don't.'

Dad has another huge brain haemorrhage and completely loses touch. He lives at home and Mum cares for him. He cries a lot. Groans when he walks and says that it hurts. Has his pain threshold fallen, or does he really hurt all over? The doctors find nothing.

Until it's too late. Until the cancer has spread throughout his body. He's admitted to hospital. His memory is very poor because of all the haemorrhages. We hang his paintings on the walls and a photograph of the house where his mother grew up. A *torp* which he has called the manor for as long as I can remember.

He tries, he pretends to follow and repeats what we say. I read for him from my latest book. I read the good reviews that it's got, and he starts to cry. He's so proud. How much has he understood? I don't know. We listen to music. Dance. But he soon gets tired. Then he stands still and holds out his arm so I can swing around it.

We talk about the past, about when he was little, and for short periods he's there. I show him photographs of his children and grandchildren, think that he knows they belong to him. I show him pictures of me from the newspaper, where I'm posing in a ski jump position. Dad starts to cry again. Is he happy? I don't really know, he cries all the time now. But singing is good. He remembers the words. We sing 'Fairest Lord Jesus' and folk songs. I start to cry. He pats me on the head. 'It'll be all right,' he repeats several times. 'Everyone has their trials and tribulations.' Does he know that he's going to die? He can't die.

Then one day I think: he has to die. I creep into his bed and lie there beside him. I think I have to be close to him and save the moments.

One warm night in the middle of summer, my father dies. I haven't been to see him for a while. I've been running a course for new writers and am at the cottage, on my way to see him the next day. The ticket is lying ready, my bags are packed. I've enlarged photographs of his grandchildren, as his eyesight is so poor now. I'm looking forward to seeing him.

I have a very restless night, as if I'm angry in my sleep. In the middle of the night, Mum phones to tell me that Dad has died. But she doesn't say died. She says 'has left us'. Or does she say that we have lost him? I don't really hear. She's been at the hospice all night, and now she's going home to rest. I wake Lolo.

My flight isn't until midday. Everything is as planned, only the person I'm going to see is no longer alive. I can't get back to sleep. I go out into the garden in my pyjamas and cry and pick flowers. They're for Mum. Because she had the strength to call me in the middle of the night and tell me herself. Because she sat with him and told him he didn't need to suffer or be in pain. She told him he could die. And then he did.

I pick a flower and look at it. As if it had also been alive and lost its life here in my hand. The sight of a butterfly increases the volume of my tears. I am careful to walk in the patches of morning sun, as if they were stepping stones. Nothing in nature is black. I suddenly remember Dad's words. I suddenly want to tell him that I agree.

I run the two kilometres down to the water. Take off my pyjamas and dive naked from the rocks into the rippling waves. Dawn breaks.

Torvald meets me at the station. He's crying. I haven't seen him cry since we were children. When we get to the hospice, I see that the flag is flying at half mast. That's for Dad, I think, and start to cry. I walk into the room and see Dad lying dead in the bed. It's so real. It's like seeing someone who isn't there. 'You can give him a hug,' Torvald says. I gently stroke his cold, yellow-tinted cheek. He, who was always so warm. I embrace him. Feel his beard scratching, like when I was a child. Torvald asks if I want to be on my own with him. He goes out and I really am alone in the room. I sit down on a chair beside the bed and sing. Dad doesn't sing with me.

I take Kiril for a walk on the lead round all the blocks of flats where I live. It's not easy to follow a cat. I don't dare take her off the lead. But in the country, she's allowed to run free and dashes past like a sprinter. I now often leave my workspace and events early because I feel that she wants company. I know that you shouldn't humanise animals. But I do all the same, and I'm sure that Kiril catifies me. She wakes me every morning. Rubs against me and gently bites my ear. I don't get up. She continues. She forces me up. But this closeness also creates problems. I get asthma. I'm allergic to the very thing I love. I've stopped giving her contraceptive pills. I don't have children myself, but would love her to have kittens.

I'm woken in the middle of the night by a terrible noise and leap out of bed. Kiril has tried to mate with a brown paper bag. The handle is stuck round her tummy. The whole bag stinks and is flecked with God knows what.

I take the hint, it's time to go to the country. Time to find a nice tomcat. We take the first bus the next morning. I've barely opened the door to the carrier before she's off like a flash to the neighbour's, where the white, deaf tomcat Tusse lives. Soon they're back in our garden. I've got a film camera with me and follow them around. At first, it seems like Tusse doesn't twig. Kiril lies on her back in front of him and wriggles. Tusse looks away. Kiril runs in front of him, stops and checks that he's following. Finally he gets it, she scampers off and he follows. They play the whole day, but nothing more happens. They lie beside each other and look expectantly at each other, but don't touch.

It's a real spring day, with unfurling leaves and birdsong.

The next day, the glass veranda is full of white hairs. There's been a fight here. When I go out I see Kiril over by the wood block, she's lying down with her backside in the air and a white cat on either side. Does she have two? I get the camera. It's such a good image with little grey Kiril between the two big white toms. They run towards me. Kiril in front, her two suitors behind. Kiril is taken on the step. Not by Tusse, but the other one, Tusse's father, Simon. Tusse sits beside them and yowls. Kiril yowls as well. The whole thing seems so brutal. Simon bites Kiril in the neck and lifts her up from the step out onto the lawn. Then he gets on top of her and starts to pump again. Suddenly Kiril musters all her strength, throws him off and leaps away. She releases a primal scream. Mission accomplished.

Back in the city, I check to see if Kiril's nipples have started to grow. I spend a lot of time with her. We eat breakfast in bed and play hide and seek. She hides behind the shower curtain. Her tail sticks out. It swishes up and down in exultation when I find her. I film her. She hides between the sheet and duvet. Manages to lie still for a while, but then her tail starts swishing again and she gives herself away. I press her little body to my face. Lie with my ear against the purring warm soul that never ceases to enjoy herself. I feel her heart beating under her fur.

I start to piece together a film idea. I'm going to build a palace for the kittens. I'm going to film their birth and development and add a voice-over about curling parents and ordinary children.

I go to the animal hospital for an ultrasound, and film it. There are at least two tiny beating hearts on the screen. 'Tick, tick, tick,' says the enthusiastic vet, 'can you see it?' I write to the head of documentaries on Swedish TV with a short description of my idea. Two days later I get a yes. I build a two storey house for them in the living room at the cottage. There's sheepskin in all the rooms and a roof terrace. White balls hanging from the ceiling to play with.

Four days before Kiril is due to give birth, she doesn't come back in the evening. The rain is pelting down and I think that she might be sheltering under one of the outhouses. I go out into the rain and call for her. She doesn't come back the following night, nor the night after that. She should come and settle into her new home. Every word is a cry for others. She doesn't come running over the field with her tail in the air in answer to my calls. Has

271

she hidden herself away somewhere to give birth? Apparently it's quite usual. I persuade myself there's no danger, but there's a silent scream inside me. On the fourth evening, I take the scream with me out into the forest and release it. The forest is like a sieve with an infinite number of holes to hide in. It's soughing. The birds reply like kittens. It has to be as I thought. As I had planned and looked forward to. I mustn't lose it.

The neighbour's boy helps me to look. I film and he looks straight into the camera and explains: 'I think she's maybe gone this way.' He points. 'Or that. Or over there.' There's no direction left. 'But not that way.' He stops, draws a circle with his hand. 'Or she's gone like this.'

I drive around on my moped and put up notices. I put an advert in the local paper with a five thousand kroner reward, and get phone calls from near and far about cats that people have found. I don't dare look in the ditches alongside the country roads. Scared to find her run over. The old farmer's wife tells me that cats are like sweeties for the fox. And there are plenty of foxes. I'm deaf in both ears.

If I had been an animal amongst animals, or a tree amongst trees, life would have meaning. My consciousness lies between them and me. People can only exist in time. We have all snapped up a life, but none of us can keep them. Everything will be replaced by something almost the same. New, new new.

The weeks pass. I think that she'll come back with her kittens in her mouth any day. I am prepared. I leave the front door ajar every night. Fill Kiril's bowl with prawns. One morning they're gone. Has Kiril been here incognito and then left again? My hope rises.

I dream about Kiril at night. She's locked in various houses. People have closed up and gone on holiday. She's skinny. Crying for help and I can't hear her.

Am I writing or not writing? Can't write, but do it all the same. A glance. A moment. A glimpse, a flash. The inner eye, the evil eye. A blindspot. Cat mint. Cat grass. Catastrophe. Cat's eyes light up in the dark, which is why I go out looking at night with a torch and the neighbour's boy.

Kiril and I didn't talk about memories. We were together in the present. And of course we had routines. Routines, routines, routines. Real time, real cuddles, real fun and good food. Don't even know if she knew she was pregnant. Planning is my secret, my humanity. But right now, if she's giving birth somewhere, she knows everything.

I can't stop looking. Kiril, come out! Something bursts. I dream that I find her all dirty and emaciated. She's a dog. The voices that have been absent for so long force their way back. 'I'll look after you,' Emil says. 'If you don't stop looking, I'll close your eyes for good,' Erik says. 'Are you being systematic?' Mum asks on the phone. It's like mathematics. Queen of science. Systematic. I certainly go in all directions. Here and there and back again. Calling. No longer have control over my thoughts. The voices are given free reign. Am awake at night and see Tusse eating Kiril's last prawn.

I realise that I loved Kiril too much. That we were too close. The summer passes. Lolo falls in love and stays in town more and more. Sonja comes to stay, comes with me out into the cow field to look and call. She's desperate to help, thinks she spots Kiril several times. Kristin leaves her one-year-old son in Oslo and comes to visit. She wants to support me and take part in the search. On the anniversary of Dad's death, I'm certain that I'm going to find her. She must have understood somewhere that she couldn't leave me. That I can't sleep, that things are on the turn. People warn me: 'You're looking too hard. If she comes, she comes. Cats don't work like that.' But I can't stop looking. Can't stop hoping.

The summer fades and I go back to town. When I open the door to my flat, I'm sure that she's found her way there, navigated the hundred and thirty kilometres, and let herself in with her own key. That she'll come charging towards me and roll around on the doormat.

It's empty. I cry as I pick up her toys and put away her food dish. I leave the netting on the balcony, and her climbing tree. You never know. Listen to a programme on the radio where a man tells a touching story about losing his parrot. His grief was overwhelming. He had never felt anything like it. Parrots are supposed to live for seventy years. He had seen a lot in his life, but it was the parrot dying that broke him. That caused his emotions to spill over.

I tell the television people that the star has disappeared, but I'm thinking about making a film about loss, disappearance and searching, how one disappearance recalls others. I found, I found that loss looks for other open wounds. I think about Dad. He was old, had had numerous brain haemorrhages, lost his memory and had cancer. But Kiril shouldn't have died, she was only four years old. She was about to give birth.

I've been looking too hard, too deep. Too everywhere. There's a dangerous hole inside me. With only a thin cover. No one can knock.

I think about what the minister said at Dad's funeral. 'If you look at the bigger picture, take in the whole universe, then it's an exception, an enormous exception, to be alive.'

4.

I'm sitting in my workspace waiting for Sonja. There are piles of paper everywhere. I've started writing a new novel. Finished filming the Kiril film, *Things Normally Work Out*, where I find all kinds of things other than Kiril. I'm in the middle of writing the scripts for ten short films for TV. I've rented one of the most expensive cutting suites in town. The production company pulls out. Money that was never there is trickling away. The producer has got another job and just vanishes. I get myself a lawyer. Film is conflict. Film is money.

I'm impatient, can't concentrate. I'm going to have a meeting with the TV documentary team the next day and want to show some clips. The film about Kiril has to be finished. I chew a pen to pieces. My thoughts split and latch onto new ones. Wonder if anyone is guiding them. 'Loss looks for open wounds,' I write apropos nothing. I have to work. 'Write,' Prince Eugen says. 'Write yourself back into the world.' I can feel it deep down in my belly, that I'm splitting. That I have to hide myself. Further, and even deeper inside myself.

Finally Sonja arrives. She's got a caffè latte with her. Does she know anything? I see us both from outside. See Sonja's hand moving in slow motion. Then she speaks my thought. 'How are things?' 'Good,' I whisper. Sonja asks such difficult questions. Talks so fast. So quietly. So far away. Only half of me is in the room. I'm holding a cup of coffee. Am I holding a cup of coffee? Try to feel the coffee as I drink. Say thank you several times. It slips down a stranger's throat, tastes strange. Sonja is in a rush, has to get a move on. She takes hold of me, shakes me fondly and asks again how things are. I don't know.

Late in the evening at home in my flat, there's a ring at the door. It's Sonja. 'I just wanted to make sure you were okay. Have you eaten?' I lie. I haven't done anything. 'Well, I'd better be getting back to the children then,' she says. 'Everything's fine,' I lie. When she's left, I turn on the tap, maybe to do the washing up. Espen sobs.

In the morning I wake up on the kitchen floor and someone is ringing on the doorbell. I get the feeling that I need to put a hat on to keep my head together. It's Sonja again. She makes coffee and asks if I've eaten breakfast. I haven't. I tell her about the presentation I'm going to give for the TV people at three o'clock. They have to accept the changes in my film idea. Maybe I should have a shower and change my clothes, as I've slept with my clothes on. 'You don't need to,' says Erik. I go into the bathroom and pretend to shower. I find a hat that sits tight on my head. We eat breakfast. Erik talks incessantly. He's so happy about the documentary. 'It's going to be a fantastic film,' he says. Everything's fine. Then suddenly his mood changes. 'Watch yourself,' he warns. He orders me to stand in the corner of the kitchen and wave my arms. Sonja stares, but says nothing. I sit down again. My right leg is shaking. It has to come out somewhere. 'How does that feel in your bones?' Sonja asks. 'There's a long lump that's vibrating.' 'Can you sit still if you want to?' 'I don't know.' I have to be still when I meet the TV people.

Suddenly Sonja stands up and goes over to the phone. She dials and then speaks to someone. 'We've got an appointment with the doctor up at the hospital,' she says. The unit has moved since I was last there. 'Think about the film,' Erik says. 'Don't ruin everything. The people at the hospital are dangerous.' 'They're going to call back,' Sonja says. The phone rings and I answer. The man on the other end asks me what my name is and I can't remember. Sonja takes the receiver and tells him my name. They ask for my ID number. I have no idea. We start to hunt around the flat and find a nasal spray with my number on it. I rattle it off and hang up. Sonja stares at me and says: 'Don't you know what you're called?'

'Was it my dad who was asking?' I wonder. 'Your dad? What's he got to do with it? We were talking to someone at the hospital, not your dad.' 'Sounded like Dad. He can't remember who I am any more.' 'Your dad is dead. We have to go.'

I think I have the right to know who it was. 'It was a psychologist, but you don't know him,' Sonja says. 'Put your coat on.' I can't work it out. What did he want from me? I have to protect myself and know who I'm talking to. I don't even know who I am myself.

Up at the hospital, we sit and wait. I look at the clock the whole time. 'You know that I've got a meeting with the TV people at three?' I say to Sonja, again and again. We talk to the doctor at the day centre first. She asks me what month and year it is. I can't answer. 'I think you should talk to another doctor in the secure unit,' she says eventually. We have to wait again.

There's a hole under me. An empty space under the floor, where everything is alien and empty. Where the answer should be, but it isn't. Am I still me? I wander back and forth, like an impatient dream. I put one foot in front of the other and the floor doesn't break. They've told me that I'm called Eli. Who should I trust? There's just a slim strip in my head where I can trust anyone. Only the tiniest strip that belongs to reality. It feels like I'm shrinking closer to the ground. So much of me has to carry all this unknown emptiness around. That's under the floor. My right leg is shaking.

I stand up and go over to the reception. Say to one of the secretaries that I can't wait any longer, that I have to go. I've got an important presentation for the TV. It's the only thing on my mind. I take my jacket and am about to leave. Someone

282

locks the door and says that the doctor will be there any minute. Sonja phones the producer and says that I've got a cold and I'm waiting to see the doctor, but I'll be there as soon as I can.

The doctor is called Manne. We sit down in one of the consultancy rooms. A nurse, who I recognise from previous stays in the unit, comes in. He says that he's followed my progress and success as an author with delight. Another nurse comes in. His name is Olof. He introduces himself and says that he will be my care coordinator. What kind of care do I need now? 'What day is it? What month?' I have no idea. He asks if I'm sleeping at night. I think so.

My mobile phone rings. I talk to the producer, say that I will get there as soon as I can. Sonja takes the handset and says that we're at the doctor's, Eli's got flu, so we won't be coming at all. She hangs up. I stand up and want to call back. Surely this won't take that long. 'Sit down, please,' Olof says. I go out into the corridor, but am quickly pulled back in. The doctor says that I can either choose to be admitted, or I can be sectioned. 'I'll think about it.' That's not possible. 'I'll get back to you after my meeting,' I say. 'You're not going to any meeting. You're being sectioned.'

And that's what happens. We go through the glass doors and they are locked behind me. The last thing I say to Sonja is: 'Don't leave me here.' Sonja gives me a hug. 'I'll come back tomorrow, and the day after.' The following day, Sonja and I have a conversation with the doctor. He says that if I run away, the police will pick me up. I tell him that I'm a writer. He tells me that he's a musician in his spare time. We could perhaps have found a lot to talk about if the question of medication was not in the way. I don't want to have any medicine.

This will become our main source of conflict. And I am in and out of the unit for the next six years.

The chicken wire still encloses the balcony. It looks like I've got a cat. Jonathan hasn't mentioned taking it down. None of my friends have offered to help me take it down. Now it's there to stop me falling or jumping out. If Kiril could have fallen and killed herself when she balanced on the railing, so can I. I was her mother and put it up so she would survive. Now I have to be my own mother. A curling-Eli-mother. All dangers have to be swept away from in front of me.

I don't remember much from those first days. Sonja, Lolo, Tim, Harald and Lisen come. The first week is worst. I don't know the staff and am unsure of my fellow patients. I draw arrows to my ears, above and below. It's the route of the voices.

One of my fellow patients walks stiffly up and down the corridor. She's tall and thin. She's wearing white shoes, white trousers, a white shirt and has a white scarf wrapped around her head. I think of her as the pill. And then there's the old, clearly attractive, woman with grey permed hair and lacy shirt. And her endless yelling. A never-ending torrent of swearwords and abuse. Calls all the women bloody whores. Lies on her bed shouting. Sits in a chair shouting. Shouts in the dining room. She's got a loud piercing voice that never rests. We all heave a sigh of relief when there's a few minutes' silence. Then she starts again. You prick, you cunt. You arsehole, you brat. You pig.

I sleep badly despite all the sleeping pills. Go into the smoking room around two in the morning. There's a woman sitting there, fast asleep. I sit down beside her on the rickety garden bench. Furniture that is too old and worn to be kept elsewhere ends up here. There's a knock on the glass door. I get up to open it. A woman on crutches wants help to get in. She points at me with her crutch. 'The police came and got me. If they'd called me, I would have come of my own accord. My neighbours had phoned them. Said that I was ringing on their doors and calling their phones. I don't have my neighbours' telephone numbers, don't even know what they're called. And since then I've had this pain in my hips.'

But why did they come and get her? I wonder. She sits down and takes out a cigarette. She's pale. Black under the eyes. We're all wearing the long white hospital gowns with buttons down the front. 'I was sectioned,' she says, 'even though I would have come here on my own. Everything started to go wrong after I was admitted to the unit six years ago. It's Manne, my doctor's fault. He mixes my psychosis medicine with the painkillers that I get from the medical centre. I'm in pain, I've got kidney problems and problems sleeping, but I'm not psychotic. I'd have come on my crutches if they'd called and let me know. But enough is enough. I'm going to change hospital now. If I stay here and make a fuss and tell people what it's really like, I'll just be sectioned. Manne has ruined my kidneys with all the Trilafon. I've reported him four times, but filled in the papers wrong.'

'Trilafon is good,' the sleeping woman beside me suddenly pipes up. It's a three-way conversation now. 'I like Manne. Now that I've switched to Trilafon, everything is much better. Except that I shake all the time, but you do too. But you don't get toothache and put on weight,' she adds. Then she appears to fall asleep and we are two again. The woman with the crutches whispers: 'Manne's got some really dangerous patients from al-Qaida. The kind of people who should be locked up come round to my flat. I've seen them through the keyhole. Really dangerous people in full al-Qaeda gear. It's Manne who sends them.'

Suddenly I feel sorry for Manne. How can I feel more sorry for him than I do for someone who thinks they're being followed?

We've both finished our cigarettes. But meet again an hour later in the smoking room. The woman whose teeth are better has disappeared.

286

I'm woken on the morning of Christmas Eve by Hanna, the nurse. She gives me five different kinds of biscuits in bed. She often has things with her from home. Expensive chocolates and waffles for the patients. I get the traditional Christmas porridge with cinnamon and sugar, with my coffee. I lie in bed and eat my breakfast. She likes me. There are three of us in a double room, I'm in the extra bed. No bedside light, no chair and nowhere to put my things. No cupboard, no key. You never know how many petty thieves might be here. Or notorious collectors.

I phone home to Norway to say Happy Christmas. Say that I'm on holiday in Spain. In the evening, I suggest that we should all go to midnight mass. Three of the other patients want to come and we'll be accompanied by a nurse. We can't go anywhere without a chaperone. The nurse has never been to midnight mass before and thinks it might be interesting. When we reach the church, the first patient wants to go back to the unit, there are too many people here. The nurse doesn't know what to do, because that means that everyone should go back. But he lets the three of us go in and sit down. When he comes back the church is packed and the service is about to begin. Then the next patient wants to go back. The nurse says that my room-mate and I can stay if we promise not to leave. We promise. When he comes back again, the service is almost over.

It's so beautiful in the church. Real candles and an orange glow in the air. I have to close my eyes so the others can also see all this beauty. I feel Christmas inside me. It's much stronger this time than the last time I was in church. My room-mate wants to go back. I'm left on my own. I want to experience it all. Even take communion, no idea why. God ceased to prod or move me many years ago. God isn't after me any more. Doesn't look. Doesn't find.

I stand in a long queue down the centre aisle. It's uncomfortably crowded. Survival is the only thing that unites us. I have decided to stay standing. Hear the words of the boxing coach, have forgotten what the priest said. Focus, focus, focus. As long as there are holes and spaces in our world picture, we'll need God. Focus, focus, focus, that's what helps us survive. Up by the altar, I get down on my knees and think to myself that I might even say something to God tonight. But the words don't come. I leave the church by the main door, where the nurse is waiting. He didn't manage to experience much.

Back to the hospital. All three of us lie in our beds in our room on Christmas night. Then a retired night sister comes in wearing a Santa hat over her grey, curly hair. She gives each of us a present. It's a small magnifying glass. A pink one, a neon green one and a yellow one. I'm touched. Three grown women unwrapping a toy from an elderly lady with no children, who works holiday weekends for company. The magnifying glasses are flimsy, unusable. They look like they come from a vending machine. I'm the only one who needs a magnifying glass. It feels like a sign.

On Christmas Day, I'm lying on the extra bed and have just finished listening to an audio book. I'm sobbing my heart out. It's not Espen. It's me. I am Eli. Grown-up tears from a source that never runs dry.

Then Manne, my doctor, comes in. I don't say hello. Just cry. He sits down on the edge of the bed. 'Why are you so sad?' he asks after a while. At first I can't answer. Then I say: 'I've been listening to "The Christmas Oratorio" by Göran Tunström. He read it himself with his Värmland dialect. It's so beautiful. I'm crying because it's not possible to write a more beautiful book, and I've got a whole pile of audio books to listen to that just can't compare with this one.' Manne says nothing. I burst into tears again. I'm surprised that he's come in to see me over Christmas, but don't want him to say Happy Christmas. Which he doesn't. He says nothing. He takes my hand and gives it a squeeze. Then he gets up and leaves. I continue to cry. I didn't tell him the whole truth. It's not just that nothing could be more beautiful. It's because the main character loses something and ends up in psychosis.

I do a tour of the corridor, into the dining room and back again. There's nowhere to go. The chairs, tables, plastic Christmas tree, walls, rooms, beds, the worn screens between the beds, and armchairs out in the corridor. I switch off the main light. Lie on my bed. My room-mates are lying silent and invisible behind the screens.

I get up again and do the same round again. Down to the dining room. Most patients are at home on release. I help myself to a peppercake and a cup of coffee. The coffee tastes disgusting, I only take a few sips, then put the mug back. Soon I'll take another one. Look forward to it and then put it back. I go back to my room, lie down on my bed. Muse that people in prison aren't allowed to chop wood. Nor those in a psychiatric ward. That feeling of lifting the axe, hitting the wood in the right place. The sound of the wood splitting. The power. The next piece and the next. I long for the country. For the woodshed. For the chopping block and axe from Norway. And then to just sit and look into the fire. The heat and smell of birchwood.

It's mealtime again. Most people are sitting by the table. Then a long-legged older man with an unkempt beard comes into the dining room, in nothing but his underpants. He's painted his lips black. 'Please go and put some clothes on,' says one of the staff. 'Why? I am who I am. I've got more education than you. I'm a qualified doctor. It's just that they took away my licence. Could I have it back, please? The less you lot bother me, the better I am.' 'Go to your room and put on some clothes,' the nurse says again.

He stands up and dances out. Not long after, he comes tottering in in red high-heeled shoes, a minimalist black shiny skirt that barely covers his behind and a red shiny top that stops at his naval. His long hairy legs and stomach are on show for everyone to see. He looks less dressed than he did in his underpants.

The snow disappears. Spring arrives with its wet days. It doesn't make much difference in here. Nothing makes much difference in the unit. A long stretch of just being here. It just carries on. Day and night.

I want to be seen through the walls, through the ceiling in my bed, where I lie for days on end. Wait for the door to open, and some eyes, a voice to come in. For long periods I feel lonelier here with all the nurses and patients than I did on my own in my flat. Do you have to rush screaming out into the corridor to get attention? Can't someone see me where I am? In silence.

The summer comes. I'm given a partial release. Lolo has come to an arrangement with Olof, my care coordinator, that I can spend three days in the country and four in the ward. I only want to be in the country. 'I could be invisible,' I say to Lolo. 'You will never be invisible. You just have to get a bit better.'

I get depot injections of Trilafon every week. My whole body is stiff. Shaky. I move my arms in an odd way. Don't know what to do with them. What did I do before? Even have to think about how to walk. How my mouth moves between my jaws. There's a strange creaking sound when I eat. I have no will power. Nothing interests me. I look at the shed I built the summer before last. Now I can't even hammer in a nail.

I try to talk to Manne about the fact that I'm over-medicated. He won't agree to my demands for a lower dose. The threat of being sectioned hangs heavy on our conversation. I'm free, but only if I do what they say. I get depot injections because he suspects that I don't take the pills. Which is true, but not as often as he thinks. It says in my journal that I'm suspected of poor compliance, which means I don't cooperate.

Manne goes on holiday. I ask the locum doctor for less medicine. 'You'll have to wait until your regular doctor comes back.' I don't know how to get my spark back. My body, my thoughts, my presence and my independence. I run along the windy forest paths. I'm the slowest runner in Sweden. Focus, focus, focus. Stop at the cliffs. Take off all my clothes and watch the sun go down. I dive into the glittering water wearing only the plaster left on my bum after the injection.

Things start to feel stable again. I've been in and out for over two years now. I'm out again. Work is going well, I've written a novel and the whole process has been enriching. I've travelled around with the book doing readings. But the most important thing for me right now is that I have a bigger team working with me in the hospital. A support network that works. Finally. That's to say, certain nurses have a special responsibility for me, and I get to know them and they get to know me. That's never happened before. I now meet the same nurses in the day centre when I'm at home as I do in the secure unit when I'm in hospital. It's a unique way of working, which makes me feel secure, which in turn provides stability. They come to visit me at my workspace. I'm in telephone contact with them almost daily.

I would never have managed to live at home without their help. They have meetings with my friends and work with them. My friends are now received very differently than before. I'm on my way out into life. Will soon finish the film about Kiril. Start a new novel. Start boxing again. Spring is in the air. I breathe it in. The trees are no longer grey and closed. They're alive and sprouting. I look up. See children playing football and my body remembers.

I'm at a big party for Lisen's husband. It's his fortieth. I feel incredibly strong. I feel like a tree. I've got a crown of leaves hidden beneath my skull, just wait, you'll see it soon enough. I get to the party early to help. I dominate and start organising, giving everyone tasks. Point to where the chairs and tables should be. Just how strong and healthy can you be? I'm about to take off. Think the others are a bit useless. No doubt they've got their own problems.

I look after the bar for the whole party, carry food in and out, light the candelabra and put out snacks. I'm wearing Prince Eugen's green tartan, fitted suit and dark sunglasses. I feel as though I'm in a film. I feel seen and loved. See myself from outside. How I weave elegantly between the guests, my small talk. 'How are you?' Better than you think. As usual, but worse. But no, I say, 'Fine, thank you.'

I meet the head of TV documentaries and he wonders how I'm getting on with the film. 'It's going fine,' I say. Even though it's not. I've been away from it for so long. Another film-maker comes over and talks about his new film, about the aborigines in Papua New Guinea. No need for burkas there, the women are bare-chested and cast their eyes down when men speak.

Have I become MP, am I part of the plot from start to finish? Today it feels like that. Someone congratulates me on my latest book and how well it's been received. Someone asks how I am. They've heard I've not been well. Not just borderline, where they often think they are themselves, but way over on the other side.

'Yes, fine thank you.' 'That's good to hear. Really, you're fine?'

I laugh. 'You look strong.' No more questions, I think to myself. I need to be left in peace. But they keep coming. More questions. 'How are you? I hear that you've not been well. Good to see you.'

See me? What do they see? I know that I'm lying a little, and then a bit more. Answering so that I'm normal, so that I am what I think they hope I am. What do I feel? An incredible power. They talk about their children and their careers and their mid-life crises. When you suddenly realise that you will never be part of Médecins Sans Frontières in Africa. That the collective in San Francisco will never happen. It didn't happen for me either. But nor did I turn out like them.

I move between the tables. No more questions. I dance. I feel invincible in the music. But what is it I want to conquer? I don't know. Move with great energy. Alone, but with all the others around, between and with me. 'Dance, and I'll conduct,' says Prince Eugen. I look up and catch someone's eye.

I dance into the small hours. The lights are switched on and the caretaker arrives. It's time to wrap up. I meet an old friend of a friend. She's become a hypnotist. She looks at me with intense eyes and says things that make me uneasy. I've taken off my sunglasses and the bright light burns my eyes. I get her card, but already feel hypnotised. There's something dangerous inside me that is about to come out. I slip in and out of myself.

I'm on top now. Can you stay on top without starting to slide? It's my turn now. To feel whole.

The day after, I stand in my colleague's room at the workspace. 'I'm breaking up,' I say. Something breaks. I shout in my head. I search in my thoughts. 'Eli's not here. I am Erik,' I say. His voice has taken over my thoughts. My body. As though he has got inside me. I've become him and he keeps Eli at bay. Don't know how the morning has been or how I got here.

My colleague looks at me in surprise. 'Should I call the hospital?' 'No.' She rings all the same, and we take a taxi there. We have to wait to see a doctor. Erik wants to leave, but is stopped and my doctor comes immediately. I say that I'm called Erik and that Manne doesn't know who I am. Manne says that he knows very well who I am and that I know who he is. Erik denies it. 'You've never met me before. Not Erik.'

I say that Erik has to show him the suit that he has at home, that he has to go and get it. And now. Manne is completely uninterested in the suit and the conversation is soon closed. Manne doesn't have much time. Erik is obsessed with showing him the suit. 'It's not Erik's suit, he's just borrowing it. It's Prince Eugen's,' I say. 'You're not at the party now,' my colleague says. 'That was last night.' I remember dancing half the night in Prince Eugen's checked suit. I have to get back into the suit to be able to explain the transformation.

Yesterday I was Eli. Today I am Erik. Doctor Manne is wrong. He doesn't know Erik. Two nurses take Erik under the arms and lift him over the floor, up the stairs and into the unit. 'Don't leave me,' Erik says to Eli's colleague. 'We'll keep Eli, so we can let you out,' the staff say. My colleague leaves, hiding her tears in her spring coat.

Erik kicks and tries to get free. Suddenly there are lots of people in the room. 'You have now been sectioned in accordance with the Mental Health Act,' Manne says. Erik is wrestled down onto the bed. His trousers are pulled down. He is given several involuntary injections.

After a few hours on the ward, Erik is still obsessed with getting Prince Eugen's suit from home. He stands by the main door, which is locked. He's shooed away several times. But then finally, when there is no one there watching, the door is opened from the outside. He slips out. He runs fast. They shout after him, but no one gives chase. He runs all the way home, and sits down on the bench outside the block of flats where Eli lives. He doesn't have the key. The sun is shining. He leans back on the bench. Where should he go? He can't get into the flat and how is he then going to get hold of the suit? The keys are locked up in the hospital with Eli's things. He has no money either. No bag. He sits in the sun for a long time. Who can help him to get in? The police?

He sets off towards the police station which is round the corner. The woman behind the window asks what he wants. 'My name is Erik and I need help to get into my flat.' 'You'll have to ask a locksmith.' 'But I don't have any money.' 'Take a seat then, and I'll speak to the boss. What did you say your name was?' 'Erik.' 'Nothing else?' 'No, nothing else.'

He sits in the waiting room and waits. After a while, he gets restless and wants to leave. He stands up, and notices how quickly the woman darts out from behind the window and locks the door. 'You're to wait here and talk to the boss,' she says. Behind a glass wall, the head of police is making a frantic phone call.

He stands up and comes out to shake hands. He's very friendly. He's wearing a uniform. Sits down next to Erik and says: 'I recognise you from the papers. You're an author. Your name is Eli. Not Erik.' 'No, I'm Erik. Eli's not here.' One of Erik's legs is shaking. The policeman starts to talk about an exhibition he's seen. Portraits of well-known people from the arts, by a famous painter. 'And you were there. It was a good picture. It wasn't a picture of Erik. It was Eli.'

Erik starts to feel uncertain. Thinks about Prince Eugen's suit and the orange checked tie. He should have had it now. The head of police starts to talk about other artists that Erik knows. Then he interrupts the conversation with small sentences like 'where is the key to the flat?' and without thinking, Erik has said 'in the hospital.' 'Which hospital is that?' 'Doesn't matter,' Erik replies. 'Where have you come from now? You've got no coat, key or bag.' Erik looks down. They were having such a nice time.

'Are you not going to tell me?' 'No, I want to get into the flat. Can you help me?' 'We're trying to help you as best we can, Eli.' 'Erik.' 'Sorry, Erik,' says the friendly policeman. 'I've read one of your books. You've definitely got your own style and language. Who writes them?' 'Eli,' says Erik. 'She's not here.' The policeman asks if he would like a cup of coffee. 'No, I want to go home to the flat and put on Prince Eugen's suit.'

The policeman goes and gets two cups of coffee. Erik heads towards the exit. 'We're closed,' the policeman says. The door is locked.

Erik doesn't ask what they are waiting for. But every now and then the policeman's soothing, friendly chat is broken when he goes in behind the glass wall to talk on the phone. Erik drinks his coffee and is shaking so badly that he spills some. The policeman finds new subjects to talk about all the time. Is he sitting beside me because he thinks it's nice or to pass the time? What are we waiting for? There's only the two of us here now, Erik thinks.

At that moment, two enormous policemen come in through

the door and grab hold of him. The head of police snaps at them and says that it's urgent, they closed an hour ago and have had to wait too long. The tone of his voice was completely different when we were speaking. It makes me uneasy. The policemen each hold one of Erik's arms. We aren't able to say goodbye properly.

The head of police who seemed so kind has called in these gorillas. They lift Erik up and carry him out of the police station. They carry him over the street, he's as light as a feather in their hands. They bundle him into a police car. Once he's sitting upright, he tries to open the back door, but can't. The car glides silently through the city. He asks them to drive to Eli's flat. They say yes, but they're lying. They stop in front of the hospital. Both policemen are standing ready by the door when Erik gets out. He's thought about making a break for it, but it's impossible to loosen their grip. They carry him into the unit, into the farthest room, where the door to the corridor is then locked. They don't let go. Stand there holding him. He tries to get free. The staff thank them.

Erik has been legally sectioned again. The police leave and Erik has to remain in the furthest room and is not even allowed out into the corridor. A nurse who is quite new calls me Erik. She's corrected by another nurse who says that she must not play along with my psychosis. 'Here on the ward, we call her Eli.' But not everyone does.

One of the nurses comes over to me the day after to say that the head of police has called. He wondered how both Eli and Erik were.

My body is too restless to be hospitalised. Ask if I can play ping-pong in the cellar or use the staff punchbag to do some boxing. Sometimes I'm allowed, sometimes not. It depends on who's working.

I think about when I was seventeen and had moved away from home to Hild's flat in central Oslo. A block of flats with a narrow asphalted courtyard. I had started to play bandy. Put on my training gear and went down into the courtyard with my bandy stick. I am Emil. I hit the ball against the wall. A movement from the hip that extends out into the arms. I can feel it so intensely, inside the oversized sports clothes. A cap pulled down over my forehead. I'm a boy. Ten, in fact, but tall for my age. Very strong and extremely sure of the ball.

I hit and hit. Swing the stick and hit the ball perfectly. I can feel it surging through my body. It fires me up. I can feel it in my arms, my back, my legs, my hips, my willy, boy, boy, boy. Go out onto the street and into a newsagent. Buy chewing gum, my eyes barely visible beneath the cap. The woman behind the counter thinks I'm a boy. I haven't tricked her. To think there's a gender stuffed into every body.

From my medical journal: *Pat became agitated yesterday evening. Smashed glasses in the dining room, said she wanted to cut herself. She later said that she was going to harm herself and smashed her head against the wall. The staff sat with her for a long time but it was eventually necessary to restrain her.*

From my medical journal: *During today's conversation she told me that Eli had not come yet. But that Eli was fine. It is Erik talking. She is bothered by a hole in her right temple. Erik, Prince Eugen, Emil and Espen and whoever is above and controls the voices is able to read her thoughts. She finds this very disturbing. Pat is incoherent, says that someone is watching her through the window. Gives long explanations of what Erik is saying and who decides etc... Pat declares openly that she will escape from the unit at the first opportunity. She does not want any inj as she believes that Eli has taken the medicine. Erik does not want her to take any medication and has not taken any himself. It's Erik who smokes hash and generally causes a disturbance. That is why she throws things around, has angry outbursts, etc.*

Pat is clearly experiencing hallucinations.

Pat physically restless throughout the conversation, drumming her legs, banging her head on the wall, sudden outbursts of laughter, etc...

I want to go home. I want to get out. I want to get out of Erik. Out into the air and heat that's coming. Summer that never penetrates into the unit. I want to go home to Eli who decides. Out of this body into my own. Explode my head. Break it into pieces and then put it back together again. Think boxing, but it's not boxing. Hit but don't hit. Don't forget to breathe. First purity, then speed. And finally resistance. If I knew better I'd give up. But I keep fighting. It's been decided for as long as I can remember.

I am Erik and forget my visitors as soon as they've left and nothing has happened. Being where the world isn't, is my world. Locked out of myself. Endless hours in bed or out in the corridor. Mealtimes. Half an hour outside in the yard every day with two nurses. Erik does karate kicks and shadow-boxes. Days that just pass. Spring turns to summer. Flower bouquets that wilt. Someone invisible has been here and left them.

The people who come tell me that they've come to visit before. That we talked about writing and that I told them about the new book. The past in the present. I only remember Lisen's husband's fortieth birthday when I danced. My strong self. The one that's done so well. I remember the head of police who seemed so nice but tricked me and got me back here. These events seem like only yesterday, but more than two months have passed with nothing to hang on to.

My case was heard in the county court and the judgment was three more months enforced care. I heard about it one day when my doctor, Manne, passed in the corridor. I had no idea what the county court was, no one told me what it entailed. It was a humiliating situation. I didn't have a chance, my lawyer met me five minutes before negotiations started. She couldn't help me. She knew nothing about me.

I don't want to take the medication, but they force me. Don't recognise myself in their descriptions of me. Think that everything exists simply to medicate me. As soon as the ruling for three more months enforced care is passed, they relax restrictions a little. I'm allowed to go out by myself as long as I

303

say where I'm going and when I'll be back.

Gradually, I manage to catch up with myself. Gradually, the cracks in my head heal. And then one day, Erik is no longer there. Clouds of everyday voices break through. I have sunk back into myself. It feels like a release. A new start. I have become number one. The one who decides. One day I will decide everything.

I've got a desk in my room. It's Eli who writes. I fly into the words. Words become sentences. Sentences become pictures. Pictures become meaning. The text feeds itself. It pulls at me. To be writing. A wordsmith, an observer, a liar. To sit in silence and wait. Get, taste, feel, enjoy, sing, be amazed. Wait for the thought behind the thought. Not have time to think it, just suddenly see it in front of me on the paper or the computer screen. It's gone directly via my fingers.

Tell me something, I whisper to myself. Entertain me, shock me. Teach me something. Writing is a hole in the illness. I run into my room and comfort-write. Eat my way through the paper. Everything else can wait. I feel my mouth salivating. I could have been anything that didn't require good sight. A masseuse, a spice merchant, a baker, a florist, a cook, a joiner, an inventor, a violinist. Or an ambassador. I'm free. I have chosen. I have become precisely what is best for me.

I write about imagined dreams. I write that I stretch my arm straight out from reality and fish for stories, and they come.

I've got a twenty-two-year-old room mate. We've become good friends. We lie and listen to my audio books in the evenings, books that Kassandra would never have opened. She likes it. Kassandra is slim and has dyed dark hair, dark eyes and cute lips. She changes her clothes and earrings all the time and has loads of comfy clothes. She sleeps a lot during the day, which worries me. I pass her bed on my way over to the window. I stop and look at Kassandra's sleeping face. She's so sweet lying there in her turquoise clothes with a turquoise headband and turquoise earrings. I touch her cheek. She can't be woken. But she shouldn't sleep her life away. I wish I could squeeze some courage into her body so she would do something.

The past weeks have been hard for Kassandra, as her little sister and several of her friends have passed their university entrance exams this spring. Kassandra hasn't even managed to finish lower secondary. And what do you wear when your arms are full of scars? She cuts herself, has done since she was twelve. There's hardly a patch on her arms where the skin isn't scarred. She has some loose, black sleeves which cover her arms, so she can wear vests and short sleeves.

Five years ago, she was run over by a bus and was in hospital for several months. There's a big dent in her bum. She shows me her padded knickers. 'You get treated better in an ordinary hospital than you do in psychiatric,' she says. 'More respect, like.'

We drink tea. Kassandra has her own store of tea bags and I want to try all the flavours. I like Chai and Yogi Tea best. Her bedside table is covered in perfume bottles and things. She is one of the few who tries to make things personal and homey. A towel over the bedside lamp to give a softer light. Her own big turquoise teacup. The hospital ones are too small. She has put a picture of her dog over some of the worst stains on the walls. It's so easy to talk to her. Bright, sad and funny. I've got a friend.

Discharged and at home again. The days are lonely. I'm scared of the windows in the flat. They are dark routes out into the world. Think that I'm going to be sucked out and suddenly it will all be over. What if I just… I found, I found something, I found a hole. A long longed-for peace. Nothing more of anything.

The windows tempt me with their mute freedom, their freedom of nothing. I sleep with my head too close to the window in the bedroom. It feels like the bed slopes towards what is dangerous. The big African sculpture stands there as protection. I can't move along walls with windows. The extra weight that is me might trigger a landslide.

I go and lie down on the hard linoleum floor of the kitchen as far away from the window as possible, right up in the corner. Have my pillows and duvet with me. My head on the floor near the sink. I stand up and turn on the tap. One of the boys is in the running water. It's Espen the Ash Lad. 'I found, I found something,' he says, and cries himself to sleep.

'We have to work on the basics,' Jonathan says. 'Sleep, rest, work, friends, travel. Use small details to create security. When you get home, turn on the lights. Music, radio, phone someone. Smells, flowers, food, tea. Exercise and cleaning. You have to stick to routines. Then you can make great leaps if you want. But first, you need to stand on solid ground. And you have at times. We have to get back there, and move forwards. You must always bear in mind how fragile you are. You have to give yourself an appropriate level of challenge. Not leaps and bounds every so often and then collapse in a heap. A film, a book, a play. A trip to Norway. It's not the whole world.'

'But that's what my everyday is like. I enjoy it and then lose myself in it. If I go to Norway, I have to see so many people that every minute is booked.'

'You have to book minutes for yourself as well.'

'I keep up appearances. Every time I come back I think how strange it is that I live in Sweden. It's almost like I don't have a home. All the good stuff that's happened, all the people, all the playing around with my nieces and nephews, it's as though it's all blown away.'

'Yes, how to carry the joy over the river,' Jonathan says.

'It's so strong sometimes. It lives in me, but I'm like a sieve. I look out from my flat up here and I think I live in space. That everything around me could be anywhere and that what's inside is coming loose.'

'That is precisely when you need to get back into your life as fast as possible. Because it's there,' Jonathan says.

'It's in my papers,' I say. 'But not in the real world.'

'With time it will be part of the real world as well,' he replies.

I go to my workspace in the hope that I'll be able to write. I sit there with my hands immobile on the keyboard. I stare at the painting on the opposite wall. The one I've stared at so many times before. It's a painting of my family. Those who are dead are also in it, Marit, Granddad and Dad. It's painted with broad brush strokes and heavy outlines, but everyone is recognisable. We dressed in nineteenth-century clothes. The picture is of Odd's christening. He's wearing a white christening gown. Marit, Mum and Hild have big hats on, Dad, Granddad, Torvald and I, the princess, are wearing sailor outfits. I've no doubt nagged my way into it in Dad's imagination. He was the one who did the painting.

In our midst sits an ape. Your eye automatically fixes on the ape. He's himself. Whoever he is. Because he's not dressed up. No bowties or tie. He's not fixed in time. He's staring straight at the painter's hand.

I talk to my little nephew on the phone. 'Hi,' I say. 'Hi, how are you? Was there something you wanted to say?' he asks. 'Like what?' I wonder. 'Like you miss me, for example.' 'Yes, that's what I wanted to say, I miss you every day.' I go there for Christmas.

I go up to the hospital to pick up some medicine when I get back. I've spent Christmas in Norway and been skiing. It's New Year and I tell myself that everything seems a little lighter. I love skiing and seeing the children. But I don't like the actual journey. Going home and coming back home. Home? Hold my mask. Hold my breath. Hold the voices at bay. Be myself and yet not at the same time. How do you carry the joy over? Breathe out, but not so much that everything crashes. The voices are on. They talk and I answer. But I'm so used to it. I will manage somehow all the same.

I ring the bell and am let in. I don't know then that I won't be let out again for six months. I talk a bit to the staff. I have to wait for my medicine. After a while, I'm told that I have to see a doctor. I don't need to see a doctor. Get frightened.

From my medical journal: *Am asked in my capacity as doctor on call to come to the unit to assess patient. When I get there patient is extremely restless, walking up and down the corridor, crying and talking without any prompts. Talking to herself, totally incomprehensible.*

Mental state: *Awake, aware of persons and situation. Unclear whether she is aware of time.*

Contact: *Reduced formal and emotional contact. Talks about herself in the third person.*

Signs of psychosis: *Informs of auditory hallucinations and claims that there is radiation coming from the walls, is frightened and displays anxiety.*

Mood: *Mood swings, crying and laughing without motivation. Talks simultaneously about several things and cannot finish a sentence before starting another.*

Assessment: *Known patient with schizophrenia, currently in an acute state of psychosis. Undersigned offers to have patient admitted and medicated, but she refuses, threatens to kick down the doors and smash the windows if I keep her here in the unit. Shadow-boxes and high kicks. Patient shows no reliable understanding of her illness, does not want to accept the offer of care, and the risk of suicide cannot be ruled out. Given the situation, I am of the view that patient is in absolute need of hospital care in order to receive adequate medication. Detention order filled out by the undersigned at 21.15 hours. Decision to section patient in accordance with the Mental Health Act taken by the undersigned at 21.15 hours. No changes have been made to patient's previous medication.*

To be sectioned in accordance with the Mental Health Act, the patient has to be assessed by two doctors. The following day, I see another doctor and this is my chance to be discharged. I don't understand why I've been detained. The new doctor is a woman I don't know either. I talk to Prince Eugen about making a good impression. But it makes no difference.

From my medical journal: *Patient is here and has been sectioned. Patient is deeply psychotic and anxious. Says that she is Prince Eugen, not Eli. Also claims that she has to go to work in an hour.*

Contact: *Poor formal contact, does answer questions, but listens to voices and answers them at the same time. Tells me that it's Prince Eugen who is talking to her. Sits crying and sobbing during our conversation.*

Signs of psychosis: *Obvious delusions, auditory hallucinations that confuse the patient all the time. Not able to assess her own situation.*

Mood: *Anxious, desperate and frightened. Dejected.*

Assessment: *Patient is in a state of acute psychosis and categorically needs to stay here in the unit, can't understand this herself. Claims that she has to go to work and that she has to leave. Fulfils criteria for being sectioned, §6b is therefore approved.*

The days that follow are total chaos. I'm given a notepad and try to work. I'm restrained twice. I've got bruises on my arms from the straps for a week afterwards. But nothing is mentioned in my journal.

I cry. Imagine if I was to lift the receiver and call home. Imagine if I was to make myself visible in the way I did as a child and they found out what was happening. The successful Eli.

Every day I had at least one crying fit. I was thirteen years old. It might last for an hour. I couldn't stop. The source was bottomless. The trigger could be something minor or nothing at all. I was inconsolable, pulled faces and cried hysterically. Mum didn't know what to do. She said that's just the way it is with Eli.

Jonathan and I don't normally talk about what has happened. We look forwards. But now I've read my medical journals again. The first time I read any of the journals, it didn't bother me at all. Didn't think that it had anything to do with me at all. Now they've caught up with me.

'How do you feel then?' Jonathan asks.

'It's an uncomfortable view from the outside that I don't want to be there in print. Someone who has seen me when I couldn't defend myself. Someone who doesn't know that I'm Eli. A visible and an invisible twin. The one who functions, gives talks, writes books, receives prizes, the friend, family member, the citizen. There's something good and healthy in there that's been broken. It makes me sad to read that I cried. I don't know why I cried. I can't remember. I must have been upset. There are days and weeks that I don't remember at all. It's hard to know that you're visible even then. It often says that I laugh without motivation, but that's a way of communicating with the voices. A sign that I feel cornered and uncertain. That the air has changed. That the unit is a stage set. "Walk, stand, sit, wait, eat." It's like an avalanche inside. Like when I go to the supermarket and people with voices and bodies get in the way everywhere. And I can't shop, have to leave empty-handed. The worst thing is meeting doctors you don't know. I think they see me as being more mad than I actually am. It's been better recently when someone from my support team has been there. I feel safer then. But all of a sudden I can feel insecure, even when they're there. Because it's not them who decides. It was worst the first time I was forced onto the floor by several people and restrained. It was terrifying.'

'Wouldn't it be liberating to be rid of all that anxiety?' Jonathan asks.

'Yes.' I don't say any more. How can I say yes?

'Some people experience it as a break in a process they can no longer control,' he says.

'Yes, I've wanted to smash everything around me including myself, until there's nothing left.'

'Maybe that's the only way then,' Jonathan says.

'Can't talk about it.'

'But you can try. Did they try to calm you down?'

'I mean, I don't want to talk about it now.'

'Then we won't. Perhaps it might never need happen again,' he says.

I don't believe that. I know that I've been unreachable. That I've been caught in movement without words. 'I have to deal with one day at a time,' I say.

'Yes, that's right. What are your plans now?'

It's night. The only sweet things in the unit are peppercakes. They've got great tins of them in the kitchen. I ask various staff if I can have some. How generous they are varies. I go back to my room and cram biscuit after biscuit into my mouth. Can't get enough. I get up again. More tea. Another evening smoke. More peppercakes.

Tonight, someone has put out a whole tin of peppercakes beside the crispbread and tea things in the dining room. I take seven times seven. Comfort food. Compulsive eating after my Zyprexa injection. A known side effect of Zyprexa is hunger. I'm going to eat until I've filled the hole in me that wants something, but I don't know what to fill it with.

We live only for a short while without catastrophe. I listen to an audio book of Greek myths. A singing head that floats on the water. I only hear snatches. Don't mix intelligence with pleasure. I take a peppercake and jam the whole thing into my mouth. Odysseus counts those he recognises, hesitates by one of them, Tiresias the prophet; he too had to go down to Hades in the end, having lived for nine generations as a man and a woman. Things like that impress me. My granddad used to say that we should live a little in each century, so we could understand time. We should live a little as each gender, so we could know what gender is, I think.

My ruminations about changing sex have never been taken seriously. Have I taken them seriously myself? I have tried so many different therapies, but it's never been resolved. I usually mention it when I'm confused. At the hospital, they say they would never discuss such a decision with me under any circumstances. 'You are too ill.' When I was little, I wanted to be like Torvald. I wanted to be treated like him and have the same demands made of me. I wanted to have his clothes and his toys. His placid nature. I don't want to be him any more. I just want to be at peace and not waver between genders. Or continue to waver, but do it with greater pride. When I hear about research into what women and men are good at or how they behave, I don't feel that I belong to either group. I think of myself as Eli. Eli with the boys.

I lie with all the peppercakes on my duvet. Take them one by one in my hand. Press them with the index finger of the other hand. The peppercake breaks. If it breaks in three, then I can make a wish.

You didn't believe it, Kiril, but I dreamt about you last night. You were so different. At least in appearance and movements, and you said nothing, and you didn't come towards me with your tail in the air and roll over onto your back, or recognise me and own me, like you used to. You were round as a ball, like a big fat owl. You had something brown on your chest. As though your fur had changed from soft and grey to a pepper prickly winter fur. No, it was like feathers. Brown feathers. And I barely recognised your little face. It was yours, but it was different in your fatness and roundness. And your beautiful green eyes were dark and mean. Looking warily from side to side.

But if you're Kiril, you're my responsibility and I love you, no matter what. I wondered what it would be like carrying this unfamiliar Kiril around. To have an unfamiliar Kiril at home with me. One that waddled instead of stretching, running and jumping. One that could perhaps even fly. But I thought, it'll be fine. You love the one you love for always.

I have to move all the time. Run in the corridor and get repri-manded. 'Sit down!' Laugh, and they say hush. I ask if I can go out. There aren't enough staff, so no one can come with me. I dump down onto a chair for a short while. A woman in a grey hoodie has been sitting in the same armchair beside me all day. She's put on twenty kilos in two years, a side effect of the medi-cine. She has a quiet, depressed voice. Hidden in her cheeks are two dimples that I would love to fill with laughter, but I can't today. When the night shift comes, we're suddenly allowed to go out on our own, even though it says 'only out with staff' in my papers. 'Don't walk so fast,' she says. I make an effort. I laugh. Been doing push-ups in the corridor all day. Am euphoric. On the way back, we go up the longest steps in Söder. 'Slow down,' the woman says. 'I don't think I can do it.' She takes one step at a time then stops. I jump manically up all the steps on both feet.

The weeks pass. I think that I'll be allowed to go home soon. I think that I'm much better. 'We've applied to the county court for your detention to be renewed. You can't deal with the medication yourself. We can't trust you to take your psychosis medicine as prescribed.' I lie in bed. Doctor Manne is standing in the room with Nurse Ingemar, who I like a lot. I shout: 'No. Not the county court again.'

I immediately think about what I can break in here. I throw myself forwards in the bed. 'It's no fun having to tell people things like this,' Ingemar says. 'One of the drawbacks of the job.' Manne has had to hurry off, but Ingemar stays sitting where he is. He tries to joke, but I'm not in the mood. I run out into the corridor and smash up a table. Kicking and punching until each leg is broken. 'A job in a demolition company might be the thing for you,' Ingemar says, holding me in a firm grip.

One sleep train after another pulls out. I don't manage to get on, I'm wide awake. Get some more sleeping pills. I've taken ten now. Outside it's dark and raining. It's been dark all day. If only it was snow. Why do I live in a cold place where there isn't even snow in winter? All this rain and chill. The first snow is the most beautiful. You find stories everywhere, mine are hidden deep in the snow.

I pull the white sheet over my head. Imagine that it's snow and pretend that I'm sleeping in a snow cave. I can't be in what's actually here. The unit, the corridor, the mealtimes. I have to dream, forwards and backwards in time. I dream back to the ski trips and nights in the snow of my youth. Marit, Hild, Torvald and I on countless trips in the mountains. Marit, who squints up at the mountainside and says that it's maybe best just to start digging. We put snow protectors over our ski boots and start to shovel. Build a cave as it should be, with a tunnel entrance and the room a little higher up, set in the snow. Then we get into our sleeping bags, fully dressed with our hats on, and lie as closely together as we can on our mats, in the home that we've made ourselves. If we've done it right, it can be minus twenty outside, and only minus one inside. We can see our breath when we say goodnight.

No doubt there's snow in the sky. Snow and sun and you can sleep deeply in there with an angel at the end of your bed. I lie with the sheet over my head in my own home-made cave in the psychiatric unit. There's even snow here. I can't be on my own in here in the cave. I find my wallet, take out a photo-booth picture of Marit. She's thirteen. With dark plaits and clear blue eyes. Lying there with her picture in my hand is like clutching onto something that's broken.

After a week, I get a notice.

The consultant at the clinic has in the attached application requested continued detention for you in accordance with the mental health act. You are therefore requested to attend the county court in person in connection with oral negotiations. Should you fail to show or respond, the case can still be decided.

Background: *Well-known forty-year-old woman with schizophrenia.*

Current status: *The patient is in a state of acute psychosis. Talks incomprehensibly, shakes and is very anxious. Claims there is radiation coming from the walls. Feels unsafe, cries and laughs without motivation. Does not want to stay in the unit, threatens to break the windows and doors. Behaviour confused, talks about herself in the third person. Not possible to assess the risk of suicide.*

Somatic: *Not examined. Will not cooperate.*

The day of the negotiations in the county court arrives. I feel nervous. If only you could touch nervousness. Cut it out of everything. Hold it and give it courage and warmth. I didn't want to have a lawyer this time, it's a waste of public money. They can't actually do anything and don't know you. I now intend to defend myself. Kristin offers to fly over from Oslo to be with me during the negotiations. But I can't find out when the case is being heard. Between 9 a.m. and 3 p.m., it says. Mad people have all the time in the world. Kristin can't manage to get to the nursery and still make a flight for nine, so we decide that she shouldn't come.

The county court comes to the hospital and uses a room there. There's a judge, three jurors, an expert psychiatrist, the senior doctor from the unit and a lawyer who comes all the same. I meet her outside and tell her she doesn't need to say anything. I've got my mental health worker, Elsa, and Sonja with me.

The doctor explains about my need for care. Then I am given the floor. I say that I am not a schizophrenic. That I am nearly healthy again. That my doctor, Manne, says that I'm suffering from a psychotic disorder. 'Why do you insist on calling me schizophrenic? I don't recognise myself in your descriptions of me. They were written by a doctor who doesn't know me.' I say that I don't need care. That I might take the medicine. But perhaps not the neuroleptic one, as I'm frightened that it might have a negative effect on my creativity. I need my creativity in order to survive. I have to write.

The expert psychiatrist asks me some questions and I answer as best I can. But I can't express myself. Their questions break my sentences in two. I say that it's all like a dream. The expert says that she understands that it all seems like a dream. She asks some more questions and I answer in order to save myself. The picture of me, but most of all, my picture of myself inside. All this isn't true. The judge asks Sonja to give her opinion. She thinks that I need all the care I can get. She and Kristin have swapped roles after many years. Kristin thinks that as long as I can write, I have no need to be in a secure unit.

Then there is a pause in the proceedings. The jurors and judge are going to talk. We others have to leave the room. When we're called back in, the doctor doesn't come with us. He has other things to do and can't be bothered to wait for the outcome. He's sure of his case, and he's right. He's won. I am to be detained for a further four months.

The County Court has today held oral negotiations behind closed doors. During the negotiations, the consultant upheld his application for the continued detention of Eli Larsen. The County Court finds that Eli Larsen suffers from a serious psychiatric disorder. In addition, the County Court finds that she, as a result of her psychiatric disorder and personal circumstances otherwise, has indisputable need for continued care. As a result of Eli Larsen's mental condition, there is reason to believe that this care cannot be given with her agreement. The conditions for being sectioned in accordance with the Mental Health Act are thus fulfilled and the consultant's application is therefore granted.

I am taken back to the unit. Go into the dining room. No one there. Stand in front of the trolley with tea and coffee and biscuits. Think about the scalding water on my hand when I was a child. I dropped the glass without deciding to. It was a reflex. Only Granny can punish me. I take the thermos of boiling hot tea water and pour it over my head. It burns my scalp. Runs down my face and neck, down my back. The pain wakes me up. Only I can punish myself.

Lisen comes to visit me regularly. She suggests that we should write a children's book together. Can I? I feel blank. I can with a bit of help. I can. We've found a new way of spending time together. We write. I haven't written for children since I was a child myself. Lisen sits at the computer. I make things up. Lisen makes things up. I make things up. A hole in the cloud of psychosis. Deep in the world of stories, my thoughts are clear. I am creative and calm.

I find great cracks in all the sickness. The unmotivated laughter and outbursts of anger are in the dim distance. I can concentrate for an hour and then take a break and then another hour. A year ago, I was so medicated that I could only talk about what I had already written. It was impossible to create anything new. Now things are getting better and better. We discuss things. Is it wrong to manipulate a child's voice from the wings? How to enter a child's body? Give it feelings and thoughts without creating a divide between what is told and the experience of the protagonist. Should it be in the first person, which is so often used in children's and young adult fiction? We choose the third person. How to avoid making the adult the norm and the child the deviant? I'm a deviant. Can we use that in some way? Lisen refers to her own children. I feel a little jealous. Counter it by talking about my nieces and nephews.

On her way here, Lisen has seen a big painted oak, with eyes and a mouth and a broken branch as a nose. Is that an image we can use as a starting point? We dig around. Both of us carry images from our childhood eyes. We sit in the dining room. Are frequently interrupted, many are curious about what we're up to. 'We're writing a children's book,' we say proudly. Little do we know that it will in fact be the start of a whole series.

I've got a knife with me in my handbag. A sharp knife with a nice sheath. I've got it with me to defend myself. I'm on release from the unit and at home in my flat. I know that there are spy cameras hidden in the walls. I know that they're listening. There's radiation coming from the walls. It's electricity that's being sent to watch me, control my steps. Observe my movements.

I hide in my bed. They're listening to my thoughts and sending them home to Mum in Norway. Everyone can hear what I'm thinking. I listen to the same song over and over again on my earphones. It creates a wave from one ear to the other inside my head. But it doesn't help.

I ring the police and tell them that I am Prince Eugen and that I know that they're after him. The voice on the telephone knows nothing about it. She plays the innocent, asks for Prince Eugen's ID number. 'I don't know it,' I reply. She asks what he's done. 'Prince Eugen had Erik hit Eli. Made her bang her head against the wall. Got her to punch her own head with her fists.' 'Who are you?' the voice asks. 'Eli's not here. She's not allowed to come out.' 'Who are you then?' 'I am Prince Eugen,' I say in a woman's voice, which confuses the woman on the other end even more. 'Where do you live?' Prince Eugen tells her where I live, even knows my flat number. 'Do you belong to a mental health unit?' 'No,' he lies. 'You have to come and take away the spying equipment.' 'We'll see what we can do.'

When he puts down the receiver he regrets having called. Why did I do that? They're going to trick me. He checks in my bag for the knife. It's where it should be. He feels safer once he's

329

done that. After three quarters of an hour, there's a ring at the door. Should I open? What if it's a child selling raffle tickets? It isn't. The sun from the window on the stairwell assails him. The dust vibrates in the air. It's two policemen. They ask politely if they can come in. 'Okay. What do you want?' 'To see how you are.'

They stomp into the flat, a man and a woman. They're so big and have so much paraphernalia. 'How are you?' 'Good.' 'Can we sit down?' They're already in my kitchen. 'Why are you watching me?' 'Are we watching you?' 'Yes.' 'What do you think might be the reason?' 'I don't know.' 'Nor do we.' 'The cameras are there in the corner.' 'There are no cameras in the corner. Do you know what, Eli?' 'She's not here.' 'We think that you're Eli, and we're going to let you in on a secret. We don't have time to watch you. We've got other things to do. So now you know.'

I go and lie down. Fall asleep. Dream that we're a team doing a brain operation on a patient. We've got green scrubs on and mouth masks pulled up over our faces. There's something wrong with the patient's flow of thoughts. It's unstoppable. There's lots of chit-chat amongst the doctors and nurses. We try to laugh off the tension. We don't have much time. We talk about property prices. About the best buys on the market. About who has maids and who has cleaners. That we have to be finished in time to pick up our kids from nursery. I make sure that everyone is doing what they should. Give orders.

Then suddenly we all pull down our masks. There is absolute silence. Everyone was so confident to begin with but now starts to doubt what they have to do. It's as if none of us have done this before. As if we actually work in a bank and have suddenly been asked to perform this operation.

Am I the one who has to cut? Am I the one who's responsible? How do you do that again? The scalpels lie there clean and sterilised on a tray. The equipment flashes as it should. The gravity in the room is tangible. No one wants to start. All at once, I'm scared. It's me who's the patient.

It's a normal morning in the unit. Nothing going on. There are no workshops here like there were in the last hospital. No one crying, no one screaming. We sit in armchairs in the corridor. Get ourselves a coffee. Take a few sips. Put the cup down. Get a new one, and put the cup down. Talk to some of the nurses. The hours creep by. It'll soon be time for lunch. And then supper and more coffee. Then an evening snack and soon my four months are over.

I'm repaired, then fall apart. The same patients are admitted here all the time. I've got friends here. Kassandra is back, seeing her again is both sad and a joy. We sit in the corridor and play cards. She's the unit's uncrowned queen of Chicago. I show her my latest find. A turquoise hoodie with a pattern in silver and black, and a hood that reaches down to my bum. She asks if I've become a raver. 'I'm just Eli,' I reply. Think that I might give the hoodie to her. But then she says that she's now out of her turquoise psychosis. It quite simply got too much.

Nearly everyone is gathered out in the corridor. Staff and patients. Then we hear some strange noises from the ceiling. We all look up. As if something was creeping around up there. It must be a rat. A rat creeping back and forth. A huge rat. Finally something is happening, these uniform days with screams and tears, coffee and food. Card games and jigsaw puzzles. Angst, depression and mania. Psychotic rants about punishing devils and gods that it's impossible to understand or that you've finally understood. A rat in the ceiling is something we can agree on and maybe have even longed for.

We move down the corridor like a herd. We creep behind the sound in a flock. What can it be? Then a light comes crashing down from the ceiling. And shortly after a whole ceiling tile. Fortunately no one gets it on the head. No one says a word, and then suddenly, a person comes tumbling down. It's Daniel, a young psychotic lad. He lies there on his back on the floor without moving. The staff hurry off to get the restraining bed, but then leave him lying on the floor. He tells us that he got up into the ceiling from the toilet. What an inventive way to try to escape. And it's good to see that the staff let him lie there. He's not restrained, but is instead drugged and put on his own bed. He wakes up for supper. Sits beside me at the table. It's fried herring. 'This is the best breakfast I've had in a long time,' he says.

It's March and there's only a thin layer of snow that barely covers the ground. I'm going to have my portrait taken for a newspaper. I'm not allowed out without an escort, and Ingemar, my mental health worker and nurse, offers to come with me to my flat, where I'm going to meet the photographer. She turns up twenty minutes late, a dauntless young woman. She has an enormous bag and pulls out all her photographic equipment and then produces a large axe. 'I thought you could hold this.' Ingemar looks sceptically at the axe. Patients from psychiatric units are of course not allowed to have knives or axes or any other dangerous paraphernalia. Who should we pretend he is? My boyfriend perhaps.

The photographer has no idea that she's dealing with a psychotic patient who has been sectioned. I'm allowed to stand in various poses holding the axe. The photographer is not satisfied. She wants to go out into the park on the other side of the road. There has to be trees in the picture. What is Ingemar going to do now? He has to come with me.

The three of us go out. I stand up straight and hold the axe limply as though I had never held an axe before. I smile. Think about Mona Lisa's androgynous smile. Was it ordered or real? You can see lies in people's faces, the lines round the eyes. A computer program can erase it. But not well enough to prevent around 20 per cent of all people who tell the truth from being branded as liars.

Ingemar stands just outside the photo frame and stares. It's a very good picture.

*

A man goes berserk in the unit. He's naked. The corridor is full of patients and they all witness a particularly brutal act of restraint. The atmosphere is fearful and uneasy. The following day, the new boss decides that we're going to have a big meeting after breakfast and talk about what's happened. The young psychotic girl who talks to herself about heaven and hell is sitting at the front, and she repeats pensively: 'Are men gods or children?' Does she have any idea why she's sitting here?

Maybe twenty patients are gathered together in the dining room. The boss talks about the commotion the day before and wonders if anyone has any questions. There are a few. Then one by one, the patients start to talk about their own experiences of being restrained. That they use more modern restraint methods at the main hospital. Ones that allow you to move when you need to get up for a pee. The whole thing takes off. People talk at the same time. Yesterday's incident is forgotten, but there are other incidents which are not.

One of the manic girls gets up and starts to mix English and Swedish. All the swear words she knows cascade out of her mouth: 'You motherfucker. You asshole. Go to hell.' She gesticulates. 'We're at the bottom. I'm homeless, you bitch.' It's hard to understand what it is she wants to say, and there are others who always want to say something. Someone shouts: 'Where is Olof Palme?' The boss doesn't manage to keep control of who's speaking next or to answer any questions. He's rendered speechless.

Only the deeply psychotic girl is silent. Her eyes are downcast and she appears not to notice the pandemonium. The boss tries to close the meeting. He says that everyone can come to him individually to discuss their issues. I think to myself that it's probably the first and last time that the new head will arrange an open meeting with patients in a psychiatric unit. A sentence crosses my mind. In English. Is this my people? Yes, sometimes.

My body is crawling. Shaking. Especially in my right leg and my mouth. Stiff jaws that crack against each other. I'm sitting in the dining room, have just made two sandwiches. Can't get anything down. Have liked food less and less recently.

The day shift come round and say good morning. An old man in hospital clothes is sitting beside me. He has been here for a while. But not as long as me. I'm now in my sixth month. I am no longer sectioned. I'm free. I'm now here voluntarily and will be leaving soon. Home to my dangerous flat with windows that you can fall or throw yourself out of. Will I take my own life, I wonder. Take a bite and the food just swells in my mouth.

'Butter is the best thing of all,' says the elderly gentleman beside me. 'This is as close to the Scandic hotels as you can get, and butter is the best of all foods. Superior to all else. You could survive on only butter. Butter and blueberries are good for your eyes, my grandmother always used to say. It's... I think it's vitamin K.'

There's a peaceful atmosphere in the dining room. The sun shines gently in through the window. The old man seems so content. Then another old man suddenly stands up. It's his room-mate. He doesn't speak Swedish. He comes over to the old man who was just now so happy with the butter and the food, and slaps him across the face. The nurse opposite looks down into her cornflakes and says nothing. The nurse at the next table quickly gets up and shouts at the man who can't speak Swedish. 'Leg egg!' The dining room falls silent. Leg egg and then

336

nothing more. Everyone understands. The man who lashed out goes back to his place and the nurse who shouted puts her arm round the man who was slapped.

'I'll get some dental floss and strangle you,' says my room-mate in her sleep.

It's the afternoon. Sweet Kassandra, I think. Are you sleeping again? We've removed the screens between our beds, try to make things nice. She's been living in supported accommodation for just over a year, but can't cope any longer. She doesn't want to go back to the loneliness. 'You were talking in your sleep,' I say, and tell her what she said. She laughs. 'I have to save myself,' she says. 'Exactly what I've thought so many times,' I say. She lies down again and falls asleep. How can she sleep so much?

I write a little. What can I do for Kassandra? I don't think that about all the patients here, but I want Kassandra to be happy. I worry about the fact that she never does anything. I reflect that Kassandra never says that she's good at anything. She often starts sentences with: can't, don't dare, don't know. I wish I could give her a little of my self-belief. I write a few sentences, but don't get any further. There's no point in pushing it.

I fall asleep myself and am woken by Kassandra crying. 'Everything's so hopeless,' she sniffs. 'I want to die.' 'Is there nothing you'd like to do in life?' I ask. 'Study, some sort of hobby? Travel? I know that you don't dare, but just a small trip. Whatever. Meet someone.' 'Cut myself,' Kassandra says. 'Not that,' I say. She cut herself a few days ago.

'I've cut myself with everything,' she says, and pulls the duvet over her head. Then she pops up again. 'Once when we were on Gotland, and me and my sister were sitting on the beach waiting for our parents to collect us, I got so desperate. I just wanted to cut myself. I thought of using a pine cone. You might laugh about it now, but it's pretty pathetic. You feel so ashamed when you're sitting there at A&E and need to get stitches for something you've done to yourself. If no one notices, I just put a plaster on,' she says and disappears under the duvet again.

'Kassandra, think for a moment.' 'Die,' she replies and starts crying again. 'In life, I said. Is there nothing in life that you want to do?' The crying continues for some time, but then she squeaks: 'I want to shop.' I dig her out from under the duvet and give her a hug.

339

For six months I've been forced to say where I'm going and when I'll be back. Sometimes I've been allowed to go out on my own, other times not. Friends have come and collected me and dropped me off again after my boxing sessions. I've been allowed to go to my therapist Janus alone, but have to promise to come straight back. No spontaneous trips to town and shopping sprees with Prince Eugen or just wandering around by myself.

Now everything is open. I have the key to my own door. Can close it and open it as I choose. There's no structure. No times. No questions. How do you find that feeling of self again after having been sectioned? What do you do with the freedom? It's easy to feel frightened and insecure. You have to create a new foundation. New walls. A new ceiling. A room that doesn't slope.

I lie in bed and imagine that I'm sawing. I can feel it in my arm. It's a blunt saw. I imagine that I'm sawing alternately through a thick branch and through my leg. I feel nothing in my leg. Close my eyes and switch from the leg to the branch, and from the branch to the leg. See that I'm cutting through the skin and veins, sinews and nerves, and then into the thigh bone. I go back to the branch. Nearly halfway. But then the image switches to the bone in my leg again.

I put everything I've got into it. Why don't I feel anything? The blood is pouring out and hiding all the details. I have to stop, I think. I don't want the saw to damage my leg. Don't want to jump out of the window. The images keep coming. In my mind I pull open the window in the bedroom and throw myself out. Feel in my arm that I'm sawing properly. I must be finished with this branch soon. But it's not the branch. The image is of my leg again.

I've nearly sawed all the way through now and am sweaty, and wet with blood. I have to stop, I think. The picture doesn't disappear. It gets stuck in my head. What if I'm doing it? What if I jump?

'Who do you want to be now? My eyes are with you all the time, even if I'm not there. Like the eyes on an aeroplane,' Espen says. 'And now and now. Who do you want to be? I'll close your tear ducts and you can be who you want to be. I'll hide it on the shelves and in cupboards, in your files of writing ideas under the bed. In the pockets of newly bought clothes. Who do you want to be? Now and now. A girl with a mask for a face.'

We've had a meeting with my mental health team and my friends. How can we help Eli to live at home after six months in the unit? The social worker can offer support in the home for one hour twice a week. Lolo thinks she can stay over every Tuesday night. I'll have daily contact with my mental health workers. My previous doctor, for whom I did a headstand on his desk to show that I was balanced, suggests that I could live with a family who are interested in culture. Lisen is tasked with finding out more. This proves to be impossible, so I'm back to square one again, on my own in the flat with the boys' voices. My old doctor also suggests cognitive therapy, that I should swap Janus for Jonathan. I'm sceptical about pretty much everything. Move and change therapist, that sounds like too many big changes. I want everything to sort itself out naturally. It doesn't.

I've been going to psychodynamic Janus for four years now. Going to stop soon, but can't really deal with the separation. Don't dare to let go. So right now I'm doubling up. One day a week with Janus and one day a week with Jonathan. I tell Janus that I'm going to cut up the two women's voices in my right ear. That's why I've got a knife in my bag. I normally use it at the workspace to make kindling for the wood burner. Now it's in my bag. I take it out and show it to him, take it out of its sheath and feel the edge. It's sharp. The intensity of the knife. Janus asks me to put it back. I weigh it in my hand. It's almost alive. 'Put it back.' I slip it back into its sheath and put it back in my bag. Janus phones the unit and asks to talk to Elsa, my mental health worker. He asks her to come and get me. 'Eli isn't well.'

Elsa knows that I have a knife in my bag and says that she doesn't want to be with me when I have a knife. 'Come with me to the unit and get an injection, but without the knife.' Janus says that he can keep the knife for me. Reluctantly I hand it over, feel naked and defenceless without it. He puts it in his desk drawer. And I'll think about it time and again, that it's lying there.

Elsa and I take the bus and the metro across town. The women's voices aren't there. I don't want to go to the unit. But don't want to go anywhere else either. I walk beside Elsa and let her decide.

Elsa is pensive and looks worried at times. But she always has a little laughter hidden in the corners of her mouth. She's an artist at heart. I think she understands what I do. That I'm a writer. She's straightforward and puts me in my place if she thinks I've done something wrong or am not doing what we agreed.

Suddenly I feel frightened. We're crossing a zebra crossing when Elsa grabs me. We stop in the middle of the road and let a car pass. The fear generated by this sudden contact stays with me. I try to listen to what Elsa is saying: 'Sorry, it's over now.' It's not over. I'm frightened all the time. Frightened with all my body. Frightened that it will happen again. That what might happen again? I don't know. That terrifying thing. Don't remember, but can't forget.

Lying in bed. The flat isn't a safe place. I get up and approach the window. The thought races through me, that I do it, but still manage. I jump six storeys down. But there's a piece of material in the air that catches me. It rocks with less and less movement. Until I am lying perfectly still facing the sky. I listen to my body. Go through each body part and am just there. Just like Jonathan has taught me. All the parts are whole. I'm floating higher up than I would dare. They need a crane to get me down.

Every time I get off the metro on the way to my therapist, Janus, on the good side of town, the same man is sitting there begging. He's made his own little space with blankets, cushions and cardboard boxes, and a tin for money. I normally give him some change. He nods in thanks and I hurry on. I often think that one day it will be Janus who's sitting there. In his clean clothes, with his bad back. Maybe I wouldn't just give him change, but notes instead. Or what if one day, instead of going to Janus, I sat down beside the beggar and poured out my heart. He probably can't afford to be sad.

One day the beggar isn't there. His things are still there. Beside the money tin, there's a note written in big letters: Back soon. Who's missing him? He's his own master. No one will know where he's gone.

It's summer again. Lolo and I are at the cottage. My brother's daughter comes to visit, as she has done every year. She's eight now. She's going to stay with us for a week. As she has done every year since she was four. Last year she was little. A playground was all she needed. A swing, a climbing frame. She could sit in the sand with a bucket and spade and build a castle, as she had done every year before. Or be totally thrilled to ride on a camel in the interval at the circus. Or try to lie as still as she could in the mornings so as not to wake me, as she did when she was little, but eventually sighed and said: 'Sleeping makes me so tired.'

This year she's all ages. Sometimes she's three and cries and whines when she gets frustrated. Sometimes grown up. She stands there clutching a toy rabbit from a jumble sale, and suddenly asks: 'How are you coping with the financial crisis?' 'I haven't noticed anything,' I reply. 'I've got such a special job.' 'Lucky you aren't an architect. They're having a difficult time,' she says gravely, and gives her rabbit a squeeze. 'So are some people in industry,' I say. 'And young people.' 'But not you,' she said, relieved. 'Then I can have another ice cream, can't I?' We've agreed on only one ice cream a day, but I break the rule.

She's been allowed to run riot with my wardrobe. Her favourite is a black and purple leopard-skin patterned hoodie with a hood that reaches down to her bum. She looks like she's taking part in a medieval role-play. But she makes hip-hop moves with her arms and wants to dance to loud music. She desperately wants to have the same hoodie.

Her mum has said that we can go to H&M and buy a summer dress. When we get into town, we go to my special expensive shop instead and buy her a hoodie. We also buy a cool T-shirt with neon print. I buy something too. A black sweater with long yellow fur down the arms. I look like something out of the *Muppet Show*. And some vests and a pair of trousers. I've got a wardrobe full. When we get out, she says: 'Eli, shouldn't you be saving for a flat rather than buying so many clothes?' Well, that's me told. I think *ferme la bouche*, you little *besserwisser*. You're my baby, and we're going to play together for many years to come.

When I watch her throw all her clothes onto the sand and run naked out into the water with a whoop, I am suddenly struck by the realisation that I don't want her to grow up.

I have to go into the hospital every third week for my depot injection and prescriptions. I'm doing some film work, Harald and I are going to finish cutting the film about Kiril. We've taken the equipment with us out to the cottage. I feel less stiff than I did last summer. Think, as I have done so many times before, that I'm better now. Feel strong. Sleeping well, running and have got lots of energy and enthusiasm for work. I go into town, have lunch with my care coordinator, Olof, as planned. Then I go to get my injection.

Erik doesn't want to. I tell the nurse, but am persuaded. Then she says that I have to sit down and wait. 'You need to talk to the doctor,' she says. I say that I have to get back to the country as I've got work to do. She persuades me to wait. As it's summer, there are only locums on duty. The doctor is young. He sends for another doctor that I've met before. They say that I have to stay in the unit. I say that I'm fine and that I have to go back out to the cottage to finish the film cut.

When I realise that they're serious, I get frightened. I start to shake. Can they keep me there? They can keep me there. My fear escalates. I have to get rid of the voices by boxing myself in the ear. I try to keep them under control. But now I feel pushed into a corner.

I refuse to go upstairs to the unit. 'Talk to Olof,' I say. 'We've just had a lovely lunch together.' I'm not ill. I feel completely clear-headed. 'We'll call the police if you don't come with us voluntarily,' the doctor says. I don't get up. Then two muscular summer temps arrive. They carry me down the corridor to the stairs then up into the unit.

I am absolutely desperate to get out and back to the cottage. They claim that I didn't have my injection, but I did in the end. I pull down my trousers and show them the plaster on my butt. Olof comes up to unit and tries to talk to the doctors. Says that he knows me. But they persist. I sit on the floor in the corridor and a kind nurse keeps me company.

Then I start to get twitchy. I want to leave. I'm like a fish in a net. The more I twist and turn to free myself, the more entangled I become. I know that, but I can't help it. They call the doctor on duty, the night staff have arrived. We go into the TV room to talk. I don't want to talk. The boys shout at me that I have to escape. But I'm sitting right at the back of the small interview room. 'Float like a butterfly, sting like a bee.' I'm up quick as a flash. Step up and over the table in my dash to escape. The duty doctor shouts at me to come back. I don't obey. I don't obey anyone.

This is all wrong. I, who am so obedient. 'Sit down,' they shout behind me. Run, I think. I realise that I'll get more injections. I don't want any injections. The nurses leap to their feet and catch me and hold me down until more come.

I've got my room at the end of the corridor. Number thirteen, the one I've had so many times before and shared with Kassandra. She's not here. As I'm carried past the staring patients, one of the nurses says: 'Take your injections and behave like a normal person. You're sick in the head. Sick in the head, do you hear?' I'm wrestled down onto the bed. The sister comes. I count four syringes, plus the one I got earlier in the day. I'm not going to wake up to a lovely day.

From my medical journal: *Undersigned called to unit where I am told that pat is troubled, banging her head against the wall.*

Undersigned tries to talk to pat who tells that the voices don't want her to take the medicine. She doesn't want to take it, jumps up onto the table and walks away. Bangs her head on the wall. Reason for prescribing enforced medication is that pat refuses all suggested help. After consultation with duty staff, the undersigned administered:

    Inj. Cisordinol Acutard 50 mg/ml, 2 ml i.m

    Inj. Cisordinol aqueous solution 10 mg/ml, 1 ml i.m

    Inj. Akineton 5 mg/ml, 1 ml/m

    As well as Stesolid Novum 5 mg/ml, 2 ml i.m

The next morning, I call Lolo and tell her that they've kept me in for no reason. My speech is slurred. My mouth can't keep up. My neck is stiff. Lolo gets angry and wonders why they've done it. 'I'm going to report them,' she says. 'Say hello to Harald and say I'll be there as soon as I can,' I tell her. 'I have to sleep now.'

I'm woken by the locum doctor in the afternoon. He says that the side effects from the medication are so serious that he can't discharge me. He'll come back again tomorrow. I can't talk properly. My whole body is stiff. This is what they've done to me.

Mental state: *Alert. Good formal contact if very tired. Emotionally present. Hallucinatory behaviour, not suicidal. Pat is so heavily medicated that she would be a danger to herself without care. Unmotivated laughter as previously seen when I have met pat in unit. Thinks she has been sectioned. Acute polymorph psychosis with symptoms of schizophrenia (F231).*

Two days later, I leave. I am still heavily medicated and Lolo and Harald are furious when they see me. 'You were fine when you left us, now you're a complete mess!' The side effects last for a whole week. My body feels stiff and alien. My mouth twisted. I sit at the kitchen table and unfold finger after finger as if I were ninety years old. Once again, I'm passive. My mouth doesn't do what I want it to, but I've got nothing to say anyway. 'You, who's always got something to tell, come back,' Lolo says. She, Harald and Tim have written a complaint the head of the hospital, but

I'm not allowed to read it. They get a swift and apologetic reply. But the big boss doesn't know how long it takes to recover from that kind of shock medication. First the physical effects. Then the psychological. Now I have to start from the beginning again.

I get a letter in the post. The handwriting is shaky. Written by an eighty-five-year-old woman:

I dreamt about a lot of unconnected words last night. As much as I tried, I didn't know what to do with them. Then an author came. Who elegantly picked up word after word and made the most wonderful sentences. They shone and sparkled and gave me thoughts I had never had before. Pictures to be looked at from every angle. With this delightful dream, I slept on into my eighty-sixth year.

When I woke up it was my birthday. My husband was standing by my bed holding a tray with flowers, a candle, coffee, toast and a beautifully wrapped present. It was your latest book. I've now read it and it was just like my dream. You make magic with words. I found the sentences I dreamt about in your book. They shone and sparkled. Thank you for the thoughts I've been given. Just wanted to let you know. Live well.

'The reality of the world is created by us. Everyone who wants to be real must be unbound,' says Prince Eugen. Emil and Espen have no idea what he means. Erik pretends to understand. I don't know what to do other than write it down. That's my freedom.

Love is a passion for words. A love that is not threatened, bound or unbound. I am never alone, I just need to make the most of it. It's the little boys on the tip of my tongue. A distortion of language. Words on paper make sentences that give meaning.

Emptiness is unfree. Freedom is pain and joy. Dig, give and live. The drawn bow of illness. I am an arrow, not a lunatic.

The only difference between me and a mad person is that I'm not mad.

I give a talk at a secondary school. Giving talks is one of the things I love best. Standing on the stage, reading and talking about my writing, sharing serious moments and humorous moments with the audience. I am a storyteller. I tell with my whole body and don't use a manuscript. I've written down key words at home and practised with them.

I've got so much experience now that I can take the talk in different directions depending on the atmosphere in the room and what comes into my head. Should I tell them this story or that one, use that example or this one? It's such a great feeling to be caught in a kind of safe uncertainty. I have an agreement with the boys that they won't disturb me. They will get my full attention both before and after if they just keep quiet during the talk itself. On this particular day, they don't do as we've agreed.

When I'm in the middle of reading a text about a dyslexic boy, they all start talking. I can't hear myself. I try to keep the thread, but don't manage and have to stop. Say that I'm not feeling well. This has never happened before in twenty years. I've travelled the length and breadth of the country. I go to the unit. Not empty and not happy.

In the evening, I sit in the corridor and chat to a Finnish nurse who's on the night shift. He's a typical macho man, but today he's unusually gentle and kind. A guy comes towards us down the corridor. He's got a spark in his eyes. He greets me. He often goes to church and talks about the support he gets from the congregation. He sometimes even helps them by selling second-hand clothes. He hesitates a moment and looks like he's about to sit down. Is he envious of our heart-to-heart? 'You…' he says to the nurse. 'You… I'm going to get you.' Then suddenly he punches him in the middle of the face. The blood starts pouring. The nurse puts his hand to his nose and throws himself to the side where I'm sitting. We're both spattered in blood. I instinctively try to protect my bag and MP3 player.

It looks like the nurse's nose is broken. The staff come rushing, the young man shouts: 'I'll be restrained voluntarily.' They wrestle him to the floor, get the restraining bed and strap him in. The bed stays out in the corridor with some screens around it. The nurse stands up and drips blood all the way down the corridor. He goes to A&E. The nurses wipe the floor and try to keep the patients away from the corridor. Ask them to go back to their rooms so they don't witness the chaos of the man being restrained. I sit covered in blood on the sofa, feeling shaken. Am given some toilet roll and rub my bag vigorously. The stains won't budge.

Was it chance that made him hit the nurse and not me? I don't think so. I'm up all night and ask the staff on the night shift how the nurse is. I'm not told anything. The day after, the guy who hit the nurse is taken away by the police and sent to a forensic psychiatrist. I don't see him for several years. And then he is fat and puffy from all the medication. He looks downcast. 'It was too hard in the state hospital,' he says. 'But now I'm out and have started going to church again.'

Olof and I go to a course about hearing voices. There are five other women there with their care coordinators. I've never talked to others before about what it's like hearing voices. On the first day, we have to write answers to lots of questions, including when the voices first appeared. No one has asked me about this before. And I haven't thought about it myself.

I think and Olof writes. We even have to write down our medical history. It's hard. It's the kind of thing you'd rather forget. I sit with Olof all day and recall things that I've never had to formulate before. The next day, the course leaders have written up a summary of our answers. They read them out to us and they have become stories.

I find it very difficult to listen to the others' stories. It hurts too much. Then my mobile phone rings and my publisher tells me that I've been nominated for the August Prize, the most prestigious literary prize in Sweden. The worlds collide. I finish the call and listen to a woman's story about how the voices came to her when she was forced to flee from Iraq. The joy of my nomination remains outside, while the others' stories bore their way in. A sweet girl tells us how the voices popped up when she was being sexually harassed at work. None of them have jobs. They go in and out of hospital. One woman says that she often hears voices when she turns on the taps. I recognised that one. It's Espen.

I am so moved that I can't stay in the room, and have to rush out. It's cold comfort to hear how hard it's been for them. Is there any future for their dreams of a job and education? I drink some water, pull myself together and go back in. Then my phone rings again. I've also been nominated for the equivalent prize in Norway. It feels completely absurd. My books live a life outside of me, and touch people far away from me and far away from my illness.

There are two lectures the next day. It seems to me that they mainly talk about the fact that they're not going to talk for long, so there's time for coffee breaks. What does that say about us? It's all wrong. Even mad people need input and quality, not all that rubbish about us resting all the time. When the course is over we get a couple of papers that the course leaders have written based on what we've told. 'Events in your life that may be the cause of your voice.' That is when the idea of writing a book about the voices starts to germinate.

Don't know if I learnt anything. If the voices will fade out. But one day I'm going to write a book about it all. If I dare.

I'm sitting on the train north. Met Jonathan in the morning and had a good start to the day. I'm going to give a talk. I'm met at the station by the organiser, an elderly man who explains that the promised meal at a restaurant will now be at his home instead. So I can meet his wife. She is very fond of Norwegians.

What organisers seldom think of is that you need some peace and quiet to prepare for a reading, and they often organise something social instead. I sit in his home and look at the photographs of Lofoten in the midnight sun. Then we go to the venue where I'm going to give the talk. There are already a lot of people by the cake stall, mainly older people. 'Looks like it's going to be full tonight,' he says happily, and it is. Lots of questions and lots of laughter. I even get the obligatory question as to whether what I write is real. I reply that I'm an author and think: are you all real? In closing I say that they all have to cross their fingers because I've been nominated for both the August Prize and the Norwegian equivalent, the Brage Prize, which is to be announced in Oslo the next day. They promise. In my excitement over the good reception, I'm about to read another piece, but then stop myself. Better to leave them wanting more.

The organiser drives me back to the hotel, which is in the centre of the small Norrland town. I'm given a piece of paper with the door code, a 'Here you go and goodbye.' It's winter and cold, dark outside on the street and dark in the hall. It's an old house. I fumble for the light switch, take a step in and then jump. There's a piccolo in uniform standing on the stairs. I reverse out through the front door. When I've stood out on the street for a while and he hasn't come out, I try the door code again and look in. It's a statue. I sheepishly slip past him and up into the hall. There I find a light switch. There are paintings and things everywhere. Several stuffed animals that force me to think straight so fear can't creep in. On one of the signs it says: Rooms 1–10. Next to Room 7 someone has written 'Eli' in chalk and there's a key hanging on the hook. I sort myself out and get into the narrow bed. Once again alone in a hotel, I think, with a piccolo out in the hall as the only company. Where's the hotel manager?

I listen to the wind and try to tell myself I'm never frightened. I remember something Mum said: 'To think that none of my children are scared of the dark when I am.' If I could be frightened, I would be. Pull the duvet up over my head. Maybe Mum wasn't right. Maybe some of her children are scared. Maybe she can't decide for us any more. I'm curious about me. About whether fear will creep up on me. Right now it's stalking about trying to decide. I don't think it's my turn tonight. Breathe more and more carefully.

The next morning I make my way to the station in the snow. I'm taking an early train directly to Arlanda, and then a plane to Oslo and the award ceremony. I race through a snow-covered Sweden. Isn't it going a bit too slow? I don't know how fast trains should go, but my whole body feels that there's something wrong with the speed. The stops are too close together. I mustn't miss my plane. I'm all dressed up, have got myself ready to go straight to the party. Five minutes before my plane is due to take off, we arrive at the airport. I run with my suitcase, force my way to the front of the queue and beg to be let through. 'It's too late if your plane leaves in five minutes,' the staff tell me. They have no idea that I'm going to an award ceremony and that it's important. I ask again. 'No,' is the answer. I ask again. 'Let me see your ticket.'

She swipes my card. 'Your plane has been delayed by half an hour. If you run, you'll make it. I'll call the gate.'

I'm up in the air and can breathe again. I made it. This is a sign. I will win the prize for the best book of the year.

I'm sitting on the metro on my way to Janus. The police are after me. I can feel it from the walls. The radiation from the corner in the kitchen. That I'm being watched. The warm pulses hitting my body. They know that I'm sitting here now, I think, shaking. They've got surveillance cameras everywhere.

When I get off there are people everywhere. Someone's going to let off a bomb, I have to drop my bag and run. Or do we have to lie down, the thought races through my mind. Like when I was on the savannah in Botswana. It was me and Torvald and two unarmed local guides, a small private aeroplane and a canoe trip away from civilisation. They rattled off in broken English what we had to do if we met any wild animals. If it was a lion, we had to stand still. If it was a female with cubs, we had to let them sniff our legs. If it was a hippopotamus, we had to run for a tree.

We stood there in the heat and listened and realised that we would never manage to remember what to do in the different situations. Fear would override our memory. You should definitely run, unless anyone gave other orders, took the lead. Will anyone do that now? Say where we should run or that we should all lie down. Does it mean that I have to take the lead?

I'm crushed on the escalator. The police are watching my every move. When I come into the therapy room I see surveillance equipment everywhere. Janus sends what we talk about to the police. He writes it down once I've left. I look around uneasily. The pattern on the Persian carpet is impossible to understand. I've stared at it many a time. Is it child labour?

From which end has it been made? The pattern is only nearly symmetrical. Apparently it shouldn't be absolutely perfect, so as not to compete with God.

I stand up and notice the lead on the floor. Something is flashing behind a curtain. 'It's just the printer,' Janus assures me. Just the printer? Will the police storm in or are they waiting outside? They're going to lock me up in a prison out in the country. I won't be able to cope. Is there anyone who understands that I won't be able to deal with being in prison? My picture of the cell gets smaller and smaller. It shrinks to the size of the toilet at home when I was a child. To the straps around my body. To cries when my mouth is invisible.

I want to die. I feel it as soon as I open my eyes in the morning. I can't live, on repeat. I want to disappear. I can't be alone in the flat. Can't eat breakfast. Can't make anything. Can't work. Can't be with people. I think that I'm going to jump from the balcony and fall six floors down. It would be so wonderful to let go. Not to have these thoughts about wanting to die. Not to have to worry about losing control. The voices that rule me and the police that pursue me.

But what would my friends say? They would understand. My family? They wouldn't understand. But they would manage. They would think it was unnecessary. Lolo would tidy my flat and cry. Giving her that kind of sorrow is not worth it. She who has given me so much more than anyone else. She who has done as she promised and never let go. And how can I know that she doesn't need me as much as I need her? To kill myself would be like pouring iced water through her warm body. I can't do it today. I can do it today. Or wait a few days. I will do it today. I'll wait a few days.

The African statue guards the bedroom window. It watches over me. But who watches over it? I watch over it. But I have no energy. I have to wait. I get scared. Will I really do it? Yes. I throw myself down on the bed and cling onto the bedframe. I'm almost lifted out of bed. Jump. Jump. I hold as hard as I can. Save me.

I'm on my way to Janus again. I'm going to let him know that I know. I sit there shaking and talking to myself. There are too many people out and about right now. 'I'm going to let him know that I know that he tricked me,' I say. 'Not so loud,' says Emil. Janus has made me ill. Is that just a thought or do I say it out loud as well? I don't know. Can't get there quick enough. Can't take the metro. People notice and people know. And now even Mum knows.

I have to hide. All these years of doubt and voices. Of admissions and discharges, of angst and wasted time. It's the therapist's fault. There's been a misunderstanding. I am not ill at all. I've seen him on TV. Then suddenly I understood everything. I knock on the door as soon as I get there. We have agreed that I shouldn't do that. I should sit in the waiting room and wait until he comes out to get me. He doesn't open the door. A colleague comes out into the waiting room. I tell her that I can't wait. 'He'll come through soon,' she says, and hurries off to her own room. Then he opens the door and we shake hands.

As soon as we've said hello I say it: 'I've seen you on TV.' 'Please, sit down,' he says. I remain standing with my coat on. 'You're that terrible father I saw on TV. You abuse your children. And you're dangerously religious. You hit, cry and pray.' 'Take off your coat and sit yourself down,' Janus says, calmly. I drop my coat in a pile on the floor and sit down. 'Don't hit me,' I say. 'Don't hit me.' I hastily get up and move my arms around. 'I'm not going to hit you, you can sit down again.' 'You've been fooling me all these years. You've made me ill. You're deeply

365

religious at heart. Admit it. Or you're Freud. Or Freudian. You're an extreme believer, and that's been harmful for me.'

I make repetitive movements with my arms, even when I'm sitting. 'Yes, yes, yes.' Laughter. I feel confident of my case. But underneath my confidence lies a white room of doubt. I don't know. Half of reality is hidden from me. The answer is behind the walls and I can't get there.

'I am not religious,' Janus says, 'and I am not Freud.' Really? He's just saying that to confuse me. 'And I am not the father in that TV series.' We sit in silence. I feel uncertain. 'I've got a meeting at one,' I say. 'With the artistic director of Stadsteatern. I'm writing a play for them.' Is it me that's ill after all? 'I'm not sick,' I say. 'You're confused,' Janus says.

'Hang on a minute,' Erik says. 'I'm here now. Eli's not here. And I know that you've tricked her.' Erik jumps up. 'Lie down,' he orders. Now Eli's back. And she has to do as he says. I lie down on the floor. 'You can get up,' says Janus. I get up from the floor. He's tricked me over and over again. He can't save me. He, who I thought was so kind and understanding. He looks at me. Looks like he always has, but is someone else. 'Eli,' he says several times, in a calm voice. 'You normally think you are several people. And today you think that I am. I'm sitting here in this room with you and I'm your therapist. I'm the actor you saw on television and the horrible man that he plays. I think perhaps it's best if we call the hospital. Have you eaten today?' 'No.' 'Have you washed and changed your clothes?' 'No, I slept on the kitchen floor. I've been preparing to come here and expose the truth. I've been preparing for liberation. Eli is well,' I say. 'You don't need to call.'

He has already called. He's talking to my mental health worker, Elsa, and asks if she could perhaps come and get me. She can. 'You need treatment,' Janus says. 'I've got a meeting at Stadsteatern at one. I don't have time for any treatment.' He laughs. I look down at the asymmetrical carpet. He's not looked as carefully as I have, even though he practically lives there. 'I've been waiting nearly six months for this meeting at Stadsteatern,' I say. 'I don't think it will be good for your play if you go there as you are now.' He's lying. I'm not postponing anything. If I've said I'm coming, I'm coming.

There's a ring on the doorbell. It's Elsa. She comes in and rubs me over the shoulders. 'Hi,' she says. 'Can I call you Eli?' 'No.' 'Well, then I won't.' 'I can't come with you,' I tell her. 'I've got a meeting at Stadsteatern.' Elsa's read the play and knows how important it is to me. 'I think Eli needs some treatment, food and sleep,' Janus says. 'We'll go the hospital for something to eat and then we'll drive you down to Stadsteatern. It's only a quarter to eleven,' Elsa says, and looks at me. She tries to tease out a smile, but doesn't succeed. 'Ingemar is waiting in the car,' she says. 'Come on, let's go.' I follow her out. Think that I have no idea what will happen now, but maybe Elsa can decide. Maybe I don't need to take responsibility. Out in the car, Ingemar says: 'Hi Eli.' I get in and he reaches back to give me a pat on the shoulder. 'Eli's not here,' I say. 'It's Erik. I'm going to a meeting at Stadsteatern.' 'It's a very good play,' Elsa says. 'Why don't I get to read anything?' Ingemar asks. 'You can read as much as you like. But you're always a bit poorly.' 'That was an Eli remark. Eli's here,' Ingemar says. 'So we can start the car.'

We drive through the town. I feel safe in the car with Elsa and Ingemar, that they won't change and become someone else. We stop at a Vietnamese restaurant to buy food. We sit in the day centre to eat it, and I try to explain to them that the therapist has tricked me. That I've seen him on TV, that he's religious at heart. That he hits children in God's name. That I'm frightened of being hit.

367

'Eat something now,' Elsa says. 'We'll talk about it after your meeting at Stadsteatern,' Ingemar says. They start to talk about something else, joking with each other and they make me laugh. When we've finished eating, Elsa asks whether I can cope with the meeting. I say yes. For me there's no such thing as not doing what I intended. Ingemar thinks I'll be fine. But says that he has to consider whether to let me go or not. He thinks it's their responsibility to make sure that I don't do anything that might show me in a bad light. 'I'm not letting Erik go,' he says. 'Are you sure that it's Eli who's here now?' I lie. I say yes, but it's Erik.

I'm given an anti-psychotic Zyprexa injection. Erik doesn't want to have it, but thinks it might be tactical; if I don't take it, they won't let me go. Then they drive me to the meeting and I promise to come back to the unit when I'm finished. 'You're usually quite frayed after all that effort,' Elsa says, and she's right. It's good to know that I can go back there and have supper.

I've got plenty of time, so I walk up and down a bit outside the stage door to Stadsteatern before going in to let them know that I'm there. I make a deal. I will swap myself from Erik to Prince Eugen. I think Prince Eugen is better at meeting artistic directors than Erik. I ask if they can be nice, just this once. Just now. Then I'll spend time with Erik afterwards. It's fine, and with great relief, I walk up to the reception and ask to meet the artistic director.

I sit up straighter now that I'm Prince Eugen. More friendly in my manner, more sophisticated. Glide straight-backed across the floor. Then the artistic director arrives. In a pink shirt, very happy and friendly. They would love me to do a play by me. He asks if I'm politically active. Prince Eugen isn't, after all, he's a royal. But he is an artist, and that is political in a way. I sit in the armchair without shaking and talk about a number of political contexts where Eli has contributed. I look out of the window and see a train station. The conductor blows the whistle and the train pulls out. The trees and electricity lines disappear instead of coming closer and we travel back in my political life. I tell Prince Eugen, who tells some of it to the artistic director. Prince Eugen is astounded, this was before his time and so is unfamiliar to him. Has Eli really done all this?

I end up in the Soviet Union. There's a meeting in the playwrights' union and I am sent from Sweden as an observer. It's December 1991. The meeting is over and we are all about to go back to our respective homes. Then someone storms in and says that the Soviet Union has been dissolved. He tears up the minutes from the meeting. These are new times, adieu. All the way home I think that it is I who have torn apart the colossal union. That I've actually been working on it for fifteen years. I'm holding a red thread from a woolly sweater and unravel it stitch by stitch.

I started with Eastern Europe. The train stops in Hungary in the early eighties. I'm in a team of young people from the Soviet Union and the whole of Eastern Europe. There are over a hundred from the east and ten from the west. We work in a factory and on a construction site, sleep in vast dormitories, eat together and hang out in the evenings. As soon as I get a chance, I ask them about conscientious objectors and homosexuals. They don't exist. I repeat my uncomfortable question in every context. Talk about multi-party systems when we eat. They laugh and pass the vodka. Am I preaching to the deaf? They're not so deaf after all, one by one they come to me in the dark and want to talk. When the floor to what is to become the Technical University of Budapest has been poured, we have to water the concrete. Twenty of us carry buckets of water from a tap some distance away and I suggest that we get a hose so that only one person is needed to do the job. This is not well received. Do I want to create unemployment like in the west? I don't reply. I pick up my pail and make no more suggestions.

One summer I cycle from Moscow to Washington. It's a peace convoy including Russians, Americans and Scandinavians. Do our numbers on the streets and squares make any difference at all? I hand over a petition to General Secretary Pérez de Cuéllar of the United Nations, with signatures from thirty European mayors against the deployment of Tomahawk and Pershing II cruise missiles. One of the participants is interviewed on the popular programme *Good Morning America*. We gather round the television in the hotel. He's practised formulating his political views and will finally be able to talk so that all of America can hear. But the question is not political. The question is, do you have a sore backside after all that cycling? And he does. He's got blisters and can barely sit down. He loses his thread.

The artistic director sits opposite me and listens. I don't know why he asked. Is political activism in or out? Does he want my play to be political? I realise that to pull people in it has to be set in our time. Or slightly, but not too much, into the future. He probably just sees Eli. Prince Eugen is a good speaker and tells the stories as best he can. Several trees disappear. Houses and fields and someone waving from a fence. We stop in the middle of the Norwegian forest. I'm at a seminar run by The Future In Our Hands, and am learning about alternative world economies. I'm back at the end of the seventies. I'm writing pieces for Norwegian radio. About Generation X and the baby boom. I go through long tunnels. Light and dark. Backwards. Backwards. Finally end up at home in my bedroom where I am standing with a stolen vase and about to go out and sell raffle tickets. That was not political.

Prince Eugen laughs. The artistic director laughs. His secretary pops her head in and reminds him about his next meeting. Our meeting is over. He promises to get in touch the following week. I walk through all the corridors and find my own way out. I'm exhausted. Go back to the hospital for something to eat and to rest. The artistic director does not get in touch for months.

I sit on the floor in the corner of the kitchen in the flat. My fingers are vibrating. My thoughts are white and grey and white and grey. I'm being watched. Erik has hit me. He's hit my head against the wall several times. I'm going to report him to the police.

I go to bed with a big bag of crisps on my tummy, what Jonathan calls teenage temptation. 'I'll show you something,' Emil says, when I wake up in the middle of the night with crisps all over the bed. Espen is crying. I dry his tears on the duvet cover. 'Get dressed,' Erik orders. I do as he says. Outside it's snowing and cold and dark and silent. Only an ambulance drives silently past with its blue light flashing. 'Walk,' Erik says. I cross the street and go into the park. It's slippy. It starts to dawn on me where we're going.

We go down to the new bridge over the Mäleren. When they were building it, Astrid Lindgren threatened to lie down on the tracks in order to save part of the park that would be ruined by the bridge. But it never happened. She said that she was too old to threaten them with her life. Where is the boundary? We go up to the highest point on the bridge. I lean over the railing, feel the pull in my stomach. I'm wearing my pyjamas under my coat. I don't have my ID card in my pocket.

'Eli,' the boys say. 'We found, we found it.' Should I say thank you? They've shown me a place to jump from. But I've promised to ring someone before I think about jumping. I don't ring anyone.

*

I never lock the door to the flat. I walk through parks and along dark streets late at night. I'm not afraid of bird flu or mad cow disease. It doesn't concern me. I think: all danger comes from within.

Saturday morning. Olof wakes me at midday. I open the door in my pyjamas. 'They're coming,' I shout. 'They're coming.'

'Who?' Olof asks, and comes in.

'The police.'

'No, it's just me.' He hangs up his coat and gives me a bear hug. Don't want to leave that space. Olof can save me. I know that he can.

'The police are coming to get me. Can you stop them?'

'The police have other things to do. It's me who decides whether the police come to get you or not. And they're not going to come.'

My right leg is shaking. I sit down. 'The police hear my thoughts and send them to Mum in Norway. She hears that I'm writing about her.'

'When did all this start?' Olof asks.

'The day before yesterday. I couldn't sleep. They heard what I was thinking. The boys are in on it. There's radiation coming from the walls, can you feel it?'

'There's no radiation in here,' Olof says.

'I have to apologise to Janus. Don't think that there's a dangerous Janus behind the friendly Janus any more. Trying to tell him stuff makes me psychotic.'

'Maybe psychodynamic therapy isn't the right thing for you just now. That's why we've suggested Jonathan. After all, cognitive therapy is all the rage,' Olof says.

'That's enough to make you sceptical,' I say. 'I have to apologise to Janus.'

'He knows how to deal with transference, after all, that's his training,' Olof reassures me. 'I think you need a Zyprexa injection. Why don't you come back to the unit with me?'

I quickly put some clothes on and pack a bag. Something tells me that I might be staying a while. We stop in front of the hospital building. 'One day we'll leave the hospital, both you and me,' Olof says. I agree, but we're not going to do it today.

I get my injection in the bum and I get food. There's a vegetarian option left over from lunch. It's cooked beetroot with a good sauce, and a salad with a strong garlic dressing. One of the nurses made it. As they've started cutting back on the garlic, he takes it with him from home and makes his own dressing. I normally pour it over all my food, so it tastes of something.

Several of my mental health workers are on duty. I can sit and listen to music. The very fact that they are here makes me feel safe.

375

For the first time since I started going in and out of hospital, everything is perfect. Now when everything is about to be changed. Now I have several mental health workers, so I can always get hold of someone. I live at home. I go to the unit when I want to or need to, get something to eat and have a chat. I meet the same people when I'm in hospital as I do when I'm at home. They know my voices and my behaviour. They can calm me down and support me when things get a bit tricky. There's such a difference between talking to someone on the phone you don't know, and meeting someone who knows you well. Then often, it's not so bad.

I can live with this. I'm changing, but I'm still vulnerable. When I behave in a way that might seem sick or frightening to others, they steer me into a new phase. And now they're going to disappear. Now everything is going to be changed. So that it's like the rest of the country, so that it fits in with the Swedish model. It's just been a trial, a socio-psychological focus, with the patient at the centre, supported by a mental health team comprised of doctors, a care coordinator and mental health workers. A pioneering project to show to study groups from other countries.

The staff are now going to work either in the unit or in a day centre for when the patient has been discharged. They will no longer have responsibility for specific patients. Community care and hospital care will now be two separate entities. Community care and day centres could also be privatised in the future, as has happened in several places already. I think that the new system, which gives the staff less responsibility, less freedom and less variation, will lead to a deterioration in care. Perhaps I should say something. Perhaps I should contact the politicians and tell them that it's a step backwards not forwards. That all mental health care providers think so too, but don't dare to say. One of the problems is that the patient organisations for psychiatric care are so weak. Either patients are too ill, or they want to keep the fact that they've been there secret. Which is true of me, as well. I don't want to represent those who are ill. I want to be an author. But perhaps I should. Perhaps I'll dare one day.

But now I spend the day sitting, or rather lying, on the sofa. Talking a bit, listening to music. I send a 'Happy Sunday' text to Mum. I want to see what happens. What she knows and what she doesn't know. No one can see me here. I pop a smiley face in at the end of message. A reply plings into the phone. Mum says 'Happy Saturday' back. 'I'm tidying the drawers and cupboards.' What does that mean?

'She can't see you, that's what it means,' Elsa says. I look at her. 'You're so sweet,' I say. She really is sweet. Sweet and serious and wise. 'You're a professional wailer for your mum, and you have to stop that. You can't pre-empt what she's going to feel. Your mum is proud of you and the fact that you write. And she'll be proud of this book too.' 'Don't say that. It might trigger something awful. Is sacrificing a life lie worth it for one book?' Elsa says nothing.

Mum knows nothing, and whoosh, suddenly everyone can read about it. No, I don't want her to know, I don't want her ideas to be shattered. A parallel life beside a life. The voices, angst, madness and wish to die. Elsa says I don't need to decide anything right now.

*

It's suppertime. I'm sitting opposite a woman I know well. We've been here together many times. She has a borderline bipolar disorder and is as usual dressed in a grey hoodie zipped right up to the neck, with the hood on. She looks a bit stiff. She doesn't look at me when I say something to her. But I don't worry about it. Maybe she just wants to be left in peace.

It's stew today. I pour garlic dressing over everything. A nurse is sitting beside me who is a bit more alert than I am. Suddenly she leaps up and leans across the table. 'You're completely red in the face,' she says to the woman opposite and pulls off her hood. And reveals that she's wound the cord from the hood twice round her neck. She's about to strangle herself. The nurse dashes away to get some scissors and cuts the cord.

The woman is watched constantly. I say: 'You're not allowed to die. I like you.' Two of the patients I've met here in the unit have taken their own lives since Christmas. One with drugs, the other with pills. 'I know,' says the woman. 'I've got family and friends who love me, I don't want to die. But do, at the same time. And it changes so quickly.'

I stay lying on the sofa until evening. Even though unpleasant things happen here, I still feel safe in the unit, with people I know around me. I don't know whether to go home. Think they think I should go home and look after myself. Then Olof says: 'You can stay here for the night, if you want.' He's the sort of person you want to parry with and hug. Someone who whistles on his way home from work, no matter how difficult the day might have been. You feel protected when he's near. I bumped into him once when he was driving a bus to make a bit of extra money. The fact that I got on his bus was a good sign.

They give me a room. The other person in the room is out on leave, so I'm on my own. It's room number thirteen at the end of the corridor. I close the door and try the bed. I first shared this room with Kassandra over three years ago. I miss Kassandra. It's good that she's not here, but it would be nice if she was. The room feels quite isolated and lonely.

I get up to take my night pills. I get too much: 150 mg Nozinan, Stesolid, Imovane and Propavan. Plus the depot injection that's already in my system. I won't sleep more than one and a half hours tonight. That dose could knock out a cow for a week. But I'm so wired I can't be turned off.

It doesn't matter that I don't sleep. Because something wonderful happens. I'm given something. I'm given stories. Four. Often I lose the thought before it gets to the pen. But now they keep a gentle pace all the way down onto the paper. Sometimes I get frustrated, when the words and images come so fast that I can't catch them. But this time I do. Open my hands, throat and pelvis and receive. It doesn't matter where I am, I just write. I think about the old American who in his dotage was 'glad to be anywhere'. It's the same when you write. Prison or heaven, cushions or a bed of nails. If I'm writing I'm at the centre of my own life. At home in myself.

Every now and then through the night I go out into the corridor and chat to the night nurse. She's kind, happy and tired. I tell her of the gifts that I've got in the dark. That I caught them. That everything is there on paper. She says she would like to read it, and asks when the book will be finished. 'Maybe never,' I reply. And think about everything I'm still going to write. That I'm never going to stop. Never retire and never put down that final full stop until I'm on my death bed. I'm so excited by my gifts and have to celebrate. Lie on the bed and enjoy. Look at the paper. Say some sentences out loud. I certainly won't be able to sleep now. There's only a few hours left of the night.

I get up and go out into the corridor. As so many times before, I sit outside the dining room and wait for the morning coffee to be ready at a quarter past five. I'm not alone. The coffee doesn't come until six o'clock. When the sleepless patients are served, the night is over and the day has begun.

*

I wait. You get used to waiting. Just sit. Talk a little to the voices. Empty my head and stare into thin air and let time tick by. The day shift comes on at eight and breakfast is served. Three of my mental health workers are there. Olof makes porridge. Not all shifts have someone who can make porridge. It's up to each team. I love Olof's porridge with raisins, nuts and stewed apples and milk. I would never think to make something so good for myself at home. Have never made porridge.

There's a calm morning mood in the unit. I sit and chat to Olof and Ingemar. Olof tells us that he's looking after a little dog. When they went for a walk down to the square, the little dog was so frightened that it began to tremble. Olof has that kind and considerate expression on his face. 'I felt so sorry for him,' he says, 'he was so frightened.' I think that Olof chose the right job, a place where he can use his empathy. I think what an important job the nurses do. What would I have done all these years without them?

Elsa comes into the dining room with a diary in her hand. She's always planning. Wants to know what I'm thinking of doing, what I've done when. We all get our diaries out and I book a meeting with each one of them in the weeks ahead. They make my everyday easier.

Jonathan comes early. I don't like it when he comes late, but still like the fact that he's not always there on the button. There are small details that make this therapy different from previous therapies.

I hold my head in my hands. 'You've felt like your head is splitting for twenty years now. But it still hasn't actually split,' he says. 'You say yourself that when you read back through your medical journal, the voices are the same. They say the same things that they've been saying for twenty years. To put it simply, they haven't kept up. You don't need to be afraid that they're going to change.'

He's said this before and I agree. 'But what good is that? Knowing?'

'Over time, it helps to know,' he says. 'That the police are after you is just paranoia. Once upon a time you might have needed the voices to survive, but you don't any more. Say no, tell them to wait.'

They will still be there. He wants so much, Jonathan. He believes in change. At best, we know who we are, but not what we can be.

I'm running with my mental health worker, Mats. He knows everyone. Says hello with every step. He knows everyone who supports Hammarby and they live in this neighbourhood. He knows everyone who works outdoors. He's worked in the parks himself, and on the roads, as a rubbish man, clearing snow and in restaurants. A good foundation to have when you're working with mental health.

We run over the bridge. It's a long bridge. He's running ahead. Something drops in my stomach. It's the same bridge that I planned to jump from. Now, all I need to do is throw myself over the railings. Fly through the air as the last thing I do and hit the ice at great speed. Life is an obstacle. Death is a jump. Mats! I want to shout. He's over on the other side. He's too far away. My thoughts move in small spasms through my body. Now, now. Mats has to run between me and the railings. Or I'll do it. Will I do it? I've thought this so many times that soon I'll have to do it. You can't want to jump and then not do it. I wasn't thinking about it half an hour ago. It's the actual possibility that triggers a pain, a spontaneous 'want to disappear'. A spontaneous 'what if...' A door out into the air. A sleep without dreams. If I don't die in the fall, I'll die in the cold, and Mats can explain what happened. I don't need an ID card.

Is this the end? Will I never live again? I imagine that everything will be white when I die. I've thought about how it would be not to be alive. But have I thought about what it means to be dead? Will books be published and films shown afterwards? Unfinished. Will I manage to be gone forever? Dad wasn't frightened. He's gone. I'm sure Marit was frightened. Sometimes I think about all that she hasn't experienced. That she never experienced the year 2000.

Mats comes jogging back. 'I want to jump. Can feel the pull,' I say. 'Everything is dangerous and nothing is dangerous,' Mats says. 'You have to be friends with your fear and situations you can't control.' Now he runs on the outside. When we're over the bridge, he says: 'I think your new book should be called *Running Away From My Illness*.' He says that he's going to write a book. But he's barely read anything. 'That's not a great starting point,' I say. Even though that's what it was like for me. 'You won't revolutionise writing by not reading any books. Good literature is good for you.'

The flat is silent. It's night. I'm lying under the duvet, but can't sleep. 'Come on,' Emil says, in a soft voice. 'Get up and come out into the kitchen.' It sounds like I'm going to get sweets. My body is suddenly alert. I leap out of bed. When I go into the kitchen, Erik says: 'Do your movements.' Espen laughs: 'Fooled you there, didn't we?'

Drink some Coke and have a smoke. Back to bed. You're much smaller when you wake up in the night. Up out of bed again. Take a bag of crisps back with me. Seek comfort in trivialities. Get thirsty, so I get up again. Drink some Coke. Back. Listen to music. I have to sleep. Listen to the radio. Set the alarm. Now it's too late to go to bed early. Maybe I should phone someone. It's too late for that too. Could ring the unit, but don't want to. Get up and eat peanuts three times. I have to write. I sit down at the kitchen table. Light a candle. Get some paper and a pen. Remember that I need to iron some trousers, which have been lying there for about six months. Get out the ironing board. I should write. Or sleep. More peanuts. I sit down with the paper in front of me. I'm not supposed to write at night unless a story comes to me. When it just comes like a gift. Not like now, sitting here blank and waiting.

I go back to bed. Think about colours. That the colours in a room have to match and contrast in the right way. Jump up and go to the bathroom, clean the toilet. Might as well do something useful? In the end, around three o'clock, I make some coffee. I've agreed with Jonathan that I won't do that at night. But I've done it now. I have a smoke. I'm going to pretend that it's morning and I'm having a nice time. Is it really nice? Try watching the flame on the candle. Fire is calming. What is it I think is going to happen when I get up? Just a little more. Of what? Cigarettes, peanuts, chocolate, crisps, Coke, beer. Jonathan says that I should wind down before going to bed. Listen to an audio book. I should just... Is all this supposed to be helping me in some way?

I sit at the kitchen table. I've been at the unit over the weekend. I didn't sleep then either. But I was given stories, gifts in the night. I liked the little girl who was me best, the one who tells stories to her classmates on the way home from school. She pees herself. Her point vanishes in a yellow puddle in the snow that everyone sees. An entire childhood filled with yellow puddles in the snow. I've written about it, and about the unit. But I don't want to be a public patient. I comfort myself with the thought that a novel is a novel and only reflects slices of reality. How you think it was and how you wish it was. Slices of an unlived life. Selected moments, imagined moments. A story that spawns other stories. A personal story. That seems all the more real the further back in time it took place. The language. That flows into the pen when you practise. And yet writing a book is still letting a small part of me live a life I can't control. A part of me that flies around like a child that's flown the nest, and I forgot to teach her how to dress before she left.

385

I'm writing now. Now I'm writing and there's a value to the night. It's like dancing. I see puddles of pee in the snow. Like a trail all the way back to my childhood. Like yellow stories in the midst of all the white. When I was walking through the park the other day, Tim said: 'Eat the yellow snow, it might be beer.' He laughed.

I'm at home for a few weeks and then go back into hospital. I know what I want. I don't want all this medication. I get there late in the evening. Have already taken my eight-o'clock medicine, two Propavan and one Stesolid. I say over and over: 'Erik is well, Erik is well.' I walk up and down and talk.

I'm given two 15 mg Zyprexa, 100 mg Nozinan, two Stesolid and two Stilnoct sleeping pills. The nurse stands in front of me with the pills in her cupped hands, like a bowl full of sweeties. 'That's far too much,' I say. 'And also, I'm not prescribed Nozinan any longer. You can't give me all this when I haven't spoken to a doctor.' 'Just take them,' she says. 'We just want you to get some sleep.' I have to. That's the way it is, because even when I've made up my mind not to take the medicine, even when the voices have told me I don't know how many times, a kind nurse or sister can easily persuade me. I think, just this once. Get it over and done with. I don't want to make a fuss.

And here I am again. In front of a cupped hand full of pills. Then suddenly the nurse says: 'We girls should stick together.' I laugh. She laughs. What's that got to do with anything? And it only takes this slight distraction, and suddenly I've swallowed the pills. Popped them in my mouth and pretended to the boys. But there'll be trouble, I know. I go to bed with my clothes on. Don't wake up until half past four the next day.

I've slept for eighteen hours. The doctors' round came to see me, but I just said that Erik was well and fell back into the bed.

Have to pee. I feel all glued up, stiff all over. Rickety and weak. My legs have no will. My arms can't be bothered when I try to get up. I fall back down onto the bed. Heavy, as though the whole room was lying on top of me, pressing me down. The walls, ceiling, furniture, everything. I have to hold it up. Try again. Can't open my eyes. But have to pee. With enormous effort, I manage to get onto my feet, take a few steps forwards, holding onto the wall. My legs buckle under me. I fall to the floor, haul myself up and try to make it to the door. Hit the wall again. Ow, my head. Collapse and crawl across the floor until I finally get to the door. Try, but can't open my eyes. The toilet is out here on the corridor somewhere. It's got a long support handle. I pull myself up. There's even a support handle along the wall for people who can't walk properly. I think I've got the right place. Tug and pull. Try to open my eyes. See something white and shiny, but my eyelids slide down again. I take a few steps to the side. Finally, the toilet door handle. I pull open the door, it's urgent now.

I collapse. I collapse on the floor and wet myself, stay lying on the floor for a while. Manage to get up unsteadily and call the staff. I have to borrow some hospital trousers. 'Come with me to the store,' the nurse says. It really does smell like an old hospital in there. I prop myself up against the wall and force my eyes open. See restraining belts, sick bags, advent candle-sticks, a small midsummer pole, towelling tube socks, towels, disposable toothbrushes that are hard on your teeth. Nappies, razors, cups for dentures, sheets, blankets. Unisex nightgowns, old-fashioned pinafores. Grey-blue, washed-out tracksuits, size large.

And those are the trousers I'm going to have. A sack that can be tied tight round the waist. I take off my wet white trousers and change. Totter back to bed, lie there staring at the ceiling until the side effects start to ebb. Then I don't sleep for three days.

I share my room with a suicidal heart surgeon. When she realises that I'm an author, she says: 'This is the VIP room.' She's obviously not used to being a patient. I understand indirectly that she finds it difficult to talk to an ordinary, lowly psychiatrist. How can she hold on to her status here amongst all the addicts and people who have never worked? She's an ermine amongst street cats.

I can't burn off my energy here in the unit. As patients, we spend the whole time waiting for the next meal. Some medicines increase your appetite, you can almost see us swelling. My weight goes up and down like a yoyo. I change medicines all the time. My body is hopping. I shadow-box and kick. Go to boxing four times a week in a gym, but am not allowed to go by myself, so I'm taken and collected like a child by Harald. The days when I can't go out, I'm fit to burst. One of the hourly paid staff, a solid and humble young man, says he'll teach me to do prison gym. He came and shook my hand and introduced himself the day after he'd helped to carry me from the basement up to the unit. 'Having to use force is one of the downsides of this job,' he says. He's training to be a therapist. We stand in my tiny room and do exercises. I'm tired and sweaty by the end of it. Sleep well that night.

The next day I'm hyper again. In the evening, I run up and down in the corridor. 'You're disturbing the others, calm down,' the nurse says. Then the German karate teacher who works nights suggest that I should go out with him. Even though patients are not allowed to go out in the evenings or at night. 'Put on your trainers.' We run up one of the steepest flight of steps on Söder. 'Come on,' he shouts. I love trainers' voices. What would I have done without all my trainers over the years?

I run up the steps until my thighs are burning. Then I carry on a bit more. Up and down. This is what I've been longing for, I don't even consider escaping. The nurse would have caught up with me in a flash. We got back to the unit exhausted. Everything feels a bit better.

I write well when I'm in the unit. I've been able to borrow a small desk again, which I've put in my room. I've taken my computer with me and sit squeezed between the bed and the desk. Lisen comes to visit every day. We've been commissioned to write a TV series for children. Lisen's not that familiar with film, so she wants me to write. Scenes flood into my head, I can concentrate for longer and longer periods at a time. There are so many balls to keep in the air and I grow with the job. When Lisen is here, when we only talk about the manuscript, I feel a clarity that I don't have for the rest of the day. I remember my scrapbooks, collages and events. It's like burning a wire. The flame rushes on and all that is left is red, knotted copper wire. A secret relationship between a boy and a girl, where, towards the end, they have to defend their friendship and shared fantasy world with their lives.

I sit in the corridor with my coat on. Want to leave. Have an appointment with a skin specialist, have got a rash. 'You can cancel it,' says Jonathan, who's come to visit. 'What's decided is decided,' I say. 'I'm not going to cancel.' If things don't happen as planned, I crack. Ask Mum. 'You have to learn to cope with changes. Practise saying no,' Jonathan says. 'No,' I say, defiantly. I'm determined to go. 'You don't decide. You're here now,' Jonathan says.

I can't let go and listen to his side of the argument. Suddenly he stands up. 'All our work is in vain, I don't have time to sit here and listen to this nonsense. I've got forty other patients to look after.' He's obviously irritated and almost shouting. Then he rushes out. The door clicks behind him. I'm locked in. What if he doesn't come back? He comes back.

I've been discharged again and am out running with Mats. We've got a circuit that takes about an hour. I'm the slowest runner in Sweden. It's great to be running, and I would never have done it on my own, if Mats wasn't there talking me on. We've run in all kinds of weather. Winter and summer. In rain, snow, sun and dark. We've been doing this for more than two years now. It's great, once we're over the dangerous bridge. Sometimes I run as far away from the railings as I can, with Mats on the outside. A shield between me and my thoughts.

When we get about halfway along the lake, I want to swim. I tell Mats that I'm going to take off more than he's comfortable with. I haven't really thought about it, it's more of a joke. Think that it doesn't matter to him how much I've got on. He carries on running. When he comes back ten minutes later, I've thrown myself naked out into the water and am fully dressed again. He says nothing. He says nothing for the rest of our run.

When we get home, he says what he always says: 'Remember your three-step routine. Stretch, shower, eat.' I can feel that something's wrong. Then he says: 'I don't want to run with you any more, after what you did. You don't swim naked in the middle of the city. You knew that I wouldn't like it, and that I could lose my job as a result.' 'I'm sorry,' I say, surprised. He seems to mean it. This is serious. He doesn't want to run with me any more. I didn't realise it was so risky. 'I accept your apology, but we won't be running together any more.' And that was his final word.

I don't know what to say. I want to defend myself, but don't know how. I go in to the flat and lie in the bath. I start to understand, but don't understand all the same. You can't swim naked in the middle of the city with your carer. I'm a grown woman. Not what I feel, which is neuter. For me, it could easily have been Espen, aged six, who was swimming. Mats should have said: 'No, you can't.' He ran off. He didn't see me naked, but it wouldn't have bothered me if he had. I don't understand that seeing a woman naked can trigger all kinds of feelings in men. When I'm in the unit, I pull my trousers down and bare my arse to male nurses without thinking about it, so they can give me injections. I lie in the bath for a long time. Should I call him and apologise again? Have I learnt a lesson or am I just sad that we won't go running any more? I feel a knot in my stomach. I realise that I've made a mistake. I duck under the water and hold my breath.

I feel better and want to cut down on my medication. In fact, I don't want to take anything at all. 'This is one of the leading clinics in the country,' Olof says. 'Yes, at pumping people full of medicine,' I reply. My doctor, Manne, is in a good mood and wants to negotiate. We do this regularly and I always leave with the feeling that I've lost. He'll reduce the Trilafon, if I take Cisordinol, Acutard and Stesolid as injections. I agree to the deal as they only stay in your system for three days, whereas the Trilafon depot injection lasts for three weeks.

The day after, I go to a vernissage. I stand outside the small gallery with some friends. I can feel that my jaw is completely stiff, and moving without me wanting it to. My neck locks. I've got a glass in my hand and raise it to my mouth. I can't control my lips and drink properly, it runs onto my jacket. I don't know what to say. Can I speak at all? We're in the middle of an interesting conversation. Does it show? I've just arrived. I have to go again. I don't dare to talk. Have to hide away. Have to go home.

I go into the gallery and wave to the artist. 'Are you going already?' she asks. I nod. I run to the metro, sit in the carriage, grinding my teeth. My mouth twitches uncontrollably. Saliva dribbles down onto my shirt. It's as though my face is twisted. When I get home I look at myself in the mirror. My cheek is being sucked into my mouth on one side. I go to bed and try to sleep. It hurts and my mouth keeps moving. I hear my jaws crunching. Get up and take some Akineton to help with the side effects and more sleeping pills. I will never take those injections again.

Phone Lolo and talk to her. I'm just slurring. It's difficult to talk when you can't control your mouth. I'm trembling from somewhere deep inside, as though my nerves were strings that are vibrating. 'Yes, yes, yes, yes.' One of the boys wants to come out. 'Get up,' Prince Eugen says. I quickly stand up. 'Go into the corner of the kitchen and move your arms.' The shaking continues. I do as he says. Lift my arms up and down, from my knees to over my head. 'Again.' I do it again. 'You'll go to pieces if you don't do what I say. Carry on. You can't be anywhere other than the corner.' I don't know how long I've been standing there. I don't know how to stop. But in the end I'm allowed to go and lie down in bed. Still shaking. Turn the volume on the MP3 player as loud as it will go, listen to music. Prince Eugen's voice lies underneath like a whisper.

I'm staying at home with my mum in Norway. We've just eaten my favourite cake with home-made ice-cream, which she baked because I was coming home. She's old now. Has aches and pains, but is still clear in the head. We talk, but there are still holes in the conversation. The ones that have always been there. I think that she's matured. That I admire her. Believe that I've got some of her strength to never give up. To never allow yourself to give up. For better or worse.

She's a survivor. Lost her own mother when she was only four years old. Grew up in Oslo during the war. In and out of the air raid shelter. Wore a red woolly hat and had paperclips on the collar of her jacket, and was interrogated by the police time and again. Got married and had children instead of studying to become a mathematician, as she wanted to. Had five children, of whom one is no longer alive. She looked after her old father and let him live with us even though there was not enough room. She stockpiled tins of food in the cellar, in case there was a war. She went to university when she was around fifty. She looked after her sick husband. Perhaps I've not wanted, but hoped she would look after me too. Didn't believe that she could.

She's lying on the bed resting. Her lined face that I'm getting closer to with time, that will one day be mine. The bedroom window is open. 'Marit and Dad are in the birds,' she says. I stand in the doorway. I don't want to think about death now. Or that the dead live in other forms of life nearby. Then Emil says: 'Can't you hear what the birds are singing? Here comes death, that's what they're singing. Here comes death.' He says

396

that they asked him to tell me. I no longer trust Emil, who once promised to help me avoid death. 'Hide yourself in the game,' he said. Perhaps I've hidden myself too well in the game. I have others to turn to now when things are frightening and difficult. I no longer need him, he weighs too little. He repeats it and I'm just as at a loss. Time will tell whether he dies before me or not. I look at my old mother and feel scared. 'They're singing about other magic things too,' Emil says. 'You can talk to them if you want.' I don't want to. Mum is asleep. When she dies, and our childhood home is sold, a new era will begin.

While Mum sleeps, I go out into the garden to dig up Torvald's trophy. The one he won in a skiing competition, when he was such a coward that he stuck to the ideal time category, which meant doing two laps in as near to the same time as possible. He went as slowly as he could. I competed in my normal category, went as fast as I could until I threw up, and got a thimble as a prize. Torvald won the biggest trophy of all. I couldn't lie in bed and look at his big cup beside all my small ones, so one day it disappeared. I was forced to bury it in the garden. Now I want to give it back. I no longer want to be him.

I think I remember where I used to put things I could no longer bear to see. But I'm wrong. Dig one hole after another and find nothing. What's done can't be undone. The people who buy this beautiful garden in the future will get a secret hole into the bargain. When they dig up the whole garden to build a bigger house, they will find my things and piece them together like a jigsaw puzzle to make a whole story.

5.

I'm at home again. The transition between being away and being home is the hardest. Stockholm, Oslo. Family, friends. Having two countries, to never be done with going home to visit. To never be done with the fact that I've swapped country. I have phantom pains in the severed root that remains in Norway.

'Go over to the dangerous window,' Prince Eugen says. 'Get up.' 'Go and sit in the kitchen corner, by the sink,' Espen says. 'Turn on the water. Then you're safe.' 'The outside world is enormously overrated,' Prince Eugen says. I close my eyes. The boys talk all evening. The same old exhortations. Then suddenly it's silent. I turn on the radio. It feels so lonely. It's the weather forecast. On sea and land. The weather makes me sad.

Then the boys are there again. They chat to each other. It's not directed at me. I am just a body for them to be in. I have no control over my thoughts, their voices run free. The words fly between them. They discuss things. 'Eat. Don't eat. Dare. Dare to jump from the bridge.' 'No,' I shout. 'Not tonight.' They stop me in my tracks when I speak. 'Shh, don't say anything. We're on the phone to each other. That's why it can get a bit confusing sometimes.' Erik laughs. I laugh. I'm an entire orphanage. I think that one day it will be razed to the ground. And I alone will be saved from the smoke-filled rooms by an enormous fireman in a smoke-diving helmet.

Ingemar, my mental health worker, comes from the hospital at around eight in the evening. He sits at the kitchen table. I'm hyper and want to say everything at once. Show him my new clothes, tell him about my childhood which I'm writing about at the moment, show him the postcard I got. I stop mid-sentence and start to talk about something else. 'You should try to wind down now,' Ingemar tells me. 'As you didn't sleep last night, you should go to bed early tonight.' I carry on telling him half stories, changing the subject all the time. Ingemar has to go soon. I take my night medication, two Imovane, two Propavan, two Stesolid, two Heminevrin and 100 mg of Nozinan. He turns off all the lights and I put on my pyjamas.

Ingemar sits by the bed and I try to sleep, but then sit bolt upright and turn on the bedside lamp. Some sentences have come to me that I have to write down. 'Turn it off,' Ingemar says. 'Lie down, otherwise the medicine won't work.' I sit up a couple more times. New sentences. Prince Eugen orders me to get up, walk across the floor and slap my hands on my knees. Ingemar tells me to stop. I creep back into bed. 'It's not the voices who decide, I do,' Ingemar says.

I fall asleep about half past eleven. Ingemar has left and dropped the keys back in through the letter box. I wake again at one, bright and alert. I take two more Heminevrin and smoke a cigarette in the kitchen. Go back to bed and try to sleep. My leg is shaking and my body twitching. Want to get away from my restless body for a while. And so the night passes, I get in and out of bed for what seems like hours. Can't listen to an audio book, can't think of anything to do apart from listening to the same old radio station as always on my headphones. The same songs and same adverts over and over again. The same vacuous presenter who tells you things like today is peppercake day. I'm addicted. Chatter that protects me from myself and the voices.

At four in the morning, I call the night shift and a couple of nurses come round. Take four more Heminevrin. Don't say anything. I should have been knocked out by all the sleeping tablets hours ago. The nurses stay for a while and talk. Say that if I can't sleep, I should phone them once every hour for a five-minute chat. They leave, and I charge around the flat. Lower the hem on a pair of trousers using a needle and thread. Turn on the computer. Ring the unit. Don't want to be awake, I want to sleep. Take four more Heminevrin. Smoke and have a glass of wine. Drink hot milk and honey, maybe it can work miracles? I try to imagine that the milk has been heated by the Finnish angel in hospital all those years ago, but now I have to do it myself. That's what being a grown-up is all about. Being good to yourself when you need it and no one else is around. I eat my third breakfast at six o'clock. Haven't closed my eyes.

The next day I call Jonathan and scream down the phone. 'Teach me to sleep.' 'Not on the telephone,' he replies. 'You can sleep. You've slept before.' We end the call. He can take his papers and lists and stuff them right there. Sleeping routine and anxiety reducing measures. It's just words. The lists might as well have been blank paper or a page from the telephone directory. I can't put them into action.

I go up to the hospital. Am cross, even though the night gave me a couple of sentences. It's not enough. I'm most angry with the sleeping pills. I get so nervous when I can't sleep, get a stomach ache from all the cigarettes. I don't find anyone to talk to in the unit, so I write a note to my doctor, Manne. 'Fucking placebo medicine. *Fata Morgana*. Give me something that works or nothing at all. Everyone's Eli.'

'We need to talk about sleep,' Jonathan says. 'Put some of the belief you have in your writing into sleep.'

'You know, when I woke up at three, I looked at my right hand,' I tell him, 'and I really felt that my five fingers were me. Espen, Emil, Erik, Prince Eugen and Eli. Espen is the pinky. But I don't know whether the index finger is Erik or Eli. And that makes me angry.' I clench my fist. It's going to go through glass. 'You have your fate in your hand,' Jonathan says. 'You, Eli, are the force that holds it together. Think that it's Eli who has the upper hand.'

'Don't call me Eli.' I feel a sudden intense irritation, a burst of rage with Jonathan. I don't want to hear him say the word Eli. It's not the first time. Sometimes something turns in me when I hear that name. I throw several punches in the air. Float like a butterfly, sting like a bee. I imagine that I ball my fist and punch with the strength of all the boys' voices. Have to stand up, the power comes from the hips. Hear my boxing trainer's voice: 'Go on, give it everything you've got. Are you here to train, or what? No relaxing.'

That applies to Jonathan as well. Why doesn't he know when he should use one of the other names? 'Why don't you say Emil sometimes?' 'Because I want to talk to Eli the adult.'

I've become a pill addict. In the drug index for prescribed drugs it says that Heminevrin should only be taken for short periods. I have been taking it for over a year now. Want to be in control, but get so desperate at night that I get up and take another one. They say that it can have the opposite effect. I ask for medicine and ask not to get it. Every time I see my doctor, I try to have my medication reduced. But he talks me out of it because we negotiate in a way I don't understand. The depot injections of Trilafon are protection, he says. But after nagging and nagging, one day I get the dose halved and feel very pleased with myself. I won a small victory there. I know that Manne doesn't think it's a good idea, but when I'm not sectioned, in principle, they can't force me. He's afraid that I won't take anything at all, and he's right.

When you sit in front of a doctor, the very situation means that one of you is below and the other is above. I fear no one. I look up to no one. But he sits there and is untouchable in some way. I always have one of my mental health workers with me, but the doctor is the authority in the room. Olof tries to persuade me to have the injection. Draws a head and a brain and a curve and tries to explain how it works. Even Jonathan, who gives the impression that he believes more in therapy than medicine, agrees with the doctor when he's in the room. Elsa and Ingemar try to convince me. Mats, whom I run with and who thinks exercise is better than any pills, has not shared his views with the doctor. When it comes to medication, they stand united, with Manne at the helm.

'Have you looked at what we agreed to about nights?' Jonathan asks. 'No.' 'Have a look in the folder now then. We've talked about sleep routines, but it appears that you've simply dropped them.'

I've only stuck to one point in the list of all the things I shouldn't do, and that is not to drink coffee. I drink Coke or hot milk and honey instead. Last night I felt that I couldn't cope with living at home. The whole year has been an endless battle. I can't do it. 'Yes, yes, yes, yes,' I say, quietly.

'What are the voices saying?' Jonathan asks, on the ball. 'That it's not working. That I can't live at home.' 'Of course you can live at home.' 'Maybe it's just small defeats in the face of great progress,' I say. 'That's more like it,' Jonathan says. 'Time you gave yourself a pat on the shoulder. And the real question is if you would do any better anywhere else. What's that saying? Wherever you go, there you are.' 'Yes, I get that. But having someone to talk to at night wouldn't be a bad thing.' 'You should sleep at night, not talk.'

'Sometimes I wake up in the morning and can't remember what I've done during the night, and the bed is full of bits of melted chocolate. It says in the agreement that I shouldn't eat chocolate at night. But I have to treat myself. The other night I spent a hundred kronor on sweets.' 'That agreement was the dream scenario,' Jonathan says. 'We'll just have to start again. Tibetan monks can sleep in the middle of a Manhattan rush hour, but I don't think we're there quite yet.'

'I get so frightened and restless when I can't sleep, or wake up

407

after only a few hours. I think that there's people in the flat, or I feel terribly lonely and adrift in space, with no connection, no links anywhere, and I think that I'll never be able to sleep again.'

'If you absolutely must speak to someone and there's no answer at the unit, you could perhaps try the Internet,' Jonathan suggests. 'There are lots of places in the world where it's day in our night.' 'I've never in my life chatted,' I reply. 'You have to think that you're the world champion in sleeping. You can sleep. You have slept. We know that. You have to make friends with your insomnia and accept that sometimes you can't sleep. Sometimes you blame your disorder for problems that belong to the healthy you, to life. Problems that we all share with you. Like not being able to sleep. Like being lonely. Half the problem is worrying about being worried.' 'No,' I say. 'Every night I think that I'm going to sleep. The opposite is a surprise.' 'You'll have to start training yourself not to listen to the voices before you go to sleep. You'll have to find a way to make them agree. They have to sleep as well. At night, they're not allowed to feed you with compulsive thoughts and violent fantasies. You have to practise saying no. Instead you should have positive daydreams. Active daydreams. I dream about a South Sea island,' he says. 'What kind of grapes I'm growing, what the weather's like, who my lover is.'

'I don't indulge in dreams like that,' I interrupt. 'You don't need daydreams when you're an author. Maybe because you're at one with your imagination. I imagine all day. I feel and experience all the time when I'm writing. But I find it hard to imagine love and sex.'

'And often it's hard to imagine the things you find hard to do. Your thoughts are sent out like signals. It shows when you're thinking about love. Look at me,' he says, suddenly. 'You're looking down too much today. Daydreams don't need to be realistic.

It's just nice to enjoy them. I'm not going to move to a South Sea island.' He laughs.

'I go to bed around nine-thirty, ten, because I don't know what else to do with myself.' 'And are you tired then?' 'No, I feel that I have to get away from the evening. If I wake up after only a few hours, I wake up in the illness. If I wake having slept all night, I wake up in wellness.'

'It's important to shorten the time that you're up. Say that it's just a little break, and that you'll soon be asleep again.' Our hour has become an hour and a quarter. Jonathan gets up, he has to go elsewhere. 'What about asking Lolo to record herself reading something calming, so that you can listen to it at night?' I think that's a good idea. 'You need to connect quickly to reality again. Reality is security, rest and sleep. I know that you can do it,' he says in the doorway.

I'm cat-sitting for Harald and we both jump out of bed. Kajsa gets some tuna and I make coffee and three pieces of toast with marmalade. My body is strangely awake, it must have been a deep sleep. Have great confidence in today, that it's okay to be alive. I'm going to get to my workspace early today. I'm going to write. It's dark outside, as it's winter. I light a candle. Am curious about how early I've woken up and go into the living room to check the wall clock. It's half past one. Half past one? That's far too early to have breakfast and coffee. I fell asleep around midnight.

And what has Jonathan said about starting up the brain? It's going at full speed now. I've told it it's morning.

Play calming music. Get into bed and think nice thoughts, so that sleep will come like the postman. I would rather train than sleep, though I know that muscles grow when you rest. That's what Kiril taught me. Kajsa has wolfed down the tuna. She sneaks back into the bedroom and lies down on the window sill over the radiator where Kiril used to lie. I follow her, sit down on the bed. Kajsa has already fallen asleep. Cats don't have insomnia.

It's more than five years now since Kiril disappeared. I'm too allergic to get another cat, and away too much. Or should I do it all the same? When the film about Kiril is finished. But I don't want a new cat. I just want Kiril.

Suddenly, I start to cry. It's Espen who's crying. Emil says that Espen is a crybaby. I dry our tears on the duvet cover. Look at the cat on the window sill. She's an outdoor cat, so she

410

gets mildly depressed when she's with me and is forced to stay indoors. 'How are you?' I ask. 'You can see that she's sleeping,' Erik replies. 'You know you shouldn't trust your mental health workers and the people who think they're helping you. You know they're lying. That they're trying to trick you. That they make you ill. The Trilafon injections make you ill. Refuse to take the injections.'

'Let's not discuss that now,' I say. 'I just asked Kajsa how she was. I'd thought of saying to her that if she sees the flat as a cage, then she just needs to change her attitude. Life comes from inside and there are people who have lived rich lives in smaller spaces than this.'

'The unit is a cage,' Erik says. 'No one can think sharp thoughts there.' But he's wrong, I've written several novels.

I see a fox that's been run over on the road near the bus stop at the cottage. It's completely flat. Its innards have been pressed out of its mouth and lie in a red pool beside it. I remember Uppsala and the taxi driver all those years ago. A latent image that has waited for me to see the real thing. When I get back into town and am about to go down into the metro, a dead pigeon comes up on the escalator. I stop. Am I really going to go down onto the platform? I'll jump in front of a train. I step onto the escalator, but immediately regret it and start to go back up at twice the speed. I have to save myself.

I've been forced to save myself for as long as I can remember. Take myself home in the middle of the night.

Elsa helps to tidy the bedroom. It's not going to be a dangerous place any more. I open a childhood drawer and find a page from a magazine. Under the heading 'Women to Women' there's a letter I wrote when I was thirteen. I read it to Elsa:

I'm scared that I will never be a real person!

I'm scared that I won't get a proper education and grow up to be a real adult. Terrified by the thought that I'll end up an alcoholic, drug addict or maybe a criminal. Did any of you who are grown up today ever go off the rails when you were young? I realise now that it was stupid to start drinking. It's even worse that I wanted revenge after a bad day and started shoplifting. You'll all be thinking that I come from a broken family or a dysfunctional home. But it's not true. My parents are kind and nice and they think that I'm open and honest with them. To me it feels more like a new age of defiance and I think my parents are stupid and old-fashioned. I've tried to talk to my mum about beer and things like that, but she just dismisses it and doesn't believe that of me. I'm glad my children don't do stupid things like that, she says. So it's not easy to make any real contact. I think school is desperately tedious. I'm not alone in that and I wonder why it has that effect on us. Don't know that working life is a bed of roses either. But still think that adults are happier and more satisfied than we are, as teenagers. I've not got anything to complain about really. When you've got a freezer full of food, clothes on your back, a roof over your head and a place to sleep, then you're better off than 75 per cent of the world's population. So why do I have this unbearable pain inside? I have to be honest and admit there have been times when I've felt so desperate that I've wanted to end my life. I've got lots of friends at school and at home. We hear about the future all the time, how overpopulated the planet is, that we have to expect a population explosion, that we will be drowning in rubbish and pollution in a few years' time. The next minute we're told that the Soviet Union is coming to get us, that Norway will soon be as middle-class and riddled with inequality as the USA. And the Christians, they scream that Jesus will soon come again and wipe out all non-believers in one go. There's so much speculation, so much is written and said, it's not surprising that teenagers feel insecure and wonder what's the meaning of it all. I've tried to be Christian, but it didn't work. Hope that my letter reaches others who feel the same, or grown-ups, preferably Christians, who have felt like I do now. From thirteen.

'That was a cry for help from the young Eli,' Elsa says. 'You had a lively intellect and if you don't feel secure, then it's not easy to make sense of your life. It's both mature and vulnerable. You just want someone to reach out and give that girl some warmth.' I look at Elsa. 'You do,' I say.

'I don't know why I wrote that I wanted an answer from Christians. Maybe God was messing with my heart,' I say. Elsa sits down on the bed. We've just thrown out all the diaries that I've kept for the past twenty years. Who will want to read about when I went to training and when I was in hospital and who I met? Now no one will know. Now it's all in the bin. 'Does he still mess with your heart?' Elsa asks. 'Not very often.'

'Did you get any answers to your cry for help?' 'Heaps, mostly from young Christians telling me that salvation was the only alternative. I struggled through the letters, but didn't reply to any.'

I pull down the note that says 'Don't sit on the sidelines of life' on it, and the whole programme. They're a blight on my kitchen cupboard doors. I want it to look nice. 'Write nicer notes then,' Jonathan suggests. 'I don't need them any longer.' 'But you have to start up the evening when you get home from work. Switch on the lights, turn on the radio. Make food. Make it normal. Don't go to bed and listen to music. Phone someone. Can't you start with your scrapbooks again?' He's referring to the art film synopses that I made. But they came to nothing because I got ill. Maybe I could start again. Maybe.

I've got better at not going to bed. At staying up with life at home. But right now I'm finishing off the film about Kiril. The one that no one thought would ever be finished now looks like it will be a moving and poetic film about life, when things don't go as planned. It's about how grief recalls other sorrows. Even Dad is in it, who died the year before Kiril disappeared. I filmed our conversations to the very end. I tried to remind him about his life, which he found so hard to remember. We talked about death. It's included in the film. I close the conversation by saying: 'We're not going to die now. We're going to go out and look at the flowers.' He replies: 'To be or not to be.' That is the last thing he says to me. I force him out in his wheelchair.

Lolo has asked me to write down every evening five good things that have happened during the day. I've got the book on my bedside table. I write: Lolo, Lolo, Lolo, Lolo, Lolo. Simply because she exists. She came this afternoon and made supper, and packed lunches from the leftovers. She's staying the night. She's said that if I wake up at night, I should only make five small and five big movements. Turning over is a big movement. Getting up is not allowed. I can't do it.

We read a children's book written by a colleague to each other. *The Fox Book*. On the first day of school, Freddy Fox gets a shock: there are only dogs in his class. We laugh. As you can imagine, he was bullied and teased. Who hasn't felt like Freddy Fox, surrounded by lots of dogs with masters, collars and a pack mentality? With Lolo in the bed beside me, I think that we're like a small pack. Or a couple of draught horses, who will never let go of one another.

I tell Jonathan that I've noticed a change in the last few months. The unruly Erik has slowly started to withdraw. I don't as often experience the uncontrollable anger moods he provokes. When there's no end to destruction. His demands that everything be smashed, crushed, splintered. His orders to punch, break and fall to pieces are rarer and rarer. I have struggled to make him disappear, in the same way that he fought to appear a long time ago.

'You've worked him out of your system. Maturity and good work, that's what I'd call it.' 'It's Prince Eugen who's taken charge now.' Jonathan leans back. He seems happy and swaps his old snus for some new. 'He just sets different traps,' I say. 'Like what?' 'Guess!' 'Relentless shopping?' We laugh. Expensive, but better suited to a wheel that's turning and life in the world. The elegant prince and I, a middle-aged woman, hand in hand. The woman boy. It's we who go out shopping.

Jonathan gets up. I think he's about to leave. Then he says: 'Do you know when we met for the first time?' I can't remember. He sits down again. 'I was new in the unit and saw you wandering restlessly around in the corridor. I tried to get your attention, and we talked for a bit, and I thought: this woman is not well. Then you interrupted the conversation and said that you had to go to a press conference because you'd been nominated for the August Prize. I thought to myself that life is made up of many dreams. And refused to let you out. Another member of staff had to come between us and say that you were allowed to leave the corridor with the locked door. If that had been today, I would have believed that you had hidden depths, but it didn't shine through a year ago.'

I walk around in my flat, in the unit, in my workspace, and the solution is always on the other side of the wall. I haven't got a chance. How can I get to it? Do all these conversations matter? I want to be completely well.

'You haven't looked on the other side of the wall,' Emil says, and laughs scornfully. 'But I'm looking all the time.' 'You haven't looked on the other side of the wall. No matter how you twist and turn, sanity and the answer are where you can't reach them. You are forbidden to go there,' he carries on. 'If you found a way out, we might disappear. Injections don't help against us. You wonder why, and there's no answer. If you found a way out through the wall, there would be another wall and the answer would be behind that.'

'I still intend to go there,' I say. 'I write, and you don't.'

It's New Year's Eve. I've been invited to dinner at Kristin's in Oslo. For the starter, we have lobster soup, with large pieces of lobster in it. The main course is tuna and for dessert, lots of delicious cheese. There are two couples at the table. Two men and two women, and me.

I float up and look down on us from above. We're as many men as women. Three and three. I can be divided. Eli, both. They each get half from me. No one needs to feel threatened. I am the androgyne and fit in everywhere. Or don't really fit in anywhere.

We raise our glasses of champagne. Soon it will be a new year. At midnight, we're going to send Chinese lanterns up into the night over the rooftops. Each one of us writes a wish on the thin, tissue-paper frame. I write, so that all the others can see, 'I want to change sex'. I don't write clearly. I don't write from which to what. It will be a surprise. Even for me.

I put on one of Prince Eugen's suits and look at myself in the mirror. I look like Eli, but am not her any more. I'm not Prince Eugen either, the prince who after much consideration and opposition went to Paris in 1887 to study art. He was determined to be an artist, contrary to all conventions. And he became a successful painter.

I look at myself from every angle. Who am I? What is visible and what is hidden? I'm older. The shirt is a little tight over the tummy of my body that used to be so slim. Women are better at driving, worse at cycling, better at everyday cooking, worse at playing chess, better at simultaneous interpretation, worse at getting pay rises, better managers. Worse at parking cars. None of these generalities apply to me. None of these generalities should apply to anyone. Female writers. Female people.

Kassandra isn't answering her mobile phone or my text mes-
sages. I start to wonder if she's alive. I text her again and again
just to give me a sign of life, she doesn't need to say how she
is. After a month, I get an answer: 'Hi Eli, feel a bit guilty that
I haven't said so before, but you're sending texts to the wrong
person. I'm from Stavanger and I'm alive.' I send a 'thank you'
to the stranger from Stavanger who's received all my worried
texts. I've changed mobile phone and had to put in all the new
numbers and addresses myself. I check on my old mobile, I've
put a seven in the country code instead of a six and ended up in
Norway instead of Sweden.

It's midnight and I write a long text to Kassandra, explain-
ing everything. And again, ask for a sign of life. Not long after
there's a pling on my phone. Another text from the stranger.
'Where in Sweden do you live?' I reply that I've been living in
Stockholm for over twenty years now. I go and get ready for bed,
it's nearly one o'clock. Another pling. Maybe it's Kassandra? It's
the stranger. 'What do you do?' 'Writer,' I reply. 'And you?' Not
long after, another pling. I'm not expecting it to be Kassandra
any more. Curious, I open the text. 'Hi Eli, been working for a
Norwegian oil company for twenty years.' It's nearly two o'clock
now.

I don't know what to reply. What are your favourite books?
Which football team do you support? I support Tottenham. My
body is hopping. Maybe this is the person for me. I don't even
know if it's a man or a woman. Which is good. I can't express
myself. Have you read Dostoevsky, Beckett, Woolf, Janet Frame,

Djuna Barnes? I like male dancers. I've got it now. I write: 'Do you ski?' I don't have to wait long for the answer: 'Yes, downhill. But not very often. Do you?' I reply: 'Cross-country, downhill and jump. I've slept in a snow cave many times.' The stranger writes: 'I've never slept in a snow cave.' S/he didn't ask any questions, so I'll have to do the asking. It's nearly three in the morning now. I lie there, making up questions and answers. I should take the initiative. But what does that look like?

Perhaps I could invite him/her to come on a snow cave adventure. Should I take Torvald with us? He can remember how to make a safe snow cave. Hild used to take us, her little brothers and sisters, with her when she went on a date. But they never worked out. I don't send any more texts, or receive any. But have saved the number in case of future sleepless Saturday nights.

Sometimes, everything in your flat breaks at the same time. Even my new mobile phone. Have to go back to the shop and complain. I've just had my hair dyed black at the hairdresser, and the colour has ruined my pillow case. I have to go back and complain. I can't cope. Everything builds up into a storm inside me. It's night-time. They're only small things, but they gnaw at me. I can't sleep. The bulb has blown. I can't seem to get a single channel on TV. I can't cope.

I get the blue glasses and start to smash them on the kitchen floor. The first glass doesn't break, I have to throw it again with more force. Then I sit on the floor in the middle of all the shards and cut my wrist. Along the vein. The pieces of glass are thick and sharp. I go into the bathroom and look for a razor blade, find a razor but can't get the blade out. I only manage seven superficial cuts, but the blood still seeps through my sleeve.

I ring the unit. I need someone to talk to. Jonathan, my therapist, is on holiday in Cape Town. I can't cope. One of the night staff, who I know well, answers the phone. He's normally pretty calm, but either something I say or the way I say it makes him uneasy. He asks me to come in. I don't want to. 'You come here instead.' 'You need to see a doctor.' 'I don't need to see a doctor.' He calls back fifteen minutes later. 'Come in,' he says.

I go out into the night. My white top is now dark with blood. It turns out that it's Manne, my doctor, who's on duty. I say that I can't stay because I want to smash the glass doors between the kitchen and dining room with a chair. If I stay, I'll just break something. I feel the need with my whole body. 'I would rather

422

not have to section you. But if you don't stay here of your own free will, I'll have to. We'll give you a Zpyrexa injection.' 'I don't want one.' Eventually I agree to have the injection if I can break one of the glass doors. I have to break something so I can get through to the other side.

As I understand it, he agrees, but the injection is given with some force. The nurses hold me down so I can't free myself and break something. They hold me until the Zyprexa takes effect and I fall asleep. I'm much calmer in the morning. But I was tricked, and I didn't get to break the glass pane.

I have to go home. It's my birthday tomorrow and I can't be here then. My mum will phone. What if she sees me through the telephone's invisible eye? I go out and sit in the corridor. A real loudmouth walks past. She screams at me. I'm scared, she's the sort of person you wouldn't want to meet in the town. The sort you would give a wide berth. The staff are always telling her to be quiet. She's called Marilyn, she looks like she's going to a carnival, with soap bubbles in her hair, like a shining crown. A small red dot drawn on her forehead and another on her chin. A yellow shawl, a glittery purple waistcoat and a purple hospital pinafore tied round her waist with the pockets to the back. Big earrings and five necklaces. She storms up to me and grabs my breasts, shouts that I look like a princess or a model. She bows to me and waves her arms in greeting, says she comes from the world's most famous country. I guess the USA. 'No, Vietnam.' Lunatic comes from the word moon. Howling at the moon. But it doesn't mean that you're not all there. Just that you express yourself differently. Marilyn talks like a lunatic, dresses like a lunatic, moves like a lunatic. What can she do? How can I and the others in the unit rest and get well when there's a loudmouth like her around?

But after only half a day I learn to listen to what she's actually saying. Her sentences have meaning. In the smoking room, in particular, all the patients are a bit better. There, it's us and them. There's no staff watching and we can talk to each other. I'm no longer scared by her flapping movements and invasive hugs. I like her in all her madness, think that she's quite fun. She's constantly changing her clothes, creative and colourful combinations, with warpaint on her face.

She screeches around and the staff are constantly telling her to shush, then she whispers a few words, only to shout again after. She spits and blows her nose in her hands then wipes them on the plants. Then she wants a hug. I have to learn to say no. When we sit on the bench by reception waiting for our night medicine, and the staff have tried to get Marilyn to bed five times, she whispers loudly in my ear, almost spits, that she wants to buy my clothes under the table. I laugh. Three nurses follow her to her room and try once again to get the wired woman to bed. I think how lucky it is that Marilyn is not out in the wind and snow, talking to the air and being ignored by everyone. She's safe in here and can be herself until it passes. Because it does. I've seen so many people come in here in a sorry state and then leave the unit after some weeks or months as a different person. One thing I'm grateful for after all these years, is that I'm no longer prejudiced and am more open to people who are different. There's always a healthy mind behind all the confusion, you just have to listen.

The woman in the hoodie sits opposite me in the dining room. The one who wanted to strangle herself with the cord. She's put on a few more kilos. She sees the dark patches on my sleeve. 'Have you been cutting yourself?' 'Just a bit.' 'I was advised to hold two pieces of ice in my hands when I want to cut myself,' she says. 'The pain was bloody awful, all the way up to my elbows.' 'Did it help?' 'No, I still cut myself. Wanted blood.'

I'm in the smoking room. I'm so scared of the transition from
day to night that I make sleep impossible. Deliberately. It's four
in the morning. See that someone has stubbed out a cigarette on
the ceiling. A woman in her sixties comes in. She emanates mel-
ancholy. 'I recognise you from the hospital years ago,' she says.
'You're the one who made the bust from medicine cups.' 'I recognise you too,' I say. She sits down. 'You've become an author
and film-maker, haven't you?' 'Yes,' I reply. 'What kind of books
do you write?' 'Adult fiction.' 'You mean porn?' I laugh. If only I
could. 'And you?' 'I live in a collective in the country. If you can
call it living. I was going to hang myself the day before yesterday. I had a long scarf, made a noose, got a chair, put the noose
round my neck and tied the other end of the scarf to the light
fitting on the ceiling. I kicked away the chair and then, crash.
I and the light fitting fell straight to the floor. An unsuccessful
murder.' 'Don't you mean suicide?' 'Yes, murder.' She nods. Suicide sounds kinder, I think. But don't know why.

Marilyn has slept well and is full of vigour again the next day.
She hasn't forgotten that she wants to buy my clothes. Only now
she doesn't want to buy them, but rather to swap her rags, half
of which come from the hospital, for my brand new designer
clothes, so that we can always remember each other.

I go into my room and lie down on the bed. I'm anxious,
have to ask the staff for help. I'm most worried about how I'm
going to get back from Umeå, where I had a reading last night.
I ask them to help me book a train ticket on the sleeper. I'm

425

scared that I might sleep in and not get off the train in Stockholm. I didn't the last time. I woke up as the train was pulling out from Stockholm Central. 'You don't need to worry,' they tell me. 'You're not in Umeå, so you don't need a ticket. You're in the unit.'

I go into the smoking room again and Marilyn is sitting there shouting. When she sees me, she gets up and comes over and talks right in my face. In the middle of a tirade about where I buy my clothes because she's going to go there as well, her top dentures fall out. She carries on slurring, standing there with her dentures in her hand. She wants a cigarette and gets one. Her upper lip hangs down, making her look old and sad. Her teeth have been so brilliant and brightened up her face. She wants me to hold her dentures while she smokes two cigarettes at once. My mental health workers have asked me to use Marilyn to practise saying no. It's not that easy. Because she wants something from me all the time. She always has an answer, like the princess who always had the last word. 'We'll give each other each other's clothes as a gift instead,' she says. 'That means good fortune.' What is good fortune? I want to write. Maybe that's good fortune.

Without wanting to, I sit there with her dentures in my hand. I'm still worrying about the train ticket. About how I can get away from here and who will help me to get off at the right station.

Jonathan is back from Cape Town. It's good to see him. He's seen lions. I tell him I was admitted to hospital again, and that it felt like a defeat. 'Turn it around,' he says. 'I can't turn it around.' 'Yes, you can. You went there voluntarily, you weren't sectioned. How about that?' 'Doesn't help.' 'It wasn't even a week, before it could be months. You're getting back on your feet again faster,' he says. 'Don't forget that. Now we're here. Before we were there.' He indicates a measurement with his hands. 'I didn't sleep last night,' I say. 'Go to bed when I've left and rest on your laurels.' 'I don't want that kind of laurel, I want the Nobel Prize for literature.'

'I don't know what to wear to Odd's wedding,' I blurt out. 'My little brother, Odd, is getting married for the third time.' 'If we therapists knew what women should wear, we'd win the Nobel Prize,' Jonathan laughs. Then we're silent for a while.

'Oh, yes,' he says. 'We've known each other for a long time now and there's something I've wondered about, that I've forgotten to ask.' What can that be, I wonder. Is he in love with me, maybe? That would be fun.

'Why do you always dress in the way you do?' he asks. 'In neon colours and black. With tassels, zips, patches and things everywhere? Like a new romantic, or punk, no, a new romantic.' 'I like colours,' I reply. 'I'm different, so I have to dress differently. I've always had odd clothes. It's like a conversation piece. Instead of a dog. I've got a jacket with valves so it looks like I can be blown up. An elderly lady asked if I got intravenous via my jacket. I have a bag with an electronic panel where the word 'hello' appears in blue. I always get comments when I'm in town or on the metro. 'Write "Kiss Me" instead,' Jonathan suggests. 'Most of the people who talk to me, or poke the valves or think my bag is wired to my mobile, are old ladies or drug addicts.'

I know that I dress in a style that's younger than my age. I don't mention the yellow and red football hat that Jonathan often wears. That's youthful as well, and the bag and the football jacket. He's not exactly grown up in his style either. We sit in silence. 'Forever young,' I say, meaning myself. 'Painful, but doable.' A tag for a boy-girl like Eli, who is not allowed to grow up. An angel. 'Yes, forever young,' Jonathan says. 'I think that you can be grown up through and through. If you want to.' 'If I dare.'

Two circles. One sick, one healthy. A figure of eight. An eternity of time and life. I draw it over and over again and end in the healthy circle. They don't weigh the same. Hope and darkness. I find my way back to the home inside me, like a bird in spring.

I haven't dared to be ill. Do I dare to be well again? Do I dare to say what everyone already knows?

I'm worried about the fact that I'm going to have less help after the reorganisation and cutbacks. I've been and talked to the boss about the changes, that my support crew is going to be disbanded. 'You should be moderately worried,' he said. He justified the organisation, said that the health service had to be more evidence-based. I realise that that is where the problem lies. In other words, they have to be able to measure what Elsa and Ingemar do when they are with me at home or in the workspace. He concluded by saying that he might perhaps have said something different if we had been sitting chatting in a pub. I understood that the decision did not come from him. I left with a pain in my stomach.

I phone Mum and tell her that I've written a book that I don't want her to read. Can she promise me that? Until now, she's read everything I've written. She promises, with some misgiving. Then she rings back in the evening. She's spoken to the woman next door and told her that I've written a book that I don't want her to read. The woman next door has promised that she'll read it and tell Mum what it's about. I'm back to square one.

I find a small cup for my independent-living man, Morgan. He just wants a little coffee. The small cups are at the top of the cupboard. I stretch up and the entire stack of cups topples over. There's a crash. The vase on the shelf below smashes. A before and an after. A moment. The green and black art deco vase that I got from Lolo at least fifteen years ago is in pieces. Why that one? I've got so many other things that could have smashed. Morgan gets some glue, he sees how devastated I am. We put all the pieces on the table. It can't be fixed. 'It's a good sign,' Morgan says. 'Things should break, it means good luck. It's the start of something new.'

Elsa comes to the workspace. I'm in the process of finishing off the book. Making a hole in the holes so the whole world can hear. Read a bit that I'm pleased with and a bit that I'm not pleased with. I say that I'm going to commit suicide when the book is ready. 'It's excruciating for everyone when they finish off a book, isn't it?' Elsa says. 'Isn't that part of the process?' 'Yes,' I concede. 'But afterwards, when it's been published, what then?

That's when I don't want to live.' 'Maybe it will give you a sense of freedom.' 'Don't think so. I'm just a writer,' I say. 'That's not enough.' We say nothing. 'I was talking to Olof before I came here,' Elsa starts. 'And do you know what we were saying? We see a new strength in you now. The difference from just a few years ago is enormous. You might never be completely well again, but you've learnt to deal with your illness so much better.'

Torvald has left a message on the answerphone. He tells me what his four-year-old son has just said. 'You're God, Daddy.' 'That's perhaps a bit of an exaggeration,' Torvald had answered. 'Oh Daddy, you have to believe in yourself,' his son reprimanded. Torvald always wants to encourage me in my writing. 'Do you think you can use that?' He often makes suggestions.

I go up to the unit to get a depot injection and to collect my prescriptions. Jonathan says that if I don't take the injections, there'll be no therapy. I think it's blackmail, he calls it a deal.

I sit in the small café on the ground floor where you pick up your medicine. It's a gathering place for lots of patients who've been discharged. Originally, the coffee was free. But some people took too much milk, or simply drank the milk. So they started to use little milk pots instead, one for each cup. Then one day, the coffee wasn't free any more, we had to pay. On Fridays, the chocolate cake was free. Then they stopped that, as too many sweet-tooths came.

The woman in the grey hoodie comes over and sits next to me. She's usually here. And I understand. I've got my workspace and my work, but I'm really the only one. 'It's the last day today,' she says. 'The café's closing tomorrow.' 'Then you'll have to take a thermos,' I say. 'They don't want us to come here. Patients who've been discharged should meet elsewhere. Only I don't know where.'

We start to talk about the fire up on the second floor of the unit. 'I was there when it happened,' she tells me. 'It's incredible that no patients or staff were hurt. No one knows when the unit is going to open again. I was lying on my bed with my head-phones on, listening to music,' she says. 'Heard all the noise and screaming, but then so much goes on in the unit all the time that you don't pay much attention. Thought that maybe some-one had set fire to a wastepaper basket. But I got up and opened the door. Saw the smoke in the corridor, closed the door, went back to my bed and pulled the duvet over my head. It wasn't until the door was thrown open by one of the staff and the black smoke billowed in that I realised it was serious. I was dragged from the bed, didn't have time to take any of my things with me. I was the last person out of the unit. They hadn't noticed I wasn't there until they counted all the patients outside. A lot of the patients had been sectioned, but they just stood there. Only the culprit ran for his life. He was a quiet man who called himself Jesus.'

'How lucky that you managed to get out,' I say, glad that I wasn't there at the time. 'Oh, it wasn't that dramatic. It was nothing really. I'd tried to kill myself with some pills in the unit a couple of days before. I'd smuggled them in under my hat, had more than a hundred pills. They usually check your bag, don't they? I've decided not to commit suicide at home. Don't want my family to find me. I locked myself into the toilet and had managed to swallow at least half of them when Ingemar realised something was up and opened the door with a master key. He always knows when I'm about to put my plans into action. I wasn't very happy that he'd found me. I kicked him. You know what I'm like, want what I don't want. But as I didn't die in the fire, it must mean it's not my time to die yet. So I've decided to live, no matter what life's like.'

We get a cup of coffee and talk about other things. It's an enormous exception to be alive.

I unexpectedly win a literary prize. From one of the biggest national papers. I'm taken out to dinner by my publisher, and it turns out to be the prize ceremony. It's a surprise and the whole of the arts section is there. There are speeches and a three-course meal. A special menu with my name on the front. I weave my way home with a cheque and a framed copy of tomorrow's arts page with a picture of me and the justification for giving me the prize. I prop it up behind the cooker. It stays there until it's illegible because of all the grease. Then I put it at the back of the cupboard.

I need the money for everyday expenses, but can't help celebrating a little. I go to a tailor and order a suit for Prince Eugen. It's black and white pinstripe with a fitted tailcoat. I show it to Jonathan. He thinks it's elegant, but that I shouldn't buy clothes for Prince Eugen. 'I buy for myself as well,' I say and sashay into the bedroom to get changed. I come out in a white skirt with fur trimmings and a white jacket with fur trimmings, have even bought myself white flared trousers to go with it. 'This is all for Eli,' I say. I've been told that I look like Elvis Presley in the white jacket and trousers and my black platform shoes. 'Now I can go to the wedding in Norway.'

It's the time of year between the bird cherry blossoming and the lilac. But I'm not aware of it. Elsa asks me to look up at the cherry blossom. She asks me to look down at the orange tulips between the pavement and the road. She bends down. 'Look how pointed the leaves are. Aren't they beautiful?' I try. 'Smell the bird cherry.' I breathe in the scent. We're on our way to the cinema. 'Have you seen the chestnut tree over there? With the vines growing up its trunk?' I haven't.

We walk past the depressing pub where I used to go for a whisky when I was in hospital ten years ago. It always fills me with a feeling of unease and a feeling of relief. It would never cross my mind to go in there now for a drink for my nerves. Nerves should be used to observe.

Elsa guides me through the city all the way to the cinema. She lifts my eyes, opens my nose. Present, present, present. I fall asleep during the film, but saw half of it and thought that half was good.

I'm practising for a talk that I'm going to give in English. Lolo is my audience. I'm serious and clear my throat. Then I begin. There's something about my pronunciation, the way I say things that makes Lolo laugh. I laugh with her. We can't stop. We squirm, about to wet ourselves. This kind of laughter has been absent for so long. And now it's back again and doesn't want to stop.

The whole summer has been good. I've slept. I haven't gone to bed during the day as I did last summer. I've made meals for Lolo and all our summer guests, been sociable and taken part. I've written almost every day. But I can't beat Lolo. She's woken me every morning with coffee and freshly baked bread, has been awake since half past five and moved plants around in the garden while they were still asleep. I don't understand how plants can thrive better in one hole than another. I love the flowers but can't bring myself to pick off dead leaves and sit there talking to them. I haven't broken the code to gardening.

But when we need to build a wall, I'm there. Natural stone and hand-mixed cement, something durable. The wall doesn't need to be cut, fertilised, watered or talked to. And it won't be eaten by the deer. But imagine if I could bake bread! One morning I try. And then I think, you don't need to be able to do everything.

I have a slight dip when I come back from the cottage. The transition to being on my own in the flat again. Hard to settle back into daily routines. Things are quite demanding now in the final stages of the Kiril film.

435

I've signed up for a music workshop with Lisen. We're going to go to Malmö and stay in her half-sister's flat. Lolo doesn't think I should go. Jonathan is doubtful. We sit in the garden outside my workspace in the late summer sun and make lists for and against. The first advantage I list is: Won't have to be at home on my own. 'That doesn't count,' Jonathan says. But then he changes his mind. 'Okay, leave it, otherwise I'm a dictator and not a therapist.' Under disadvantages, I write: Can I face meeting so many new people? Will I cope with a six-berth compartment on the night train?

But I don't want my illness to prevent me from doing what I want. I want to do unexpected things that have nothing to do with my work. I want to play the drums. I played the snare drum when I was little, in the school band, marched through the streets on Norway's constitution day and played the drum cadence. Can I still twirl drumsticks? What if my leg starts to shake under the bass drum instead of keeping the beat? I want to write lyrics. Have got a commission from a Norwegian pop-star and want to try it out. The seminar will close on the Sunday with a concert in a big venue in the centre of Malmö. What if I'm out of rhythm? The list for is twice as long as the list against. I get five minutes to think about it, and then say: 'I'm going.'

Playing is fine. It's like cycling, my arms and legs obey me. A tune somewhere in my body. A rhythm that has lain dormant. In the afternoon, we go to Lisen's sister's flat. Five cool and sweet lesbians in their twenties live there. Lisen's sister is wearing a trendy pink checked baseball cap, which I compliment. She says that I can have it, and it doesn't leave my head for the whole weekend.

The flat is big and messy. I ask if I should go and buy some food. 'We dumpster dive,' they tell me. 'What's does that mean?' 'We look in bins and containers and find our food there. There's a bakery next door. And leftovers from restaurants and shops, we live well on it.' They're vegetarians and teetotallers. Probably a good thing, as I don't think that Systembolaget, the Swedish alcohol monopoly, uses containers. Imagine if I'd known when I was twenty that you could be a teetotaller. They make food, and I eat with a healthy appetite. It's exciting to be eating rubbish. See that there's a list on the wall of who's doing the washing up, the cleaning and the dumpster diving. I become pensive. 'But tomorrow morning. What about coffee? Will there be any?' 'Relax,' Lisen's sister says. 'What happens happens. Forget your routines.' 'That's fine,' I say. 'I don't have that many.' If only Jonathan could hear me, all the routines that we follow.

I'm filled with their youthful enthusiasm. Sleep through the night. I'm grateful and think that rubbish makes you sleep well. Take a morning dip in the sea, then go to the music workshop. We're divided up into five bands, and have to write two songs, set them to music, and then perform at the concert the next day.

One of the instructors comes into the rehearsal room and tells me that the drummer's role is to keep the band in order. Help, I'm used to other people keeping me in order.

I immediately attach myself to the vocalist and guitarist. She speaks in a Skåne dialect. 'I'm going to play some mean music on my axe,' she says, picks up her guitar and goes over to the mike. I thought she was a man at first. She's got short hair, a peaked hat and a black t-shirt. She says that she's in between man and woman. Neither King nor Queen, but a Queeing fighter. 'Lots of people are,' she says, and changes from a man to a woman with a big smile that covers her face. 'I'm sure,' I say, and think: maybe me too.

I quickly write down some lines. Suddenly it's no problem to rhyme. It feels good and unpretentious, the words just flow onto the paper and soon I've written two songs. The others write the music. Make the melody, the refrain, rhythm, verse and solo.

In the last hours before the concert, I hit a big low. I'm out of rhythm, the drum solos are either too slow or too fast. Lisen has to devise a movement with the bass to help me come in at the right place. Slightly nervous, we make our way to the venue. We rehearse once before the audience arrives. It goes well. It goes even better when the audience is swaying in front of the stage.

I don't sleep well on the night train home. But it doesn't matter. Lie there eating crisps, trying to do it quietly. I feel a bit claustrophobic, but deal with it. I say no to the voices. They're just a whisper far away and I can imagine that they're helping me. The train speeds through the night. I, who normally feels homeless, who normally feels that the journey there and back is going away, feel that I'm heading home. I know that I won't lose touch any more. I know that light times lie ahead. That things will happen that I never believed could happen. That I'll grow. I lick the salt from my fingers and know that Eli is the index finger.

I speed through sleep and into the future. I've done this before. Someone is broken and I'm going to fix her. There's a bunk in the room and all the equipment needed for an examination. No windows, just pale green, calming walls. I've got a mouth mask pulled up over my face, like in a film. It's chaotic. We have to heal this person urgently. There are others waiting for their turn. This is the future. It depends on me. It depends on cooperation. I am highly competent. The scalpels lie gleaming in front of me on a tray.

I am an androgyne, I think happily. I've read that they're the best bosses. There are eight of us in the room. But every time I try to heal someone with my colleagues, it turns out that they're not my colleagues at all. And that I'm the patient. It's me that is broken.

This is a recurring dream. I'm just as surprised every time. And I thought… This time I'm certain that I'm on the helpers' side. I start as the doctor and end up as the patient who destroys the whole examination room and is restrained. I start with a feeling of competency, camaraderie and unity, centred on the patient's problems. How can we best resolve this? I can operate and I can calm people down. I know everything there is to know about medicine. I end in desperation. This is not the future.

I don't give up. I never give up. Wake up. Elsa calls on my mobile phone and I tell her about my dream. 'You are the doctor,' she says. 'Without you, you can't be healed. And you are getting stronger every day.'

I found, I found... When I get home, there's a letter waiting for me. 'We would like to invite you to give a reading in Havana, Cuba.' Something I wrote over twenty years ago has been translated into Spanish. If I can go to Malmö, I can go to Cuba. If my writing finds its way to Cuba, it can find its way anywhere.

The next day, I go to my workspace. I feel happy and proud that I managed the trip so well. I've been inspired to write lyrics, so when I sit down to write my novel, I start to rhyme.